THE GOLDEN SABRE

JON CLEARY, an Australian whose books are read throughout the world, is the author of thirty novels including such famous bestsellers as *The Sundowners* and *The High Commissioner*.

Born in 1917, Jon Cleary left school at fifteen to become a commercial artist and film cartoonist – even a laundryman and bushworker. Then his first novel won second prize in Australia's biggest literary contest and launched him on his successful writing career.

Seven of his books have been filmed and *Peter's Pence* was awarded the American Edgar Allen Poe prize as the best crime novel of 1947.

Jon Cleary lives with his wife Joan in Sydney.

Available in Fontana by the same author

The Beaufort Sisters
A Very Private War

JON CLEARY

The Golden Sabre

FONTANA/Collins

First published by William Collins Sons & Co. Ltd 1981
First issued in Fontana Paperbacks 1981
This Impression January 1982
Copyright © Sundowner Productions Pty Ltd 1981

Printed in Canada

To Eric Neal

'We could make you disappear, Cabell. Magic like that happens all the time in Russia. Who knows what has happened to our beloved Tsar? They say he is dead, but they have not produced his body.'

'I'd remind you, General Bronevich, that I'm an American citizen.'

'Then we'd make you an American magical act. Like your famous magician Houdini. I have read about him.'

'Houdini is an escape artist, General.'

'Ah, but he doesn't walk about without his head, does he? Could you do that, Cabell?'

Matthew Martin Cabell was very attached to his head. It was his wits and not his size that had brought him all the way from Chicago's Prairie Avenue to this town of Verkburg on the eastern slopes of the Ural mountains in Siberia. As a boy smaller than the other kids on his block, the only one who did not have an Irish name though he had an Irish mother, he had had to talk his way out of fights or, if it came to blows, fight dirty. His fame as a fighter of crafty viciousness had brought fight managers looking for a kid they could groom into a champion, someone of the likes of Joe Walcott, the Barbados Demon, or Honey Mellody. But the kid had been brighter than the managers: he wasn't going to get his most valued possession, his head, knocked off to make money for crooked promoters. He had gone to the Armour School of Engineering on a scholarship and for a while he had thought he had chosen the wrong profession; engineers appeared to be bigger and tougher and more aggressive than he had expected and he had thought of changing to English literature or Art History where the personalities and the wrists seemed much limper. But he had survived, again by using his wits and the occasional dirty tactic, such as a boot in the privates or two fingers in the eyes, and gone on to be a geologist in the oil fields of Texas,

Venezuela, Roumania and Baku, where sometimes he had lost a fight against a bigger, equally sharp-witted, just-as-dirty fighter. But he had never lost his head and he was determined not to lose it now.

'General, all I want is to have my truck loaded on a train for Ekaterinburg – from there I'll get another train for Vladivostok. I'm not a spy for the Bolsheviks or anyone else. I've been looking for oil around here and I haven't found any.'

'Who do you work for? Yourself?' General Bronevich put out a hand and the dwarf who stood beside him gave him a fresh cigarette from a battered silver case. The General lit the cigarette from the stub he took from his thick loose lips, then dropped the stub on the floor. The floor was littered with crushed stubs, like bird droppings, and the room swirled with smoke that smelled days old. 'You work for yourself?'

'No, the American-Siberian Oil Company of New York.'

Bronevich looked at the dwarf. 'What do you say, Pemenov? Have you heard of this company? Peregrine Pemenov is my chief-of-staff,' he explained to Cabell. 'He had an American mother, a whore who came from San Francisco to Vladivostok and married my stupid cousin. Unfortunately she only laid half an egg.'

The dwarf smiled a child's smile, as if he found the cruel joke funny. The poor son-of-a-bitch, Cabell thought, he's probably had to put up with stuff like that all his life. He was not an ugly little man, but Cabell found himself averting his gaze, as if he did not want to embarrass the misshapen Pemenov. The dwarf's mother had subjected him to another cruel joke when she had labelled him with the ridiculous Peregrine.

'The American-Siberian Oil Company is legitimate, General.' The dwarf had a soft raspy voice, as if it too were misshapen, the larynx flattened. His broad Mongolian face had a straight, handsome nose, one of the few good things his mother had bequeathed him; his blond hair was cut very short to the scalp and surmounted with an embroidered pill-box cap he had stolen from an Hussar. He wore a grey silk blouse, with the sleeves chopped off just above the cuffs to

6

accommodate his very short arms, and black trousers stuffed
into what looked to be a child's pair of riding boots. A silver
dagger was in a decorated scabbard on his belt. 'They have
been in Siberia since just after the war against the Japanese.
Never found any oil.'

'Have you found any oil, Cabell?'

'Not a drop. Now all I want to do is pack up and go
home.'

'You can do that, Cabell. But only after we have investigated you – Pemenov will do that. We can trust no one these
days, neither Reds nor Whites. I keep telling that to my wives
every day. And to my mistresses,' he said, trying to look like
a Siberian Don Juan. He was a Moslem with three wives, all
of whom he was glad to leave at home. But his mistresses
were a figment of his vanity, since no woman could stand
more than one night of him and then only at gunpoint.
'They all agree with me and there's nothing like a woman's
intuition, is there?'

*Not when she knows she'll get her head chopped off if she doesn't
agree.*

When Cabell had arrived in the Verkburg district three
months ago he had been surprised to find that the regional
commander was General Bronevich. He had been warned
before he left Vladivostok that the White Russian opposition
to the Bolshevik revolution was made up of many factions,
most of them at vicious odds with each other. The most
independent of them were the Siberian *atamans*, the Tartar
Khans with their private armies who saw the civil war as the
greatest opportunity for large-scale raping and looting since
the hey-day of their ancestor Genghis Khan. Cabell had
thanked his luck that he had managed to pass unmolested
through the domain of the worst of the *atamans*, General
Semenov. The White forces of Admiral Kolchak, the
commander-in-chief, were already retreating east to Omsk
and Cabell had had doubts about going on. But he had been
assured before he left the States that there was little or no
fighting in the area where American-Siberian were sending
him and they wanted to know whether oil was there. If there
was, American-Siberian, blessed with executives whose
loyalty to governments was as slippery as their product,

would come to an arrangement with whoever won the civil war.

Cabell had taken his truck off the train at Ekaterinburg, carefully not letting his curiosity get the better of him in the town where the Tsar and his family were said to have been murdered. He had put the truck on a branch-line train and come a hundred miles south-west to Verkburg and found that another *ataman*, intent on building an even worse reputation than Semenov, had moved west and taken over this region. Up till now Cabell had not been disturbed in his work, since he had spent all his time out in the hills west of town. He had found no evidence of oil and last week his employers had sent word that, because it seemed they could not pick the winner of the civil war, though they did not say that, he should give up and head back to the United States. So he had driven into town this morning, dropped off the two local men he had hired, gone to the railroad station to see about putting himself and his truck on the next train for Ekaterinburg and within ten minutes found himself in General Bronevich's office in the town barracks.

'Am I under arrest, General?'

'That would mean putting you in prison, Cabell, and having to feed you. Food is short, as you know —' Bronevich ran his hands down over his fat belly, tried to pull some creases into his uniform to suggest he was underweight; he failed, looked up at Cabell and smiled. 'Well, food is short for some people, shall we say? No, Cabell, you will be free to walk around — you will have the money to feed yourself, I'm sure. If Pemenov's investigation finds you are not a Bolshevik spy or an American spy or any other sort — the investigation may take weeks, of course, because there are so many spies —' He smiled again, an expression that did nothing to endear him to anyone who witnessed it. He had the broad Mongolian face, a completely bald head, a mouth full of gold teeth and eyes that looked as if they could cut glass. It seemed to Cabell that he must have made a career of his ugliness, matching his character to his looks. 'If you are cleared, you can take the train for Ekaterinburg. I shall see you get a compartment to yourself. The fare will be — What do you suggest, Pemenov?'

8

'Two thousand American dollars.' The dwarf's intelligent blue eyes seemed to gleam with malicious humour.

'Where did you learn to speak Russian, Cabell?' said Bronevich.

'I worked down at Baku for eighteen months before the war with the Germans. Will the two thousand dollars pay my truck's fare, too?'

'Ah no. What room would there be in a railway compartment for a truck?'

'You shouldn't be trying to rob me, General. I don't know if you know it, but America is supposed to be on the side of the White armies.'

'But we don't need the Americans, do we, Pemenov?'

The dwarf smiled his child's smile. 'Not here in Verkburg, General.' He addressed Cabell directly for the first time, spoke in English: 'We don't need the Americans anywhere at all in Russia, Mr Cabell.'

'Are you a Bolshevik, Mr Pemenov, and the General doesn't know it?'

The child's smile flickered again on the big adult face. 'Don't be stupid, Mr Cabell. You're too far from home and all alone – being insulting isn't going to help you. No, I'm not a Bolshevik. I just hate Americans, all of you.'

Cabell looked at him, feeling a reluctant pity. 'Your mother must have been a real bitch.'

'She was, Mr Cabell. A real shit of a bitch.'

'What a beautiful language!' Bronevich blew out a cloud of smoke, rolled his head in ecstasy at the music he had been listening to. 'I could listen to English all day. What a pity I don't understand it.'

'Two thousand dollars, Cabell,' said Pemenov, this time in Russian. 'The General will be waiting for it – after we have investigated you.'

Two minutes later Cabell was out in the square that fronted the barracks. The August sun pressed down like a bright golden blanket; the air was dry but so hot that it seared the nostrils and dried Cabell's lips almost instantly. The bell in the tower beneath the green onion dome of the church at the far end of the square tolled noon; the iron notes hung on the heavy air as if cloaked in velvet. Soldiers

9

lolled like dark shocks of corn in the thin midday shadows; a row of them looked as if they were stacked ready for loading on the two military trucks parked by the barracks wall. But Cabell noticed that each truck, decrepit antiques, had a wheel missing: the axles were jacked up on bricks. He knew then that he would never get his own truck on the train for Ekaterinburg. Battered though it was, it was still in better shape than the two military vehicles and General Bronevich wouldn't let it slip out of his hands.

Shopkeepers were locking up their stores, getting ready for lunch; in a town full of soldiers they had learned to leave nothing unattended. Shutters were closing on house windows, locking out the heat. A peasant crossed the square at a slow walk, bent over beneath the load of firewood on his back: the heat didn't fool him, he knew winter would have no memory of today and would freeze him if he was not prepared against it. An open carriage drawn by two black, sweat-shining horses came round the square and broke into a trot as Cabell, eyes blinded by the white cobblestones, stepped out of the shade to cross the road.

The horses were abruptly pulled up, rearing high, one of them almost knocking Cabell's head off as its front hooves pawed at the air. Cabell fell back, just managing to keep his feet, and leaned against the side of the carriage as it came level with him. He looked up into the sun and dimly saw the shape of a woman pulling hard on the reins.

'For crissakes, lady, why don't you watch where you're going?'

'Watch it!' said the lady, let go of the reins with one hand, swung her handbag on its long strap and whacked Cabell across the ear. 'If you're going to use that sort of language, you're not getting an apology out of me. Out of the way, you lout!'

The carriage swept on and Cabell jumped back to avoid being run down. He held a hand to his ear, glad to find it was still attached to his head; his other ear was still ringing with the echo of the sharp voice that had spoken to him in English. It was not his day; first a general who suspected he was a spy, then a dwarf who hated him because he was an American, now an English-speaking woman who thought he

10

was a foul-mouthed lout. He stood in the middle of the square, looked around him, wondered where he might find a friend; but two thousand miles of isolation stretched away from him in all directions. All at once he realized that he was sinking very rapidly into a very serious situation.

He walked across the square, still feeling his sore ear, swore at a dog that lazily snapped at him, and came to the line of plane trees under which he had parked his truck. It was not strictly a truck; it was a 1914 Chevrolet car which had had its rear seat and bodywork stripped away and a high-sided platform substituted. It had done more than its fair share of hard travelling and Cabell did not dare to guess how many more miles it had left in it before it fell apart from the battering it had taken in the past five years. It was a car that had been built for the soft dirt roads of America and not for the jungle tracks of Venezuela and the trackless rocky ground he had driven it over here in the Urals. The tyres, worn to condom thinness, had had forty punctures in the past three months; the brakes, when applied, were just a plunger pressed into a well of wishful thinking. He had intended taking it home more for sentimental reasons than because he thought it had many more years of usefulness left in it.

But it was useful now. He knew that the next train for Ekaterinburg did not leave for another three days; by then General Bronevich might have decided that he was indeed a spy. He turned his mind against any thought of what might happen to him. Houdini, the greatest escape artist of all time, always made sure that he did his magic in front of a friendly audience. He never attempted anything where the nearest applause was two thousand miles back in the stalls.

As Cabell approached the Chevrolet a soldier rolled out from behind the shadow of the tailboard, stood up, lethargically brushed the dust from himself and asked Cabell where he thought he was going.

'Can you drive?' Cabell said.

The soldier squinted and pondered, decided he understood the question and shook his head.

'General Bronevich wants the truck round in the barracks

yard. You better let me drive.'

The soldier looked around for guidance, saw that he was alone, squinted and pondered again. Then he shook his head and raised his rifle threateningly. It was a Krenk, an ancient one that looked as if it might go off without its trigger being touched.

Cabell smiled, feeling that his lips were splitting and his teeth falling out of their gums. 'You can ride with me.' He patted the front seat. 'Right up there with the driver, Ivan. That should do wonders for your prestige with the girls around here.'

The soldier squinted and pondered once more. Then he abruptly nodded and was up in the front seat so quickly it was almost a feat of instant levitation. Cabell went round to the front of the truck, swung the starting handle, got the engine to fire at the first couple of turns, got in behind the wheel and let in the gears. He drove slowly round the square till he came to the street that headed out to the main road to Ekaterinburg. The gasoline tank was half-full and there were eight four-gallon cans packed in boxes in the back of the truck. If the tyres held he could be in Ekaterinburg in just over two hours, three at the most. A British consul was stationed there and perhaps he could be persuaded to shelter an American till the latter could board the first train going east to Vladivostok. Cabell decided he would make the Consulate a present of the Chevrolet.

As they reached the far side of the square Cabell, glancing across past the broken plinth that had once held a statue of the Tsar, saw General Bronevich come out of the barracks with Pemenov. There was a yell from the General and next moment a shot; a bullet hit the soldier in an arm and he dropped his rifle and screamed in pain. Cabell stepped on the accelerator.

'Sorry, buddy,' he said in English, 'I think you'll be safer on the ground.'

There were no doors on the truck. Cabell reached across, gave a hard shove as he took the truck round a corner, and the soldier went tumbling out and hit the cobblestones with a thud that made Cabell flinch guiltily. But there was no time for conscience or sympathy. He put his foot down hard and the Chevrolet leapt away up the road towards Ekaterinburg.

In the square General Bronevich was shouting Mongolian obscenities, than which there is nothing more obscene. An officer appeared out of the shadows and, hampered by his heavy riding boots, galloped across to the line of slumbering soldiers who, startled by the shot, were blinking themselves awake and looking for the enemy. The officer kicked them to their feet, yelling at them and himself, urged on by the yelling of General Bronevich. The soldiers, still only half-awake, stumbled towards the barracks stables and their horses.

General Bronevich, no runner, waddled back into the barracks and through to the barracks yard; Pemenov, following him, looked more agile despite his tiny legs. The General's driver, having taken both front wheels off the General's car to repair the tyres, had lain down in the shade of the car and fallen asleep. He had taken off his boots and in his sleep, dreaming of his wife's sister, was sensually wriggling his bare toes. General Bronevich, beside himself and everybody else with rage, shot off three of the driver's toes and waddled back into the barracks and out into the square as half a dozen soldiers, mounted now, thundered out of the stables and took the road for Ekaterinburg.

'Get my car fixed!' General Bronevich bellowed to Pemenov. 'I want that American's head fitted to the radiator!'

'Yes, General!' Pemenov whirled and his short legs blurred as they carried him back into the barracks at surprising speed.

Two miles up the road, the outskirts of the town already behind it, the Chevrolet was bowling along like the excellent car it had once been. Cabell, feeling better already as the wind drove in to cool him, began to think of home. In another month, six weeks at the outside, he would be driving down the road to Bloomington. His mother had died three years ago and since then his father had moved from Chicago to just outside Bloomington, where he had a small general store. If he was lucky he might even be home in time to take his father to see the White Sox play in the World Series. The Old Man's last letter, picked up in Verkburg only this morning, had been dated June 1; but Jack Cabell had already been claiming then that this White Sox team was the greatest of all time, would be sure to make it to the World Series. Cabell had not seen a major league game since May 1912 and he was looking forward to seeing the men his father acclaimed, Eddie Collins, Shoeless Joe Jackson, Shineball Eddie Cicotte.

He was dreaming of heroes of the past, Ty Cobb, Christy Mathewson, Honus Wagner, thinking what a nice clean war baseball was compared to this civil war going on around him, when the off-side front tyre blew out. The car swerved violently and it was only with tremendous luck that he managed to keep it on the road. He had just got it under control and on a straight course again when the other front tyre blew out.

[2]

Eden Penfold dusted herself off after the truck, its horn blasting at her, had sped by. The horses had shied, but she had managed to steady them, though they were still trembling and nervous as she got them back into a steady trot. Beside her the children were brushing dust from themselves and Frederick was cursing in Russian.

'Watch it!' she snapped in English.

'But I don't know any English swear words —' Frederick was twelve; a handsome, dark-haired boy with a slim frame, an innocent expression and an attitude towards life that suggested his education had begun some years before his actual birth. 'You are always saying, Miss Eden, that one should never hide one's true feelings —'

'There's a time and place for everything, even feelings.' *Ah dear God, if I could only express my true feelings.* After six years she had begun to doubt that she had a true vocation as a governess. Sometimes she found herself thinking thoughts that were as revolutionary as those being trumpeted in Moscow right now; though hers were social and romantic rather than political. So far she had managed not to reveal any of her thoughts to her two charges.

'You have a double standard,' said Frederick. 'One law for

14

the rich like us and another one for you.'

'How on earth can you stand him?' Eden asked Olga.

Olga, ten years old, already beautiful and waiting for the world to be laid at her feet, shrugged. 'He'll get worse, I'm afraid. But by then I shall be married and living on the French Riviera.'

'You have a little while to go before that happens, my girl.'

Ah, what dreams we women have! But at ten she, living in the semi-detached house in Croydon, south of London, had been dreaming of nothing more than being the bride of the boy next door who, she remembered now, had had adenoids and a tendency to nervously pick his nose when spoken to by a girl. She had never thought of herself as of the stuff of which French Riviera beauties were made. But then she had also never thought that she would finish up here in Russia and Siberia as governess to the children of a Russian aristocrat.

It was another hour before they came to the first fields that marked the border of the Gorshkov estate. Once a month Eden drove into Verkburg in the carriage to see if any mail had arrived for herself or the children; it was a twelve-mile drive each way and she did not enjoy it in the summer heat. There had been no letter today for her from her parents, but there had been one each for the children from their mother and another one for her. The children had read theirs with excitement and delight; she had read hers with growing trepidation and despair. She turned the horses in through the white pillars of the gateway and drove up the long avenue of poplars and wondered how much longer she and the children were going to be isolated here, the children separated from their parents and she from the England that she had now begun to pine for.

She pulled the horses to a halt in front of the Gorshkov house. The house, built of a white-painted stone with a Palladian façade that had been added by the children's grandfather, looked out of place amongst the wooden barns that surrounded it. Grandfather Gorshkov, the first Prince Gorshkov to add wealth to his title, had tried to buy taste at a time, in Europe, when taste was not at its highest. The

Palladian-fronted house in itself was attractive; he had just not known enough to complement it with the appropriate surroundings. Plane trees threw shadows that softened the grey drabness of the barns and cow-sheds, and a few lilacs, faded now by the summer sun, added a touch of colour in the yard between the main barn and the house.

The Gorshkov estate covered fifteen thousand acres. It had been founded originally by a Prince Gorshkov who had been one of Catherine the Great's lovers; he had lasted three months and had been known as the Wednesday Man, that being his day to perform. Arriving one Wednesday and finding he was in a queue, he had decided his time was up and left St Petersburg, exiling himself before Catherine disposed of him more permanently. He had come east, established himself and died here on the estate, leaving a wife, a son and two daughters. Following generations had built up the estate and in 1860, in the reign of Alexander II, they had moved back to St Petersburg and built themselves a small mansion just off the Nevsky Prospekt. The young princes had been educated in the Cadet Corps; the princesses went to the Smolny Institute. Though their names were never entered in the *Livre de Velours,* they were close enough to flutter like loose addenda to that almanac of nobility. Princess Gorshkov, the children's mother, whose family had been in the *Livre de Velours,* had impressed all th:s on Eden when she had first arrived in St Petersburg. Eden, who had not even met the Mayor of Croydon, had been suitably impressed at the time, though her awe had since worn off.

Far out on the rear boundary of the estate Eden knew the farm workers would be bringing in the harvest; tomorrow the traction engine in the threshing yard would be started up and today's somnolent peace would be gone. This would be the first harvest since Prince Gorshkov had gone off to fight with General Denikin's army. She wondered if the workers would demand it as their own property. No one knew these days what the workers were going to demand next.

As she got down from the carriage Nikolai Yurganov came across from the stables and took the horses' heads. 'Miss Eden —'

She turned back as she was about to follow the children into the house. 'What is it, Nikolai?'

'There's a man in the big barn – I think you should see him —'

'A man? What sort of man?'

'A foreigner, Miss Eden. He has a motor car —' Nikolai Petrovitch Yurganov was a young man convinced already that he would not last to be old. He was a Cossack from the Don who had come east to avoid the fighting and carousing that had been his family's main pursuits. He had pale brown hair, already starting to thin, a long bony face, a body to match it and a soft girlish voice. He had a pathological fear of horses and one small glass of vodka stunned him like a blow with a rifle-butt. At his birth he had set the Cossack tradition back a millennium. 'He drove in here a while ago. His tyres are punctured —'

Eden stood irresolute. In the nine months since Prince and Princess Gorshkov had gone off to Georgia she had had no major problems to face; the war was a long way from here and even General Bronevich's soldiers had not come out of town to worry her and the children. Once she had been myopic to consequences, the essential talent for any sense of adventure; she would, if she lasted long enough, stand gasping with admiration for the sunrise on Judgement Day. But today's letter from Princess Gorshkov had brought a sense of foreboding.

'Can't you get rid of him?'

Nikolai shook his head. 'He won't take any notice of me, Miss Eden – no one ever does —'

'Oh damn!' she said under her breath and, carrying her parasol, stalked across to the main barn and into its cool dim interior. She saw the strange truck at the rear of the barn, next to Prince Gorshkov's car under its big canvas cover; then she saw the man in a blue shirt, bib-and-tucker overalls and a flat-crowned cowboy's hat sitting on the running-board of the truck. 'What are – Oh, it's you!'

'Well, well, if it isn't the old handbag whirler —' Cabell felt his bruised ear. 'I'd like you beside me some time in a bar-room brawl.'

'Just the sort of place where I spend most of my time.'

17

Why am I sounding so tart? She should be welcoming this man, whoever he was; he was the first non-Russian she had spoken to in over two years, ever since the Gorshkovs had fled St Petersburg for this estate. 'I'm sorry, Mr —?'

'Cabell.'

'What are you doing here?'

Somehow he had suggested to her that he would be garrulous, as long-winded as Trotsky, whom she had once heard speak; instead, in what seemed to her no more than half a dozen sentences, he told her who he was and how he had arrived here in the Gorshkov barn. But even his brevity landed like a weight on her.

'You can't stay here! I have the children to think of —'

'Miss Eden.' Nikolai stood like a trembling shadow in the doorway of the barn. 'There are horsemen coming up the avenue!'

'Oh Jesus,' said Cabell. 'I better be going —'

'Going where?'

'I'll try and make it out there to the wheat-fields. Maybe I can hide—'

'Stay where you are.' Even as her decision was forming in her mind she wondered why she was making it. Was it just because the man spoke English? Did her charity lie only in her ear? She could not imagine herself being so impulsive about helping a Russian. 'Put the horses away, Nikolai. And keep your mouth shut – you know nothing, you understand?'

She went out again into the glare, opening her blue parasol and raising it against the golden brightness. As the half-dozen horsemen galloped into the broad area in front of the house, Frederick and Olga came running out of the front door. 'What's going on? Why the soldiers? Are we being attacked?'

'Be quiet,' Eden said, and looked up at the sergeant leaning down at her from his horse. She recognized the men for Siberian Cossacks, the worst of all Cossacks. They wore their karakul hats, dirty grey uniforms and expressions that made her quail inwardly; sabres hung in scabbards from their saddles and all of them had rifles. The horses, crowding in around her, looked as wild as the men. 'To what do we owe this honour?'

The sergeant peered and leered at her, split between appreciating this rich plum of a girl and wondering what she was doing here. A Turkic-speaking gentleman, he also only vaguely understood what she had said to him in Russian. He straightened up and nodded to one of his younger soldiers.

'Question her.'

The young soldier pressed his horse forward, likewise leered down at Eden. She felt she was being visually molested as the horsemen crowded round her; Nikolai had warned her what might happen if these Tartars took it into their heads to come out from Verkburg and pillage the estate. Now here they were and if they found the man they were looking for, God help him. And, what was worse, God help her and the children.

'I am in charge here —' said Frederick.

Eden hit him with her handbag and the soldiers laughed and cheered. Frederick drew himself up and almost got another whack with the handbag. 'Shut up, Freddie. What can we do for you, corporal?'

'We are looking for an American in a motor car —'

'That must have been he who passed us and covered us in dust,' said Olga.

'Children should be seen and not heard,' said Eden, trembling inside, seeing two of the soldiers now leering at Olga. 'Of course it was he, who else could it have been?' She looked up at the young corporal. 'He was travelling north at a great speed, out there on the Ekaterinburg road. He went by us in a cloud of dust and disappeared up the road.'

The corporal conveyed this information to the sergeant, who peered and leered again at Eden. She and the children were still tightly encircled by the horsemen. She felt more threatened now than ever before in her life; somehow she felt more endangered now than in the Revolution riots two years ago in St Petersburg; even the flight from that city had not had any close moments of danger. These Tartars, savages on horseback, could do what they wanted with her and the children and there would be no one to stop them. The estate workers were too far away, the house servants were probably already cowering in the cellars; Nikolai, she knew, was a reliable coward and the American, who had brought these men here, was an unknown quantity. She felt suddenly overcome by fear and the heat and was ready to collapse. She would be unconscious when she was raped for the first time, which was probably the best way to be.

The sergeant straightened up, snapped something to his men in his own tongue and all six of them suddenly whirled their horses about and went galloping off down the avenue, disappearing like evaporating ghosts into the shadows of the poplars. Eden, halfway to fainting, came back to full consciousness.

'Just as well they decided to go,' said Frederick. 'I'd have shot them with Father's gun.'

'Just what we need,' Eden said to Olga. 'A stupid twelve-year-old hero. We'd have all been dead before you could have loaded the gun.'

'It's already loaded,' said Frederick. 'I've had it loaded for weeks, just in case.'

'I had mine ready, also just in case.' Cabell came out of the barn carrying a Winchester rifle. 'Those bastards looked—'

'Mr Cabell, could you please moderate your language?'

Cabell took off his hat and inclined his head. 'Sorry. I've been talking to myself for so long, I keep forgetting . . . Thanks, Miss Eden. You could have given me up to those guys, you know. I wouldn't have blamed you.'

'Never!' Frederick was a one-boy defender against the invaders. 'Those men are barbarians!'

'Do be quiet, Freddie,' said Eden. 'Mr Cabell, where were you intending to go?'

'I was heading for Ekaterinburg. But I'm not going to make it now – when I blew my tyres I bugg – messed up the wheels. I'll have to go on foot, unless I can buy a horse from you.'

'We shall sell you a horse,' said Frederick. 'We have dozens—Ouch!'

Eden hit him with her handbag, but did not give him a glance.

'Mr Cabell, if you go by horse you will have to travel at

20

night. They will be watching for you all the way to Ekaterinburg. As soon as those men get back to Verkburg they will send a message through on the telegraph to all the villages and towns between here and Ekaterinburg. These White armies do fight amongst themselves, but they also co-operate with each other sometimes. We'll give you a horse and you can leave after dark.'

'Miss Eden, you are a peach. And very resourceful, if I may say so.'

Eden blushed under the compliment and Olga said, 'I love to hear a man compliment a woman. It is the way things should be.'

Cabell raised an eyebrow, then bowed. 'At your service, Miss —'

'Princess,' said Olga. 'Princess Olga Natasha Aglaida Gorshkov.'

'I am Prince Frederick Mikhail Alexander Gorshkov,' said Frederick, not to be out-ranked.

'And I am plain Miss Eden Penfold.'

'Not plain,' said Cabell, smiling. 'And I'm delighted to meet a fellow proletarian. As for you two aristocrats, buzz off while I talk to Miss Penfold.'

'We stay,' said the two aristocrats. 'This is our house —'

Eden raised her handbag again, but Frederick and Olga moved back out of range. Cabell looked at the two children, then shrugged. 'Okay. Are there any servants here besides that guy Nikolai?'

'There are four in the house, but they can be trusted,' said Eden. 'It is the workers out in the fields I'm not sure about.'

'One of them is a Bolshevik,' said Frederick. 'That fellow Vlasov. He spits in the dust every time I pass him.'

'So should I if I were not a lady. That doesn't make me a Bolshevik. But Freddie is right – there are some out there who are not to be trusted. Nikolai has told me of some of the talk that has been going on lately.'

Nikolai had come across from the stables and stood just behind the two children. He did not understand the conversation in English, but he looked as worried as the others. He kept glancing down the avenue, waiting for the Tartars to come thundering back and kill them all.

'The car under that cover in the barn,' said Cabell. 'Does it go?'

'It hasn't been driven since Prince Gorshkov went off to the war last December,' said Eden.

'What sort is it?'

'A Rolls-Royce Silver Ghost,' said Frederick. 'There are only nine Rolls-Royces in the whole of Russia and the Tsar had two of those. But Father's is the fastest of them all.'

'A Rolls-Royce, eh? Then that means I couldn't borrow it or buy it?'

'Exactly,' said Eden firmly. 'You will take the horse and leave tonight.'

Cabell smiled. He was not much taller than Eden, just medium height, and though he had wide shoulders there was not much beef on him. Had the managers been able to sweet-talk him back in the days of his youth he would now be a middleweight, maybe fighting the likes of Mike O'Dowd and Harry Greb; whomever he fought, the situation would be less dangerous than this. He had black hair and a black moustache and sun-darkened skin that accentuated the white exclamation of his smile. His movements were a physical illustration of his personality, quicksilver in a tube that occasionally spilled its cork. Eden liked what she saw.

'I won't embarrass or endanger you, Miss Penfold. I'll be out of here tonight. In the meantime I better start covering up my truck some way, in case those soldiers come back.'

'Afternoon tea will be at four. I'll send one of the servants for you.'

Eden had recovered her poise. She was perhaps a little stiff and starched, but that, Cabell guessed, went with being a governess. Under her straw hat he could see blonde hair drawn back in a bun; the style was severe but it showed her long graceful neck. She had dark blue eyes with heavy lids that made it hard for her to turn a glance into a stern stare; she had a slightly indolent look about her that was deceiving, an odalisque who cracked a whip; had Croydon had harems she might never have left England. Her figure was the sort that promised much even under the high-necked shirt and long brown skirt she wore; it was an unspoken and, to her, unrealized invitation to carnal thoughts in men.

Cabell, who could have carnal thoughts with the best of them, shrugged philosophically. This was no time for getting randy.

'Come on, children, time for your music lesson.'

'I think I shall stay with Mr Cabell,' said Frederick; then backed off as Eden raised her handbag. 'Don't you dare do that again! When we have won the war I'll see that you go to jail with all the other Bolsheviks—'

'Inside!' snapped Eden, and after a moment's further rebellion Frederick followed his sister into the house. 'Forgive him, Mr Cabell. He's not really a bad child. He just thinks, with his father away, that he has to be master of the house.'

'Where are their parents?'

'Princess Gorshkov is down in Tiflis, in Georgia, and Prince Gorshkov is somewhere with General Denikin's army. I have no idea when they will be back,' she added worriedly. 'Princess Gorshkov wants us to join them in Tiflis. But how does one get from here to there, a thousand miles away?'

'A good question,' said Cabell; but he had his own problems.

'I'll be ready for tea when you call me. And thanks again, Eden.'

No man had called her plain *Eden* since Lieutenant Dulenko had called her that and *my darling* five years ago; not even Prince Gorshkov departed from the formal *Miss Eden* when he addressed her. But Igor Dulenko was long since dead and the love she had felt for him had withered away. It was strange that a strange man, using her given name so casually, should have reminded her of Igor and what she had once felt for him. For a moment she felt unutterably sad and she turned away from Cabell and went into the house without a word.

Cabell looked after her curiously, then he went back to the barn with Nikolai and began to think of ways of hiding the Chevrolet.

Cabell had been in the barn half an hour, had, with the willing help of Nikolai, pushed the Chevrolet right to the back of the barn and hidden it from casual sight behind stacked bales of hay. He had taken off his shirt from under his overalls and his skin, covered in dust, was streaked with a dark wash of sweat. He leaned against the shrouded Rolls-Royce and took the pannikin of water Nikolai brought him.

'How is the war going, Nikolai? Are the Whites or the Reds winning?'

'I don't know, sir. We hear nothing down here. We have enough to worry about with that General Bronevich and his savages. As soon as the weather gets cooler they'll start riding out this far and then we'll —' He did not finish the sentence, but shuddered.

'Have you worked for the Gorshkovs a long time?'

'Only three years. I am a Cossack from a little village on the Don.'

'Then you'd be a good man to defend Miss Penfold and the kids.'

'I doubt it, sir. My father used to say a fart would knock me down. He was a very vulgar man, vulgar and violent. He had seven sons, I was the youngest, and he said his spunk had run out by the time he got to me. When he was drunk he used to wail that he was the only Cossack along the whole Don River who had a fairy at the bottom of his garden. That was where he used to make me sleep, in the wood-shed.'

'Well —' said Cabell; but was left with nothing else to say. 'Well —'

Then they heard the sound of a car coming up the avenue. Nikolai raced to the doorway. 'It's General Bronevich and his soldiers!'

Cabell grabbed his shirt, hat and rifle and scrambled up the ladder to the loft of the barn. He heard the car grind to a halt, its engine whistling for a moment, then wheezing into silence; then he heard the jingling of stirrups and the murmurs of men as they steadied their horses. He crept

24

across the loft and peered out through a crack in the timber walls.

The car's driver had jumped down and opened the door. General Bronevich got out, followed by Pemenov. The sergeant and the horsemen who had been here earlier had returned, but they had not dismounted and remained in the background as the General went up the steps of the house and banged loudly on the front door.

Inside the house the servants, ears alert as yet-undiscovered radar, had once again fled to the cellars. Eden waved the children back up the stairs in the main hall and went fearfully to the front door and opened it. General Bronevich almost fell back down the steps in surprise.

He had been expecting some servant, as dumpy as himself, to open the door. Instead here was this pretty girl with hair the colour of Siberian buckwheat honey, a bosom that reminded him of the lower foothills of the Yablonois, and a body perfume composed of rosewater, starch and fear. He turned to Pemenov on the steps below him and said, 'Come back for me in an hour. I shall interrogate this girl myself.'

'Will it be safe, General?'

'For me or for her?' Bronevich's smile was as obscene as an open fly, except that it was golden.

'Yes, General. What about the men?'

'Tell them to wait down by the front gates. I do not wish to be disturbed in my interrogation. You may take the motor car. Go for a drive and run over some peasants.' He laughed loudly this time; he was suddenly in both high good humour and high tumescence. The afternoon was going to be better than he had expected, he had already forgotten why he had come here. 'Get lost, as they say back in Skovodorino.'

Pemenov smiled, saluted, went down the steps, gave an order to the horsemen, climbed into the car and was driven off, followed by the six mounted soldiers. Eden watched all this, puzzled and still fearful, holding on to the front door for support while her legs seemed to get thinner and more brittle, so that she felt if she moved they would snap like dry twigs beneath her. She swallowed, trying to moisten her dry throat, while the palms of her hands felt as if they were holding a pint of water each.

General Bronevich gave her his bullion smile: gold gleamed in his mouth like a newly-opened reef. 'I am General Bronevich,' he said in Russian. 'I am here to service you.'

Oh my God, Eden thought, does he really mean what he's just said? She swallowed again, forced some words out of her arid throat: 'What can I do for you, General? Your men have already been here —'

'I am coming in,' said the General and pushed past her and kicked the door shut behind him. He looked up and saw Frederick and Olga leaning over the balustrade at the top of the stairs. He hated kids, especially the kids of these namby-pamby Russian aristocrats. He bellowed 'Back to your room! I don't want to see you again! Go!'

At the top of the stairs Frederick drew himself up; but Eden got in first: 'Freddie, Olga – do as the General tells you! Go on, go back to your rooms – at once!' Then she added, her voice thinning with the fear that was taking her over completely: '*Please.*'

Frederick hesitated, then abruptly he grabbed his sister and the two of them disappeared from the top of the stairs. General Bronevich winked approvingly. 'You know how to handle children – good, good. Sometimes I think they should all be strangled at birth. But then we shouldn't be here enjoying each other, eh?' The gold came out again, carats of good humour. 'Well, let's see where we'll have our little interrogation. Are there any bedrooms downstairs?'

'No, General.' *Should I scream for help?* 'Let us go into the drawing-room.'

The General, disappointed that he might have to take second best in the way of a comfortable rape, followed Eden into the drawing-room and shut the double-doors behind him.

It was a long, high-ceilinged room with a parquet floor on which rugs were scattered. A big blue-patterned ceramic stove stood in one corner; there was also a marble-surrounded fireplace in which logs were already stacked as if winter might strike at any moment. The furniture, painted white with gold trim, was solid rather than elegant; but the

26

white grand piano in one corner stood on graceful carved legs and apologized for the heaviness of some of the other furniture. When the Gorshkovs had fled St Petersburg they had brought no furniture, but they had come heavily laden with ornaments. The rugs on the floor were Bokhara's best, brought from the house in St Petersburg; a Corot and a Watteau, bought by Princess Gorshkov on one of her visits to Paris, hung on the walls; several minor pieces by Fabergé decorated the mantelpiece. But Bronevich, a man with a crude eye, saw none of these better adornments.

He walked to the piano, opened up the keyboard lid and struck the keys with hammer fingers. He nodded admiringly at the discord he had created, then looked around him. He saw the long couch facing the open french windows and the view of the wheatfields beyond. It was not as good as a bed, but it would do. He put his belt and holstered pistol on a side table and took off his jacket.

Eden, not quite believing this was happening, said, 'General, what are you going to do?'

'You,' said the General and exposed his member, which, slant-eyed and bald-headed, looked as Mongolian as the rest of him.

Out in the barn Cabell, having seen Pemenov in the car and the six soldiers on their horses go off down the avenue, was wondering what was happening in the house. Down below him Nikolai had come back into the barn and was wandering up and down in a frenzy of fear and worry.

Cabell called down to him. 'Go across and see what's happening.'

Nikolai's upturned face showed eyes as white as a terrified horse's. 'He will kill me —'

Then there was a scream from the house. Cabell, clutching his rifle, tumbled down the ladder, went racing out of the barn and across towards the open french windows. He leapt up the steps and plunged into the drawing-room as General Bronevich tried to plunge into the wildly evasive Eden.

Cabell shouted and the General, letting go his trousers, spun round and grabbed for his pistol on the table beside the couch. His trousers fell down round his ankles, he stumbled and fell forward on his knees and Cabell hit him hard behind the ear with the stock of the rifle. The General gave a grunt and went down on his face, twitched and lay still. Cabell kicked him over on his back, saw the General's erection and modestly kicked him over on his face again.

Eden sat up on the couch, gasping for breath as she pulled her skirt down over her exposed legs. Her hair had tumbled down from its pins and hung wildly about the torn shoulders of her shirt; she looked nothing like the starched governess Cabell had talked to out in the barn. She glanced down at General Bronevich and saw the huge lump behind his ear from which blood was welling in a dark bubble.

'Oh my God! Is he —?'

For the first time Cabell realized what he might have done. He dropped down on one knee and felt the General's pulse. Then he rolled the Tartar over on his back, grabbed a rug and threw it over the now limp weapon that had threatened Eden, and bent his ear to the General's broad fat chest. Then he straightened up, wondering if today wasn't someone else's nightmare that he had wandered into.

'He's dead!'

Then the door burst open and Frederick, a double-barrelled shotgun held at the ready, stood there with a wide-eyed, terribly frightened Olga at his shoulder. The two children looked down at the dead General, then Olga pushed past her brother and ran into Eden's arms. Eden tried to comfort her while trying to pull herself together. Too much had happened in the last five minutes, she had been raped emotionally if not physically.

Cabell crossed to Frederick and took the gun from him. The boy stared at him, but there was no dispute. He would have fired the gun if there had been need for it; he was prepared to kill but he was not prepared for death. He had seen dead men before, the bodies of soldiers glimpsed lying beside the railway tracks as they had fled from St Petersburg, but he had never seen death up close. It was even more horrifying to have it here in the house with them.

'We've got to get away,' said Cabell. 'When will that dwarf in the car be back? Eden, I'm talking to you!'

Eden's senses, which seemed to have left her, started to work again. 'The dwarf? Oh – he told him to come back in an hour. But —'

'No buts. We're getting out of here. You, me and the kids.'

Frederick drew a deep breath, took his eyes off the corpse on the floor and tried again to be the man he thought he was. 'How? You said your motor car won't work —'

'We could go on horseback,' said Eden. 'But not to Ekaterinburg —'

'There's a British consul there – you'd be okay —'

'But not the children —' Her mind was in gear again. 'The local commander in Ekaterinburg would not let the children go —'

'Then we better head somewhere else. Does that Rolls-Royce work?'

'Of course,' said Frederick. 'Every week I run the engine – Father asked me to do that. But we'd have to put the wheels on. Father took them off and put them in one of the big wine vats with french chalk on them, to stop the tyres from perishing,' he said.

'Okay, you come with me. Eden, you and Olga pack a bag. You better tell the servants to get the hell out of here – they don't want to be in the house when the dwarf and those soldiers come back and find him.' He nodded down at the dead General, just a mound beneath the Bokhara rug. 'Can you see the road from upstairs?'

'Yes, from the main bedroom.'

'Olga, you stay at the window and keep an eye on the road. Let me know in a hurry if those soldiers start coming up from the gates. Eden, when you've packed your bag, get some food and water together. But first, get rid of those servants. Come on, Freddie.'

Cabell had no idea where he would head once (if) he got the Rolls-Royce started. But going on foot or on horseback would be futile; it would be like galloping off on a treadmill that would gradually grind to a halt beneath them. General Bronevich had probably been on the telegraph line to Ekaterinburg before he had left Verkburg; patrols would be on the alert all the way up the main road. To head west would mean going up into the Urals, into mountains that would offer no refuge; to go east would take them into the semi-desert steppes where they might run into another Tarter *ataman's* army. The only imperative need was to get away from here and trust to luck that some road would open up to safety.

As he crossed the yard towards the barn the full impact of what he had just done hit him. He pulled up sharply, as if it were a physical blow; then he hurried on, trying to shut his mind against the killing of Bronevich. He had injured men in fights, been injured himself; he was no stranger to violence in the often violent world in which he worked. But he had never killed a man before. What worried him was that as he had swung the rifle butt at the Tartar he had *meant* to kill him, though he hadn't expected it would happen. He had never even thought of killing any of the men he had fought; but those fights had been over private, personal differences, some trivial. He had never fought over a woman. But it struck him now that he had meant to kill Bronevich because of what the General had been trying to do to Eden. He went into the barn cursing his chivalry.

When he threw back the cover from the Rolls-Royce he was amazed at the condition of the car. Its royal blue paintwork and huge copper-domed headlamps gleamed; its leather upholstery was uncracked. It looked ready to be driven off at once, except that it had no wheels and was mounted on wooden horses.

'Nikolai washes and polishes it every week,' said Frederick. 'It was Father's pride and joy and he told Nikolai he expected it to be as good as new when he came home from the war.'

In the next half-hour Cabell came to admire and bless the absent Prince Gorshkov, who had such blind faith in the future that he wanted to ride into it in the same style as he had ridden out of the past. He had left instructions that would have done credit to Henry Royce himself; nothing had been overlooked. The tyres, kept in french chalk, were in perfect condition. There were five of them with inner tubes, plus four others stuffed with sponge rubber balls. There were six four-gallon cans of petrol, a two-gallon can of Castrol oil and a box of spare parts. And there was a small single-shaft, two-wheeled wagon that could be attached to the back of the car.

When the car was ready to go, Cabell stood back. 'Your father had some purpose for all this – he didn't get all this ready for nothing. Did he ever tell you what he had in mind?'

Frederick shook his head; but Nikolai answered, 'His Highness told me, sir. He said if ever the war was lost he was coming dack here and was going to drive the family to Vladivostok.'

'Father would never have said such a thing,' said Frederick. 'He wouldn't think that we could lose the war.'

Poor kid, Cabell thought. His Old Man protected him too well. The Russia of Rolls-Royces, even just nine of them, was gone forever. But Prince Gorshkov, wittingly or not, hadn't bothered to tell his children. 'We're not going to try for Vladivostok,' he said.

'Where are we going then?' said Frederick.

'Christ knows. I'll drive the goddam thing around in a circle and we'll see what direction it comes out.'

Then Olga appeared at the doorway. 'One of the soldiers is coming up the avenue!'

'Where's Miss Penfold?'

'Here.' Eden, dressed like Olga in a travelling suit, came into the barn carrying two large suitcases.

'Where are the servants?'

'They've all gone out to the fields. Quick – we must hurry!'

'Is there any back road out of here?'

'Yes – it goes down through the fields and out through the estate village.'

'Goddam!' Cabell went to the door, looked slantwise down through the poplars; the soldier, horse at a slow trot, was no more than a couple of hundred yards from the house. 'If he sees us drive out of here he could cut across the fields and head us off. Nick!'

Nikolai was slow to respond; he was thick with fear. 'Sir?'

'Go out, see what he wants. Try and get him to come into the barn. Offer him a drink of vodka, wine, anything. But get him in here! Eden, get yourself and the kids out of sight. Come on, for crissakes move!'

Eden pushed the two children ahead of her towards the rear of the barn. Nikolai turned to follow them, but Cabell grabbed him and spun him round.

'I told you – get out there and bring that soldier in here!'

'I can't, sir – I'm just jelly —'

'You'll be pulp if you don't do what I tell you!'

'You don't have to do it, Nikolai,' said Frederick gently. 'I'll go.'

He spun away from Eden and before she or Cabell could stop him he had run through the doorway and out into the yard. Cabell called to him in a low voice, but Frederick took no notice. Tears sprang into Nikolai's eyes, ashamed that a boy had gone out to do what he had been afraid to; yet he still couldn't move, stood there and wanted to die. Out in the yard Frederick stood with his back to the barn as the horseman came slowly out of the shadow-latticed avenue into the bright white dust of the yard.

'Good afternoon.' Frederick's voice broke, ending on a high note; he cleared his throat and tried again. 'Good afternoon, soldier. The General does not wish to be disturbed.'

The horseman was Pemenov. Thirsty, tired of driving around in the bone-shaking car, he had come back to the gates down on the road, where the six horsemen sprawled in the shade of the poplars. He had not wanted to drive up to the house in the car for fear its noise might disturb the General before the latter was finished whatever or whomever he was doing. He knew from experience how the General hated to be distracted while raping; it was one of his few sensibilities. The walk up the long avenue was too far for Pemenov's short legs, especially on a day like this; so he had borrowed one of the horses. He had shortened the stirrup leathers and one of the soldiers had lifted him into the saddle; he knew that they laughed at him behind his back, but they would never laugh at him to his face while he was the General's favourite. Now he sat above this arrogant aristocrat boy, his short legs sticking out on either side of the saddle, knowing he looked ridiculous and daring the boy to laugh. He would kill him if he did.

'I want water,' he said. 'A drink.'

'Water?' Frederick was still having trouble with his voice. Cabell, listening to him, thought, *The kid's scared stiff*. He looked angrily at Nikolai, but the anger died at once. Nikolai was still crying and behind the tears there was a look on his face that puzzled Cabell.

But Frederick was still managing to fool Pemenov: 'Get down, soldier —'

'Don't keep calling me *soldier*. I am a major, Major Pemenov.'

This funny little man a major? But Frederick couldn't laugh. 'Major . . . Get down and come into the barn. There's water there. And some of my father's vodka, too.'

Pemenov nodded agreeably. 'Vodka? That would be better.' He smiled and Frederick gave a tentative smile in reply: they were like two children getting to know each other. 'But with water, too.'

He slipped down from the saddle, landing with unexpected grace on his tiny feet. Leading the horse, he followed Frederick towards the open door of the barn. Frederick, for his part, suddenly realized he had no idea what Mr Cabell had in mind.

He faltered, stumbled, and the dwarf, still smiling innocently, as if eager to be a friend, reached forward and steadied him. Then they passed from the bright sunlight into the dimness of the barn.

Pemenov blinked, caught a glimpse of the gleaming big motor car, one he had never seen before, standing in the middle of the barn floor. He said, 'It's dark and cool in here.'

Then he saw the American coming at him. Cabell hit him with the starting handle of the Rolls-Royce and he went down into an even darker and cooler state. He dragged the horse's head down with him as he fell face forward; it stumbled but kept its feet and finished up astride him, its hooves pawing nervously on either side of him. Cabell wrenched the reins free of the dwarf's hand and threw them at Nikolai.

'Tie the horse over there! Okay, everyone in the car!'

Eden pushed Olga up into the rear seat, dumped the suitcases in the trailer and clambered into the front passenger seat. Cabell dragged a tarpaulin over the loaded trailer, tied it down with rope. Frederick had already jumped up into the driver's seat, closed the air tank switch and was pumping up pressure on the dashboard gauge. Cabell flooded the carburettor, then went round to the front of the car while Frederick set the mixture control to *Strong,* put the ignition control to *Late* and the governor control to *Midway.* Cabell gave the starting handle two complete turns, then Frederick switched on the engine.

'Here we go,' said Cabell. 'Say your prayers!'

There was no need for prayers. Henry Royce's engine started up at once, purred like some satisfied women Cabell had known. He ran round to get into the driver's seat, but Frederick had one hand on the wheel and with the other was reaching to let off the hand-brake.

'Out of there!'

'I understand this car better than you! My father taught me how to drive it —'

'Jesus, sonny, you'd turn the Virgin Mary into a Bolshevik! In the back, you hear!' He stood on the running-board, reached down and Frederick, with a yell, went backwards over the seat and into the rear beside his sister. 'You argue with me again and I'll hit you with the goddam handle!'

He dropped into the driver's seat, reached for the brake-handle and saw Nikolai standing in front of the car. 'Sir —'

'For crissake, Nick, get out of the goddam way!'

'Sir, I want to come with you —'

'There's no room! You'll be safer here – just disappear for a while —'

'Let him come,' said Eden. 'We can't leave him here. He's a foreigner, even to the people on the estate – just like you and me —'

'Oh Jesus,' said Cabell. 'Okay, in the back!'

He let in the gears and the Rolls-Royce glided out of the barn, the only noise that of the small trailer bouncing along behind it on its iron-shod wheels, did a wide turn and went down between the barn and the cow-sheds and out on to the narrow dirt road that led down through the tall yellow sea of wheat.

'Okay, we've started. Now where the hell do we head for?'

'Mr Cabell, would you mind moderating your language?'

'I will when I know where the hell we're going!'

'I think we should head for Tiflis,' said Eden.

'Jesus wept,' said Cabell and lifted his eyes skywards. The immensity of the sky seemed to reflect the distances that lay ahead of them. He had always had love affairs with horizons, but this was heading for the edge of the world. 'Tiflis!'

[4]

Pemenov got slowly to his feet. His head, always too big for his body, felt even bigger and heavier. He looked around, saw the tyre-marks of the Rolls-Royce as it had gone out of the barn into the yard. He felt the back of his head and cursed softly; he would kill the American when they captured him. Then he remembered the General.

He ran out of the barn and across to the house. He hammered on the front door, but there was no response. He raced down the front steps, round the side of the house; he came to the long narrow terrace and the open french windows. He went in, still running, and pulled up so sharply he skidded on the parquet floor.

It took him only a moment to learn the General was dead. He knelt beside the corpse, pulled the trousers up and covered the limp instrument that had led the General to his death. Tears came into his eyes as he looked at his uncle's ugly, brutal face. The General had laughed at him, made cruel jokes; but he had killed three men who had made the same jokes at Pemenov's expense. Pemenov's mother had killed herself when she realized what she had borne; his father, always a drunkard, had been killed in a drunken brawl when the cruelly named Peregrine had been only five years old. For the next twenty-five years Yuri Bronevich had cared for his unfortunate young cousin, treating him as a nephew. He had laughed at him, abused him, belted him, but he had protected Pemenov against what the rest of the world would have done to him.

Pemenov threw the rug back over the body. He took

Bronevich's pistol from where it had fallen, went out on to the terrace and fired two shots.

In less than a minute the horsemen came galloping up the avenue, followed by the General's car with its driver and, beside him, the soldier whose horse Pemenov had borrowed. Pemenov, who had now slung Bronevich's gun-belt across his chest like a bandolier, shouted orders for someone to look after the General's body; then he clambered up into the car and snapped at the driver to follow the tyre-tracks that led out of the yard. The driver let in the gears and the car, an ancient Mercedes that had never been properly serviced, wheezed out of the yard and down the narrow road that led through the wheat-fields.

It had gone no more than half a mile when its engine coughed, spluttered and died. The driver, a hulking youth who had never ridden in a car till a year ago, looked helplessly at the little man beside him. 'No petrol, Major. I forgot to fill the tank when the General rushed us out here —'

Pemenov's first reaction was to hit the driver with Bronevich's pistol. But some inner caution, always on the alert from past experience, held him back; his only protector was dead back there in the house. He sat there in the car, in the midst of the blinding yellow glare of the wheat-fields, and wanted to weep tears of rage and frustration. Then, looking back, he saw the horseman galloping at full pelt along the road after them. He stood up on the front seat and waited.

The soldier reined in his horse in a cloud of dust. 'We found a motor truck in the barn – it is the American's! The Englishwoman lied to us!'

Pemenov almost fell off his perch in a swoon of rage. First the American who had knocked him unconscious, then the Englishwoman who had tried to protect the American. The foreigners had to be driven out of Russia. Or killed . . . 'Give me your horse!'

The soldier reared back with his horse. 'Why should I? Who are you now—?'

Pemenov levelled the General's pistol at the man: Bronevich, though dead, still lent him some protection.

'Bring your horse here by the car! Give me the reins. Now get down!'

The soldier glared, but swung down from his horse and backed away. Pemenov stepped up on to the side of the car and vaulted into the saddle. He gestured to the driver. 'Give me the General's rifle and the bandolier and his binoculars!'

The driver, careful of the gun pointed at him, did as he was told. The rifle was a Mosin-Nagent, better than the ancient Krenk in the saddle scabbard. Pemenov took the Krenk from the scabbard, unloaded it and flung it into the wheat. He adjusted the stirrup leathers, then he was ready to leave.

'Don't follow me or I shall kill you. Give the General a decent burial.'

He dug in his heels and turned the horse south. He had no idea where he was heading, except to follow the tyre-tracks in the dust for as far as they might go. If he lost them, he would just keep riding south anyway, into the steppes and oblivion if that was the way it had to be. He could not stay here: his life would be hell. Better to head south, ride after the American, kill him. He owed it to the General who could no longer protect him.

CHAPTER TWO

'Tiflis is over a thousand miles from here, you know that?'
They had left the estate wheat-fields and were on a narrow
country road, bowling along under the immense blue glare
of the late-afternoon sky, a long trail of dust whirling out
behind the Rolls-Royce and its bouncing trailer. 'Where
does this road lead?'

'It goes round south of Verkburg, then up towards the
mountains. No one will be looking for us south of
Verkburg. That's why I suggested we should head for Tiflis.'

'Why not Cairo or Capetown? Goddam women! You put
'em in an automobile and they lose all sense of distance, they
think they're on some goddam magic carpet!'

'Watch it!'

'Put down your handbag! I'm not going to apologize –
you're enough to make Jesus Christ Himself swear!'

'I wish you wouldn't keep bringing the Holy Family into
your conversation. The children are good Orthodox
Christians. So am I. Well, not Orthodox – Church of
England.'

'I'm an orthodox lapsed Catholic. I'm not driving this
thing all the way to Tiflis – tomorrow I'll take the Holy
Family and myself and head north and take my chances.
We'll talk about it when we stop to have a meal – where's the
food basket and the water?'

'Oh my goodness!' Eden slapped a hand to the top of her
head, as if her hat were about to blow off. 'I left the basket
and the water-skin on the table in the kitchen!'

Cabell looked at her with wry disgust. 'What do you want
me to say now? Oh my goodness?'

They had gone fifty miles, were south of Verkburg and
heading up into the hills when a rear tyre blew out with a
blast like that of a small cannon. The car skidded, but Cabell
kept it under control and ran it gently off the road and in
amongst a stand of fir trees.

'There'll be twenty or thirty more of those before you get

to Tiflis,' Cabell said as he got out to fit the spare.

'We could fit the tyres with the rubber balls in them,' said Frederick, who had now got over his pique at being relegated to the rear seat.

'You can save those for the really rough roads.'

'You talk as if you've already made up your mind you're not coming with us.' Eden was careful not to sound aggressive. She had had time to think about what lay ahead of them and her early confidence had drained out of her as if a plug had been pulled.

'Let's say I'm looking for an alternative.' Cabell stripped off his shirt and hung it on the tonneau of the car. He saw Eden frowning at him as he pulled his overalls straps back over his shoulders. 'Okay, don't start lecturing me about my dress, Miss Penfold. I'm not going to get my shirt all sweaty and dirty just to shield your maidenly susceptibilities.'

'I wasn't thinking of mine. I was afraid for Olga's.'

'Does my bare chest worry you, honey?'

'Princess,' corrected Olga. 'Not at all, Mr Cabell. Naked men are beautiful.'

Eden gasped. 'You haven't seen any!'

'In books. With fig-leaves on.'

'There,' said Cabell to Eden. 'I could even get by in front of the Princess with just a fig-leaf . . . Relax, Miss Penfold. Take your corset off.'

'Not in your company, Mr Cabell.' Eden, aware that she now had to court Cabell into staying with them, tried to smile. But it was like a strip of lemon pith.

'Oh, you and I are going to be like an old married couple by the time we say goodbye.'

'How romantic,' sighed Olga. 'Love at first sight.'

Cabell grinned, patted her shoulder. 'That's one of the dangers of myopia, honey. Get Miss Penfold to explain that to you in one of her lessons.'

He was taking the spare tyre out of the trailer when he stopped and gazed down through the trees. Almost a mile away, perched on the side of a steep hill above a narrow pass, was a village, a collection of log huts strung along a single street and behind them the log stockades surrounding their gardens.

'Nick —' He took some roubles from the purse in his overalls pocket. 'Get along to that village and buy what food you can. Meat, bread, potatoes, whatever you can get. And see if they'll sell you a couple of water-bags.'

'What do I say if they ask who I am? Everyone is so suspicious these days.' Nikolai would much rather have remained to help fit the tyre.

Cabell looked at Eden. 'You know this area. Who could he be?'

'I don't really know it at all – we've hardly moved off the estate.' She was feeling more helpless by the minute and that annoyed her; she had always prided herself on being resourceful. But she tried: 'Nikolai, tell them you are up in the mountains with a prospecting team. There are one or two small iron mines up there, I think.'

'I'll go with you, Nikolai, and help you,' said Frederick, and Nikolai looked at him gratefully.

'You'll stay where you are,' said Eden.

Nikolai went off reluctantly, moving slowly down through the trees as if hoping the village would have disappeared by the time he reached it.

'Okay, Freddie,' said Cabell. 'Hop out and give me a hand with this jack. You ladies get out, too.'

'Mr Cabell,' said Frederick, 'if you wish me to do something for you, *ask* me, don't order me. I *am* a prince —'

'Freddie, you are a small stuffed shirt. Princes are a dime a dozen in Russia and don't let anyone tell you different. Down in Armenia and Georgia there are more princes than sheep. Now get out and get to work on that jack or I'll boot your aristocratic ass up through your aristocratic gut!'

Frederick stared at him, then looked at Eden for support. But she, while not agreeing with Cabell's choice of language, agreed with him in principle. There might be more than enough lords and ladies back in England, but at least they did not call themselves princes. It was a subject she had never raised with her employer, but princes for her were proper royalty. She could never bring herself to see Frederick on the same level as the Prince of Wales. Six years in Russia hadn't worn away even a thin layer of her Englishness.

'You had better do what Mr Cabell says.'

'Damned proletariat!' said Frederick and skipped aside as Eden swung her handbag. 'Wait till Father hears of this!'

'Is there anything I can do, Mr Cabell?' Eden said stiffly.

Cabell looked around. The sun had passed beyond the mountains above them and it was cool and pleasant here in the thick stand of firs. Some wild flowers, anemones and gagea, bright scattered trinkets, grew out of soft patches in the rocky earth. Nature's music, a soft wind in the tree-tops and the whispering trickle of water over rocks, suggested a peace that he welcomed after the events of the day. It would be dark in another two hours and it might be an hour or more before Nikolai returned with the food and water.

'You and Olga clear a spot for us to camp. We'll stay here tonight and move on first thing in the morning. If you don't mind soiling your hands, Princess —?'

'One had better become accustomed to working,' said Olga and picked up a twig between thumb and forefinger and threw it away with a fastidious grace that didn't bode well for her future among the workers.

Cabell and Frederick, the latter in sullen silence, changed the tyres. Then Cabell went looking for a place to wash and found a narrow stream dropping down over steps of rocks through the forest. He was out of sight of the others and he stripped off completely and washed himself down with the clear cold water. He wiped the water from himself with the palms of his hands and stood for a moment breathing the cooling air, smelling the forest and watching the green dusk ever so slowly start to creep up between the trees. A blue-grey waxwing bounced from branch to branch looking for supper and a red squirrel slipped like shifting bark up and down the trunk of a tree. This, as much as making a living from the search for oil, was what brought him to these remote spots. He had not left Prairie Avenue just for money alone.

His father had been an adventurer whose courage ran out when he was only 500 miles from home. Jack Cabell had come down from Quebec heading for the Amazon and then the Andes; he had wanted to see jungles and really great mountains. He had got as far as Chicago and his nerve ran out. From then on he had travelled in books, safe in hardcovers against storm, disease, cannibals. He had kept the books for his son and Matthew Martin, always called that by his mother who had an Irish taste for long-windedness and no liking at all for long distances, had followed his father's vicarious journeyings. But Matthew Martin had had more courage than Jack Cabell; and horizons called to him like houris. But, unlike most horizon-chasers, he always appreciated what he passed along the way. He smelled invisible flowers, heard silences, saw more than his eye told him. He knew that his job, if he was successful in locating oil, would bring men and equipment to spoil the very things he had enjoyed. But by then he had headed for another horizon and never looked back. That would only bring a sense of guilt and he was not perfect. The world, he hoped, would always be big enough to stay ahead of its despoilers. But sometimes he felt he was whistling into a wind that had not yet begun to blow, that was still beyond time's horizon.

He pulled on his clothes, donning his shirt again, and went back to where Eden, Olga and Frederick had cleared a space around the car. The air was cooling by the minute and he knew it would be cold here tonight. The climate could do that here on the eastern slopes of the Urals; the difference between midday and midnight temperatures could sometimes be fifty degrees Fahrenheit. He looked at Eden, wondering how warm she would keep a man.

'There's a stream over there,' he said. 'You can all go and have a wash.'

'Is that an order or a suggestion, Mr Cabell?' Eden had taken off the jacket of her travelling suit; her once-white blouse was grey with dust and there were dark stains of perspiration under her armpits. She was tired and testy and still upset by the day's events and she forgot about wooing Cabell to remain with them. Her voice once again was full of governess' starch.

'You can take it any way you want,' said Cabell, a little surprised: he had thought they had declared an unspoken truce. 'But while I'm stuck with a female nanny, two uppity kids and a limp-wristed Cossack, there's sure as hell not going to be any other boss but me around here.'

'You have a knack for putting people in their place,' said Eden, still not retreating. 'Are there any American Tsars?'

He grinned after her as she stalked off with the two children in tow. Goddam, he thought, how did General Bronevich keep his erection in the face of such scorn? She'd freeze the blood of a cantharides-crazy gorilla. How could he have wondered about her keeping a man warm?

Half an hour later Nikolai came back with two legs of mutton, two loaves of coarse bread, a small bag of potatoes, two full water-skins and three blackened and dented iron pots. And a load of high indignation.

'Those villagers are capitalist robbers! They saw I was a stranger and everything doubled in price!'

'You two kids peel the spuds,' said Cabell; then raised his hand threateningly. 'Get a move on! There's going to be no loafers in this commune. Everybody works!'

'Bloody Bolshevik tyrant,' said Frederick and ducked just in time as Eden's handbag came round in a swift whirl at his head.

The meal, when it was finally ready to be eaten, did no more than fill their bellies. 'We eat much better than this at home,' said Frederick.

'Kid, stop complaining. You're eating now what the workers in this country have been eating for centuries. Sometimes they didn't get as much as this. If you don't like it, just tie a knot in your digestive tract and live on air and your memories of what you had back home. But for crissakes shut up and don't complain!'

The boy sat very still for a moment, then suddenly he sprang up and walked off into the trees. Then Nikolai said quietly, 'Excuse me,' and got up and went after Frederick. There was silence for a long moment and Cabell put down the plate of mutton stew. He had three tin plates in his own cooking gear and he had doled out the stew on them, keeping a plate for himself and letting the other four share the other two plates between them. He chewed on the last piece of meat in his mouth and it tasted like soft alum.

'I'm sorry.' He looked across at Olga, who sat as stiff and white as a china doll. 'I didn't mean to hurt Freddie like that.'

The child said nothing; then she, too, got up and ran off to join her brother and Nikolai. Eden put down her plate. 'You say a lot of things that are right, Mr Cabell. You should learn to say them so that they don't hurt people so much. Especially children. Freddie and Olga aren't old enough yet to be blamed for what's wrong with Russia.'

'I know. I'll go and apologize —'

'No, leave them while they're with Nikolai – he'll comfort them. Talk to Freddie in the morning.' She stood up, began to gather up the plates. 'Perhaps it would be better if we went on alone to Tiflis. I don't think we're very compatible.'

He looked up at her. She was flushed by the firelight, strands of her hair had fallen down about her face: goddam, he thought, she's beautiful at times. 'I'll sleep on it.'

Later the children came back, said nothing to Cabell but quietly went about helping Eden with the washing-up. Nikolai, also silent, brought in more wood for the fires. Cabell sat with his back against a tree, feeling as much an outsider as he had ever felt in his life before. Once, as Frederick passed by him, he said, 'Freddie —'; but the boy ignored him and walked on. Cabell felt a flash of anger at being ignored by a child, but he swallowed it. He had learned diplomacy the hard way, but amongst men. Children were a whole new race to him and it was a wonder to him that he had ever belonged to them. He sat quietly against the tree till everyone had settled down for the night, then he got out his sleeping-bag and prepared to crawl into it.

'Good night, Mr Cabell,' said Eden from the rear seat of the car. 'Thank you for all you've done today.'

She and the children were sleeping in the car, she and Olga in the rear seat, Frederick in the front. Nikolai, covered with the trailer's dusty tarpaulin, slept on one side of the car; Cabell in his sleeping-bag was on the opposite side. None of them was comfortable or really warm; the children grumbled sleepily and Eden shifted restlessly. Only Cabell and Nikolai, the one grown accustomed to discomfort, the other born to it, went off to sleep at once.

Eden lay staring at the patches of stars showing through the tops of the firs. She could hear grunting and movement

44

in the forest, but Cabell and Nikolai had lit four small fires around the car and she hoped they would prevent any wild beasts from coming too close to the car. On reflection she was surprised how calmly she was taking the possibility of a bear or wolf coming into their camp. But then the hazards of living had been building slowly ever since August 1914.

She had come a long way from Croydon. Her father and mother, school teachers both, had not objected when she had applied for the advertised job in the *Daily Telegraph*; after all, they had encouraged her to read about faraway places and other people's customs. Of course, being Tories, they had been thinking of the Empire and good solid English-speaking stock such as Australians and New Zealanders and had seen her as the governess to some rich sheep farmer's family; they had visions of her rounding the Australians' sat-upon vowels and weaning them away from their aboriginal habits. Her mother had had a fit of the vapours and her father an attack of xenophobia when she told them, after the letter had gone off, that the job was with a Russian family in St Petersburg. Foreigners were best left to themselves to find their own way out of their ignorance; Russians were not only foreigners but barbarians as well. Better that she should become a missionary and go out and teach the Zulus or the Australian blackfellows; at least the Empire would gain something from that. But she was a stubborn romantic, the best sort; and in the end she had prevailed. The job was for two years and she had promised to return home at the end of it.

She had applied for a passport, something she had never heard of up till then, Russia and Turkey were the only two countries in the world that required travellers to have them. She had bought a steamer trunk and a suitcase and in September 1913 sailed on a German ship for St Petersburg. The adventure had begun.

She wrote home to tell her parents that the Russians, or anyway the Gorshkovs, were not barbarians. She told them that they would be surprised at how civilized the Russian middle and upper classes were. French (or sometimes English) was often the first language in a household; one spoke Russian only to the servants. The gentlemen bought all their clothes from English shops in St Petersburg; the women went to Paris to buy their dresses, their underwear and their cloaks; only fur coats, for men and women, were made by Russians for the Russian gentry. Why, Prince Frederick, the boy she was teaching, even wore Norfolk jackets, knickerbockers and Eton collars. She had been acclaimed as a gourmet chef when she had given the cook her mother's recipe for English trifle; the French governess, from the house next door, invited to tea, had thought the trifle was some sort of culinary joke; but she did not tell her mother that. She had written them not to worry: she was in circumstances every bit as civilized as those in Croydon. She did not mention that she was living in a good deal more luxury. She did not think it fair to compare the 20-room house in St Petersburg with the semi-detached house in Croydon. Nor the Corot, Watteau and Fragonard paintings in the big salon with the Landseer and Holman Hunt prints on the parlour walls. Nor did she think it fair to tell them that she could not see herself ever coming home to Croydon to live there forever.

Then August 1914 had come and Igor, Lieutenant Dulenko, went off to war. Her parents had not known of him; she had still been feeling her way, if that was not too indelicate a way of putting it, with a particular man. Then he had gone away...

But now memory failed her, was not strong enough to keep her awake: she fell asleep, worn out by the day. She slept fitfully, memories nibbling at her like mice, and when she woke she was stiff and cold and for a moment completely lost.

Then she sat up and saw Nikolai warming up one of the legs of mutton on a rough wooden spit and Cabell going off to fill the water-skins from the stream. She woke the children and told them to follow Mr Cabell and wash the sleep from their faces.

Cabell had filled one of the water-skins and was dipping the second into the stream when Frederick and Olga came through the trees. He said good-morning to them, but they just nodded stiffly. They knelt down to wash their faces. And the wild boar, grunting and whistling with terrifying

46

loudness, came barrelling down the slope straight at them.

Olga screamed and fell into the water. Frederick jumped across the stream, leaving the way open for the boar to come straight at Cabell. He swung the half-filled water-skin; it hit the boar on the snout and burst open on its tusks. The beast skidded to a stop, blinded by the water; it let out a horrible sound of rage, shaking its head to clear its sight. Cabell grabbed up Olga, flung her over his shoulder and raced for a tree that had fallen down across a gap between two big boulders. Out of the corner of his eye he saw Frederick haring off through the trees towards the camp and he hoped the boar would not follow the boy.

But the boar had already marked its target. It grunted and whistled again, then came straight after Cabell. He knew how fast the beast could move, had gone hunting them north of Baku; but he had never been as close as this to one before. He staggered up on to the nearest boulder, clutching hard at Olga as she slipped off his shoulder. He lost his footing and fell back as the boar came in beneath him. He landed on its back, heard Olga scream right beside his ear; somehow he managed to keep his footing and didn't fall over. He leaned back against the boulder as the boar, thrown off balance by his landing on its back, went down on its nose and rolled over and over like a circus dog. Cabell scrambled back up on to the rock, hands scrabbling at its rough surface, his knees scraping against it, and fell on to the fallen tree, only just managing to hang on to Olga as she tumbled forward off his shoulder. She was screaming, seemingly without stopping for breath, and her hands were clawing at him like birds' talons. Somehow he turned round on the tree-trunk, straddled it, feeling the rough bark against the insides of his thighs, and faced the boar as it came up on to the boulder. It paused, grunting and whistling at him, its tiny eyes red with hate, the tusks bobbing up and down as if already tearing into his guts.

It was no more than ten feet from him as he inched carefully back away from it; he could smell it, felt the heat of it. He was frantically trying to keep his balance on the narrow trunk as Olga still screamed and struggled in terror across his shoulder. He could feel his legs and arms beginning to tremble and he wondered if he was going to have the strength to get off the log if the boar hurled itself at him.

It kept putting tentative hooves on to the log, then drawing back. It wanted to be at him, to tear him to pieces with its tusks; but instinct told it it could not keep its footing on the thin round trunk of the tree. Frustration made it rage even more and Cabell, slowly easing his way back, the bark wearing away at the insides of his legs, never taking his eyes off the animal, waited for the boar to hurl itself across the intervening space. Which it all at once did.

He saw it coming at him like a giant blunt-nosed shell; then there was a shot. The boar's head seemed to blow apart; the hurtling beast slipped sideways in the air. It hit the tree-trunk only two feet in front of Cabell, bounced off and thudded down between the two boulders. It twitched, then lay still.

Cabell, clinging to the still screaming, struggling Olga, saw Eden come out of the trees, one hand holding her shoulder, the other the double-barrelled shotgun. With her was Frederick and, some paces behind, easing his way cautiously out from behind a tree, was Nikolai.

Cabell brought Olga forward from his shoulder, sat her facing him on the log and gently slapped her face. She gasped, drew in her breath; then her screaming quietened to a soft whimpering. Cabell patted her arm, then nodded down at the dead boar beneath them.

'He won't worry us any more, Olga. Relax, honey – it's all over.'

Olga whimpered, gulped, still trembled. Then Nikolai, overcoming his fear, certain now that the boar was dead, came in beneath the tree-trunk and Cabell lowered Olga down to him. Then, very conscious of his chafed thighs, Cabell lifted himself up and walked off the log and slid down the boulder to stand beside Eden and Frederick as they came up to him.

'Thanks, Eden. We're even.' He looked at the dead boar. 'He even looks a bit like General Bronevich.'

She was massaging her shoulder; trembling a little, too. She would never make such a lucky shot again; she hated to think what would have happened if she had missed. Or if her shot had been wide of the boar but not of Cabell and Olga. 'I've never a fired a gun like this before, only a light one.'

She gave the gun to Frederick, went to Olga and comforted her, leading her away through the trees and back to the camp. Cabell looked at Frederick. 'That was quick thinking, Freddie, getting Miss Eden here with the gun.'

The boy wanted to be a hero but he was too honest. 'She was already coming this way with the gun. As soon as she heard Olga scream —.'

Cabell put his arm round the boy's shoulders; only then did he realize how much Frederick had suffered at seeing his sister in danger. The wiry young body was trembling as much as Olga's had been; all the juvenile arrogance was gone. He wanted the comfort of an adult.

'Freddie . . . About last night. I'm sorry. Sometimes my tongue gets away from me. It won't happen again, if I can help it.'

'Will you be coming with us then?'

Cabell sighed. 'I'm afraid I may have to.'

They walked back to the camp, he with his arm still round the boy's shoulders, while Nikolai, a coward but not insensitive, quietly followed them.

[2]

Pemenov rubbed the insides of his short thighs, feeling the chafing there. It was months since he had ridden a horse for such a distance; he had always travelled with General Bronevich in the car. But he would have to suffer the soreness till he became accustomed to the saddle again: there was a lot of riding ahead of him.

He had picked up the trail of the car he was chasing on the road that skirted south of Verkburg. He had pulled his horse into a farmhouse and, producing the General's pistol and instantly wiping the derisive laughter off the farmer's face, had demanded food, a water-bag and the farmer's own straw hat. The farmer, aware now that this strange little man was quite capable of killing him and his family, had hurriedly obliged. Then, under questioning from Pemenov, he said yes, he had seen a motor car heading down this road. Yes, this was the only road till it joined the main road ten miles farther on. No, he did not know much about the main road except that his brother, who worked in Verkburg, said that it was the only road that went south and these days not many people travelled it.

So Pemenov headed south and now in the cooling evening he was making camp amongst some trees just beyond where the secondary road joined the main route. When he had eaten he wrapped himself in the stinking blanket that had held the soldier's saddle roll and settled down to sleep between the two fires he had lit. The horse was tethered to a nearby tree on a lead-rope long enough to give it room to move if it was attacked by a bear or wolves.

Pemenov put the loaded rifle beside him, closed his eyes and went off to sleep at once. He would need an early start tomorrow and it would be a long ride. He knew that motor cars, though they travelled faster, broke down more than horses. He fell asleep absolutely certain that he would catch up eventually with the American.

[3]

'We'll have to get more food. Some fruit and jam and honey, things like that. And some tea or coffee. Mr Cabell, are you listening to me? You haven't spoken since breakfast.'

They had had their meagre breakfast, none of them having any real appetite after the encounter with the boar; then they had re-packed the trailer and got on the road again. As they had driven out on to the road Cabell had seen the crows already coming in above the trees to the spot where the dead boar lay.

They had driven through the village where Nikolai had bought the mutton and bread. The villagers, alerted by the shouts of their children and the barking of their dogs, had come out of their wooden houses to stand and stare at the car as it rolled grandly down the single street. They saw only the occasional truck and never a car here; the outside world did not intrude, even the civil war was a war between strangers. The children and some of the women waved and one or two of the older men saluted: they had no idea who was in the car or whom it belonged to, but it was a symbol. Hands had been touching forelocks for centuries: it was a habit, good for one's health.

'I'm thinking about how far we have to go,' said Cabell. 'I wish to hell there was some quicker, safer way. An airplane, maybe.'

'That's wishing for the moon, Mr Cabell. I don't think we should pray for miracles. I didn't think lapsed Catholics ever did any praying.'

'It's a reflex action. You got any suggestions about what we should do?'

'Just keeping heading south and hoping for the best.'

'That's constructive. How about this war that's going on? It's all over the place. We've got no way of knowing whether we're going to run into a battle. I don't want to be caught in the goddam middle.'

'Watch it!'

'You have a knack for making anyone swear, Miss Penfold.'

'Were you in the Great War, Mr Cabell?' Frederick had recovered from his fright at seeing the danger his sister had been in. He was also recovered from his hurt at what Cabell had said to him last night. But he was still the little aristocrat, sitting upright in the back of the car while Cabell, the chauffeur, took him out for his morning spin. Despite what the American had said last night, he was not going to descend from prince to commoner overnight. His mother had coached him too well in his rank. 'The war against the Germans?'

'No. I was searching for oil.'

'That wasn't dangerous, was it? Not like fighting in a battle.'

'No, it was a joy-ride. Just like the last couple of days.'

'My father fought at Tannenburg, where he was wounded, and at Stanislau.'

Prince Gorshkov seemed to have had bad luck with his battles: Cabell wondered what other defeats he was presently headed for.

'Bully for him.'

The reply left Frederick nonplussed: his ear was still too young for an adult's sarcasm. But Eden looked at the American and wondered how he felt about his not having been in the Great War. He sounded as if he had some guilt about it. She herself had seen none of it, but she had seen the results of it. She had been at the station in Petrograd (she would never get used to that new name; St Petersburg had a ring to it, even if it was a German ring) when the hospital train had brought home the body of Igor. There had been other bodies covered with threadbare grey blankets; and wounded men, the sight of whom had depressed her more than the shrouded corpses. Men without limbs, a boy with half his face blown away; she had felt more pity for them than for the dead, even for Igor. For him she felt a terrible sense of loss; then realized later, with a sense of shame, that she felt sorrier for herself than for him. He had gone eagerly off to war, as he might have gone to the Swiss Alps to climb, which he had told her he did every summer; he would have died as he had wanted to, a hero in battle, died for Russia. She sometimes wondered, however, what had been his absolutely last thought just before death took him. Did men in battle really die as heroes or did they go out fighting death as fiercely as they had fought the other enemy?

But Cabell was not thinking of the past war. He had no regrets at having missed it, but he was irritated when someone suggested he should have been in it. He was more concerned with the present war:

'We have no idea where the armies are —'

'General Denikin's army is in the Ukraine,' said Frederick. 'That's where Father is.'

'There's a dozen damned armies. White ones, Red ones, private ones. At least back home *our* Civil War was pretty straightforward. What about you English?' He looked at Eden.

'We English don't fight amongst ourselves. At least not for three hundred years.'

'You fight the Irish. What about the Scots and Welsh?'

'They try to fight us. But we'll just ignore them.'

'And they'll all go home and be quiet?'

'Eventually.' But she really didn't believe that, only wished for it. Though she had never lost her Englishness, England was becoming like a foreign country to her. Her parents, in the infrequent letters that got through since the Revolution, told her that England had changed during the War. Perhaps when she eventually reached home – how soon? Next month, next year? – she would not recognize the country she had left.

They were still on a mountain road, passing through pine forests, but now the road began to dip as it swung slightly south-east. The car was behaving beautifully, rolling smoothly along without effort, everyone in it marvellously comfortable. Cabell, a man who had never wished for riches, suddenly was seduced; he wanted to be an oil millionaire, have a car like this. He would chase horizons, follow beckoning roads in the grand manner, a vagabond with style.

Then the forest thinned out and they saw the narrow-gauge railway track running up to the mine cut into the side of the mountain slope. A wagon loaded with ore was being winched down the track to two wagons, drawn by oxen, waiting on the road.

The half-dozen men standing by the ox-wagons stiffened in surprise as the Rolls-Royce came round the bend in the road and glided to a halt beside them.

'Good morning,' said Eden. 'Is there a town or village up ahead?'

The men glanced at one another, then a thickset, bald-headed man said, 'Who wants to know?'

Cabell, half-turned in his seat, saw that Frederick was about to let the men know who he was. 'Shut up, Freddie,' he said in English.

The foreign language caused a stir amongst the men. They had been examining the car, their expressions a mixture of amazement and admiration. Now they stopped dead and looked at the man in the wide-brimmed hat who spoke a strange tongue.

'Who's he?' said the bald-headed man.

'He is an American engineer,' said Eden. 'I am an English teacher.'

'Who owns such a motor car as this one?'

'I do,' said Cabell, and borrowed some of Frederick's arrogance for the moment. 'Good-day to you, gentlemen.'

He let in the gears and drove the car on before the men could move to stop him. Farther along the road, when they were out of sight of the mine, he said, 'Those guys were asking too many questions.'

'They are iron miners,' said Nikolai. 'Miners are different people from anyone else. It is the working underground, I think.'

'Who do they work for – themselves?'

'I don't think so,' said Eden. 'Probably for some land-owner who lives in Moscow or somewhere far from here.'

'They might work for my Uncle Vanya,' said Frederick. 'Father once said that Uncle Vanya owned everything for a hundred miles south of Verkburg.'

'Freddie will inherit it all when Uncle Vanya dies,' said Olga. 'He is Uncle Vanya's favourite nephew. I'm his favourite niece.'

'Well, you're not my favourite passengers,' said Cabell. 'I have an idea your Uncle Vanya wouldn't be those miners' favourite boss, either. Just keep your mouths shut about your relatives, okay? Stop playing Prince and Princess and be just plain Fred and Olga.'

'Mother won't like it when she hears of it,' said Olga.

'Your mother's safe in Tiflis.'

The children said nothing, just looked at each other and sat back stiffly in their seats. But Eden said quietly, 'You didn't have to say that, Mr Cabell.'

'I know,' he said just as quietly; he increased the speed of the car, hoping the wind would make the children deaf to what he said. 'But I haven't had much experience with kids.'

'That's very evident, Mr Cabell.' But she smiled when she said it and he grinned back at her.

Goddam, he thought, she's a good-looker and she looks as if, with the right feller, she'd enjoy . . . But with two kids and a namby-pamby Cossack in the car, what could a feller *do*?

Ten minutes along the road they came into a large village. There was a main street and side streets running off it; a white stone church sat on the slope above the wooden houses, its golden dome dull and patchy. Children and dogs appeared from nowhere; then doors opened and men and women stood there. Excitement made the warm lazy air come alive; no one had ever seen such a magnificent car. Cabell and the others floated down the main street as Cleopatra's barge might have floated down the Nile.

The main street ran into a square halfway through the village. On one side of the square a row of walnut trees fronted the entrance to a small railway station. Old men sat on benches beneath the trees, sometimes poking with their walking sticks at the hens that scratched about in the dust; they sat in silence, gossip and comment exhausted. Half a dozen women stood waiting their turn at the well-pump in the centre of the square, chatter spouting with the water. Several dogs rose up out of their torpor and began to bark as the Rolls-Royce and its procession came into the square and pulled up.

'You do the shopping, Miss Penfold.' Cabell got down from the car, smiling broadly at the gathering crowd like a politician gathering votes. 'Take the kids and Nikolai with you, get a good supply. Don't waste time. I'll have a talk with these old guys, find out what lies south of here.'

The old men sat up straight on their benches as he approached them. They looked remarkably similar in their loose blouses and baggy trousers, as if they had all shrunk to a uniform size inside their clothes. Their only difference was in their headgear: some wore caps, one or two had straw hats. They peered at him with their rheumy eyes, recognizing him as a foreigner but knowing no maps on which to place him. Their eyes retreated into the gullies of their faces and he felt he was walking into an ambush. He was aware that the crowd, those that hadn't followed Eden and the others, had fallen silent. He had a sudden premonition that he should turn back, get into the car, pick up the others and drive on. But it was too late now.

'Good morning, gentlemen.' Their gaze sharpened even more with suspicion; you could combine all their ages and no man in that time in this village had been called a gentleman. That was for the absentee land owners, the men who had come every year like the summer 'flu and been just as welcome. 'What is the name of this village?'

The old men looked at the man who sat in their middle. They all had beards or moustaches, but he had the most magnificent beard of all, a white explosion of hair that hid everything below his nose. He had once been tall but the years had shrunk him; but as he stood up there was no bend in his back. He wore a roughly woven straw hat, baggy blue trousers and a grey blouse from the breast of which hung a brightly polished medal on a faded ribbon. He didn't lean on his stick but held it as a gentleman might hold a staff of rank.

'Drazlenka is the name of our village.' He had a surprisingly young voice, as if time had not been able to get at his throat. 'Who are you, sir?'

'My name is Cabell. I'm an American, driving down to Tiflis and then to Batumi to catch the ship for home.'

'I know Tiflis, I was there once. On my way to my second war, the one in the Crimea against the English.'

'Your *second* war?'

The old man chuckled, like birds chirruping in the nest of his beard. 'I fought for our Tsar Alexander against Napoleon Bonaparte, I was a drummer boy.'

Napoleon and Alexander? That had been over a hundred years ago. The old man's mind was wandering; but he was obviously the one who had to be spoken to. He was the village patriarch, the other old men looked to him for their words. In the background the crowd was still silent, their faces no longer laughing and excited but blank.

'Does the road run right through to Tiflis from here?' said Cabell, humouring the ancient.

'One can always find a road,' said the old man. 'Perhaps not for the horseless carriage, but for one's feet. I walked the journey.'

'A thousand miles? Each way?'

'It took time. When one was young one had plenty of time.' Somewhere in the white jungle of beard Cabell guessed the old man might be smiling. 'Where do you come from now?'

Cabell hesitated, then decided that General Bronevich had probably not come this far south. 'From Verkburg.'

'The woman and the children are your family?'

Again he hesitated: would it be safer to lie to the old man? But there was no time for an answer. There was a hubbub across the square behind him. He turned round and saw Eden, Nikolai and the two children being hustled towards him by a group of men. Leading the group, now and again giving Eden and the others a rough shove, was the bald-headed miner.

'Ah,' said the old man and Cabell thought he heard the chuckle again. 'Here comes Comrade Keria. He will ask the questions now.'

He sat down again on his bench and the other old men nodded to him, pleased that he had displayed their authority and dignity. They sat there like honoured guests at some formal function waiting for the festivities to begin. Cabell, watching the group approach, aware of something in the atmosphere that he couldn't quite grasp, suddenly wondered if the festivities would include a lynching.

The whole village seemed to be gathered in the square now. People flowed out of doorways and streets and lanes, coming quickly but with scarcely a sound other than the clatter of their wooden-soled boots on the cobbles of the square. They crowded in behind the group escorting Eden and the others and for a moment Cabell thought he and the old men were going to be swamped. Then, only two or three yards from him, the miners and the crowd came to an abrupt halt. Eden grabbed the two children and with Nikolai moved to stand beside Cabell.

'What's going on?' he said.

'I don't know. The miners came rushing down the street in a lorry. They saw us going into a shop and they pulled up and grabbed us.'

Cabell saw the scared faces of the children and he put an arm round Frederick's shoulders. He said in English, 'Now remember, Freddie – keep your mouth shut.' Then he looked at the bald-headed miner and said in Russian, 'I am told your name is Keria.'

Keria twisted both little fingers in his ears, a disconcerting habit. 'Yes, I am Maxim Keria. Chairman of the Drazlenka Soviet of Bolshevik Workers.'

Cabell noticed that only the miners nodded approval of what Keria had just said; the rest of the crowd remained silent and expressionless. But he opened his arms, stepped forward and embraced the bald-headed Bolshevik. 'Greetings, citizen! Why didn't you say who you were back up there at the mine?'

Keria's surprise and puzzlement was no less than that of Eden. She stared at the traitor, wondering how she could have begun to trust him, even to like him. But Cabell, his back to her and the others, had guessed at the consternation that had gripped them. He stepped back from embracing Keria and without turning round said in English, 'Play along with me. Don't bugger this up or we're going to have our asses kicked in.'

'Watch it,' she said automatically. 'And you have the wrong revolution. They were citizens in the French Revolution. They're comrades here.'

'Nerves,' said Cabell, and he was full of apprehension. 'I lost my cue for the moment.'

Keria, suspicion replacing surprise, making his ugly face even uglier, said, 'Who are you?'

'I am Comrade Cabell and I bring you greetings from Big Bill Haywood and the Industrial Workers of the World. Big Bill said to me, Comrade Cabell, he said, go out there to Siberia and tell the workers there that the IWW is right behind them. And, by God we are! Aren't we, Comrade Penfold?' He reached behind him, pulled the stunned comrade forward. 'This is Comrade Penfold, who's come all the way from England to bring greetings from George Bernard Shaw!'

As he looked at Eden, out of the corner of his eye he saw the white beard twitch in the region of the patriarch's mouth. Was the old son-of-a-bitch smiling?

'Greetings from George Bernard Shaw and Keir Hardie and Sidney Webb!' Eden shouted in a wobbly voice. If her mother and father, the Tory true-blues, could only hear her now . . .

But Keria was unimpressed. 'Who are these Industrial Workers of the World? Who is this George Bernard Shaw?'

Eden looked sideways to Cabell. 'I'd hate to be in England

58

now. I think an earthquake might have just happened.'

'An earthquake named Shaw? I wish he were here now. We could do with some of his arguments.'

'What are you talking of in your foreign language?' Keria demanded. 'Why do you have a magnificent car like this? Workers don't ride around in such cars.'

'They do in England and America,' said Cabell, trusting to the ignorance of isolation; but out of the corner of his eye he saw the huge white beard twitching again. 'Soon everyone here in Russia will do the same.'

He sounded ridiculous in his own ears; but he had no other weapon. He tried desperately to remember some of the rhetoric he had heard from the Wobbly organizers on the Texas oil fields, but all that came to mind was the apathy of the workers they had been adressing and the brutal antagonism of the oil-field bosses. Phrases came back to him – 'Workers of the world unite!', 'Sell your labour, not your life!' – but the iron miners of Drazlenka remained as unmoved as the oil workers of Texas. He might have been Big Bill Haywood addressing a Republican convention.

At last he threw up his hands and looked at Eden. 'I don't think I'm getting through. You got any messages from Karl Marx?'

But Eden had messages from no one. She had no ear for political oratory; all she could remember of Trotsky and Kerensky was that they were boring. She gestured helplessly.

'Well, that's it, Comrade,' Cabell said to Keria. 'Greetings from the Great Outside World.'

'You are not comrades,' said Keria and behind him the miners nodded their heads. But the crowd said nothing, did not move. 'You will be executed after you have been tried.'

'You have the verdict before the trial?'

But Keria was deadly serious: he had no sense of humour. 'Just as it was under the Tsar.'

Behind him Cabell felt Frederick stir and he stepped back and put his heel on the boy's toe. 'Sorry, kid.'

'Who are these children?' Keria demanded, scrutinizing them for the first time. 'They don't look like the children of workers. And who is the scrawny one?' He jerked his head at Nikolai.

'The children are mine,' said Cabell. 'Their mother was Russian but unfortunately she came back for the October Revolution and fell prey to the charms of a workers' chairman from Georgia. That's why we are on our way to Tiflis, to ask her to return to our family circle. You want your mother back, don't you, children?'

The children were a little slow to respond to their substitute father and Eden answered for them. 'Of course they do.'

'Why are you travelling with this man?' Keria glared at her. 'Are you his mistress?'

'Watch it,' said Eden. 'Not in front of the children.'

For the first time the crowd showed expression. It looked disapproving: adultery was a bourgeois habit. 'What about him?' said Keria, jerking his head again at Nikolai.

'A fellow worker,' said Cabell. 'Trotsky himself lent him to me. His very own godson.'

He's gone too far, thought Eden. But some of the miners looked at Nikolai with new interest and some murmured approval. But Keria was all suspicion. He was trained for the future: trust no one. 'He can prove that at the trial. Take them away!'

But the Drazlenka soviet had never had any prisoners to try: it did not know where to take them. There was no village jail or police station, no army barracks: they had authority but none of authority's conveniences. They looked at Keria in bewilderment and he stared back at them, bewildered by his own command. Cabell suddenly wanted to laugh, but he knew the situation was far too serious for any merriment.

Then the white-bearded old man stood up. 'Put them in the railway waiting room. There is no train for another two days.'

So the enemies of the proletariat were carted off to the railway station. The crowd surged along behind them. Any stranger coming on the scene would have thought that he was witnessing the departure by train of the village's favourite family. There was no booing or jeering, just laughter and shouting; it was as if now that Keria had made the decision for them, the crowd had come alive again. But if the crowd was now merry, none of its merriment communicated itself to Cabell. With one eye never leaving Keria, seeing the sense of power all at once beginning to swell the man, he knew that the bald-headed miner intended to have an execution if it killed him. He would only be following in the tradition of Russian history: drastic solutions for minor problems. The Tsars had been better teachers than they knew.

Cabell, Eden, Nikolai and the two children were herded into the dusty waiting room. Keria gave instructions to two of the younger miners, then he left, closing the door behind him. Outside the crowd drifted away, but some children remained, their faces pressed against the grimy windows of the waiting room. The two young guards, uncomfortable in their unaccustomed role, sat down on a bench beside the door. The prisoners, equally uncomfortable but for a different reason, stood awkwardly for a moment, then they, too, sat down on the benches around the grimy walls. Above Eden's head was a fly-spotted time-table; but someone had painted a rough red hammer-and-sickle on it. Behind the red paint of revolution were the schedules of trains that might never run again. Cabell wondered where the train due in two days would be heading, wondered what its passengers would think if they saw five corpses hanging by the neck from the walnut trees outside. But maybe train passengers all over Russia were familiar with such sights now. He just didn't know. He began to feel more and more remote, as if the real world were sliding away from him.

'I want to go to the lavatory.' Olga was pale under her perspiration, afraid and trembling again.

Eden put the request to the two guards. They looked perplexed, not knowing what privileges a prisoner was entitled to. Then the door opened and the white-bearded old man came in. The two youths stood up, but he ignored them. He looked at the prisoners in turn, then he smiled at Eden.

'A pretty girl. You make an old man feel young again. Or wish he were young.'

'Thank you, Grandfather —' Eden wondered if thanks for compliments were in order in such circumstances.

'My name is Delyanov. Alexander Dmitri Delyanov. I was named after Tsar Alexander. The first Alexander.'

'Comrade Delyanov —' One of the guards felt he had

better start acting like a guard. 'Comrade Keria said no one was to come in here —'

'Stuff Comrade Keria,' said Comrade Delyanov. 'I am one hundred and twenty-five years old and I am not going to be ordered about by infants like you. I am wearing trousers older than you —' He gestured at his baggy patched pants. 'Get outside! Go on – out!'

Cabell hardly saw the young men exit. He was gazing at Delyanov, trying to make his eyes believe what his ears had heard. He knew of tales of men who lived to a great age in southern Russia; but they had been men from the hills and mountains of Georgia. Perhaps no one had come here to the southern Urals looking for ancients; but he still could not believe that Delyanov was as old as he claimed. A man who had seen Napoleon . . .

'Did you – I mean are you really as old as all that?'

Delyanov smiled. 'You think I am a liar, don't you, Cabell? You are one yourself, a liar with lots of imagination. It was a pity you were wasting it on clods with no imagination. Yes, I am one hundred and twenty-five years old.'

Frederick gasped and Olga opened her eyes wide. Cabell said, 'Did you actually *see* Napoleon Bonaparte?'

'Of course.' Delyanov was not offended; he had been asked the question a thousand times. 'I was at Tilsit in 1807 when the Tsar and the Corsican met on the raft in the middle of the Niemen River. I led the Tsar down to the boat that took him out to the raft, playing my drum. He pinned that medal to my tunic himself.' He patted the medal on his breast. 'He was a strange one. He could have been the greatest of them. But —'

'I want to go to the lavatory,' said Olga with a full bladder and no sense of history.

'How many wars have you fought in?' said Frederick.

'Three. The war against Napoleon, the one against the Turks and the one against the English. I missed the last two, against the Japanese and against the Germans. I volunteered, but they laughed at me. They laugh at old men sometimes for the wrong reasons.'

'How have you lived so long?' Cabell still could not bring himself to believe that Delyanov was as old as he claimed. He looked like a well-preserved seventy at the most.

'The right food, the right thoughts and baggy trousers.' He pulled out his trousers to show their bagginess. 'Tight trousers cut off the blood to your crotch. That's where a man's youth is, in his crotch.'

'Watch it,' said Eden, nodding at Olga.

'My dear —' Delyanov bowed to Olga. 'I apologize.'

'Will that awful man Keria really execute us?' said Frederick.

The old man nodded. 'He wants to make a name for himself. A name for himself in this village!' He laughed and for the first time there was the sound of age in his throat: it was an old man's cackle. 'When you have seen emperors, as I have . . . Keria is a little man with little ambitions.'

'Killing us is a big ambition in my eyes,' said Cabell. 'Who owns this village? Don't people have any say?'

The old man shrugged. 'This village used to belong to a prince, Prince Vanya Gorshkov.' Frederick and Olga raised their heads, but Delyanov didn't notice. 'He won't come again. None of those princes will.'

'Are you a Bolshevik?' Cabell said.

'No more than you are, Cabell.' Delyanov's beard twitched. 'I am a realist. The past is past, so I am a Bolshevik if they say I am.'

'But surely the people won't let Keria kill us?' said Eden.

'Who knows? They are a strange people here. I wasn't born here – I came here sixty years ago. I am here more years than most of them have lived, but they still say I came from outside. They want to build a wall round Drazlenka now, shut out everyone. This was always a village that hated outsiders. Now that the Prince won't be back . . .'

'Can you help us escape?'

'I want to go to the lavatory,' said Olga. 'I can't hold it any longer.'

'I can't help you escape,' said Delyanov, 'but I can escort the young lady to the lavatory.'

He opened the door, stood back to let Eden and Olga go out. He looked back at Cabell and the beard twitched again. 'You and the boy and the scrawny one will have to attend to your own bladders. Everyone pisses on the railway tracks.'

He went out, closing the door behind him. They heard him snap something at the two young guards, then the door opened and the two youths looked in and jerked their heads at Cabell.

He, Frederick and Nikolai went out on to the small station platform and stood there in a row relieving themselves. Cabell looked south down the railway line, wondering how far it went. Was there another town further on, one where outsiders were hated as much as in this one? He began to appreciate for the first time that they were heading into a part of the Russian Empire that had never really been fully conquered, where the people did not, and possibly never would, see themselves as Russians.

'I wish they would stop calling me the scrawny one. They all sound like my father.' Nikolai shook himself, pulled up his trousers and turned back towards the waiting room. Melancholy and insulted, he eyed the two guards who stood watching them. 'Shot by Bolsheviks. He'll never forgive me for that.'

'I doubt if he'll get to hear of it.' Cabell tried to sound comforting, a little difficult in the circumstances. 'How are you, Freddie? You've kept your mouth shut pretty well.'

'I'm going to let them know who I am.' Frederick waved a strong stream in the air, a golden rapier stroke. 'So's they'll know whom they're murdering.'

'Whom? That's good grammar, Freddie, but poor politics. We've got to start thinking of getting out of here.'

Crossing the square with Eden and Olga, Delyanov fluffed up his beard and said, 'You're a remarkably pretty girl.'

'Thank you,' said Eden, and refrained from saying he had already told her that. She had met lecherous old men before, but never one as ancient as this. She changed the subject away from herself: 'You sound as if you might have been educated, Mr Delyanov.'

He nodded proudly. 'I educated myself, taught myself to read when I was forty years old. I met Pushkin – you know, the poet?'

'I know him.' She had discovered him when she had come to Russia, almost swooned over Tatiana's love letter to Onegin.

'I didn't agree with everything he wrote. Too much about freedom – that was what I thought then. Now – well, maybe he was right. I met Tolstoy too. On my hundredth birthday I made the journey all the way to Yasnaya Polyana to pay my respects. He talked to me, called me Uncle – he thought he was getting old till he talked to me. He talked to me about what he believed in. I began to see that things had been wrong —' He shook his head and the beard quivered. 'You are a hundred years old and one day you discover you've been blind all your life.'

'It's not too late.' But Eden felt ridiculous telling him so.

'No.' He fluffed up his beard again. 'I can save you from being shot. Marry me.'

Eden stopped by the well in the middle of the square, leaned against its stone wall while she splashed water on her face from the dribbling pump. There were still people in the square: the half-dozen old men still sitting under the walnut trees, seve   conferences of crones, children slipping like drops of mercury from one group to another. The heat pressed down on her like a soft invisible weight; it came up from the cobblestones and the dust as sharp white lights that made her eyes ache. Everyone in the square, even the old man immediately in front of her, seemed to hang suspended in shimmering sunlight. She was going to faint; or fall into the mirage with them. Yesterday a Mongolian general had tried to rape her; today a centenarian was proposing marriage. Perhaps she was already in the mirage.

'Don't you already have a wife?'

'I've had four. They're all gone. You're a pretty girl, you'd be good to look at in my old age. Keep me company. All my children are dead, too. All twelve of them. Took after their mothers, all died young. None of them lasted past seventy.'

Eden wanted to laugh. She could feel hysteria taking hold of her like a fever. She looked wildly around for some grasp on reality, heard Olga say, 'I want to go to the lavatory.'

'Here it is.' Delyanov led them up a lane past log houses, opened the gate in a rough wooden fence and pointed to an out-house in the middle of a vegetable garden. Olga, walking carefully but quickly, went along the garden path to the lavatory and disappeared into it. Eden leaned against the fence, recovered slowly.

'If you marry me,' said Delyanov, 'Keria won't shoot you.'

'But you don't *know* me – we have only just this moment met —'

'I like your looks. At my age one cannot afford to waste even a day.'

'At my age one doesn't marry at a moment's notice. You will have to give me time.' But she knew that back home her mother already thought she was on the shelf for good: twenty-six and no husband in sight. But she couldn't see herself taking a centenarian bridegroom home to Croydon.

'There is not much time. You may be dead by tomorrow afternoon. This man Keria is very impulsive.'

She had heard the phrase *a shotgun wedding*, something that Americans evidently went in for. But this was terrifyingly ludicrous: a firing-squad wedding. 'I shall have to talk to Mr Cabell.'

'Is he your lover?'

She hesitated, then nodded: any port in a storm. 'He won't like it.'

'He will if you save his life and the children's. What does he do besides tell lies about being a comrade?'

'He's an engineer, an oil engineer. A geologist.'

'They're practical men,' said Delyanov, as if the engineers he had known put romance to some mathematical test. 'Ah, here comes the little girl. That better, my dear? A little bladder relief does wonders.'

Olga gave him her princess look. 'One does not talk about such things in polite company.'

Delyanov smiled in the depths of his beard. 'You'll be a great lady some day, my dear. May you live long enough,' he said, and winked at Eden.

He escorted them back to the railway station, exhorted Eden to consider his proposal as a serious one and left them in the care of the two young guards. Eden closed the waiting-room door on the youths, leaving them sitting on a bench in the sun. They didn't protest but sat there dumbly, now and again looking at each other as if expecting some flash of intelligence that would tell them exactly what their duties were. They had heard all the theory from Comrade Keria, but this was the first lesson in the practice of revolution and they were at a loss. The revolution, Keria had told them, was a Russian affair, a war against the Tsar and all the reactionaries who had supported him. And here they were guarding two foreigners, a couple of kids and a scrawny one who sometimes walked like a girl.

Eden sat down on a bench in the waiting room and said, 'The old man wants me to marry him.'

'He is far too old for you,' said Frederick. 'He would be impotent.'

'Watch it!'

'What sort of education did you give these kids?' said Cabell; but it was only a mark-time remark while he took in what she had said. 'The old son-of-a-bitch must be senile. It's – it's indecent!'

'What is the matter?' Nikolai said in Russian.

Cabell told him and the Cossack rolled his head in shock and despair.

Eden said, 'If I marry him, he says he can arrange it that you four go free.'

'No!' said Cabell and the two children echoed him. 'It's all a bluff. That guy won't have us shot.'

But later that night, trying to sleep on one of the hard wooden benches, Cabell felt no optimism at all about their fate. He had heard of the wholesale killing by both sides in this bloody civil war and he knew and understood some of the hatred that fired the revolutionaries. Keria was one of them, recognizable at a glance, a man looking for a way out of a hole in the ground to a place on top of the mountain. Cabell had seen the coal miners on strike in the hills of Pennsylvania, the men who had inherited the fierce passions of the Molly Maguires of the 1870's. Miners had the seeds of revolution ingrained in them as deeply as the mine dust in their lungs. He could not blame Keria for the way he felt. He just did not want to die as a way of proving Keria's revolutionary zeal. And there was also the villagers' hatred of outsiders . . . Tomorrow there would be no one on his and the others' side at the trial, no one but a randy old man offering to marry a girl young enough to be his great-granddaughter.

He turned over to go to sleep and saw Eden sitting up on her bench, her head and shoulders outlined against the moonlit window. Quietly he got up and went and sat beside her.

They spoke in whispers, not wanting to wake the children and Nikolai. 'What am I to do?' she said. 'I keep thinking of the children. And you,' she added. Then added further, lives weighing on her like sacks of potatoes: 'And Nikolai.'

'It's not worth the risk,' he said. 'The old man can't guarantee we'd be let go.'

'Perhaps I could save my own life. I'm ashamed that I keep thinking of that.'

He felt for her hand, found it. It was the first time he had touched her and both felt the immediate intimacy; but their hands were stiff one within the other, arthritic with caution, wary of the circumstances that had brought them this close. 'When he dies – it could happen tomorrow, the day after, any time . . . What happens to you then?'

'They'd probably kill me then.' Her fingers were just dead bones in his hand.

'I'm not going to let that happen. Not to any of us.'

'What are you going to do?' Then she started to weep. It was something she hadn't done in a long time, not since the first lonely weeks when she had first come to Russia and then when they had buried Igor Dulenko. She had never thought of tears as a sign of feminine weakness, but somehow she had survived without them till now. When Cabell put his arms round her she didn't resist but leant her head against his shoulder and let the tears come. It was so long since he had held a girl like this one in his arms that he felt awkward; there had been girls in his arms but they had been paid for and none of them had asked for gentleness or sympathy. He brushed his lips against her hair, but said nothing.

On a bench opposite them Nikolai watched them and wept, too. For himself alive today as much as for himself dead tomorrow. He longed for love, but there was no man who would comfort him.

In the morning the villagers came early to the square, like a football crowd eager to get good seats for today's big match. They brought chairs with them and set them up in a hollow square in front of the railway station. The sun climbed through a brilliant sky and the tree-shrouded mountains flickered with flashes of green as the trees stirred in the slight morning breeze; to the east clouds lay on the horizon like the white negative of another dark range. The breeze suddenly dropped as the sun got higher, the trees in the square drew their shadows into themselves and the heat already began to sear like an invisible flame. Two ravens appeared out of nowhere, materializing like black spirits, and flapped lazily on to the roof of the railway station. They croaked miserably as the prisoners were led out of the waiting room and Cabell, looking up, thought of the line (was it from *Hamlet*?): *The croaking raven doth bellow for revenge.*

But there was no look of revenge on the faces of the crowd sitting on their chairs, standing in orderly groups. They looked uncertain this morning, as if during the night they had dreamed of the enormity of what they wanted, the death of the outsiders. The old men sat in the front row, some of them with their wives.

Delyanov rose from his chair and came forward. He carried a bunch of red roses and, taking off his hat with a sweeping gesture, he handed the bouquet to Eden. 'Everyone knows of my proposal. I announced it last night. You will be welcomed by all as my wife.'

'Silly old bugger,' said an old woman in the front row and chomped her gums at him.

Delyanov turned to her. 'You are only jealous, Natasha Mihalovna, that I did not ask you to be my bride.'

'Who would have you?' said Natasha Mihalovna. 'It takes you all your time to pee, let alone use it for anything else.'

'Do you mind?' said Eden. 'There are children present.'

'Holy Toledo!' said Cabell, careful for once of the children.

'What's the matter, Mr Cabell?' said Eden.

'Nothing, nothing.' He shook his head, wondering if the heat had got to him already. By tonight it wouldn't matter what was discussed in front of the children, they would only be corrupted by worms. 'Here comes Judge Keria.'

But Keria was not the only judge. The village soviet had stayed up half the night planning this trial; it would be done in the proper way, even if the verdict was already decided. Keria and two other miners sat down behind the table that had been placed outside the entrance to the railway station. The five prisoners were sat on chairs placed to one side; opposite them sat two more miners, the prosecutor and his assistant; there was no counsel for the defence. The walnut trees threw impartial shadows on all of them; the spectators sat in the open sun but seemed oblivious of it. Keria rapped the table with his gavel, a short pick-handle, and the trial began.

The prosecutor, a burly young man with close-cropped black hair and a look of intelligence that had never been allowed to flower, rose to his feet, conscious of the occasion and his position in it.

'The charge is that these five strangers are enemies of the State.'

'You have no evidence,' said Cabell.

'I second that,' said Delyanov.

'Shut up, you old fool,' said Natasha Mihalovna and some murmurs in the crowd seconded her advice.

'You were the same at the priest's trial,' said Delyanov. 'You're not interested in justice, just in satisfying your spite.'

'You don't know what you're talking about,' grumbled the old woman, not sure herself what he was talking about. What was justice? No one in the village had ever known it.

Cabell looked for a priest amongst the crowd, but there was none; then he looked across the square and up past the houses to the white church on the slope above the village. Its doors were closed, planks nailed across them. Had the priest been driven out of the village or had he, too, been executed? He stared at the church, then his eye caught sight of something else on the crest of the slope. A horseman stood there gazing down on the scene in the square. The rider was small (a boy perhaps?) and he sat without moving. Was he waiting, Cabell wondered, to take a message of their execution to another village?

Cabell looked back at Delyanov. 'What happened to the priest?'

'They drove him away,' said Delyanov. 'Drove him away with stones.'

'Good riddance!' cackled Natasha Mihalovna.

Keria banged the pick-handle, called for order. 'Go on,' he said to the prosecutor.

But the prosecutor was too slow. Delyanov was back on his feet, speaking directly to the tribunal this time.

'The young woman, if she has any sense, is to be my bride. So I say you cannot execute her friends, because they will be my friends, too. I move the trial be ended.' He looked at the old men on either side of him. They stared back at him, neither denying him nor supporting him. He drew himself a little straighter, then turned and stared back at the crowd, challenging it. 'Well? You have heard me speak. Let me marry the girl and let the others move on!'

There was silence for a moment, then Natasha Mihalovna chomped her gums and suddenly screamed, 'Sit down, you old fool! The trial goes on!'

There was another moment's silence. Cabell looked out at the crowd, realized with a sickening sudden emptiness that Delyanov was alone. Then someone clapped. The clapping spread through the crowd, hesitatingly, never loud, the hands hollow so that the sound, too, was hollow. It was an answer; but not the answer Delyanov had expected. He looked around him, bewildered; suddenly, after sixty years, he, too, was a stranger again. Abruptly he sat down, looked as if every one of his years had all at once fallen in on him. Jesus, Cabell thought, they've just executed him!

The prosecutor, given back the floor (or the roadway, for he stood in the middle of it), put the case against the prisoners. The foreigners had no proof that they were who they said they were; the children were half-Russian, as admitted by the American, but they did not look nor sound even half-worker. Compare them with the children of our village . . .

He swept an arm around the square and Exhibit A, a hundred or more children of all ages, beamed like a hundred small suns. Frederick and Olga gazed at them with such superior stares that the hundred suns suddenly split and tongues were poked at the two junior prisoners.

'People like this cannot be allowed to run loose! Trust no one, says Vladimir Ilyich – Lenin has the right idea! We must protect the Revolution!'

'Now just a minute —'

Cabell, counsel for the defence, stood up. Then he remembered his manners; maybe a little graciousness wouldn't go amiss. He bowed to the three judges; two of them involuntarily inclined their heads, but Keria remained unmoved. Then Cabell bowed to the crowd, and after a moment's hesitation they bowed back, all the heads dipping like huge sunflowers suddenly wilting; then the heads all snapped up again, as if the crowd had just remembered that it no longer had to bow its head to anyone. Cabell noticed that Delyanov was the only one who hadn't moved: his head was already bent, his chin sunk on his chest. It was impossible to tell whether he was indifferent or asleep or just plain dead.

'Our friends speak of the Revolution being protected,' Cabell said. 'Does it need such protection? Revolution never fails if it has the proper target and the aim is straight – that is why Lenin and the men in Moscow can't be defeated! But are we —' He waved a hand at himself, Eden, Nikolai and the two children. 'Are we proper targets? Should you waste bullets or rope on strangers?'

'Why not?' asked Keria. 'We have plenty.'

'I plead not for myself but for this lovely lady, every inch a socialist from her head to her toes. For this young man, godson of Leon Trotsky —' He wondered if anyone here knew that Trotsky was a Jew. Did Jews have godsons? 'And for my two beautiful children, deserted by their mother, uninterested in war and revolution, wanting only their mother's loving arms about them again —'

In his mind's eye he stood off and looked and listened to himself. Only the Misses Lilian and Dorothy Gish were missing; he wished he could whistle *Hearts and Flowers*. This whole event was a nightmare, a caricature melodrama: at any moment the US cavalry would come galloping to the rescue . . . He was light-headed with the heat and despair. His oratory had fallen on unsympathetic ears. It suddenly struck him that the crowd had not the slightest interest in Lenin, Trotsky or any of the other revolutionaries in Moscow: they were letting Keria conduct the trial because he was the only organizer amongst them. Cabell's and the others' only crime was to be outsiders. He looked at the judges, the prosecutor and the crowd. Every eye was dry and cynical, he could have been selling salted peanuts to a mob dying of thirst.

'I think you should sit down,' said Eden. 'But thank you, anyway.'

He slumped back in the chair beside her. Beyond the heads of the crowd he could see the Rolls-Royce parked beneath the tree where he had left it yesterday. He wondered if the Winchester and the shotgun were still in the car; or were they in the trailer? He couldn't for the life of him (he laughed sourly and silently at that) remember where he had put them yesterday morning. He looked covertly about him. He could see no one carrying a gun; the guns would be produced later for the firing squad. If he chose the right moment, moved quickly enough . . . But he had forgotten Eden and the children and Nikolai. And why did he think the villagers would sit still and wait for him to start up the car? Oh, for a self-starter, the key to an instant get-away! Why wasn't the Rolls-Royce a Cadillac, a car that already carried that marvellous energy-saving (life-saving, in this case) device? But, as Eden had told him yesterday morning, he was wishing for the moon. It was useless to think of escape. He could not go without them, even if he did manage to start the car. And there was no chance in hell of his taking them with him.

The prosecutor had finished his spiel. The villagers sat and looked at the judges, waiting for the verdict; and Cabell sat and looked at the villagers. They had, yesterday as he had driven down the main street through them, all seemed harmless, pleasant country folk; the sort of folk he might have found in Wisconsin or Indiana or Kansas. Even till this morning he had not believed that they would really allow him and the others to be executed. Now he saw that they *wanted* the death of the strangers: it was written on their broad, sunburned faces as plainly as words spelled out in any language you cared to name. He looked up towards the church again, saw its plank-barred doors. Then he saw the horseman still sitting his horse on the skyline, still waiting to carry his message.

Jesus Christ, he thought, what had bred this implacable hatred of strangers in the villagers? Was this village really part of the domain of the children's Uncle Vanya? Or was it, despite the fact that it was less than a hundred miles from Verkburg, that a road and a railway ran through it connecting it to other places, was it no more than a tiny enclosed community in its own tiny world, where the image and the words of Lenin might be respected but where, if he himself appeared here, he might find himself a stranger, suspected and therefore to be killed?

Only God, who presumably had also been driven out, knew how many strangers had passed through here in centuries past. The Mongols on their way to massacre the Volga Bulgars; the Golden Horde of Tamerlaine; the Genoese traders branching out from Marco Polo's route; the Muscovite emperors expanding south and east: this village might have begun as a camp for stragglers from any one of those invasions. Suspicion of strangers, an urge not to belong to the outside world, had probably been inherited, like a language. He and Eden and Nikolai and the children were to be killed not because they might represent the Tsar and what he had stood for but because they represented the unknown. Cabell wondered how often Prince Vanya Gorshkov had dared come here.

Keria banged the table with the pick-handle. 'The court will now decide its verdict. The prisoners will tell us their names for the record.' He opened a school exercise-book. Cabell leaned forward, but could see no names on the open first page. 'The little girl first. Stand up. What is your name?' Automatically, before Cabell could stop her, Olga stood up and said, 'Princess Olga Gorshkov.'

Suddenly everything and everyone in the square stilled.

Oh Jesus, Cabell thought, that's it! They'll kill her and Frederick first.

Eden jumped to her feet; her hat fell off in her agitation and she grabbed it and pressed it back on her head. 'You can't blame her for her name! We've done nothing but come to your village to buy food —'

'You are enemies of the State.' Keria was the first to recover from the shock of knowing who at least one of their prisoners was. The phrase came out so pat it was almost as if Keria were reading it from the book in front of him. He wrote down Olga's name in a laborious hand, asked for the others' names. Frederick gave his next, lifting his chin as he said his title. The crowd stirred, leaned forward, drew in its breath with a hiss of hate. The taking of Cabell's, Eden's and Nikolai's names was an anti-climax.

'You will be executed this evening,' said Keria and closed the school-book; the lesson was over till another trial. 'You will be shot.'

Olga whimpered and Eden put a comforting arm about her. Nikolai and Frederick, faces equally stricken, looked at Cabell, who stared at them helplessly. Then slantwise to them, he saw Delyanov still slumped in his chair in the middle of the old men. The head lifted just a little; between the brim of the straw hat and the great white beard an eye winked encouragingly. Cabell stood up.

'We'd like to plead the court's indulgence. We'd prefer to die at dawn.'

Eden looked up at him, said in English, 'What's the difference? Let's get it over, for God's sake!'

Keria also said, 'What's the difference? Dead is dead, today or tomorrow. We have to go back to work in the morning.'

'You can have the execution early, before you go to work.' *How the hell can I be talking so calmly and yet so irrationally?* But Delyanov's winking eye had suggested a gleam of hope. Their death had to be put off . . . 'It's an old American custom and I'd like to die like an American. To die at dawn is to die with grace.'

'To die is to die,' said Keria stubbornly.

'I wish he wouldn't keep saying that.' Nikolai was in the

depths of Russian despair, than which there is nothing deeper. Heaven or Hell, neither of which he desired at the moment, loomed in front of him.

'Let them die in the morning,' said the old woman who had demolished Delyanov. 'It will be a good start to the day!'

'Yes!' The crowd was now on its feet; it was going to get what it wanted. 'Let them die in the morning!'

Cabell turned towards the crowd, bowed with exaggerated gratitude. It was all hollow bravado on his part; but he decided he was going to die large, not small. Fatalism was part of the Russian character; he would show them that an American could be fatalistic, though off-hand he could not think of a single famous American fatalist. His countrymen were diseased with optimism. But, in that final moment of truth, when the coin was stood on edge, perhaps optimism and fatalism were the same. Well, he'd know in the morning. Unless the wink from Delyanov's covert eye meant something else but death might come with the dawn.

The crowd began to break up, to move away. The two young guards told the prisoners to start moving back into the railway station. As he went in the doorway of the waiting room Cabell looked up towards the hill where the church stood. The horseman was gone.

Now they were to die they were fed better than they had been last night. It was as if the villagers, having made their decision and got what they wanted, were ready to hold no other grudges. They brought lunch: red cabbage pie; *pryaniki*, the little cakes made with honey; goat's cheese and black bread; oranges and grapes and a white wine that, with the afternoon heat and the fact that they hadn't slept well during the night, put them all to sleep as soon as they had finished eating. Cabell, the last to doze off, was glad that he had insisted the children should have a full glass of wine each. He had no idea what dreams roamed in their skulls, but for the moment they looked relaxed and unworried. Eden and Nikolai had also dozed off, but their dreams, or nightmares, were there on their pinched and restless faces. In their sleep they were counting the hours they still had to live.

Four women brought them supper just as the sun went down behind the mountains. The dust-shot air in the square outside turned purple; the people seemed to slow, moving through it as if all the excitement of the morning had exhausted them. In a wild-lilac on the other side of the single railway track a nightingale, on early shift, sang to the night coming out of the desert steppes. Keria came with the women, bringing no song with him. But he had with him Cabell's rifle.

'A fine gun. I personally shall use it tomorrow morning.'

'A Winchester. The same kind as President Roosevelt himself used.'

'President Roosevelt – I have heard of him. A capitalist oppressor who rode his horse over the American peasants.'

'That's him,' said Cabell, weary now of Comrade Keria. 'All the way up San Juan Hill.'

The door opened behind Keria and Delyanov walked in carrying a large ceramic vase full of water. He ignored Keria and walked to the bench where the roses he had given Eden this morning, wilted now by the day's heat, still lay in a bunch. He picked them up, arranged them in the vase, then set the vase in the deep ledge of one of the windows. He stood back, nodded admiringly, then at last seemed to recognize that he was not alone in the room.

'Ah, Comrade Keria, the boy executioner.' He nodded at the Winchester. 'Is that what you're going to use?'

'Yes!' Keria was belligerent and angry; but he was also uncertain. 'You have no right to be here, Comrade Delyanov.'

Delyanov seemed to have recovered his poise, he had shrugged off the years that had been flung on him this morning. 'I am not your comrade, Keria, nor anyone else's. I am Alexander Dmitri Delyanov, my own man. I have played the drum for emperors, fought four wars for Russia . . . A scum like you can never call me comrade!'

'Get out!'

Keria raised the Winchester. The four women who had brought supper had retreated to the open doorway; behind them the two guards, different young men from those who had been here yesterday, stared in over their shoulders.

Eden quietly pushed the two children into a corner, stood in front of them to shield them from whatever was going to happen. Nikolai was still sitting in a corner, hunched on a bench to make himself as small a target as possible if bullets should suddenly start whipping about the room. Cabell had not moved, but he had eased himself off his heels, was ready to jump at Keria.

Delyanov took a step forward, lifted the barrel of the Winchester and looked directly down it. It was a marvellous act of defiance; but Cabell wondered if Delyanov would have done such a thing a hundred years ago. Then he pushed the gun aside, reached inside his blouse and took out a silver-handled long-bladed knife. He plunged it up through Keria's spleen to his heart; Comrade Keria died with a wide-mouthed gasp of shock. Delyanov grabbed the Winchester and tossed it to Cabell, who recovered quickly enough from his own shock to catch it. One of the women screamed and Cabell jumped the doorway and aimed the rifle at the two young guards, who were as shocked and bewildered as the women at what had happened. They dropped the ancient guns they carried and came into the waiting room, their hands raised, pushing the women roughly ahead of them as if eager to surrender.

Cabell motioned with the rifle and the four women and the two young men sat down on a bench along one wall. Keria lay on the floor in the middle of the room, face down and with blood spreading out from under him. Eden, acting as quickly as Cabell had done, had brought the children forward to stand just inside the door. Nikolai was on his feet, but seemed unable to get his legs working. Delyanov stood over Keria, but it was impossible to tell what expression was hidden behind the great white beard. Then he bent down and slowly and deliberately wiped his knife on Keria's backside.

He straightened up and said, 'You had better go. Your motor car is still out there in the square. Do not shoot any of the village people unless you have to.' He glanced at the four women and the two youths. 'They are not bad people.'

The six villagers stared back at him, their faces still blank with shock. Then one of the women frowned, looked down at the dead Keria, then back at Delyanov. Suddenly she spat at him. He wiped the spittle from the leg of his trousers with the blade of his knife and just shook his head sadly.

'Thanks, Alexander Delyanov.' Cabell wasted no time in effusive gratitude; he had seen people coming across the square, attracted by the scream of the woman here in the waiting room. 'Get out to the car, Freddie – you know what to do. Come on, all of you, quick!'

Nikolai suddenly got his legs working, went out of the room on the run, pulling Olga with him; Frederick went after them. Cabell stepped out of the waiting room, rifle aimed at the growing crowd in the square, and waited for Eden to follow him. She picked up the two guns the guards had dropped, bundled them awkwardly under one arm. She took a single rose from the vase and raised it like a toasting glass to Delyanov.

'I shall keep it always.'

'I would have made you happy,' said the old man. 'Even if only for a few weeks.'

'What will they do to you?'

Delyanov took the two guns from her, bowed and gestured for her to go out the door and followed her. The square was crowded with people now, but they were all pushed to one side by the threat of Cabell's Winchester. He had eased himself away from the station doorway and now stood in the middle of the roadway, halfway to the Rolls-Royce. Frederick was behind the wheel of the car, Olga was in the back seat and Nikolai was frantically trying to wind the starting handle.

Delyanov dropped one gun on the ground, raised the other and covered the crowd with it. 'Please go quickly, young lady!'

'Come with us!'

'Yes!' Cabell shouted from the middle of the roadway. 'They'll kill you!'

Delyanov raised his head, the great white beard seemed darker in the gathering dusk: he could have been a younger man, young enough for his second, third or fourth war. 'Let them! I know more about dying than any of them – it's nothing to be afraid of!'

'Good luck,' was all Eden could say.

Then she ran across to the car and jumped into the back seat with Olga. Nikolai swung the handle again and the engine started. Cabell backed towards the car, the Winchester still covering the crowd; Delyanov remained in the roadway, his gun aimed at the crowd. Nobody moved: in the deep dusk on their side of the square they looked like a long low rock formation, grey and unyielding. But unmoving, too. Nobody was going to risk his life to stop the strangers, the outsiders, from escaping. They would bide their time, take out their revenge on Delyanov, the old man who had seen more of life and the outside world than any of them.

'Come with us!' Cabell yelled in one last plea to the old man.

But Delyanov shook his head, put a hand under his beard and fluffed it up in that gesture of his that courted both young ladies and now death. 'Go!'

Cabell jumped on to the running-board, rifle still covering the crowd. 'Drive it, Freddie! Straight down that road ahead!'

Frederick started up the car as smoothly as Cabell himself might have driven it. It glided along the side of the square while on the other side, beyond the well, the villagers stood in ranks like an army being reviewed; Cabell, gun at the ready, stood on the running-board and inspected them carefully. They went out of the square, pursued only by the night, and Eden looked back over the tonneau.

Delyanov raised the gun he held in salute. He was just a fading figure in the fading light, even the white beard was indistinguishable. He melted away into the purple dusk and it seemed to Eden that faintly, an echo over a hundred years of a man's life, she heard the roll of drums.

She raised the rose she still held and pressed it to her lips. 'Don't ever laugh at old men,' she told Olga.

'Never.' But Olga, even when she was old herself, would always dream of young men.

Pemenov was too late. He had spent the afternoon hidden behind the deserted church on the hill, but always with the village in sight. He had had a tiring ride and he knew that very soon he would have to see about getting a spare horse. But he would keep going, even if in the end he had nothing but his accursed tiny legs to carry him after the American.

He had guessed at what had gone on in the square this morning: another damned workers' trial. Well, he would rob the workers of their victims; or anyway of one of them, the American. So he had waited patiently for nightfall, but then the commotion had occurred at the railway station and he had known he had to act now. But by the time he had dragged his horse to the rear steps of the church so that he could clamber up into the saddle, he was too late. As he rode out from behind the church he saw the car driving out of the square.

He urged the horse down the hill, only just managing to stay in the saddle as his tiny legs kept losing their grip. He clattered down the main street and into the square, the General's Mauser pistol raised threateningly. He drove his horse straight into the crowd as it moved slowly, like lava, towards the white-bearded old man who stood holding a rifle in the roadway outside the railway station. He rode right up to the old man, swung his horse round so that he, too, faced the crowd. He pointed the pistol in the crowd's direction, but he spoke to the old man.

'Where have they gone? The people in the motor car?'

'Who are you?' said Delyanov.

'I am their friend.' Pemenov was still watching the crowd, seeing the smiles beginning to appear on their faces. He'd teach them to laugh at him, he wanted to kill them all. But he knew that he couldn't, not with just the pistol. 'I have to catch up with them.'

Delyanov said nothing for a moment, looking carefully up at the dwarf. Then: 'They are heading for Tiflis.'

'Tiflis?' He would be riding forever . . . A child laughed at him and he raised the pistol and aimed it.

'Don't.' Delyanov's voice was quiet; but his rifle was aimed straight at Pemenov's head. 'If you would shoot a child, you can't be a friend of the American and the others.'

The dwarf lowered the Mauser, smiled his child's smile. 'I was only joking, old man. Thank you for your information.'

He swung the horse round, cantered across the square towards the road that led south. When he looked back he saw the old man lower his rifle and just stand, like a sentry at ease.

Then the first stone was thrown.

[6]

Once they were outside the village Cabell took over the wheel from Frederick. The boy did not protest; he recognized now who their leader was, even if he had no rank. Night had fallen and they drove south behind the yellow-white prow of the headlamps' beam. The road, little more than a wide track, wound through thin fir forest. Startled saiga antelope, a dying breed like truly ancient men, raced across the road in front of them; once a wolf bared its teeth at them in the glare of the headlamps and skipped aside just in time as Cabell drove the car straight at it. Owls sat on branches above the road like traffic lights waiting to be invented; they passed a bear that seemed to be leaning against a tree like a fur-coated drunk. Then the forest abruptly ran out and the road came out on the edge of a spur. Cabell pulled up, certain that they were safe now from pursuit.

'We'll sleep in the car. Nikolai, Freddie and I will take turns at guard.'

'We can do our share,' said Eden.

'You women will be doing the cooking,' Cabell said. 'If and when we find more food.'

He took the first turn at guard. He got out of the car, taking the Winchester with him, took his leather jacket from his bag in the trailer and put it on against the night's chill. He walked to the edge of the steep drop below the road and sat down on a rock. The moon, a great golden coin, came up over the horizon, out of the deserts and the mountains, out of Mongolia, out of China. The steppe below him stretched away for distances he could only guess at, one vast carpet of gold beneath the golden moon. No lights showed from villages, no shadows suggested houses. Somewhere out there he knew there would be the faded brown tents of the nomads, the wanderers of the steppes who carried their own frontiers with them; but the tents and the camels and goats, the wealth of the nomads, were lost in the great golden haze. Cabell shivered, not with the night's cold but at the beautiful loneliness of what lay below him. Cities, he hoped, would never destroy it.

But his hope was already lost. Already, in minds far to the north-west in Moscow, ideas were being born, cities were being planned. In twenty-five years' time, less than a hundred miles to the north of where he now sat, there would be a city of 200,000 people, built with the aid of American engineers; steel furnaces burning the night, tall stacks belching smoke, the air smelling of nothing but progress. The antelope and the bear would have retreated, the nomads gone further into the deserts, another horizon shrunken.

At the end of two hours Frederick, rousing himself, came to relieve him. 'I couldn't sleep, Mr Cabell.'

'Will you be all right on your own?'

'Of course.' He had brought the shotgun with him. He sat down on the rock and looked up at Cabell. 'Why did those people hate us so much? Was it because of who I am, and Olga?'

'Partly. But mainly because we were outsiders. In a different way, maybe they were as scared as we were.'

The boy pondered this while he stared out at the moon, now losing its golden hue. 'Why did all this have to happen? The Revolution, I mean. My father is a good man. So was the Tsar.'

'It's not just your father. Nor the Tsar, not the last one.' From what he had heard, Nicholas II had been a weak, foolish man who had always been too late to recognize what was happening; he had held sacred the principle of autocracy but seemed never to have really understood the responsibilities of it. But it was too late now to explain all that to a twelve-year-old boy who still believed in the system. Christ, he thought, why must I explain to the kid the death of the system he belongs to? That's his father's job, not mine. 'I don't think I'm the one to explain it, Freddie. I'm prejudiced. I come from a country where we don't believe in princes and tsars and kings.'

'Do you dislike me because I'm a prince?'

Prince Gorshkov, where the hell are you? You've given this son of yours love and comfort, but you've never given him the truth. 'It's not the individual, Freddie – do you understand what I'm saying?' The boy nodded. 'The old Russia was just dying – Do you know what cancer is?'

'I heard my mother speak of it. My grandmother died of it, I think.'

'It's a disease that eats away at the body. Well, Russia had – has cancer. The cancer of oppression. The people don't have as much freedom as they should, they don't own as much as they're entitled to . . . I hate to say it, Freddie – I hope your father will forgive me for saying it – the old Russia, your Russia, is finished.'

After a moment's silence the boy said, 'Will the new Russia be any better?'

'I don't know. I honestly don't know. But I think it's worth a try.'

Again the boy was silent. Then: 'Is America perfect?'

'Oh Jesus!' He laughed softly, shook his head. 'No, it's not. Far from it. But like I said about the new Russia – we think it's worth a try.'

Frederick sighed. 'I've always wanted to be grown up. But now I'm – I'm frightened, Mr Cabell —'

He couldn't leave the boy to his fear and sadness, not now. He settled down on the ground, put his back against the rock. 'I'm not sleepy. I think I'll stay here with you a while, okay?'

'Thank you, Mr Cabell.' Frederick slid down off the rock to sit beside Cabell. 'You're like my father, a good man.'

'Only sometimes,' said Cabell, and wanted to weep for the boy and what lay ahead of him, being grown up.

In the morning they drove on, feeling the reaction to yesterday's escape and feeling hungry, too. Then they saw

84

the railway, two tracks meeting in a junction; one set of tracks headed south, the other came in from the west through a gap in the mountains. Even as they watched they saw the train, an engine and four carriages, come out of the gap on the western line and head north.

'There's your train, Mr Cabell,' said Eden. 'The one you wanted to catch out of Verkburg for Ekaterinburg.'

Cabell pulled up the car and they watched the train, a mile away, chugging its way steadily north, the smoke from the engine's stack laid back along the carriages by the morning breeze. It was cooler this morning, with thunderheads building like another dark range behind the iron-grey mountains to the west.

'You could chase the train and catch it,' said Frederick very quietly, without enthusiasm.

'Do you want to get rid of me?' Cabell had said it as a joke, but instantly he was sorry. Frederick looked embarrassed and hurt. 'Sorry, Freddie – I didn't mean that.'

'We shouldn't blame you if you do want to catch the train,' said Eden. 'But—'

'But what?'

'But we'd like you to stay with us,' said Olga, and the other three nodded.

Cabell gazed at the distant train. Against the vast steppe beyond it it seemed almost motionless, as if it were slowing while he made up his mind. Two days aboard it and he would be in Ekaterinburg, safe with the British consul while he waited to board the Trans-Siberian to Vladivostok and home. But even as he gazed at the train he knew he would not be safe aboard it. General Bronevich's men would board it at Verkburg, interrogate all the passengers; he would have to start running all over again, if he were lucky enough to get off the train in the first place. No, he would be better off, or at least no worse off, right where he was. But he knew it was more than just the question of his own safety that influenced his decision. He looked around at them and grinned. My family, he thought. Goddam!

'I haven't got a ticket,' he said and started up the car and drove on.

Everyone laughed, suddenly happy and Eden looked at

him and smiled. 'When we get to Tiflis, Mr Cabell, may I take you to tea?'

'I can think of no better way of celebrating.' But he could, though she probably wouldn't agree, would probably tell him to *Watch it!*

They came to a fork in the road at the rail junction. Cabell didn't hesitate: he continued south, following the line that led in that direction. 'You didn't even stop to consider,' said Eden.

'No. You probably didn't see them. There were soldiers on the last carriage of that train, with a machine-gun. If there are more soldiers up there in the mountains —' He nodded to the west. 'If there are, I don't want to run into them. If I can manage it, we're going to stay clear of soldiers all the way from here on to Tiflis.'

Ten miles down the road the offside front tyre blew out with the familiar bang. It took Cabell and Nikolai half an hour to remove the burst tyre and fit one of the tyres filled with sponge rubber balls. They drove on for half a mile and Cabell found the steering had been affected. They pulled up again, this time for an hour. He and Nikolai changed the tyres round, fitting two pneumatics to the front wheels and two ball-filled tyres to the rear wheels. Then they drove on once more and Cabell wondered how many more punctures there would be before the end of their journey. He had become quite attached to the Rolls-Royce and he wanted to see it, as well as themselves, arrive in Tiflis in good working order.

It was mid-morning before they saw the small town on the ridge ahead of them. They had stopped by a small stream and drank from its clear waters; but now hunger was beginning to make empty pits of their bellies. Cabell pulled the Rolls-Royce off the road into a small stand of larches. They had passed no dwellings, but now they could see farmhouses and paddocks where cows grazed and several fields where harvest hands were at work amongst the wheat and corn.

'That town's probably the terminus of the railroad,' Cabell said.

'No,' said Frederick. 'I remember Father telling me – the railway goes on and finishes up nowhere. They stopped

86

building it when the Great War started. But that town would be as far as the train goes. I think Father said it was called Oblansk, something like that. The Ural river comes down somewhere near here. We can follow that right down to the Caspian Sea.'

'You taught him his geography pretty well,' Cabell said to Eden.

'He learned all that himself. I only taught him about the rest of the world.'

'I know all the capitals of the world by heart,' said Frederick.

'Who cares?' said Olga. 'I'm hungry.'

'You and I are going into town, Nick,' said Cabell. 'Unhitch the trailer and empty it. I'm not taking this car into any more towns or villages if I can help it. I don't want to run into another mob of Bolsheviks or any Cossacks, either. You and I are going to be a couple of field hands working for another minerals prospector.'

'I'm beginning to wish I'd stayed home on the Don,' said Nikolai. 'Even my father was safer to live with than this.'

Cabell topped up the car's tank with petrol from the spare cans in the trailer, then put the empty cans back in the trailer. He retired behind a bush and took off his bib-and-tucker overalls, put on the trousers of his only suit and his best shirt. He left off his celluloid collar and rolled up the sleeves of the shirt; by the time he reached town sweat and dust would have camouflaged the quality of the shirt. His boots were American, but they were scuffed and dirty and maybe they would not be noticed. He tossed his flat-crowned Stetson into the car. He knew that a sharp eye would detect him at once as a foreigner, but he hoped that any sharp eye he met amongst the storekeepers in the town would be blinded by the desire for a profit. He had heard that even in Moscow, right under the noses of Lenin and all the other socialists, the small storekeepers still believed fervently in the profit motive.

'Be careful,' Eden said when he and Nikolai were ready to depart.

He smiled at her reassuringly. There were moments when he forgot their immediate circumstances and looked at her as he had once looked at the girls walking down Prairie Avenue. She was a good-looker, no doubt about it, a real peach; even now, with her face coated with dust and strands of the dark golden hair hanging down over her ears. Her skirt was too long for him to see what her legs were like, but she had good hips, a small waist and a bosom that would more than fill a man's hands if he could get it out of her blouse. She would have to be a virgin, he guessed, but she didn't have the look of a girl who wanted to be a life-long one. He just wondered why someone as good-looking as she hadn't been snapped up by some randy Russian. Old Delyanov could not have been the first man who had put a proposition to her.

'Eden – that's a lovely name. Have you known any original sin?'

Instead of taking offence, she blushed: all her governess' starch had disappeared. 'Watch it, Mr Cabell.'

From that moment he knew they had moved on to different ground. With the kids and Nikolai in their pockets, there would be no opportunity for any romancing; he could put that out of his head right now, forget about the merits of baggy trousers. But from now on he knew they would co-operate with each other, that each of them was going to be concerned for the other's safety. He suddenly felt even more glad that he had decided not to chase the train this morning.

'If Nick and I don't come back within three hours, don't come looking for us. Just get in the car and keep going.'

'No.' She shook her head emphatically. 'We'll want to know what happened to you.'

He could see it was useless to argue with her; if she and the children should disappear he knew he would go looking for them. 'Okay. But give us at least three hours. We have to walk in there and back and I don't know how long it's going to take us to do the shopping.'

It took him and Nikolai almost an hour to walk into the town. As they trudged along the road, pulling the trailer behind them, dust and sweat soon coated them. They passed horse-drawn wagons, and several decrepit-looking trucks rattled past; a postman came towards them on a bicycle, nodded and swept by. Women came out of the town along the road, baskets on their heads, bundles slung over their backs. Half a dozen men, scythes over their shoulders, went by on the other side of the road, the scythes glinting like scimitars in the sunlight. But they saw no soldiers and no one looked at them with suspicion and they entered the town, feeling safer with every step. This seemed a town beyond the war and not afraid of outsiders.

They found the town market without much trouble and then Cabell realized why no one had looked at them curiously. The town was not a big one and he had wondered how it earned its income. But when he and Nikolai came into the big square he realized that it was no more than a market town. And strangers, buyers and sellers, had probably been coming to this market for centuries.

The square was large, surrounded by two-storeyed wooden buildings with an occasional one built of stone. A church stood at the northern end, its doors open, its copper onion-shaped dome catching the sun which came in shafts through the gathering clouds. Stalls had been set up in rows and traders bargained loudly with buyers. To Cabell's first quick glance there seemed to be stalls for everything: food, clothing, kerosene and petrol, furniture, carpets, pots and pans, guns and knives, jewellery, herbs, spices and drugs. The traders' horses, carts and camels were lined up behind the stalls; half a dozen mules were tethered to one side, like eunuchs put in their place. A hundred smells hung in the humid air, a dozen small worlds at the end of one's nose. Street musicians played: a cithern, a flute; one even had an upright piano and sat before it, cap pushed back on head, reminding Cabell of honky-tonk piano-players he had seen in bars in East Texas and Louisiana. But this was not East Texas, nor even Russia as most Europeans and Americans thought of it. This was an eastern bazaar, this was where southern Asia washed against the shores of Europe like a great ocean.

'Wonderful!' said Nikolai. 'I could spend a fortune here. If I had a fortune.'

'First things first,' said Cabell and set about buying food.

He had always carried plenty of cash with him, preferring to risk being robbed than to being penniless because a bank draft had not turned up in time. Revolutions and civil wars can devalue a bank's efficiency as much as they do the money inside it; a shot fired in a street can close a bank's door quicker than those of a lawyer's office, which usually runs a close second. So Cabell carried his own bank, a money belt that had been stowed in his bag in the trailer and had escaped the attention of the villagers of Drazlenka, who had been more concerned with taking his life than his money.

When he had bought enough food and two large baskets in which to carry it, he then sought out the seller of kerosene and petrol and filled his empty cans with several gallons of the latter. He had worked out that with the 28-gallon tank of the car, plus the spare cans, he would have enough petrol to take them possibly another 450 miles before their supply ran out. That distance would take them down to the eastern shore of the Caspian Sea and there he expected to find towns or villages where petrol would be sold, if not for cars and trucks, then for motor-powered boats. The road south-west, he hoped, would not deviate too much from the flight-line of a crow. There would be no spare petrol for detours and he fervently hoped there would be no necessity for them. He had found himself praying an old prayer this morning, asking St Christopher for a little help along the rest of the way.

With the essentials packed in the trailer he and Nikolai moved on to other stalls. From a Turkoman seated amongst his copperware, the beaten and polished metal reflecting a light that turned him to a copper figure, they bought a samovar.

'Miss Eden should have packed a samovar before she packed her clothes,' said Nikolai. 'No Russian goes any-where without his samovar.'

'Okay, you're in charge of it from now on. No matter what happens, always save the samovar.'

Nikolai smiled, enjoying himself, forgetting the depression that had burdened him. He liked this American, but he knew he could never tell him so.

They haggled with an Uzbek, who kept polishing his bald head with his hand as if afraid that hair would grow there while he bargained with them; he sat amidst an arsenal of daggers and swords and finally, with an exchange of smiles that said both of them had enjoyed the haggling, Cabell bought two knives and two daggers from him. Then Cabell saw Nikolai holding a curved sword, stroking it as if it were a long-stemmed flower.

Cabell was surprised. 'Are you feeling war-like, Nick? Would you like it?'

'Not for myself, sir. Prince Frederick has always wanted one – he was always admiring his father's sword. But I have no money—'

It was a beautiful sword, a *shaska*, a sabre only slightly curved, its handle inlaid with silver. It was spoiled only by the painted decorations on the blade, as if its previous owner had decided he would no longer use it as a weapon. Cabell took it from Nikolai, weighed it in his hands.

'It would be too heavy for him. This was a big man's sword.'

'Too heavy now, perhaps. But Prince Frederick is going to be a big man himself when he grows up.'

'You think they'll still be fighting with swords then?'

'Who knows, sir?' said Nikolai, who would not fight even with a willow wand.

Cabell looked at the Uzbek. 'Where did you get it?'

The stall-owner shrugged. 'It came to me. A soldier said he had picked it up beside the railway between Orenburg and Tashkent. There was a battle there last year. He was a deserter, said he didn't want to fight any more. That was why he painted it.'

'He spoiled it. How much do you want for it.'

'Twenty roubles, sir. It is a king's sword, as you can see. The silver-work on the handle —'

'I'll give you fifteen.'

'Sir —' Nikolai stepped forward hesitantly. 'He is asking too much. I could never afford so much money – that is four months' pay —'

'I'll lend it to you.'

'I could never repay you —'

'I'm already in your debt, Nikolai.'

There was more haggling with the dealer, then it exchanged hands and Cabell passed it to Nikolai.

'It's yours to give Freddie. Just tell him to be careful with it.'

'I shall tell him who bought it —'

'No.' Cabell was quiet but firm. He had begun to realize that Nikolai's feeling for Frederick was more than just the affection a servant sometimes felt for the children of his employer; this was real love and it disconcerted him. It would not hurt to allow Nikolai to care for Frederick for the rest of the trip. What happened after they got to Tiflis would be the concern of Frederick's mother and father. 'It's your gift. Mention me and I'll chop your head off with it.'

Nikolai smiled gently. 'Thank you, Mr Cabell.'

They moved on. They bought clothes from two women, one a pretty, plump girl with flashing eyes and enough invitation to have accommodated a regiment, the other an old hag with one eye and one tooth who snarled at them all the time she was serving them; the pretty flirt tried to rob them and the old hag gave them a discount. Finally they bought five soft hand-woven rugs to protect them against the cold nights. As they trudged out of the square, the trailer stacked high, they looked like traders themselves, heading for another town, another market. No one had questioned them, asked them who they were, where they had come from. The Revolution and the civil war were of no apparent concern to the townsfolk here; the only loyalty was to a profit. And strangers were commonplace in a place where traders came and went like the seasons.

Cabell and Nikolai were a mile out of town when the storm broke. Clouds, suddenly gathering speed, thundered across the sky. An army of silver lances turned the dust of the road to mud. The ground seemed to shake under the sky's bombardment; blazing lightning blue-blinded their eyes. Dragging the trailer through the rapidly increasing mud, they raced for the shelter of a barn beside the road. As they stumbled in through one wide open doorway a man came running in through a rear door driving half a dozen cows ahead of him. He swept the rain from his face with a huge hand, then showed a wide mouth of broken yellow teeth. It was not his fault that the smile was more threatening than it was welcoming.

'Siberian storms!' he bellowed above the thunder. 'The greatest!'

Cabell could only nod acknowledgement. 'It sounds like a dozen battles!'

'The only battles we ever have around here!' The man walked to the doorway, looked out with pride as if he personally was responsible for the rain, the thunder and the lightning. 'Listen to that!'

He was suddenly lost in a blinding blue flash as lightning felled a tree beside the barn; the walls of the barn seemed to shake and the thunder went right through Cabell's head. He fell over as the terrified cows milled together, ready to stampede but not knowing which way to run. Nikolai dragged him to his feet just as a cow stumbled and was about to fall on him. They dragged the trailer into a corner and huddled behind it as the cows milled and mauled about the barn. Cabell looked towards the door, expecting to see the blackened form of the farmer lying there. But he was still on his feet, throwing his arms high in the air in appreciation of an extra-loud clap of thunder or a blaze of lightning. Siberian storms were evidently his theatre.

At last the thunder rolled on south, the lightning flickered away and the rain ceased. The farmer, disappointed that the drama was over, turned back into the barn.

'I love the storms – they are our only excitement!'

'But what if they do damage? Ruin your crops or kill your cows?'

The farmer was herding the still frightened cows out into the field at the back of the barn. 'One has to pay God for what He gives us —' He blessed himself with a hand that could have felled a cow with one blow. 'He gives me the storms . . .'

Well, thought Cabell, every man to his own entertainment. 'You said the storms are the only battles you ever have around here.' He was cautious; he did not want to be taken for a spy. 'Hasn't the war come this far south?'

The farmer shook his head; water sprayed from his lank hair. 'Who cares about the war? What do the Muscovites mean to us?' He spat on the ground. They haven't changed, Cabell thought: the Muscovites, Romanovs or revolutionaries, had never really conquered these people east of the Urals. 'Yesterday a small train came through here. If it had stopped in town, the people would have killed whoever was on it — just because we don't want soldiers here, we don't want their war. They tell me the station-master said there were Cossacks on it. Not many, a dozen or so, that was all.'

'Where did it go?'

The farmer shrugged. 'South. Who knows after that? The line finishes no more than fifty miles from here. It just *stops* —' he made a chopping motion with his hand. 'Where can the train go?'

'Where indeed?' Cabell picked up the shaft of the trailer, ready to go.

'You're not from around here, are you?'

Cabell said cautiously, 'No. We are mining surveyors. Our truck broke down out along the road. We're working up in the mountains.'

'Who for?' But the farmer didn't sound suspicious.

'Ourselves. And whoever wins the war.'

'Hope you don't find anything,' said the farmer amiably. 'Mines spoil the countryside. Where do you come from? You're not one of us. Or a Muscovite, either.'

'America.' Cabell felt now that the big man could be trusted.

'America, eh?' For a moment the farmer's face clouded over. They're all the same, Cabell thought hopelessly, the Russians, no matter where they come from, suspect all foreigners. But then the broken-toothed smile appeared again. 'What sort of storms do you have over there?'

'Big ones,' Cabell said; then added diplomatically: 'Not as big as the Siberian ones.'

The farmer nodded proudly. 'No, we must have the best.'

He went back to the field behind the barn and stood there staring after the retreating storm as it hurtled up into the mountains. Cabell and Nikolai left him and went out along the road. The trailer slid and slithered in the mud; several times they lost their footing and fell over. It took them well over an hour to get back to where Eden and the children waited anxiously for them. Eden and Frederick had put up

94

the hood of the Rolls-Royce and they had managed to remain dry during the fury of the storm.

Cabell was moved by the relief that showed on Eden's and the children's faces at his and Nikolai's safe return. They were now a group who, though they might continue arguing amongst themselves all the way to Tiflis, were in agreement on one aim: they all had to survive.

Eden prepared lunch from the food Cabell had brought back from town. There was sausage to be fried and potatoes to be sliced and fried in the same fat; thick slices of coarse-grained black bread; honey, yoghurt, and yellow plum jam; and tea brewed in the samovar by Nikolai. Frederick brought wood for the fire and did his best to help; Olga, told by Eden to stay out of the way, just sat by and waited to be waited upon. Oh honey, thought Cabell, are you in for shocks when you grow up! But as if reading his thoughts Olga looked across at him and smiled, sure of her place, now and forever.

After breakfast, having re-packed the trailer, which now resembled a steppe trader's overloaded barrow, they all changed into the clothes Cabell had bought.

'The Rolls is always going to be our give-away. But maybe we'll look like peasants who pinched it from their boss. The thing is, we don't want to look like toffs out on a picnic.'

'I hardly thought we looked like that,' said Eden. 'I haven't felt so dirty since I don't know when. I think we should next look for somewhere to have a nice big bath.'

'Oh sure,' said Cabell. 'All in together.'

'Watch it!'

By the time they were ready to move on they did make a passable imitation of a group of peasants, even if slightly effete ones. Nikolai was the only true man of the land amongst them and even he did not look as if he could keep a plough on a straight course. Cabell, darkened and leathered by years in the sun, hands calloused by countless rocks, looked more like a peasant than any of them.

He looked down at his loose blue blouse with its rucked sleeves, his broad leather belt and his baggy blue trousers shoved into calf-length boots. He replaced his Stetson with the beaded Uzbek skullcap he had bought and tossed the

95

broad-brimmed hat on the front floor of the car. Once they were beyond the town he would put it on again against the beat of the sun.

'Cabell the Magnificent!' He produced the curved sword, forgetting who was supposed to have bought it, and at once there was a gasp from Frederick. 'You admire my sword, my son? It has carved my way from the Pamirs to here, chopped off the legs of a hundred men –' he swished the air with it '–seduced a score of women —'

'Absolutely magnificent! Jolly marvellous!'

Then Cabell saw the disappointed look on Nikolai's face, cursed himself for his forgetfulness. He abruptly reversed the sword, held out the hilt to Nikolai. 'No, it's not mine. It's Nick's – he bought it.'

Nikolai took the sword, looked hesitantly at Cabell, who nodded. Then he held the sword out to Frederick. 'I bought it for you, Your Highness – you always admired your father's sword —'

Frederick took the sword, blinked as if he were afraid of crying. Cabell watched the boy and Nikolai closely; then saw that Eden was just as intent. She knew what Nikolai was; and she, too, was afraid for Frederick. Cabell caught her eye and gave just the slightest shake of his head.

'Do you like it?' Nikolai's face seemed to have broadened, taken on flesh with pleasure. Christ, Cabell thought, it's probably the first time in his life he's ever given anyone something.

Frederick carved the air with the sword. 'Oh, I could be Frederick the Great!'

'All right,' said Eden, 'come down to earth. If you and Mr Cabell are trying to pass as peasants, the last thing we want is for you playing at emperors.'

Cabell grinned at Frederick, ending their little game. 'Women never understand, do they?' Then he included Nikolai in the smile. 'Only men have imagination, right?'

Nikolai was bursting with happiness. 'Oh yes, Mr Cabell!'

'Pooh,' said Olga, already in the car and ready to go, a peasant empress. 'Men never grow up, that's what Mamma says. Thank God,' she added.

'Did your mother say that?' said Cabell. 'Or Miss Eden?'

'I think we should be moving on.' Eden blushed and Cabell wondered just what topics a governess discussed with her charges. 'Do we keep on this road?'

'It's the only one,' said Cabell. 'Unless we look for one going through the mountains.'

'There is none this far south.' Nikolai had rarely said anything when any plans were being discussed; he had waited till he was spoken to. But the last few hours, even the last few minutes, had given him a feeling of being *accepted*. The children had always accepted him, even if they had never treated him as an equal; but all adults, even his own father and mother and older brothers, had never made him feel as if he belonged to their circle. 'I came here from the Don through these mountains. There are only tracks fit for horses, no roads for motor cars such as this one.'

'How did you come?' said Cabell. 'By horse?'

'I walked.'

Jesus wept, Cabell thought. What rejection had driven this weedy, effeminate boy to walk a thousand miles through the Urals into Siberia? Had he had to put those mountains between himself and his family, those who had driven him out because he was not man enough for them? Cabell was sure now that Nikolai was homosexual, though the boy had probably never had a relationship with any other man.

He had all the American male's revulsion of such men; they got up to practices that turned a decent man's stomach. There had been none along Prairie Avenue when he had been growing up; the Irish there were still wondering if it was sinful to try a few simple variations on the old heterosexual positions. He had been simple enough himself; when a French-Canadian waitress he had taken out had suggested some *soixante-neuf* he had wondered at first what mathematics had to do with the basic thing he had in mind. He had met his first homosexual face to face in Baku in 1914, a Roumanian gem merchant who had sold Cabell some diamonds and then put a proposition to him, offering a discount. Cabell had put a fist in the man's face, as any decent chap would, thrown the diamonds at him and taken his money back. Now he felt miserably sorry for Nikolai, felt the beginning of another aspect of his education.

'Then we'll continue south.' Cabell was a little brusque, embarrassed by his thoughts about Nikolai. Maybe he was misjudging him after all, the occasional effeminate gesture didn't mean a chap had to go all the way. 'You ride up front with me, Eden. Watch out with that sword, Fred.'

Frederick put the sword back in its scabbard, climbed into the rear seat and sat beside his sister, the sword between his knees and his hands resting on its hilt. Cabell glanced back at the two of them, then looked at Eden.

'I don't think we'll ever make peasants out of them. You've done your job too well.'

'Oh, you should have seen them when I first met them. They were just too blooming aristocratic and snooty to be true.'

'I was only four years old then,' said Olga defensively, feeling that perhaps a little proletarian modesty was called for. She was an actress and wished she could act a peasant. But she was also a princess and, despite what Mr Cabell had said about princes and princesses, one couldn't hide one's breeding. Or so Mamma had said.

'You were a pain in the neck,' said Eden.

A pain in the ass is the correct expression, thought Cabell. He looked sideways at Eden, saw the swell of her bosom under the blouse she wore (had he deliberately bought one that was too small for her or had it been an honest mistake?) and wondered what sort of ass she had under the thick peasant skirt. Cool down, Cabell.

They drove on, out of the forest and down the road towards the town. They went through the town at speed, Cabell blowing the horn to clear their way. He swept the car round two ox-carts, braked sharply as a flock of geese scuttled across in front of him, squeezed between two coveys of children who converged in from either side of the street to gape and shout at the magnificent motor car, the like of which they'd never seen, as it whirled by them. Olga waved a regal hand and Frederick nodded right and left and the town children's cheering turned to booing: they had been hailing the Rolls-Royce, not a couple of snooty kids like themselves. Then the Rolls-Royce was out the other side of town and they were bowling along the rapidly drying road, under an

98

afternoon sun that brought a steamy haze out of the ground and made mirrors of pools lying in the fields. They passed the last of the farmhouses and Eden turned and waved to two women who came to the door to stare after them.

She had put her fears and doubts to the back of her mind, even if only temporarily. She had always dreamed of adventure, though, innocent in its pursuit, she had always ignored the probability that it would entail dangers. They had certainly had their share of danger so far; and she wanted to repeat none of it. Yet she could feel the excitement in her, a low bubbling pleasure that she had never felt before; and felt guilty about it. She was responsible for more than the education of Frederick and Olga now; she was responsible for their lives, for their safe delivery to their mother in Tiflis. God knew what dangers lay ahead of them and she should be anticipating those instead of feeling this – this feeling of escapism? Yes, that was it. She was never really meant to be a governess, but that had been her only means of escaping from Croydon and the school teacher's life her parents had meant for her. She had dreamed of something else but spending her life looking after other people's children: of being Igor's wife, for one thing. But she had remained with the Gorshkovs, waiting for the chance to go back to England, see her parents, then escape again. But to where, she had had no idea.

'Your eyes are sparkling,' Cabell said. 'You're another girl, now you've got out of those governess' clothes.'

She looked down at herself, saw how tight her blouse was. She was surprised to find she wasn't shy about her bosom and how it showed under her blouse. Igor had often told her how beautiful her bosom was. 'Perhaps I'm a peasant at heart.'

'I'll believe that when I see you in a haystack.'

She didn't say *Watch it,* but she looked at him warningly, giving a hint of a nod back at the children. She liked this flirting, even if he went too far sometimes. But they still had to be careful of the children.

They had been driving for an hour when they saw the river coming in in a broad sweep east of them. At the same time they saw the railway again. It came out from behind a low hill, ran in a straight line down towards where bridgeworks had been started on the north bank. But it had not reached the embryo bridge; work had stopped on both projects when the rail tracks were within a quarter of a mile of the river. As the farmer had told Cabell, the railway line just *stopped*. There was no terminus, not even any final buffers. The tracks just finished, as if the railway workers had downed tools and disappeared in mid-shift. There were no piles of sleepers beside the tracks, no rusting stacks of rails, no loads of ballast: scavengers had been here and picked the place clean.

There was no warning sign that the track abruptly ended. Any engine-driver would have been glad of such a sign, especially the driver of the engine that now rested its own length beyond the end of the rails, its big wheels buried a foot deep in the soft earth. Behind it, still on the rails, were a passenger carriage, a closed goods wagon and an open-slatted horse wagon. The passenger carriage was tilted forward, its front bogies having followed the engine into the ground, but its rear bogies rested firmly on the rails.

Beside this small train were a dozen horses and their riders, already swinging round to come galloping across towards the road.

'Cossacks!' Nikolai suddenly screamed from the rear seat. 'Drive! Drive fast!'

CHAPTER THREE

But the Cossacks were experienced warriors or bandits, whichever they were. They had not come directly at the road in one bunch. Half of them were galloping at an angle towards the road as it swung down towards the river; the other six came in behind the Rolls-Royce as it gathered speed. The car lurched and skidded on the loose surface as Cabell tried to gather speed too quickly; he had to fight it as it threatened to plunge them off into the rocks on either side. He realized he was not going to be able to keep the car at speed on such a treacherous surface and he slowed down as he saw the Cossacks already coming to a halt across the road ahead. As he stopped the car the other half a dozen horsemen came racing up, aiming their rifles in the air and letting off a small barrage that immediately sent Nikolai to the floor of the car.

'Do we fight them?' Frederick's hands gripped the handle of his sword.

'Be quiet,' said Eden; then said softly in English to Cabell, 'What are we now? Cossacks despise peasants. Especially ones who steal their master's motor car.'

The car was surrounded by horsemen, all of them crowding in close to look at the Rolls-Royce and its occupants. Their fierce broad faces showed as much curiosity as hostility. They were all young men, some of them no more than youths; but their leader was a middle-aged man with a black scrubbing-brush of a moustache and black nailbrushes as eyebrows. He took off his karakul hat, exposing a shaven head with short black forelock; he scratched the forelock, then put his hat back on. He leaned into the car from his horse and glowered right into Cabell's face.

'Who are you – peasants like you riding in a motor car such as this?' His breath was vile; Cabell reeled under a poison-gas blast of onions. 'I have seen such a motor car in St Petersburg, but it belonged to the Tsar.'

Cabell took off his Uzbek beaded cap, took his Stetson from under his feet and put it on. The Cossack had sat up straight again in his saddle and Cabell took a quick breath of fresh air while it was available. 'I am Matthew Martin Cabell, American, rodeo champion of Texas and special riding instructor to his young Excellency, Prince Frederick Gorshkov.'

'Prince Frederick Mikhail Alexander Gorshkov,' said the prince, hands clasped on the hilt of his sword.

'I am the Princess Olga Natasha Aglaida Gorshkov,' said the princess.

'Another of my riding pupils,' said Cabell.

'And who are these?' said the Cossack leader, gesturing at Eden and Nikolai as the latter slowly unwound himself from the floor of the car. 'Your manure gatherers? Give me no horseshit, as we Cossacks say.' One of the horses obligingly illustrated, depositing a small heap of steaming manure on the running board of the Rolls-Royce. *Who are you?*'

'Can you ride?' Cabell said in English to Eden.

'Yes. But not like a Cossack.' Eden's excitement had run out of her.

'What are you saying? What language is that?' The leader suddenly produced a whip and struck Cabell across the back of the neck with it. 'Who are you? Tell us or we kill you!'

'We are who we said we are.'

Cabell, rubbing the back of his neck, feeling the weal under his fingers, tried to keep his voice cool, but he felt far from calm. He recognized that these Cossacks would be from one of the White armies, that they would have no Bolshevik sympathies at all. He could not tell the difference between the various Cossacks, those of the Ukraine, the Don, the Urals or the Kuban; but if this leader had been in St Petersburg and seen the Tsar in his Rolls-Royce, then he must have belonged to one of the privileged regiments. The Cossacks were as independent as any people in Russia, but they had always been reactionary, defenders of the Tsar and believing themselves several classes above the peasants.

'This is Miss Eden Penfold, an English governess to the Prince and Princess. She also teaches riding English style.'

'And who's this weed? A Don Cossack?' The car was surrounded by laughter.

Nikolai almost fainted, but Cabell was not going to throw him to these wolves. 'He is my stable boy. And what I have told you is the truth.'

'We shall see. Get out of the motor car.'

Cabell and the others alighted, keeping close together. The afternoon sun struck slantwise, so that those horsemen against it looked huge and threatening. The horses, Cabell had noted, were not the shaggy steppe horses but a finer breed. He had seen the Orloff Blacks, the Cossack horses bred from steppe horses mixed with Arab blood. But these looked even better, wilder, stronger and more mettlesome.

'You have fine horses,' he said to the leader. Flattery might get him nowhere, but it seemed they were going nowhere anyway.

'They are Kabardian horses,' said Frederick. 'My father says they are the very best in all Russia.'

The Cossack leader looked at him approvingly, almost as if seeing him for the first time. 'You know your horses, boy.'

'Your Highness,' Frederick corrected. 'If you are a true Cossack you would call me by rank.'

Oh Jesus, thought Cabell. The Cossack let out a roar, half-shout, half-laugh, pulled his sword from his saddle scabbard and slashed the air only inches above Frederick's head. The boy sprang back, brought up his own sword, stood defiant; only Cabell, standing right beside him, could feel the fear quivering in him. He gently took the sword from Frederick, making sure not to damage the boy's dignity, and handed it to Eden. The Cossack reached down for it but Eden shook her head and backed away.

'I shall give you the sword when we've surrendered,' she said. 'We haven't done that yet.'

'Very spunky, Miss Penfold,' Cabell said in English. 'But don't let's get into another war. We're a long away from reinforcements.'

The Cossack tapped Cabell on the shoulder with his sword. 'Speak Russian.' Then he looked back at Eden and smiled. He was surprisingly handsome when he did that, all the dark threat suddenly disappearing from his face. 'Keep the sword, woman. But don't try sticking it in any of my men or all of them will have your pants down before you can say Ivan Rabinovich. They haven't had a woman in almost six months.' Olga gasped and he leaned down and patted her on the head with his sword. 'Don't worry, little princess. My men don't rape little girls, only big ones.'

'I'll thank you not to talk like that in front of the children.'

Eden was trying hard to do her governess' duty, but she knew she was fighting a losing battle. She was more than a governess now, she was a protectress and polite words were not going to protect Olga from a little crudity and whatever else threatened her.

The Cossack looked at Cabell. 'You have a rare one there. Is she as stiff-backed as that in bed?'

'No,' said Cabell, but didn't look at Eden.

'Well, is she as stiff-backed when she rides a horse? Let's see!'

He barked an order to one of the riders, who immediately swung down from his horse and handed the reins to Eden. For a moment she was nonplussed. What was she expected to do? Jump on the horse and go galloping off, vaulting from one side of the saddle to the other in imitation of those circus tricks Cossacks sometimes indulged in? She looked at Cabell, who hesitated. He had no idea how well she could ride, he might well be asking her to break her neck. But the risk had to be taken, if she was willing. He nodded and Eden handed the sword back to Frederick.

Cabell held the horse's head while Eden put her foot in the stirrup and looked at the young Cossack for a lift up into the saddle. He obliged at once, squeezing her rump as he did so, grinning hugely. She settled herself sideways in the saddle, then whacked him over the head with her handbag. He staggered back and she looked at the leader.

'Tell him not to pinch my behind again or I shall run him through with the sword.'

Then the horse suddenly reared, aware now that someone other than its master was on its back. The Cossacks shouted and roared with laughter, even the youth who had been clouted by the handbag, and Cabell swept the children and Nikolai back out of the way of the pawing hooves. But Eden stayed in the saddle, got the horse down again and held him in check. Then, sitting side-saddle, holding the horse on a tight rein, she took him at a prancing walk up the road.

Cabell looked up at the leader. 'Does she ride well enough for you?'

The Cossack nodded. 'Let's see how she rides at the gallop.'

Four of the horsemen abruptly took off at a gallop, swept in, two on either side, behind Eden's mount and clouted it across the rump. Startled, it reared high, came down running. Eden's head jerked back, but she managed to hold on. The five horses went up the road at full stretch, the Cossacks yelling derisive encouragement to Eden as she quickly settled herself to the rhythm of her mount. She had never ridden till she had come to Russia, but in six years she had become an expert horsewoman. She had a natural sense of balance and something in her hands that communicated itself to a horse. Now that she had this horse under control, she felt an exhilaration as the wind tore at her, freeing her hair, and she felt the power and energy thundering away beneath her. This must have been one of the better horses; and her light weight helped. She gradually began to draw away from the other riders. For one wild mindless moment she wanted to ride on, keep the horse speeding along till only exhaustion would bring it to a halt. Then sense and sanity came back. She drew rein, brought the horse down to a canter, turned him round as the other riders caught up with her. They had stopped shouting and were smiling now. They snatched off their hats and waved them at her; two of them rode close and patted her on the back. She had not meant to prove anything, but she had just done so. The Cossacks had tested her in a skill that was as natural to them as breathing and she had come through.

But as she rode back down the road it was just as natural to her that she should feel embarrassment for Nikolai, the covert Cossack who couldn't even stay on a horse. She must not let him see that she guessed his shame.

She swung down from the horse and looked at Cabell, feeling she had proved herself to him and pleased at the thought. He in turn looked at her, admiring her and stirred by her. Her hair hung down about her face and shoulders, her cheeks were flushed beneath their sheen of sweat; she looked almost as wild as the Cossacks themselves, anything but a starched governess. Miss Eden Penfold was coming out of her corset.

'You were marvellous!' Frederick exclaimed. 'You showed them!'

Olga danced and clapped her hands. 'Oh, they shouldn't laugh at girls, should they?'

Eden looked up at the Cossack leader, who nodded. 'You were good. I am Felix Pugachov, Captain. You will stay with us till I decide what is to be done with you. Bring your motor car across to the train.'

[2]

'Have more vodka. We have plenty, gallons of it.' Pugachov lolled back in his seat. 'Plenty of food and drink. And something else.' He winked broadly, but didn't elaborate.

'Something else?' said Cabell.

'Ah, that would be telling.' Pugachov winked again. His elbow had been continually bent for the past hour; he drank vodka as if it were water. But its effect was beginning to show on him now. 'That would be telling.'

'Have you been in the war?' Frederick asked.

'Have we been in the war, Your Highness? We have been fighting for five years. Or I have – some of my boys are too young to have seen it all. First the Germans, then the Bolsheviks. All this year we have been with Admiral Kolchak's army along the Siberian railway. A good man, but weak. He's all at sea on land.' He lay back and laughed, spilling vodka down his blouse front. 'That's good! I make good jokes, eh?'

Cabell, Eden and the two children were in the passenger carriage right behind the derailed engine. The tilt of the carriage, with its front bogies off the end of the rails, was not too uncomfortable, though those on the higher seats had a tendency to slip off. Pugachov and his guests or prisoners (Cabell hadn't quite decided what they were supposed to be)

106

were in seats at the higher end of the carriage; at the other, lower end half a dozen of the Cossacks sat drinking on the hard wooden seats. Outside the other Cossacks were preparing a meal, helped by the still-fearful Nikolai.

The sun had just gone down behind the mountains and the sky was streaked with coral reefs, like the reflection of a distant tropic sea. The tops of the pines and larches down by the river were gold-green, as if autumn had come early. A steppe eagle was crucified for a moment on a shaft of sunlight, then it planed down to its nest on the far side of the river. The wind had dropped and Cabell, looking out the window, once again felt the peacefulness that always attracted him to these remote places. Except that there was no suggestion of peacefulness in the carriage.

The men down at the end of the carriage had had too much to drink; they were not yet quarrelling amongst themselves, but their voices were getting louder, argument almost on the end of their tongues. Pugachov had loosened his belt, loosening a stomach that was bigger than Cabell had suspected, and he lolled back in his seat behind an increasingly smeared smile. Outside, the Cossacks round the camp fire had also been drinking and now were resting against their saddles while Nikolai finished the cooking.

When Nikolai at last called everyone to supper, Pugachov, staggering a little, led the way out of the carriage. The mutton stew and potatoes did nothing to settle the drink in the Cossacks; they washed every mouthful down with a swig of vodka. Cabell had accepted a mug of the drink, but he had surreptitiously managed to pour most of it into the ground beside him. No drink had been offered to Eden or the children, but the soldiers had forced several mugs of vodka on Nikolai and he looked ready to fold at any moment.

Frederick got up, said he was going for a pee, and ducked between the carriage and the wagon immediately behind it. Cabell, sitting on the running-board of the Rolls-Royce, looked at the wagon and for the first time saw that its sides were armour-plated. He wondered what was in the wagon – ammunition? But where had Pugachov and his men thought they were heading with a wagon-load of ammunition?

Then Pugachov got up, had some difficulty in keeping his balance, bowed to Eden and Olga. 'So you do not think I am a rude Cossack, I shall go and piss in private.'

'Do that,' said Eden.

He ducked awkwardly between the carriage and the wagon, crawling on his hands and knees beneath the coupling and banging his head on it. He swore loudly, looked owlishly back over his shoulder and apologized to Eden and Olga. The apology was spoiled by the fact that he passed wind loudly at the same time.

On the other side of the wagon Frederick, having relieved himself, was inspecting the armour-plating, tapping his knuckles against the iron plates. Pugachov crawled out from beneath the coupling, pulled down the front of his trousers and watered the wheels of the wagon. As he pulled up his trousers he saw Frederick watching him.

'Ah, Your Highness – what are you staring at? You have never seen a Cossack cock before?'

'I was looking at this wagon,' said Frederick, offended by the man's coarseness; Eden had taught him some lower-middle-class English gentility. 'Why are the sides armour-plated?'

'Ah!' Pugachov made an attempt to tap the side of his nose, missed and hit it hard with his second try, bringing tears to his eyes. 'You're a bright boy, aren't you?'

'I am a prince,' said Frederick, who bored other people with his preoccupation with his rank but never bored himself.

'I know plenty of stupid princes.' Pugachov leaned against the wagon and looked blearily at Frederick. There was still light in the sky and dusk had not yet swamped the day. The boy could see that the man, though drunk, was shrewdly sizing him up. 'You are not a top prince, otherwise you wouldn't boast about it.'

Frederick was hurt, but said nothing. He was still a long way from being an adult, but he was approaching the frontier; childhood was falling behind him, like a country he was reluctantly fleeing. It never would have occurred to him to think of his mother as a snob, but in the nine months since he had seen her he had begun to realize, if only vaguely and only occasionally, that some of the things she had taught him and Olga were wrong.

'Are you for the Tsar?' Pugachov said.

'Of course. I don't believe he is dead. The Bolsheviks didn't kill him, they have him and the Tsarina and his family hidden away somewhere. They wouldn't dare kill him.'

'Oh, they'd dare, all right.' Pugachov seemed to be trying to sober up. 'Bolsheviks can be just as stupid as princes.'

'Do you think the Tsar is dead then?'

Pugachov pondered that a moment. It was hard to tell whether he had not previously considered the question or whether he was too drunk to grasp it quickly. Then he nodded. 'He's dead, all right. It's been too long – someone would have told us by now if he was still alive. No, he's dead. All of them, the whole family. That's why we took this.' He thumped the side of the wagon with his fist. 'They won't need it any more.'

'What's inside it?'

'Ah!' Again Pugachov tapped his nose, doing it at his first attempt this time. Then he leaned forward, dropped his voice. 'Can you keep a secret?'

[3]

Pemenov hobbled the two horses and set about preparing his evening meal. He had bought the second horse, holding his gun at its owner's head, from a farmer he had met on the road. The price he had paid would not have bought a small dog if the transaction had been honest, but he felt he owed the farmer something. There were odd moments in his life when he had an attack of conscience; it irritated him, like eczema, and he wondered if he had inherited it from his mother. It would be just like her, the American bitch, to do anything to make him uncomfortable.

He had no memories of her, only those passed on to him by General Bronevich. His only memory of his father was that the latter, in his rare sober moments, had lavished affection on him; but then, having done his duty and been worn out by it, he had gone off to get drunk again. Peregrine (a name he had wanted to discard but which his protector had insisted he keep, as if it were some sort of challenge to a world that would abuse him anyway) had learned at a very early age that, even with Bronevich to shield him, he would always be alone.

So that now, as he sat down to his meal in the forest on the hills above the town a mile or two ahead of him, he felt no loneliness. Though he did not know it, it was one thing he had in common with the American he was tracking. He had a love for lonely places. His reasons, however, were different from those of Cabell. He loved the lonely places because they allowed him to be himself. There was never anyone else around to remind him that he was a freak.

[4]

'Are you sure?' said Eden.

'I saw it, I tell you!' Frederick's voice was hoarse with excitement and with the effort of keeping it low. 'The wagon is full of gold bars and jewels and things like that. It's part of the Tsar's treasure!'

'I think we should get out of here,' said Eden.

'How?' said Cabell. 'These guys are drunk, but they're not all fast asleep. Pugachov is no idiot. He's got them lying across the doors at either end.'

'We could get out the windows,' said Frederick.

'Have you tried opening them? I tried – they're stuck fast. We'd have to smash the glass and that'd wake every-one and we'd have bullets flying around in here like blow-flies.'

'They might kill each other then,' said Olga.

· 'Honey, they might kill us, too. No, we stay quiet and see what tomorrow brings. They might even let us go.'

'You don't really believe that, do you?'

Cabell wished that Eden hadn't asked that question. He ignored her and looked at Frederick in the dim light of the two oil lamps which lit the carriage. Pugachov was stretched out on the floor of the aisle between the two rows of seats. Eden and Olga were trying to make themselves comfortable on two of the hard wooden seats; Cabell and Frederick were opposite them on the other side of the aisle, equally uncomfortable. Only Nikolai was comfortable physically if not mentally: he was curled up in the car outside.

'Freddie, how much gold is there in the wagon?'

'Lots.' Frederick raised his hand about three feet above the floor. 'On both sides of the wagon, all the way down either side. Between the stacks of gold are the boxes with all the jewels in them.'

'It must weigh tons. Why doesn't it all drop through the floor?'

'The floor is all iron plates, too.'

'Did Captain Pugachov —' Pugachov stirred in his sleep, as if he had heard his name. 'Did he say where he was taking it?'

'No. He just showed me the treasure, then all of a sudden he dragged me out of the wagon and shut the door again.' Frederick had just reached the age when wealth had begun to take on some meaning; he was like an innocent who had just discovered sin and found it had its attractions. Since Pugachov had opened the door on the gold mine in the railway wagon, his young mind had been trying to comprehend what he had seen and he had been torn between greed, instinctive in all of us, and a sense of duty. Dutifully he now said, 'There is a fortune back there, Mr Cabell. I think we should try and recapture it for the Tsar.'

'Freddie, the Tsar is dead. And even if he isn't, his treasure isn't going to help him. Not stuck 'way out here in the middle of nowhere. Let's go to sleep.'

The sun, coming up out of China through the dirt-streaked windows, woke Cabell. He sat up, wondering why all his bones had turned to iron during the night; he moved his arms and legs, heard rusty creaks. Then he was fully awake and he slowly eased himself upright in the seat, waited for the blood to start flowing again and lubricate him. He looked down at the aisle floor and Pugachov, wide awake, gazing up at him.

'I was not asleep last night. I heard you. You know about the gold.'

Cabell decided there was nothing to be lost by being frank. 'Yes. How much is there in that wagon?'

Pugachov got slowly to his feet, belched, jerked his head. 'Come outside.'

As Cabell stepped out into the aisle he saw that Eden was awake. He shook his head at her and followed Pugachov down the slope of the carriage floor. Pugachov kicked his men, growling at them, and they all slowly stirred themselves. Cabell stepped over them and jumped down from the rear platform of the carriage. Pugachov leaned against the platform steps.

'That wagon is only one of twenty-nine that were in Admiral Kolchak's treasure train. We took it. The other twenty-eight are somewhere on the Siberian railway, God knows where. Nobody knows we have that wagon, we got away with it before Admiral Kolchak started his retreat to Omsk.'

'Is it really the Tsar's treasure?'

Pugachov nodded. 'Oh, it's his, all right. I was with the original troop that guarded it when it left Kazan, on the Volga. It had been taken there from St Petersburg when we were fighting the Germans. When we started fighting with the Bolsheviks, they decided to ship all the treasure to Omsk. It had been in Kazan all that time and the Bolsheviks had been sitting on it and didn't know it. Makes you wonder about them, doesn't it?'

'What happened?'

'We drove them out of Kazan and then the fighting started over who was going to get all the gold. Our side started fighting amongst themselves, I mean. No bullets flying, nothing like that. Just bureaucrats arguing. In the end it was all loaded on a train and we took it to Omsk. We sat there with it in the railway yards and it was almost as if everyone forgot about it. I didn't – I tell you, I was tempted every day to do something about it. Then one day we got word that things weren't going well with Admiral Kolchak's army and he was retreating towards Omsk. I could see what would happen. The treasure would be put on the line again and we'd head east with it and maybe eventually finish up in Vladivostok and all the bureaucrats would start arguing again and God knows who would get it all in the end. Not the Tsar – I knew he was dead.'

'So what did you do?' Cabell looked along at the armour-plated wagon, still unable to visualize the fortune that it contained.

'I got my boys together – they are only boys and they'll follow me anywhere. One night we stole an engine, that carriage and the horse-wagon, hitched them on to the last wagon of the gold train and headed west from Omsk. The army was going east and we just kept passing them, going the other way. One time we drew into a siding while Admiral Kolchak went past in his train. He was standing on the platform of his carriage, looking very sorry for himself. My boys and I fired our rifles as a salute —' Pugachov laughed, pleased at another of his jokes. He was rich, he was happy, he would go on laughing and making jokes for the rest of his life. 'Then we started getting too close to the Bolsheviks and we had to look for a railway running south. We found this one and – *here we are!*'

He stopped laughing and gestured angrily at the engine buried in the soft ground.

'How much is the treasure worth?'

Pugachov shrugged. 'I'm only guessing. The gold and jewels and money on the whole train, the twenty-nine wagons, were said to be worth one billion, one hundred and fifty million roubles, give or take a million.'

Cabell whistled, his mind racing like an abacus about to fly off its spindles. 'Over nine hundred million dollars!'

'Dollars?' Pugachov shrugged again, as if a dollar were worth nothing. 'I have done a little arithmetic, Cabell. I estimate there is almost forty million roubles' worth of treasure in that wagon. My men and I will be rich for the rest of our lives! If only —' He kicked a wheel of the engine, let out a curse.

'Captain Pugachov,' Cabell said cautiously, 'why are you telling me all this?'

'Because I want to use your motor car.'

Cabell shook his head. 'It wouldn't work. The springs aren't built to take that sort of weight. For crissake, you've got a whole wagon-load of it and the wagon's got an iron floor —'

'The young prince is a smart fellow, very observant.'

Pugachov had now led them away from the train; they stood on a bluff looking down towards the wide, dark-green river. 'I'm not proposing to take all the gold. Just my share, one-twelfth of it. I share everything with my men.'

Like hell you do. You're not going to share the Rolls-Royce with them. 'The car still wouldn't take that much weight. A few gold bars and maybe some of the jewels – that's all you're going to get away with, Captain.'

'Get away with?' Pugachov bridled.

'That's what you want to do, isn't it? Sneak off while your men aren't looking. They'd catch us on those horses of theirs – with all that weight, plus you and me and the girl and the kids and – and my stable boy, I couldn't drive fast. They'd catch us before we'd gone a couple of miles and they'd kill us all.'

'I wasn't thinking of taking the girl and the children.' He didn't mention Nikolai at all: he was a peasant, not even to be considered. 'There'd be just you and me.'

'Then you're not taking me.'

'I could kill you,' said Pugachov conversationally.

'If you did that you'd have no one to drive the car. You can't drive it, otherwise you wouldn't have told me all you have.'

'Bright, aren't you? Just like the little prince.' Pugachov scraped the ground with his boot, stared down towards the river. Several fish jumped, then disappeared again, leaving dark weals on the green surface. At last he said, 'It's a goddamned nuisance, isn't it? Nobody told me this railway wasn't finished. It was supposed to go all the way down to the Caspian. There's another railway on my map – it's further south, a hundred miles or more. It was built by the Emir of Bokhara in the last century.'

'Where were you taking the gold?'

'To Baku. I intended taking the treasure across the Caspian by boat. The English are there in Baku, supposedly backing General Denikin. But I don't think they care one way or the other who wins – they're tired of war. They would buy the gold from us. At a discount, of course – they are the toughest traders in the world, the English, they make the Jews and the Armenians in our market towns look like

114

priests handing out alms. My wife's father was a fur merchant from St Petersburg. He used to tell me when he'd go to England, the English used to skin him as if he himself were a bear.' He nodded his head, pondering on the perfidies of English traders. 'They'd buy the gold, all right, and take it home to England and not ask questions about it.'

Cabell wasn't sure that the English were quite as mercenary and unprincipled as Pugachov thought. He knew that they, like the French and the Americans, had grown tired of waiting for a White Russian victory in the civil war; he had learned that when he had landed in Vladivostok several months ago. They were ready to settle for any victor, so that they could take their troops home and get on with the job of recovering from the bigger war that had finished a year ago. The British (or the French or the Americans or any government for that matter) might have been interested in buying Admiral Kolchak's entire treasure train at a discount: after all, almost a billion dollars' worth of bullion and gems was not to be despised by any nation's treasury. But he doubted that they would compromise themselves, either with the Whites or the Reds, whoever should prove the eventual winner, for a mere forty million roubles. Thirty-six million dollars, give or take a million.

'I think you're stuck here with it, Captain.'

'I'll find a way,' said Pugachov stubbornly.

'In the meantime, what happens to us? We're no use to you. Let us go on.'

Pugachov shook his head, pulled on his thick moustache. 'You might run into some of General Denikin's men. They'd come up here and take the treasure from us. No, you stay with us.'

Cabell shrugged hopelessly and walked back to the camp fire on the other side of the train. Eden and the children, now out of the train, looked at him expectantly, but all he could offer them was a shake of his head. He saw the despair cloud their faces and abruptly he determined he would get them all away from here. But how?

Despair also seemed to have taken hold of the Cossacks. They sat around listlessly or walked down to the engine and grumpily kicked at its half-buried wheels. Pugachov sat alone on the rear platform of the carriage, staring moodily at the treasure wagon next door.

'I'm taking the children down for a bath,' said Eden and took a towel out of her suitcase in the trailer. 'We're all filthy.'

Pugachov scowled down at her. 'You look all right to me. Stay where you are.'

'I shall not. I don't know what sort of women you spend your time with, Captain, but I believe cleanliness is next to godliness.'

'Attagirl,' said Cabell, grinning at her but admiring her, too.

'I said you stay where you are!' Pugachov roared as Eden herded the two children ahead of her up past the rear of the train.

Eden took no notice of him and Cabell said, 'Let them go, Captain. Where the hell can they run to, for crissakes? If it makes her better to feel clean, what harm does it do you? I could do with a bath myself.'

Pugachov scowled at him, the thick black eyebrows coming down, but sat back in his seat. 'You stay here. She and the children can go, but you stay here.'

Eden walked the children down to the river, found a gravel stretch along the bank where they could wade out into the water. 'Be careful of the current. Freddie, you bathe first. Strip off and give yourself a good wash.'

She and Olga sat on the bank while Frederick stripped off, soaped himself and enjoyed himself in the cool river. He came out, dried himself and put on the fresh shirt Eden had brought down. She combed his long dark hair, stood back and nodded approvingly.

'You're a very handsome lad, Freddie. But you probably know it.'

'Oh, he does,' said Olga.

'All right, go back up to the train while Olga and I bathe.'

'I'll wait,' said Frederick, who had often wondered what Miss Eden would look like without her clothes. 'Just in case some of the soldiers come down to spy on you.'

'We'll be all right,' said Eden firmly, reading the look in his eye. 'Back to the train – now!'

116

Frederick went reluctantly. Then Eden and Olga undressed and went into the river, careful not to go too far out into the strong current, going in only to their hips and then squatting down. Eden felt dirty, a state she hated, and she scrubbed herself as if she had just emerged from a coal-mine.

Up on the carriage platform Pugachov had shifted his position and was watching the scene down by the river through his binoculars. He nodded appreciatively and wondered what the ripe Englishwoman would give him for a bar of gold.

'Don't do that, Captain,' said Cabell quietly at the bottom of the steps leading up to the platform. 'Do you have a wife?'

Pugachov lowered the glasses and actually managed to look embarrassed. 'I have a wife, yes. I was just admiring Miss Penfold. No harm in that, is there?'

'No. I admire her myself. But not when she has no clothes on.'

'Isn't that the best time?' Pugachov laughed.

Down on the river bank Eden had come out, dried herself and dressed in a fresh blouse and was now drying Olga. She straightened up as she finished, telling Olga to dress herself, and caught a glimpse of movement in a clump of trees almost half a mile upstream. She squinted, trying to make out what had caused the movement. Was it one of the Cossacks spying on her and Olga? Then she made out the shapes of two horses amongst the trees, but could see no sign of a man. Feeling uneasy, she said nothing to Olga but hurried the child through her dressing, then went back up towards the train. As she reached the railway line she looked back towards the trees, but could see nothing now.

'Feel better?' Cabell said.

He had come to the end of the train to meet them. She sent Olga on, handing her the wet towel. 'Hang that out to dry. I want to talk to Mr Cabell.'

'If it's about trying to get away,' Cabell said when Olga had moved away, 'I haven't thought of anything yet. We're like this train – we're stuck.'

Without turning round Eden said, 'There's someone back there along the river, in the trees. Could it be someone who is after Captain Pugachov?'

Cabell looked over her shoulder towards the distant trees, but could see nothing. 'If it is, we better be ready to duck as soon as the shooting starts. Don't move around too much – and keep the kids close to you. Sit in the shade somewhere and as soon as the shooting starts, lie down flat.'

'And pray?' She still felt uneasy, yet she smiled.

'And pray.' He smiled, took her hand and pressed it. 'You're all right, Eden. When we get to Tiflis, you and I are going out to dinner. No afternoon tea with the kids. Just you and me.'

'I'll look forward to it – What do I call you? Matthew Martin?'

'My mother did. Most people call me Matt.' He looked over her shoulder again, but could still see nothing moving amongst the trees.

'Don't forget. Keep close to the ground.'

'Do we tell Captain Pugachov?'

'Not yet.'

He left her and went along to where Pugachov still sat on the carriage platform. 'Could I borrow your glasses, Captain? I thought I saw some ducks over there along the river. We might have duck for supper.'

Pugachov handed down the binoculars. Yesterday's drinking had had its effect on him and he had no interest in food this morning, least of all greasy duck. 'I'm not going to let you go shooting, Cabell. You might shoot me or one of my men instead of a duck. But you can have a look. Enjoy the view.'

Cabell went back to the rear of the train, aimed the glasses at the clump of trees. The glasses were strong and at once he saw the two horses set well back in the trees. Then he saw the figure, short and thickset, kneeling beside one of the horses. He steadied the glasses: no, not *kneeling*. It was a man standing upright, the dwarf who had been with General Bronevich, the man he had knocked out when Frederick had brought him into the Gorshkov barn.

'Shitabrick,' he said softly.

He lowered the glasses and walked slowly back to the group sitting and lolling beside the main carriage. He handed the glasses up to Pugachov. 'I was mistaken, Captain. No ducks.'

'Then you're not disappointed I won't let you shoot them?' Pugachov laughed and belched.

'Captain – What are you going to do? Just sit here and hope for some sort of miracle?'

'I'm thinking, Cabell.' But thinking had given him a headache; he scowled again. 'I may have to go north again, steal another engine and find some other railway line.'

'The troubles of the rich,' said Cabell sympathetically.

'The poor just don't appreciate them.' But Pugachov smiled; his sense of humour hadn't entirely left him.

Cabell moved across and sat down beside Eden in the morning shade thrown by the treasure wagon. 'Did you see anything?' she said.

'Yes. It's that dwarf who was with General Bronevich. The one who came into the barn.'

'Good heavens! What does he want?'

'Us, I should think. Things ain't healthy, honey.'

'Don't call me *honey*.' She said it automatically; she was more concerned with the man lurking in the trees half a mile away. 'Don't you think you should tell Captain Pugachov?'

'I don't know. It's six of one and half a dozen of the other.'

'But that dwarf might want to kill us!'

'So might Pugachov.' He didn't tell her that Pugachov had already said he didn't need her and the children and Nikolai. 'He's not on our side, don't start thinking that. We'll just sit and wait a while. The dwarf isn't going to start anything in daylight, not while all these Cossacks are around us.'

The sun climbed higher and the morning wore on. Nikolai, for want of something better to do, got permission to go down to the river and bring back a bucket of water; he was now washing the car. Down in the trees along the river bank Pemenov watched the strange scene: a train stuck at the end of a railway line going nowhere; a dozen Cossacks and their horses looking lost and restless; a shining royal blue Rolls-Royce emerging from its coat of mud as a man washed it. And the two children playing catch with the American in his broad-brimmed hat, tossing some sort of ball to each other. He watched patiently, waiting for night. He would go in when everyone was asleep and kill the American. He probably would be killed himself, but the prospect didn't disturb him.

It was midday when those by the train heard, on the still air, the shouts and the thin music of a pipe. Then, out of the trees up along the road, there came a caravan. Two men on horses, a dozen men and women walking, children scampering along to the tune on the pipe, eighteen camels plodding in single file and a third horseman bringing up the rear with two mules on a lead-rope. They were at least three hundred yards from the train but even at that distance their shock was evident when they saw it. The horsemen in front pulled up sharply; the walkers congealed in behind them; and the file of camels concertinaed into milling confusion. Everyone immediately turned to bringing the camels under control before they bolted.

Pugachov was on his feet at once, tumbling off the carriage platform and yelling to his men. All their horses were bridled but none was saddled; the Cossacks, led by Pugachov, jumped on the bare-backed horses and took off towards the road and the caravan.

Cabell also jumped to his feet. 'Get the handle, Nick! Start the engine!'

Eden grabbed the two children and pushed them into the car. Cabell leapt in behind the wheel, set the controls and waited for Nikolai to swing the starting handle. He took a quick look towards the road and picked out the way he would take across the rough ground. Nikolai swung the handle; the engine wheezed but did not start. He tried again, already beginning to sweat; the engine took, purred sweetly. Cabell, shouting for Nikolai to jump into the car, reached for the brake.

But he had under-estimated Pugachov. The Cossack captain had looked back, seen what was happening and two horsemen were already galloping back towards the train and the car. One of them raised his rifle and a bullet went over Cabell's head and smacked into the side of the treasure wagon, ricocheting off the armour-plating and whining away into silence.

Cabell switched off the engine and looked at Eden. 'Not this time, I'm afraid.'

Eden was looking up towards the road. 'I'm not afraid for us. It's those people in the caravan . . .'

No one in the caravan had been foolish enough to fire on the advancing Cossacks. They all clustered together, men, women, children and livestock in one big group; the camels and horses and mules moved restlessly, but they were under control. Those in the car could hear shouts from Pugachov and his men but couldn't distinguish what was being said.

Cabell looked at the two Cossacks who were now ranged one on either side of the Rolls-Royce. They had dismounted and had their rifles levelled at Cabell and the others. These were Mosin-Nagent guns, newer and more effective than the ancient Krenks, and he began to appreciate that Captain Pugachov had a very efficient unit under his command. There was a Maxim machine-gun mounted on the engine tender and another on top of the horse-wagon at the rear of the train. He had noticed them earlier and cursed himself now for not having jumped up behind one of the machine-guns and annihilated the Cossacks while they were riding towards the caravan. But he knew even as he thought of it that, once behind the machine-gun, he could not have fired it. He could not have massacred a dozen men, no matter how dangerous they were, in front of the children. Oh Cabell, he thought, when it comes to pulling the trigger of a gun you're as lily-livered as Nikolai.

'Relax, fellers,' he said in Russian. 'I was just testing the engine.'

'Horseshit,' said one of the Cossacks; they were both young, neither of them over twenty. 'Sit there and put your hands up. All of you!'

They kept their hands up for twenty minutes, till their muscles stiffened and ached and Olga began to cry; then Pugachov came back and swung down from his horse. Behind him the caravan, escorted by the Cossacks, was coming towards the train.

'So you thought you could sneak away, eh?'

Cabell didn't answer him. He was looking at the caravan

121

people as, fearful and quiet, they came towards him. Their camels he recognized as the shaggy Bactrians, the hardy beasts of burden from the deserts of central Asia. The people were Uzbeks, the men wearing their embroidered skullcaps and, because of the heat of the day, their striped, padded *khalats* worn as a cape over their shoulders. The women had their faces hidden behind black veils, but some of them wore bright skirts or trousers, red or blue, beneath the enveloping black *chador*. The children were bright-eyed, torn between fear and curiosity. Cabell guessed the group were traders, probably inter-married, on their way home, to Samarkand or Bokhara, from the market in Oblansk.

'I am making a trade,' said Pugachov. 'I am giving these Uzbeks the train and I am taking their camels. A bargain for them, eh? What other Uzbeks will have their own train?' He had regained his good humour. 'You may put your hands down. I know you're not going to run away.'

But he would not allow Cabell and the others out of the car. They sat there under the guard of one Cossack and watched the treasure being taken out of the armour-plated wagon. The gold was packed in boxes which took two men to lift them; other boxes, much lighter, held the jewels and gems. There was a yell and two of the soldiers dropped a box of gold. The box burst open and ingots, all stamped with the Imperial seal, where scattered around like yellow bricks. The Uzbeks gasped when they saw what the heavy boxes contained; even the Cossacks themselves paused, suddenly overcome by their first real sight of their booty. It was if the Holy Grail had just been dumped at everyone's feet.

'Leave it,' said Pugachov as the two Cossacks went to pick up the gold bars. 'There's plenty more.' He glanced at Cabell and grinned. 'Oh, what it is to be rich, eh?'

The Uzbeks were still staring at the gold; a child knelt down and shyly touched one of the ingots. Pugachov looked at them, then moved up to the wagon and looked in at the remaining boxes. His face seemed to droop with disappointment and chagrin, then he sighed loudly. He looked across at Cabell, smiled wryly.

'There's still so much we can't take.' Then he said to the Uzbeks, 'It's all yours.'

None of the Uzbeks moved. Fear held them back: this was some trick, they knew of the Cossack cruel sense of humour. Pugachov picked up one of the bars and handed it to the child who had touched it, a small girl about eight or nine.

'It's all yours, sweetheart. Buy yourself a doll.'

The Cossacks had stopped loading and were looking at Pugachov, not sure that he wasn't joking. Then one of them said, 'Why do we have to give it to them, Captain?'

'Because we can't take it all with us,' Pugachov snapped. As much as any of them he hated to be so charitable. 'We can only take what the camels can carry.'

The Cossacks, after some rebellious looks amongst themselves, went back to loading. The boxes were loaded two to a camel, the ropes slung between the two humps on the animal's back; the camels had been stripped of all the Uzbeks' goods they had been carrying. When the loading was finished and the camels had struggled to their feet, there were still just as many boxes of gold left in the wagon.

'Oh, it hurts more than a sabre wound,' said Pugachov, 'but we must leave it behind. Do you think I should leave some men here to guard it and come back for it? Make several trips?'

'Can you trust them?' Cabell said.

'Ah, there you have a point. You saw the look on their faces just then when I offered the gold to these traders. I would trust my boys with my life. But not, I think, with this gold.' He looked at the burdened camels. 'A pity. I am not going to be as rich as I had hoped. These damned traders will be richer – there are less of them to divide the spoils. I think I'd do better to kill them. Then I shouldn't envy them, eh?'

'Then there will be blood on your gold.' Eden tried to speak calmly, but she was fluttering inside. She had seen the faces of both Cossack and Uzbek when the gold had spilled out and the ugliness of their greed had shocked her. She wondered what the look had been on her own face. 'That will bring you bad luck. The very worst sort of luck.'

'Perhaps you are right.' Pugachov took off his hat, pulled on his forelock. Up on the train two of his men were dismantling the machine-guns, rendering them useless; in a few minutes they would be on their way again and he did not want his men shot in the back as they left the train. The Uzbeks might not be satisfied with the fortune he was leaving them, they might want the lot. He reached into a cavernous pocket in his trousers and took out an emerald-studded gold egg almost as large as an ostrich egg. He handed it to Eden. 'May this bring you good luck.'

'Oh, I couldn't!' But Eden saw the look in Pugachov's eye and knew she could, indeed *had* to. 'It's a Fabergé – I saw one once in St Petersburg.'

'The Tsar had dozens of them.' Pugachov was beaming at Eden's open-mouthed admiration of the gift. He must remember to take one home for the wife. 'Open it.'

Eden pressed a catch and the top half of the egg opened up. Inside was another, smaller egg, this one studded with diamonds. She took it out, pressed a catch and its upper half in turn opened, revealing a third egg, this one decorated with rubies. When she had finished opening the small treasure chest, seven eggs lay in her lap; diamonds, emeralds, rubies, sapphires gleamed in the golden nest. Frederick maintained a princely disdain, but Olga leaned over and picked up the smallest egg and cooed over it as if she had laid it herself.

'May she have that one?' Eden said to Pugachov.

'No,' said Frederick. 'It belongs to the Tsar.'

'It used to belong to the Tsar,' said Pugachov. 'Now it belongs to me and I can give it to whoever I wish. You may have it, Princess. It goes with your beauty.'

'Thank you,' said Olga, no beauty to deny her looks.

'Traitor,' said Frederick. 'Father will make you give it back.'

'Mother won't,' said Olga, who knew where the real power lay in the Gorshkov family.

Then Pugachov gave the order for his caravan to get on the road. It started off: eighteen camels, twelve horsemen, the Uzbeks' three horses carrying food and camp equipment. And the Rolls-Royce.

'This car is not going to be able to travel at the pace of those camels,' said Cabell. 'It will just wear out the engine.'

Pugachov pondered the limitations of modern

technology. A magnificent machine like this which could not travel as slowly as a camel: it made one wonder if the world was not going backwards. He looked towards the two mules which, as a true horseman, he despised and had intended leaving with the Uzbeks.

'We shall not use your engine. The mules can pull the motor car.'

'That's ridiculous—' Cabell saw Pugachov's face harden '—ly easy. What an intelligent idea!'

'Every other inch a hero,' said Eden in English.

'Every inch a realist,' replied Cabell and smiled at Pugachov.

'Miss Penfold is agreeing with me about your splendid idea.'

Ropes were produced and the mules were hitched to the front of the Rolls-Royce. It was a teaming that would have had Mr Henry Royce blowing a gasket had he known. Pugachov plucked Frederick from the car and set him on his own horse. Then he got into the front seat beside Cabell.

'We shall ride together.' He looked up at Frederick sitting erect in the saddle, the sabre held over his shoulder. He had not asked the boy if he could ride; he had taken it for granted that any prince, no matter how young, should be able to sit a horse. 'Lead the way, Your Highness.'

Frederick moved his horse forward and the mules, responding to the long rope reins held by Cabell, fell in behind him. The Rolls-Royce eased forward, began to roll smoothly. They went up towards the road, the mules straining against the traces, following the main part of the caravan, then they were on the road and the long journey south was once more under way. Eden, in the back seat with Olga and Nikolai, looked back.

The Uzbeks had not moved or said a word as the caravan had started off, had stood silently beside the train, the glittering litter of ingots still at their feet, still unable to believe they had been left a fortune such as their dreams had never been able to encompass. The afternoon sun blazed in their faces as they stared after the departing caravan; it struck the gold and for a moment it seemed to Eden that they all stood in a bright yellow pool. Then suddenly they moved.

The women and children scooped up the scattered ingots; the men scrambled into the wagon. Shouts of laughter, screams of delight, floated across to those in the departing car; even at a distance one could hear the hysterical, slightly mad note in the excitement. One man had climbed to the top of the wagon and was dancing up and down the length of the roof, whirling his *khalat*.

'Twenty million roubles,' said Pugachov. 'I should be canonized for such charity.'

'How will they take it home with them?'

'Oh, they'll manage. They'll probably cart it up into the mountains, box by box, and bury it, then come back later with another caravan of camels.'

'Why couldn't you have done that?'

'No, Cabell, we can never come back here. We are Grebentsky Cossacks. No one loves us, least of all the peasants of Siberia. I have only eleven men. We could take on a hundred and kill them all. But not a thousand. And there are other Cossacks looking for us – they'll probably know by now we stole that wagon. If Admiral Kolchak has retreated all the way to Omsk, he'll have his bureaucrats checking the train again. No, we have to keep going south to the Caspian and then across to Baku.'

'And where then?' said Eden.

'Ah, where? America perhaps?' He glanced at Cabell. 'Are rich men welcome in America?'

'A few.' But he couldn't see a rich Cossack at home in the States, except perhaps in Texas. 'You think the Bolsheviks are going to win here in Russia?'

'Never!' That was Frederick, sabre at the ready.

Pugachov glanced back at Eden, gestured at the optimism of youth.

'His Highness can't read the writing on the wall. You should have taught him better.'

'I taught him English, not pessimism,' said Eden; yet she felt her own lack of faith in the future. The Russia she had come to six years ago was doomed and, looking beyond the family which had treated her almost as one of its own and

126

for whom she prayed there would be no tragedy, she was glad to see it die. She just wasn't sure that the Bolsheviks, as crudely violent as those they were trying to supplant, had the answer. When she got back to England she must take more interest in politics. Then she found herself looking at the back of Cabell's head and wondering if she might not go to America instead.

Pugachov shrugged. He had no interest in politics; he had been a fighter. But now he was middle-aged and he was tired. 'I think I prefer to be a rich pessimist. But somewhere else but Russia.'

The car came to the top of the last rise before the road wound down to follow the river. From there they had their last sight of the Uzbeks. They were hauling the treasure boxes out of the wagon as fast as they could work; the image crossed Cabell's mind that they were like rats tearing the insides out of a huge dying beast. Then the car rolled forward, Cabell putting the brakes on to prevent it rolling over the top of the mules, and the crest of the rise suddenly shut out the Uzbeks, the train and the fortune that would make them happy for the rest of their days or haunt them for generations.

Cabell had looked for the dwarf back along the river, but he had not appeared. But Cabell knew he had not gone away, that he would still be following them.

[5]

Pemenov saw the caravan start off from the train and he shivered with rage. He had seen the Uzbeks arrive and seen some sort of slow commotion when they had been brought down from the road to the train; but he had been too far away to see what was going on. Now he could see them jumping in and out of a wagon in the train, hauling out boxes and behaving like children on a picnic. He waited till the Cossack caravan had disappeared over the crest, then he led his horses down till he found a shelf in the river bank. All his life it had been a struggle for him to mount a horse; he still cursed each time he had to do it. He drew his saddle horse in beneath the shelf and jumped on its back, hurting his crotch as he did so. He was far from happy as he headed the horses up through the trees towards the train.

The Uzbeks, intent on their fortune-gathering, did not see him till he came round the rear of the horse-wagon and pulled up his horses. He held his pistol, aiming it at a middle-aged man who seemed to be the leader.

'Where are the Cossacks heading for?' He spoke in Turkic, not in Russian.

The man raised his hands, shook his head. 'We don't know, sir. They have just gone, going that way —' He nodded towards the south.

The Uzbeks, even the women and children, stood in front of the boxes, trying to hide them with their legs and bodies. Pemenov, still angered at losing the American for yet another day, was blind for a moment or two to what they were trying to do. Then he saw the gold, the fallen ingots now stacked back in their box but with the lid of the box still open.

'Is that gold?' He jerked the pistol and the leader, after a moment's hesitation, took out an ingot and handed it up to the dwarf. 'In all those boxes, too?'

The leader reluctantly nodded. 'The Cossack captain said we could have it, what was left. He has taken a lot of boxes with him.'

Pemenov turned the ingot over in his hand, saw the Imperial seal. His small hand had trouble holding the gold and a child snickered. He jerked his head to look at the small boy, almost falling out of the saddle as he did so; which made the other children laugh. His head swivelled, his face suddenly dark with anger: the children did not realize how close they came to being massacred. Then he regained control of himself but only with a tremendous effort; a week ago he would have killed them all. But he could not waste time and bullets here: his quarry was disappearing down the road south. He stuffed the gold ingot into his saddle bag, gestured for the leader to give him another one, with which he did the same.

He looked at the gold in the open box and at all the other boxes. He could not even begin to guess what the fortune was worth; whatever it was, it would make him the richest dwarf in the world. Perhaps even the richest dwarf in history: his mind swirled with the vision. No one would laugh at him, not even children; he would be surrounded by heads bent lower than his own. They might call him names but they would be with respect: Little Midas, Little Croesus . . . He uttered a half-sigh, half-curse: what was the use? The gold was as secure here as if it were still in a reef a hundred feet below the ground.

He turned his horse, rode straight through the surrounding Uzbeks, scattering them out of his path. When he had killed the American he might come back this way and see if the Uzbeks and the gold had disappeared. Then he might track *them* down. He rode on up to the road, dizzy with thoughts of other roads he might be taking in the future. The gold bars nudged his legs, like solid promises.

[6]

The caravan camped that night beside the river amongst a grove of wild pear and wild apple. Some bustards took off through the long grass in flapping indignation at being disturbed and a fish hawk swooped by to whistle at the intruders. The sight of the osprey gave Cabell an idea.

'I think I'd like fish for supper.'

He burrowed around in his gear, produced a reel of fishing line. 'Are you always so well prepared?' Eden asked.

'If I were always well prepared, would I be where I am now?' He bounced the reel in his hand. 'I've been pretty close to starving a couple of times, when I've got lost. Once in Venezuela, the other time in Mexico. This line saved my life. Unfortunately, I don't think it's going to do the same in this situation.'

Eden tried to hide her shock. 'You really think Captain Pugachov will kill us?'

'Why not? He doesn't need us. We're just amusement for him. He'll get rid of us as soon as he tires of us.' He checked the line for any tangling. 'There's the dwarf, too. He's not chasing us to give us that food and water you left behind in the kitchen . . . Sorry. I didn't mean that the way it sounded.'

She could see that beneath his calm exterior he was worried. During the slow, dreadfully slow, afternoon's journey, she had had time to think about their predicament. The thought of the dwarf trailing them had troubled her; it was so totally unexpected that she could not quite accept the idea that he wanted to kill them. Too, she could not bring herself to accept the same intention by Pugachov; he had been so friendly and generous during the caravan's trek, like an uncle enjoying a day out with his nieces and nephews. Like so many other romantics she was prepared to believe the best of people if they showed a better side of themselves: the dark side did not bear thinking about. But Cabell was obviously thinking about it and she would have to do the same.

She followed him down to the river's edge, watched him while he dug around and found some worms, attached one to the hook and cast the line out into the water. 'There are lots of fancy flies, but worms are still a fisherman's best friend.'

Eden knelt down and washed her face with her handkerchief. She had for the moment forgotten about the children; they could look after themselves. Then she felt a stab of conscience and looked up towards the car to see if they were all right. Frederick was unsaddling Pugachov's horse, talking to the Cossack captain just as if he *were* a favourite nephew. Olga, every inch a lady, sat on the running-board of the car admiring her jewelled egg. In the background Nikolai, trying to make himself inconspicuous by making himself useful, was gathering wood for a fire.

Cabell sat down on the bank and looked up-river. On the opposite side there was a small promontory jutting out; in its lee he could see a reed-spiked swamp. Mallards were gliding down ramps of sunlight into the swamp, hitting the water in small silvery explosions. The countryside stretched away beyond the river, bronzed with summer; there were occasional clumps of trees, but the forest had thinned out on that side. A faint breeze came out of the steppes, promising the cool of evening.

'Peaceful, isn't it?'

'Not when one is thinking about being shot or having one's throat cut.'

'That won't happen to you.' There was a tug on his line and he began to haul it in; a two-pound perch came floundering up the bank. 'With your looks, Pugachov will either take you for himself or give you to one of his men. Grab the fish!'

Eden made several grabs at the perch, clutched it and awkwardly extracted the hook from its mouth. Cabell put another worm on the line and once more tossed it out into the river.

'You can start cleaning that.' He took the clasp knife from the clip on his belt and tossed it to her.

She rolled up her sleeves, clumsily began to clean the fish. She had done nothing like this before, the Gorshkovs had always had more than enough servants for such tasks, but she was determined to show Cabell that she could be as resourceful as he. But why am I trying to prove myself to him? she asked herself. And lowered her gaze from his, concentrating on the fish, as the answer came only too readily.

'Have you had much experience with men?'

The question was so unexpected she almost sliced off a finger. 'What? I – I've had enough. I had a —' She almost said *lover*, a word she had never used before. 'I was engaged. Well, not officially. He went off to war.'

'An Englishman?'

'A Russian. He was wounded at Tannenburg and died on the train coming back to St Petersburg.'

'Five years ago this month,' he mused. He had been looking out at his line, but now he turned his head to look directly at her. 'Has there been anyone since?'

'What business is it of yours?'

'None, I guess. I just think, with your looks and figure, you shouldn't have wasted all those years.'

'You say some rather ungentlemanly things to a lady, Mr Cabell.'

'Eden – I'll always treat you as a lady, no matter what I say. Has there been another man since your Russian?'

'No–o.' Why was she telling him all this? But her head and her loins knew, if not her heart. He was male and he was company and she was sick and tired of chastity and loneliness. Well, not chastity; was continence the word? She had lost her virginity to Igor Dulenko and been amazed at her own enjoyment of it. And now she was beginning to feel that way again, the way she had felt when she had said yes to Igor's pleas. The discovery was so sudden that the knife slipped again and this time she did cut her finger. 'Damn!'

'Watch it!' He grinned, took her hand in his and looked at her bleeding finger. 'It's not deep. Wrap your handkerchief around it. You'll live.'

She sucked on her finger, looked down at the knife in her other hand and told him what she thought of him.

'What'd you say?'

She took her finger out of her mouth. 'If Captain Pugachov doesn't kill you, I'll do it myself!'

She dropped the knife at his feet and went scrambling up the bank as Nikolai came down to Cabell. 'What is the matter with Miss Eden?'

'She's cut her finger. Women get upset about little things.'

'Oh, don't they! I could never live with a woman.'

Cabell felt the moment was awkward, even if Nikolai didn't. Then another fish jumped at the end of the line and the topic was forgotten. In the next half-hour Cabell landed three more fish. They had enough to invite Pugachov to dine with them. It was a gesture that had an effect on Pugachov out of all proportion to the thought that had prompted it. Last night he had been their captor and host; he had almost thrown their food at them. Tonight was different. Eden, without thinking of the protocol, had sent Frederick to offer the invitation. Pugachov, though it took them some time to realize it, was a social snob. It was the first time a prince, even if only a twelve-year-old and a minor prince at that, had invited him to dine.

They sat there in the twilight by the river and ate fish and boiled potatoes and washed them down with vodka; Eden watered hers and drowned Frederick's and Olga's. Pugachov became expansive and told them stories of his term of duty as a young man at the Winter Palace in St Petersburg.

'The magnificence there! Such a palace! The Tsar and Tsarina lived quietly, but, oh, those other people around them – the balls, the parties! What a way to live.'

'It is the only way to live,' said Olga, who had not even begun.

Pugachov, who had mellowed with the vodka, shook his head sadly. 'It is all finished, Princess. I was in St Petersburg and Moscow in 1913, when the Romanovs celebrated three hundred years on the throne – I was part of the Tsar's guard. It was wonderful. And there was the Thanksgiving service in the Kazan Cathedral – God smiled on us all that day. Then the Tsar went down the river to Moscow. We rode behind him into the Red Square and you never saw such crowds – one could believe they would love the Tsar forever. But it was all just theatre, make-believe like an opera – it was a farewell, but we didn't know it. It's all over, Princess.'

'No!' Frederick shook his head fiercely.

But Cabell knew it *was* all over. He was no Bolshevik but he knew the Tsars had asked for what they had eventually got; in the three hundred years of the Romanovs there had been too many tyrants. He wondered if Prince Gorshkov, fighting in the Ukraine or wherever he was, had as much faith in the future as his son.

'Yes, Your Highness,' said Pugachov, 'it is over. You should stop thinking about being a prince – Ah yes.' He held up a hand as Frederick went to protest. 'I respect princes – and princesses.' He looked at Olga and she inclined her head graciously. 'But you should think of another profession. Be a man who searches for oil, like Mr Cabell. Is there a future in oil, Cabell?'

'Unlimited,' said Cabell. 'Some day the whole world will run on oil, it'll be so cheap every man will be able to afford even to run a motor car. There are over seven million automobiles in America even now.'

'Seven million!' Pugachov rolled his head in wonder. 'There can't be that many horses in Russia!'

'How much oil is there in the world?' Eden asked.

'We just don't know – we've only just begun to tap it. There may be more oil than there is coal. Some day the whole world will run on it. Automobiles, ships, trains, power stations – everything!' He looked at Frederick. 'If ever you want to stop being a prince, let me know. Some day

133

there'll be oil kings and they'll rule the world.'

'Perhaps I should sell my gold for an oil field,' said Pugachov.

'You could do worse,' said Cabell.

Later, before turning in, Cabell went down to the river to relieve himself. The moon had just come up over the rim of the horizon; the river flowed like liquid metal (or golden oil?) past him. Out in mid-stream a fish jumped; for a moment droplets of gold hung in the air. Somewhere an owl hooted, underlining the lonely silence. Then there was a footstep behind him.

'I hope I didn't scare you.' It was Eden.

'No—o.' But he was embarrassed: he had finished relieving himself but his penis was enjoying the night air. He turned away, hastily adjusted himself, put it away for the night.

If Eden saw what he was doing, she gave no sign. She was looking out over the river and country beyond. 'You like this loneliness, don't you? I've seen you admiring it. Were you born in country like this?'

'No, I was born on a street called Prairie Avenue in Chicago, but it hadn't seen the prairie in fifty years or more. When I looked out our front door all I saw opposite was stores or houses exactly like ours. There were kids yelling on the sidewalk and old women arguing and drunks fighting. And when all that noise stopped, you could hear the clanging of the street-cars down on Fifty-first Street. I never heard an owl hoot or a bird sing till I was twelve years old and my father took me on a camping trip. That was when I started to think about places a bit further than the end of Prairie Avenue and I started to read books my father gave me. Yes, I like wide open spaces – this loneliness, if you like. It beats the hell out of living in a city.'

He had sounded almost eloquent as he had talked and she recognized the depth of his feeling and responded. 'I don't know if I could go back to Croydon – that's just south of London. The childr – the kids don't yell on the – sidewalk? – and there's certainly no old women arguing and drunks fighting. But . . . Travel broadens one, but it spoils you, don't you think?'

'Maybe. Depends what you want from life.'

'What do you want?'

'I'm not sure. Eventually a wife and kids, I suppose.'

'And you'd cart them round the world after you looking for wide open spaces?'

'The right wife wouldn't mind.'

'There must be a word to describe men like you, but I don't think anyone has coined it yet.'

'I'm sure you're working on it.'

'Oh, I shall, Mr Cabell, I shall. Now would you excuse me?'

'Oh, sure. But you and I will have to have separate bathrooms in future. We're getting too intimate.'

'Watch it!'

He took her arm, turned her towards him. He half-expected her to draw away, but she didn't. He leaned forward and kissed her on the lips. She still didn't draw away, though there was no response in her lips. He put his hand behind her, drew her into him and increased the pressure of his kiss. Her lips relaxed, then her mouth opened. Down in his baggy trousers things began to warm up; she felt him against her and for a wild moment was tempted. Then she gently pushed him away.

'Not here, Matt. Maybe when we get to Tiflis.'

He stared at her, then kissed her gently on the cheek. 'Good night, Eden.'

Later, she in the car and he in his sleeping-bag on the ground beside it thought of each other before they dropped off to sleep. Neither mentioned the word love in his or her mind. But there was doubt about the feeling each felt for the other, the doubt about how far to commit oneself. And love, like hate, can begin as doubt.

In the morning the strange caravan got under way again, this time with the mule-drawn Rolls-Royce heading the procession. Pugachov rode with Cabell again and Frederick rode the Cossack's horse. The camels plodded along with their flat-footed walk, the leaders of them right behind the car. Eden would occasionally look back into their cynical, mournful eyes; they would open their great ugly mouths and slobber their indifference. Only when she thought about it did she realize that she never looked beyond their ugliness to the treasure they carried on their back; it was as if all the boxes of gold and gems were valueless. But her hand still clutched tightly the large handbag that now held the gem-studded golden egg.

The road still followed the course of the river, winding its way through forest-covered slopes. Now and again the Cossacks, tiring of walking their horses, would suddenly yell and dash on ahead, racing each other to the top of a rise; then they would come cantering back, faces flushed, smiling widely and throwing some respectful banter at Pugachov. There was no doubt that he was the leader of this band and they would follow him to wherever he led them. But to America? Cabell wondered.

Occasionally he glanced back over his shoulder, looking beyond the caravan; but he saw no sign of the dwarf, yet felt sure the little man was there beyond the crest of the last rise. He was tempted to ask Pugachov to send some of his men back to check; but caution held him back. For some reason he could not name, he did not want to be beholden to Pugachov. The Cossack had been affable enough ever since they left the train, but Cabell had seen how rapidly a Russian temper could change; in their own way the Russians were every bit as volatile as any Latin. They could be dull, stupid, stolid; but not the intelligent ones like Pugachov. And what would happen if the dwarf did appear, told Pugachov how Cabell had killed a White Army general? The Cossack might ask himself, if the American could kill a general, why shouldn't he try to kill a captain? And Cabell could guess at what means Pugachov would take to prevent that. Kill the American first.

In mid-morning the road came to the top of a long slope. The trees fell away and one could see for several miles, the road still winding on through the trees and the river going round in a long shallow curve. In the far distance Cabell could see a long boat (a ferry?) crossing from one bank of the river to the other. He pulled on the reins of the mules, put on the car's brakes.

'I can't take the car down this hill behind the mules, Captain. It would wear out the brakes and we'd just roll straight over the top of them.'

The whole caravan had halted behind the car. It was a steep descent that lay ahead of them and the horsemen had dismounted and were checking the ropes that held the treasure boxes on the backs of the camels. Frederick had got down from his horse and was walking up and down, easing his legs.

Cabell, without waiting for an answer from Pugachov, got out of the car and untied the ropes that had been the mules' traces. His mind was revving quicker than the Rolls-Royce's engine at top speed. He led the mules to the back of the car, handed the reins to Nikolai.

'Make sure you don't let them go,' he said casually and, with his face turned away from Pugachov, winked at Nikolai.

'We wouldn't want that to happen,' said the Cossack and took his pistol from its holster. 'No tricks, Cabell.'

'I'm offended, Captain. I thought we were friends now.'

Pugachov smiled, wiped a knuckle along his moustache. 'We are, we are. The best of friends. But even friends sometimes fall out, don't they?'

Cabell climbed into the car, set the ignition. More by good luck than intention he had pulled up the car on a slight incline; if he let off the brake it would start rolling downhill at once. He checked that Frederick was close by the car and hoped the boy would be alert when called. He set the gears in neutral, then looked at Pugachov.

'I shall need the starting handle, Captain. It is under your feet.'

Pugachov bent down and in that instant Cabell hit him. It was a street fighter's punch, short and dirty, full of power. It hit Pugachov where his jaw met his ear; his head jerked sideways and he dropped his pistol. Cabell grabbed the gun, tossed it into the back seat, not looking to see who caught it. He let off the brake and grabbed the wheel. The car started to roll, slowly at first, then gathering speed. The mules, their reins stretched, started to break into a gallop behind the car.

'Nick, let them go! Freddie – quick, for crissake!'

If Frederick, in his years ahead, ever had to go to war he would make a good soldier, alert to any emergency. As soon as he saw Cabell hit Pugachov he had jumped up, grabbed his sword from the saddle of his horse, run and jumped on to the running-board of the car. He scrambled over the door, fell in with Eden and the others in the rear seat.

Nikolai let go the ropes and the mules swerved away to the sides of the road. The Rolls-Royce, gathering speed at every turn of the wheels, had gone forty or fifty yards before the Cossacks realized what was happening. Cabell threw the car into top gear, gauging that the speed was right; there was a momentary jerk, a cough, then the engine started. The car went down the long slope and Cabell concentrated on taking it round the curve at the bottom of the hill as the first bullets hit the dust of the road behind them.

Pugachov sat up slowly, holding his dislocated jaw. Eden leaned forward, the pistol held steady in both hands. 'No tricks, Captain. Even though we are friends . . .'

He stared at her, tried to smile, found it hurt too much and lay back in his seat nursing his jaw. He mumbled something, but he could not open his mouth and Eden didn't understand what he said.

Then Frederick, peering back through the train of dust they had raised, shouted, 'They are coming after us!'

Pugachov raised himself and looked back, then looked at Cabell. There was no mistaking the message in his dark, angry eyes: *You'll never get away.* But the car had reached the bottom of the hill, had gone round the bend with the rear threatening to break away on the loose surface; the trailer keeled over on one wheel but, miraculously, didn't topple over; they swept out of the bend and on to the flat. Cabell put his foot down and felt the car surge ahead. He knew the horsemen could never catch them while the car continued to run. All he had to pray for was that the ferry, which had been coming in to this side of the river when he had spotted it (if it was indeed a ferry), had not yet begun its return journey to the opposite bank. He prayed with all the fervour of a lapsed Catholic beating at the church door to get back in; his re-conversion was instant, Saul hit by a second shaft of light on the road to the Damascus ferry. Holy Mary was hailed as he hadn't hailed her in years; the Silver Ghost sped along under appeals to the Holy Ghost. In her grave his mother was spinning in religious ecstasy.

There was no sight at all now of the pursuing Cossacks; they were lost behind the dust spinning out from the back of the car. Cabell kept his foot down on the accelerator; he had to reach the river in time to get the car on the ferry (if it was a ferry). If the boat was not a ferry it would mean finding another road (if there was another road) and keep going. He was not going to abandon the car to escape just to the other side of the river. They still had too far to go: Tiflis was not on the opposite bank.

Suddenly they shot out of the trees, were in the open. Ahead he saw the ferry (it was a ferry!) just about to pull away from the bank. He blew the horn, kept his hand pressing on the big rubber bulb. He saw the ferry stop, then nose back into the bank.

Cabell saw the boarding planks come down as he topped the rise above the landing. He stood on the brakes, held the car against its swerve and took it down without stopping, straight up the planks and into the midst of the cows that were the ferry's main cargo. But the trailer, its wheel-base narrower than that of the car, fell between the planks and hung precariously from the end of the ferry's decking.

Cabell and Nikolai jumped out of the car and then down into the mud of the bank. They struggled desperately to push the trailer up on to the ferry; but it was too heavily laden and they could get no purchase in the slippery mud. Cabell looked up, saw the Cossacks come thundering out of the trees a quarter of a mile back. He jumped back up on to the ferry, pulled Nikolai after him.

'Move!' he yelled to the ferryman.

The latter, a burly grey-haired man, was bewildered by this strange car on his ferry and this foreigner shouting at him in Russian. He was a Turkoman and he had only a few words of Russian. But he understood bullets. When the first one from the approaching Cossacks smacked into the wooden railing beside him he knew what to do. He started working the long pole; he made room for Cabell as the latter rushed to help him. The ferry was flat-bottomed, a long blunt-ended scow attached to a long rope that stretched from bank to bank and prevented the ferry from drifting downstream with the current. Its only propulsion was the long-bladed pole and the ferryman and Cabell worked it back and forth like madmen, men who had discovered they were going the wrong way across the Styx and wanted to get back before their time ran out.

The Cossacks had arrived at the top of the bank, jumped down from their horses and were taking aim with their rifles. They were still breathing hard from their desperate riding: the first bullets went high above the ferry. But the scow was only halfway across the broad stretch of river; its progress was handicapped by the trailer half-dragging in the water from the stern. Eden, still in the car, abruptly scrambled over into the front seat. She shoved the pistol into Pugachov's ribs.

'Stand up, Captain! Up there on the seat – right up!'

Pugachov frowned at her, not getting her meaning at first; then he understood what she was exposing him to and he glared at her. But there was a look of grim determination on her face that told him she might, just might, put a bullet into him if he did not do what he was told. Shakily, still holding his jaw, he stood up on the seat of the Rolls-Royce and faced back to the bank where his men were aiming their rifles straight at him. They had calmed down now; their bullets would hit home this time. Pugachov stared back at them a hundred yards away, unable to shout either an order or a plea at them. He saw the half-dozen rifles aimed straight at him. What would his boys do? Did they love him, respect him, need him? Yesterday morning they had been dreaming of splitting forty million roubles twelve ways; this morning the fortune had been reduced to less than twenty million. If they killed him the split would be only amongst eleven; how was he to know there wasn't someone amongst them aiming for an even smaller number of share-holders? He had seen what greed could do to men of all classes; it had been the one common denominator in the civil war. These boys of his were no different. He was forty-five years old, an old man to them: he would never be missed. He opened his mouth to shout and almost fainted with the pain. He stared back at the rifles, closed his eyes and waited for the bullets to strike him.

Then Frederick shouted, 'They're not going to shoot!'

Pugachov relaxed, felt the sweat suddenly break on him.

He steadied himself as the ferry at last bumped into the far bank, sat down heavily in the seat as Cabell got in behind the wheel.

'Your men showed some sense then, Captain. Give them my regards when you go back.'

Pugachov showed his surprise; he had supposed he was going to be kept prisoner, taken with them in the car. He tried to say something, but again his dislocated jaw prevented him. He mumbled, grimacing with pain.

Cabell waited till the cows had been driven off the ferry. Then, with Nikolai and the ferryman pulling on the trailer, manoeuvring it up on to the ferry's decking, he eased the car forward. When the trailer was up on deck, he then drove the Rolls-Royce off and up the bank past the curious peasants who were waiting by the landing stage. He got out of the car, went back and paid the ferryman double the fare, then returned to the car. He motioned to Pugachov to get out.

The Cossack stepped out and Cabell took his face in both hands, running his fingers gently down the jawline. 'I had this happen to me once – a big Texan hit me when I wasn't looking.' He couldn't admit to a defeat, not to this Cossack; actually, the Texan had toyed with him and hit when he had finally felt like it. 'I don't think it's broken, Captain. Now hold still – this is going to hurt.'

He expertly clicked the jaw back into place and for a moment it looked as if Captain Pugachov, hero of a dozen battles, rapes and lootings was going to faint. He leaned back, his legs sagging, and Cabell grabbed him by the front of his blouse and held him up. The Cossack recovered, blinked, rolled his head and gently worked his jaw. Then he nodded.

'Thank you, Cabell. You are not taking me with you?'

'Captain, what would we do with you? You can catch the ferry back on the next trip.' Cabell put out his hand. 'Enjoy your fortune.'

Pugachov, after a moment's hesitation, shook hands. Then he saluted Eden, Frederick and Olga; Nikolai, his fellow Cossack had he but known it, was the only one who missed out on a farewell. 'May you reach Tiflis. God will take care of you.'

Cabell, lapsed once again now he was safe, shrugged off the Divine assistance. He felt confident, able to do it on their own. 'We'll make it.'

Pugachov looked at them all again, nodded a reluctant goodbye. He had come to like the American and the Englishwoman and the children; he would have killed them if it had had to be done, but that wouldn't have meant he disliked them. Some day, perhaps soon, he might be spending the rest of his life amongst people like this; a rich man wouldn't want to spend his retirement amongst a lot of uncouth Cossacks like himself. He wished he had been able to keep them prisoner, used them to start him off on the right social course in Baku.

He went down to the ferry, stood at its stern as it went out into the stream. He opened his mouth to shout 'Good luck!'; but his jaw still hurt and he shut it again. He took off his hat and waved it and slowly he went away from Cabell and the others, backwards across the broad river to the opposite bank where his boys and his fortune awaited him.

[7]

Pemenov had followed the caravan at a discreet distance, not travelling on the road but threading his two horses through the trees some fifty yards parallel to the road. When he saw the caravan halt at the top of the rise within sight of the river he had pulled up and watched. Then he had seen the car start rolling down the hill, heard the yells of the horsemen and saw six of them leap on their horses and start in pursuit.

He took his own horses farther up into the forest, quickened their pace and took them as fast as he dared through the trees. It was not easy riding, but he had to stay out of sight of those Cossacks who had stayed with the camels; if they saw him, one or two of them could jump on their horses and chase him and he knew he could not out-distance them. So he stayed up amongst the trees and rode as fast as he could, which wasn't fast enough to satisfy him. When he came out of the trees and saw the ferry already halfway across the river, the Rolls-Royce standing out amongst the cows on board like some elegant, new-fangled milking machine, he wept with rage. Then he saw the Cossacks, now dismounted, aiming their rifles at the ferry.

He rode down out of the forest, keeping behind a low rise that separated him from the road. He came to a dry creek-bed, pulled up and watched the river. He saw the Cossacks lower their rifles, saw the ferry nose into the opposite bank and, after about five minutes, the car was driven off it. Five minutes later the ferry started its return journey.

The car drove off from the opposite landing stage before the ferry was halfway back across the river. He waited till the scow nosed into the bank; a Cossack came ashore, pushing his way through the peasants who had crossed with him. He was greeted with slaps on the back by the six horsemen who had been waiting for him. He was an older man, the obvious leader of the troop, and he kept touching his jaw, as if he were having trouble with it. He swung up on to a horse, two Cossacks doubled up on another horse and all seven men went galloping off back along the road. When they had disappeared into the trees Pemenov rode out of the creek-bed and down to the ferry.

The ferryman looked up as the dwarf, riding one horse and leading the other, came down the bank and up on to his ferry. He was getting some queer ones today as passengers; he wouldn't be surprised now if the Tsar himself turned up. But he took the little man's fare and pushed the ferry out into the river again.

Pemenov remained in the saddle, despite the fact that his legs were aching. He did not want to get down, for fear that he might not be able to remount without having to ask for help. He did not want to waste time shooting some peasant for laughing at him.

CHAPTER FOUR

'You should not have taken it,' said Frederick. 'It doesn't belong to you.'

'It was a present.' Olga, lolling back in the seat as the car rolled along, turned the golden egg over and over in her hands. 'Just like Miss Eden's.'

'She shouldn't have taken hers, either.'

'Who's *she* – the cat's mother?' said Eden over her shoulder. 'Stop worrying about the eggs, Freddie. There's more to worry about than those.'

'What will you do with yours?'

'I shan't sell it, if that's what you're thinking. I'll keep it as a memento of – well, of what Russia once was.'

But she felt guilty saying that. The old Russia really meant nothing to her; her fondest memories would really be of the Gorshkov family. She had seen only the tail-end of Tsarist Russia and it had not compared well with the England she had come from. Her sense of the romantic had been thrilled by the exotic in St Petersburg, the borrowed fashions of France and Italy taken to excess by the Russian taste for the baroque; her genteel feeling for what was good taste, fed into her like rolled oats by her parents, had been dealt a healthy kick in the ass, as the man beside her would say. She had loved the sight of all the uniforms in the city, the broad cruel-looking faces of the Tsar's Siberian soldiers, the darkly handsome Georgians; traitorously, she had begun to think of the Grenadier Guards back home, whom she had seen only once on parade, as pink-cheeked boys playing at soldiers. There had been visual excitement galore for her in that first year in St Petersburg. But . . .

With the start of the war against the Germans had come the beginning of her disillusion. Brought up in a home where even her mother's colour scheme was Tory blue, insulated by middle-class snobbery that always looked up rather than down, she had been only dimly aware of the wide gap between the classes in England. Travelling up from Croydon by train to London she would look out on the backs of tenements just south of the Thames and realize there were perhaps millions of people who did not live as well as even she and her parents; but she had had no social conscience in those days and she had never attempted to project her imagination into the dark, cold rooms of those tenements and wonder exactly how the people there actually did live. She had sometimes made afternoon excursions to Mayfair and Belgravia and admired the town houses of the rich; once, when she was seventeen, her parents had taken her to a fête in the grounds of a grand country house owned by a Conservative earl and she had joined her mother in swooning at the rarefied atmosphere they had been permitted to enjoy. She had known nothing of the industrial north of England and hadn't wanted to know.

Her education in social conditions did not begin till the first year of the war against the Germans. Then she began to realize that, whatever the gap between the classes in England, they were a cohesive, chummy lot to what she now discovered in Russia. When the Revolution came in 1917 she understood the reasons for it, even if she did not appreciate the excesses of revenge it brought. Tsarist Russia could no longer be justified; but she had never uttered a word of what she thought to anyone in the Gorshkov household. They had treated her well and she had always prided herself on her loyalty. It was a splendid English trait, whatever foreigners might say about perfidious Albion.

Now she could see disillusionment beginning · in Frederick; but the boy was fighting it as if it were some fatal disease. He was growing up too fast; she had the feeling that by the time this trip was over he would no longer have need of a governess; she would be able to teach him nothing that would help him in the new social order. His tutor, if anyone was teaching him anything on the trip, would be the man sitting beside her, Matthew Martin Cabell. Who had begun to teach her a few things about herself.

'What's a memento?' said Olga; and Eden told her. 'Oh, *that*. Well, I don't want a memento. All I want is *things*. Pretty things like this.'

Olga could not be taught anything; she already knew all she wished to know. Oh sweetheart, Eden thought, what heartache you're in for! Yet even as she pitied the Olga of ten, twenty, thirty years hence, she wasn't sure that her pity wasn't misplaced, might not be needed. Some people, she had learned, had an aura of survival about them. And Olga, even so young, looked like one of those.

'We'll stop for lunch soon,' Cabell said. 'How's the food holding out, Nick?'

'There is plenty, sir.' Nikolai, now they were out of danger, was once more enjoying the trip. He sat in the back of the car, relishing the breeze on his face, and for the first time in his life let himself dream of luxuries. The ultimate dream would be to stay with Prince Frederick, care for him in whatever new life lay ahead of them, to ride around in a car like this, not as a yard servant but as a beloved companion, to wear silk instead of rough wool, to eat delicacies instead of mutton stew . . . 'Perhaps we can catch more fish.'

'If we find another river.'

They had left the big river behind and were travelling through rolling, thinly forested country. They passed through a hamlet that appeared deserted; no one came out to herald their passing, not even a dog. But frightened eyes watched them from behind the closed shutters and out in a field at the back of the houses freshly-turned earth rested on the eyelids of three dead men.

Then at last the forest stopped and the Rolls-Royce was in short-grassed country where its occupants could see for miles ahead of them. The road dipped towards a depression, a mile or more wide, and at the bottom of it, running beside a narrow river, they saw another railway line.

'That must be the one Pugachov spoke about,' said Cabell. 'The one built by the Emir of Bokhara last century.'

'I think we are still too far north for that,' said Frederick.

'Okay, kid, no geography lessons.' In his present mood Cabell did not want to be put right by a twelve-year-old know-all.

'I wonder if there are trains running on it?' said Eden.

'What are you thinking?'

'Well —' She hesitated to criticize his judgement. She was enjoying this trip by motor car (well, enjoying the safe moments such as now); but she had come to realize the hazards of such a method of travel. If she had been alone with him, she would not have chosen any other way of getting to Tiflis. But she had to think of the children, get them safely to their parents. 'It might be safer if we could pick up a train.'

'What do we do? Pull up a train and ask the driver where he's going? What happens if we pull it up and only then find out it's full of soldiers going somewhere to fight the war? Would you want to get on the train then?'

'No—o.'

The railway line was on the far side of the narrow river, running parallel to it. The road ran down to a ford in the river, where white rocks showed like the bald heads of underwater swimmers. They were fifty yards from the river when the two front tyres blew out as if on an order from Mr Dunlop to fire a barrage. The car swerved violently and for one awful moment Eden thought they were going to topple over. But Cabell, unlike his grandson, if he should ever have one, came of a generation that drove with one ear continually tuned to an explosion at any of the four corners of the car. He turned the reluctant front wheels into the skid and they slithered down the loose dirt of the road and came to rest twenty yards from the bank of the river. As they did so, Cabell heard a flapping sound under the bonnet and knew either the fan-belt or the generator-belt had gone.

'We'll eat first, then we'll fix the tyres.' A clump of willows grew on the low bank, offering shade from the hot glare of the sun.

'Don't you think we should fix the tyres and drive on further?' said Eden. 'Just in case Captain Pugachov catches up with us.'

Cabell sighed, wondering when female back-seat drivers had first made their influence felt. Had Moses been given unwanted directions coming out of Egypt? Had Lot's wife looked back merely to tell him he'd taken the wrong turning? Had the Khan of Khokand listened to his three thousand wives and concubines when he had journeyed through the Fergana valley?

'Nick and I will be doing the tyre-changing and we'll do it in our own good time. We don't work in the heat of the day.'

'But what about Captain Pugachov?' said Frederick.

'Another county heard from.' Cabell was irritable and knew it; but couldn't help himself. He was all at once exhausted by his responsibilities; never before had he had to care for other people's lives. Treacherously, he suddenly wanted to be free, to go off on his own. But he looked again at Eden and at once put that thought out of his mind. 'Captain Pugachov is in no hurry. He has all the time in the world – that fortune of his isn't going to lose its value, no matter how long he takes to get to Baku. Who knows, it may even increase in value if there's inflation. And unlike us, he doesn't have to stick to the road. He's not going to worry us, not any more.'

'What about —?' But then Eden changed her mind, didn't mention the dwarf. The children and Nikolai knew nothing of him and she did not want to add to their worries.

'What about what?' Frederick didn't miss much nor did he want to.

'Nothing. Let's get lunch. While the two tyre-changers have a nice rest in the shade.'

Cabell, already heading towards the shade of the willows, paused and bowed. 'You're getting that rasping wife's note in your voice again.'

'Will there be a wedding?' said Olga.

'Mind your own business and help Freddie peel the potatoes!' Eden busily burrowed around in the trailer like a cook who had suddenly been told she had to feed a regiment. 'Go on, get on with it!'

Cabell smiled to himself, passed under the willows and went along the river bank. He saw a fish leap in the water and he decided then that they would camp here for the rest of the day and night and move on first thing in the morning. He had no idea what sort of country lay ahead of them, except that from here on the country would flatten out and become drier. His maps had vast areas where details were scanty; the farther south one went on a map the vaguer it became. But he knew that very soon, within the next few

148

days, they would be driving down into the clay and sand dune country of the semi-desert steppes. They might not find as pleasant a camping site as this till they reached the shores of the Caspian Sea.

He was not worried about Pugachov's catching up with them. The camels, burdened as they were by the treasure, could not be pushed too far and too hard in a day. He thought about the dwarf – What was his name? Pemenov? Something like that – and decided that he, too, would be too far behind to catch up with them. If he had been close enough to see the Rolls-Royce cross the river in the ferry and then drive on, he might already have decided that the chase was futile and turned back to Verkburg.

'We'll have lunch, Nick, then fix the tyres and I'll fit a new generator-belt. Then I'll catch some fish for supper and we'll camp here.'

Nikolai settled down on the thinly-grassed bank beside Cabell. He felt a little conscience-stricken that he was not helping prepare lunch, but that was forgotten in the pleasure at being accepted as another man by this American gentleman. He just wished his father could see him now.

[2]

Twenty miles back along the road Pemenov came into the hamlet through which the Rolls-Royce had passed. His horses were weary and one of them was lame. He pulled up, sat his horse while he looked around at the dozen or so wooden houses, all of them with their shutters closed tight on their windows. Some hens scratched the earth between the houses and a rooster sat on a post and jerked its head at him, as if telling him to move on. Then he heard a dog bark in one of the houses and he moved the horses towards the house and kicked on the front door.

There was no answer at first and he kicked again, shouting for whoever was inside to come out. Then the door opened a couple of inches, then slowly slid back. Three women edged out of the doorway: a grandmother, daughter and granddaughter, the family resemblance even more pronounced by the common fear smearing their faces. They looked mutely up at him and he waited for them to laugh; now he was alone, without General Bronevich's protection, he expected to be pelted with laughter at every meeting. But these women had no laughter left in them: they were miserable and afraid.

'Where are your menfolk?' he said in Turkic.

The women looked at each other, as if afraid of giving something away. Then the granddaughter, a girl of about twenty, plain beyond hope of being anything better, said, 'The soldiers came and took them away. After they had killed my father and two other men.'

'Which soldiers?'

The women looked at each other again, then all shook their heads. Weren't all soldiers the same? 'We don't know. They came two days ago and took all our men. My father and some of the men tried to fight them . . .' Her voice trailed off; behind her her mother choked off a sob. 'It's the same with the women in the other houses. There's no one here now but women and children.'

'Has anyone else passed through here? Today, I mean.' He was not interested in the soldiers and what they had done. War was war: women never seemed to realize that.

'A motor car – a grand one. We saw it go past, but it didn't stop.'

'How long ago?'

The women looked at each other once again, then all shrugged. What was time? Just sunrise and sunset, the four seasons. 'Not long.'

Then Pemenov heard a horse whinny somewhere behind the house. 'Do you have horses?' The women's faces closed up and he angrily repeated: 'Do you have horses? Answer me!'

'They are all we have left to pull our ploughs and carts.' The mother spoke this time; she looked as old as her own mother, aged by grief. 'Please don't take them —'

Pemenov rode his horse round to the back of the house, pulling the lame horse on its lead-rope. In a barn he found three horses: a draught horse and two small sturdy horses such as the nomads often rode. They were not as big as his own horse, but he knew they would have as much stamina. And they would be a damned sight easier to mount if he couldn't find a convenient rock or log to use as a block. He slid down from his horse and began to unsaddle it. The saddle was heavy and he almost dropped it. He had forgotten the gold bars in the bags.

The three women came hesitantly to the door of the barn. 'Are you going to take all our horses?' the granddaughter said.

'Just these two. I'll leave you mine, so I shall not be robbing you.' He felt almost pious, shivered with his own generosity. 'I'll want food and water, too. Fill my water-bags.'

The women, beginning to accept the fact that he was not intent on raping or looting, moved to do as they were told. All their lives they had done the bidding of their menfolk; they were accustomed to being ordered about. The mother and the grandmother went into the house to get what food they could spare and the granddaughter took Pemenov's water-bags across to fill them at the well by the corner of the house. In ten minutes he was ready to be on his way again.

He found a box, used it as a mounting block to swing up into the saddle of one of the steppe horses. He waited again for the women to laugh, but none of them did. So he smiled and did not know how charming his child's smile was. The women smiled back and he had one of those rare moments when he felt some warmth towards someone.

Then he turned the new horses south and went after the American again.

[3]

They rose early the next morning, had breakfast and were re-packing the trailer when the first bullet hummed over their heads and smacked into the willow tree.

'Down!' yelled Cabell and grabbed Olga and pushed her down into the dust beside the car.

Eden, Frederick and Nikolai acted with equal alacrity, all three of them flattening themselves as if they had been

151

scythed down with the one sweep. Cabell reached up, swung open the door of the car and pulled out his Winchester. He told Eden to keep herself and the others where they were, then he raced in a crouching run towards a shallow trench in the slope above the river. As he did so the second bullet slammed into the trailer itself. He had no idea where the shots were coming from, but he wanted to draw the fire away from those huddled on the ground by the Rolls-Royce. He did have a very clear idea who was firing the shots and he was sure he was meant to be the target. When the third bullet thudded into the earth a foot from his head as he dived into the trench, he knew his guess was right.

He looked back along the river, certain now that that was the direction from which the shots were coming. More willows grew along the bank about a hundred yards upstream and behind them a low bluff rose, crested by a line of scrub. Birds were rising in small clouds from behind the bluff: cranes, herons, geese, screeching and honking as they wheeled away across the river and the railway line. Even as Cabell looked at the line of scrub he saw the puff of smoke and at the same instant the bullet hit the side of the trench above him, showering him with grit and dust.

He worked his way backwards out of the trench, then scrambled higher up the slope towards the road. A low patch of wormwood grew here, just high enough to hide him as he raised his head and took a bead on the crest of the distant bluff. He had never fired at a man before and the thought still worried him; he was just glad that his target was so far away. He waited for another shot, but the dwarf (for he was sure it was he) had lost him for the moment and was searching for him. Then the shot came and down below him Cabell heard the bullet ricochet off the car and whine away. He squeezed the trigger, aiming at the spot in the scrub where he had detected the hint of a movement. An answering shot came at once and he ducked down out of sight.

He called down to Eden. 'Are you all right?'

'So far.' Her voice sounded steady. Christ, he thought, she's some girl. 'But I think he can see us.'

'Okay, start crawling. Keep flat on the ground and don't put your asses up in the air. Come this way. Shitabrick!' He was showered in dirt as the bullet hummed by only inches above his head, bouncing off the ground just above him. He hunkered down even lower, gestured to Eden and the others to crawl in below him. 'Keep your asses down!'

In a few moments, asses down, they were all safe in the dip below the road and Frederick looked up and said, 'The word is arses, Mr Çabell.'

Cabell looked down and grinned and the boy grinned back. He was showing off, being grown-up, but Cabell was not going to belittle him. He was learning, remembering what it had once been like to be a boy who wanted to be a man. 'I'll remember that in the future, Fred.'

'Just watch it in future,' said Eden. But she had something more serious to worry about than language in front of the children: 'Is it the dwarf, you think?'

'It can't be anyone else.'

'The dwarf?' said Frederick. 'The little man who came to our house? How are you going to stop him from shooting at us?'

'That's the problem. It's all open country between us and him. He'd pick me off like a rabbit as soon as I tried to make a run for it.'

'We can't stay here all day,' said Eden.

'We may have to. The only thing in our favour is that he can't get any closer to us without coming out in the open. That's his first mistake. If we're patient, maybe he'll make another.'

'You would have made a good general, Mr Cabell,' said Frederick.

'Who wouldn't?' said Cabell, thinking of some of those who had sacrificed men in France in the recent war.

On the distant bluff Pemenov, no general and not even a good major, had realized his mistake and was cursing his lack of field experience. He had seen plenty of action, but always with General Bronevich planning the tactics; and he had always been only an observer, never an active participant. The General had always kept him out of the firing line, using him as a messenger; and he had never felt any urge to prove himself as a soldier, always afraid that he would be laughed at. He could not handle a rifle from horseback, as all the Cossacks could, and the General's troops had never been in any action where they had gone to earth for any prolonged period. Not as he was now.

He should have charged the camp as soon as he had seen it in the first light of morning. He could have been on the American and his party, used his pistol and been out of the camp before they had realized what was happening. And the American would now be dead.

It looked as if he would have to wait till nightfall. He lay stretched on the ground, the Mosin-Nagent propped up in front of him, his shoulder aching from the recoil of the shots he had fired. He had done his best to pull the butt in hard against his shoulder, but his arms were too short and the harder he pulled the more the barrel wavered. He had had to settle for steady sighting and then the jolt as the butt hit him.

He rolled over and looked down at the two horses tethered in the thin scrub below the crest of the hill. He felt thirsty and he wondered if he dared risk leaving his position here to go down and get his water-bag. Then he heard the train-whistle.

Cabell also heard it. He looked down-river, towards the south, and saw the train, an engine and ten or twelve carriages, coming up the line. In a few minutes it would pass within a couple of hundred yards of them, on the other side of the river.

The car was ready to go. He and Nikolai had spent all yesterday afternoon repairing the inner tubes, changing the tyres, fitting a new generator-belt; he had also cleaned the plugs, changed the oil and lubricated the wheels and all those joints he could get at. The road conditions from now to the Caspian Sea would be the worst they would experience and he wanted to guard against breakdowns if he possibly could. There would, he knew, be a breakdown or two somewhere along the road, but he did not want them to occur because of some negligence on his part.

'Nick! Crawl to the car and get the starting handle fixed!'

'But, sir — ' Nikolai did not like the thought of being so exposed.

'For crissake — ' Then Cabell gentled his tone. He was

154

learning quite a lot on this trip, one item being an understanding of another man's cowardice. 'If you stay low, you'll be okay. If you're in front of the car, you'll be out of his line of fire. Get down there, quick!'

Nikolai hesitated, then on his belly, his arms and legs working furiously, he slid like a shell-less crab down towards the car. He reached it, swung open the door and took out the starting handle. Then he crawled to the front of the car, inserted the handle in its slot and lay there, looking for all the world like a peasant who hadn't made it across the path of the speeding Rolls-Royce.

Cabell was watching the train steaming slowly up the line, the smoke from its stack curling lazily back over it in the still morning air. He could see the machine-guns mounted on the roofs of the first and last carriages, each gun manned by two men who were stretched out at their leisure as if convinced that they were far from attack or ambush. With his surveyor's eye he was taking various lines of sight. The willows would screen the Rolls-Royce from those on the train; if Eden and the children could get down beyond the willows, on the river bank, they would be screened from the view of the dwarf further upstream. The non-military man, who up till a few minutes ago had never fired a shot at another man, was proving better at tactics than the soldier upstream from him.

'Eden, get down there on the other side of the willows. Leave the kids here with me. Start waving at the train, try to get it to stop.'

'What are you going to do?'

'As soon as it stops, we start moving. If the dwarf fires at us again, I'm betting those machine-guns will open up. They'll be expecting him to shoot at them and they'll want to get in first.'

'What if the train doesn't stop?'

'Will you get down there and do what you're told! Move!'

She gave him a look that was intended to render him speechless. But she did not stop to argue, at once went crawling down towards the willows, disappeared into their trailing curtains. Cabell looked down at Frederick and Olga just below him.

'You kids be ready to jump into the car soon's I give the word. In the meantime keep your heads down.'

'What if the train doesn't stop?' said Frederick.

'If I had a handbag I'd belt you over the ear. Don't you goddam Russians ever have an optimistic thought?'

'You're swearing a lot,' said Olga.

'Honey, I haven't really started yet. Now just shut up and be ready to run when I tell you!'

He was on edge now that he had conscripted Nikolai and Eden into helping him in his scheme. He guessed he would still have been nervous even had he been alone, but at least then he would have been responsible only for himself. He had no guarantee at all that his scheme would work; for all he knew, the machine-gunners on the train might open up on Eden as soon as they saw her; perhaps he should have gone down to hail the train himself. But that would have left no one up here to cover the dwarf if he should decide on a last-minute suicidal rush to get at them.

The train came chugging up the line, doing no more than twenty miles an hour. He could see now that it was a troop train, its carriages crowded with soldiers. They would not be Reds, he guessed; the Bolsheviks had not got this far south. They would belong to one of the White armies; but which one? He would place no bets that these troops would welcome him and the others any more than General Bronevich had.

Then he heard Eden shouting. He could not see her, but he could imagine her jumping up and down, waving her arms and generally acting a maiden in distress. Anxiously he watched the machine-gunners; it was a moment or two before they saw Eden. Then they sat up, but didn't man their guns. They waved back and at the same time a hundred hands appeared at the windows of the carriages, fluttering there like pigeons outside a moving loft. The engineer blew his whistle and faintly there came the shouts of the soldiers approving the pretty girl who was waving them on to war. But the train did not slow.

'Jesus Christ!'

Cabell watched the train go slowly by immediately opposite him; in a few moments it would be opposite the bluff where the dwarf was hidden. There was nothing else for it: he was going to have to risk wounding a man against whom he had no grudge at all.

He shouted to Eden to come back to the car, yelling to her at the top of his voice. For a moment he thought she hadn't heard him and he fretted with impatience at goddam women who wouldn't listen. Then she came crawling back through the willows and lay on the ground beside the still prostrate Nikolai in front of the car.

He waited till the front of the train was opposite the dwarf, then he lifted the Winchester, took aim at one of the machine-guns on the roof of the front carriage. He prayed that he wouldn't kill or wound one of the men; what he wanted was a miraculously lucky shot that would put the gun out of action. He squeezed the trigger and the miracle didn't happen. One of the machine-gunners jerked, then grabbed his leg and rolled back in agony, almost falling off the roof of the carriage.

It was a moment before there was any response. Then the second man grabbed the machine-gun and opened fire; at the same time the machine-gun on the last carriage opened up. Bullets raked the bank, sending up explosions of dirt; Cabell heard the *thwang* as the car and the trailer were hit. The train didn't slow but tried to pick up speed. It went on up the line, taking the machine-gunners, still firing, further and further away from Cabell and the others. The gunners evidently could see no one, so they sprayed this side of the river, intent on keeping the ambushers down while the train sped on to safety. It was what Cabell had planned for but had hardly dared hope would succeed.

The machine-gun fire had passed on, was now raking the bluff where the dwarf was hidden. Cabell slid down the slope, jumped into the car and switched on the ignition. The engine took at the second swing of the starting handle, purred contentedly in low revs while all the humans clambering aboard it were ready to explode. Cabell let in the gears, swung the wheel and took the car down the slope, the wheels skidding as he tried for too much power too soon. The car hit the water, lurched as the wheels bounced on the smooth stones of the ford. Water sprayed out in a glistening

157

fan as the Rolls-Royce ploughed through it; then they were climbing the far bank, the tyres slipping in the mud. But Cabell kept the car steady and it went up the slope. Then they were heading south once more and he pressed down on the accelerator, trying for as much speed as there was beneath his desperate foot.

Back in the dip of the bluff Pemenov, flat on the ground beneath the hail of machine-gun fire passing only a foot above him, caught a glimpse of the car speeding away along the road, escaping from him once more. In his rage he almost stood up into the gunfire from the train; but a bullet clipping the top of his straw hat forced him down at once. There was a final burst of fire, then the train had gone on and he was left alone and furious by the river. He stood up, staring down the road, watching the small tornado of dust, all he could see of the car's progress, disappearing into the distance.

Then he looked down at his horses and was relieved to see that they were still on their feet, moving restlessly in their hobbles. They had been hidden from the river and the railway line by the sloping shoulder of the bluff and any bullets that had missed the bluff where the dwarf had lain had passed right over the horses.

He walked down to them, took off their hobbles, led the saddle horse to a nearby fallen tree. He clambered up, turned the horses south and once more set off. As he often did, he wondered what and where he would be if he had been a normal-sized man. Such thoughts occupied him, as other men dream of riches or beautiful women beyond their reach.

[4]

The Rolls-Royce bowled along under the morning sun, out in open country now. A few sparse clumps of trees stood like mourners above the graves of dry creeks; but on both sides of the narrow road coarse grass stretched away as a still, yellow-green sea. Half a dozen saiga antelope watched the speeding car from a low ridge; then they raced away, making the skyline shimmer with their movement. The dust spun out behind the car, obscuring the road already travelled; ahead of them the road ran on into a sky as blank as the landscape. This was the beginning of mirage country, where the far horizons could be as deceitful as the songs of sirens.

They travelled for twenty miles, through country that didn't appear to change its character, before Cabell brought the car to a halt. 'I want to see if any damage was done. Those machine-guns put some bullets into the car and the trailer.'

He got out, looked at the car first. There were half a dozen bullet holes in the near-side of the Rolls-Royce, one of them only two inches above the petrol tank. He was inspecting the bullet hole when he caught the smell of petrol. He had to take only one step to discover the source of the smell.

'Goddam! Holy Jesus!'

'What's the matter?' Eden caught the note of despair in his voice, didn't chide him for swearing.

'The gas cans – every goddam one's got a hole in it! We're out of gas except for what we've got in the tank!' He stood for a moment staring at the petrol cans, breathing deeply, as if trying to knock himself unconscious with the fumes. He knew he was to blame: he should have anticipated the chances of the machine-guns doing at least *some* damage. At last he looked at Eden and the others in the car. 'Sorry about the language.'

'It's understandable,' said Eden, handbag at rest in her lap.

Cabell and Nikolai cleaned out the trailer, making sure that none of the food had been contaminated by the leaking petrol. One of the ball-filled tyres had been rendered useless by several bullets; Cabell took it out and bowled it away down into a gully beside the road. The rugs were soaked with petrol and would have to be washed; some of their spare clothing was also wet. And one of the water-skins, punctured by a bullet, was empty.

'How much petrol is in the tank?' Frederick asked.

Cabell put in the dip-stick, measured the level of petrol it showed, did some calculating. 'Enough to take us a hundred and fifty miles, maybe.'

'Where will that put us?' said Eden.

Cabell looked around from horizon to horizon, shrugged. 'Maybe out in the middle of nowhere. Like this, only more so.'

The sun had already burned off the cool of the morning. In the few minutes the car had been stationary its metal had become hot to the touch; the copper-domed headlamps looked as if their metal was molten. The white dust of the road hurled back the hot light so that one tended to lift one's face up and away from it; but then the brilliant sky assaulted the eyes; Cabell felt engulfed by the blazing sunlight, drowning in it. He looked out across the steppes, saw the first mirage: a dark line of moving people and livestock walking across a shining lake. He closed his eyes, opened them and looked again: the mirage was gone. The horizon had begun to fade in haze, steppe and sky melting together in the cauldron of sunlight.

'We better put up the hood.' He and Nikolai pulled up the hood, locked it in position. Twice he burned his fingers as he touched the metal, but managed to bite back the curses that sprang to his tongue. He and Nikolai got back into the car. 'Well, what do we do?'

Eden said, 'What's the alternative?'

'Going back, at least as far as the river, the big one. The ferryman might be able to tell us where to get some gas.'

Eden opened the neck of her blouse and fanned herself with her handbag. The sun struck down through the canvas hood as if it would soon burn its way through it; in the meantime the glare from the road seemed to intensify as if to make up for the shade that had been provided by the hood. Her eyeballs ached, pierced by white splinters of light; she could feel her nostrils and mouth drying out as the air itself began to burn her. Sweat was running on her under her clothes. ('Perspiration, dear,' her mother would have said. 'Only men and horses sweat.' She felt a wild urge to tear off her clothes, ride the rest of the way in only her chemise. It shocked her to think that if she were alone with Cabell she might even have risked it.

'That would take us back to the dwarf and maybe even Captain Pugachov. I think we should risk going on. We may find a village where they have some petrol.'

Cabell looked at those in the back seat. 'What do the voters back there say?'

'What are voters?' said Olga.

'You are the leader, Mr Cabell,' said Frederick.

Cabell looked affectionately at the boy. 'Whatever you say, Prince. But I'd have settled for a little democracy right now.'

'You want us to make the decision,' said Eden. He grinned at her and nodded and she said, 'All right. We go on. Let's *do* something instead of just sitting here and being baked to death.'

Cabell looked back over his shoulder at Nikolai. 'Nick? You going to vote?'

Nikolai was surprised that even he should have been asked; but he wasn't going to presume by offering an opinion. 'You're the leader, Mr Cabell.'

'That's what I was afraid of.' But he let in the gears and drove on.

The breeze created by their passage blew in and dried the sweat on their faces even if it did little to cool them. Whenever the car slowed to negotiate a bumpy section of the road the dust caught up with them and they choked in it. But the car was still running smoothly and Cabell kept it at a steady thirty miles an hour, not wanting to waste petrol. He thought of all the cheap oil lying beneath the earth's surface, perhaps beneath this very road over which they were travelling, and he dreamed of the day when cars would be cheaper to run than a horse-and-wagon, when there would be gas stations never more than fifty miles apart, no matter where one went in the world. But even as he dreamed he saw what would happen: the lonely landscapes he loved would disappear beneath countless roads, forests of gas pumps would blossom where pine and fir and oak had once grown. He squinted out at the wide bright horizon, hating it now for its lack of promise yet not wanting to see it ruined.

They stopped for lunch by a creek where some thin willows and tamarisk trees grew. The latter told him they were now approaching dry country; he saw that the earth here was part clay. He said nothing, but he began to feel even more dispirited. He and Nikolai washed the rugs and the petrol-soaked clothing in the stream and hung them out to dry on the car and trailer; when they got on the road again an hour later the sun had baked the rugs and clothing dry. They headed south through the blinding yellow-white light of the afternoon, passing nothing, not even a solitary farmhouse. At one point they drove down the road watching an eagle drifting in the sky ahead of them, like a corpse floating in the mirage of a distant sea.

In the late afternoon Cabell began to look for a place to camp. The petrol was running low; he reckoned he must have enough for only ten miles at the most. The engine began to cough, then stopped when they were a mile from what appeared to be a low line of bushes crossing the road up ahead. Cabell switched off the engine and as the car rolled to a halt he peered ahead through the slanting sunlight.

'I'm not sure whether that's a line of bushes or the tops of trees in a ravine. But it must mean there's some water around. Okay, everyone out. We're going to push from here on. Not you, Princess. You stay in the car and steer it.'

'I think it would be better if I did that,' said Frederick.

'Oh, pooh,' said Olga. 'You think I can't do anything.'

'Of course you can,' said Eden, but knew that Olga would never have any ambition to prove herself. Being just herself was her only ambition.

Even on the flat road it was no easy task moving a two-ton car and a trailer that carried a couple of hundredweight of gear. But somehow they got the Rolls-Royce rolling and, sweating and gasping for breath, the dust on them turning to grey mud, they pushed it down the road while Olga sat behind the wheel and exhorted them not to stop working.

'Keep it going! Keep it going!'

'I'll murder the little bitch,' Cabell muttered, the words turning to mud in his mouth.

Eden looked at him out of a grey mask. 'Not Olga. I think you secretly admire her. Even if she was my age, you'd still have her up there behind the wheel and I'd be back here pushing.'

'I think under all that dust you're a Bolshevik.'

The mask cracked under the pressure of a smile. 'I can tell

you, right this minute I feel like a serf.'

Cabell's own mask cracked in reply. 'Bear up. Only three or four hundred yards to go.'

'Keep it going!' Olga encouraged. 'Keep it going!'

'Thank Christ she doesn't have a whip,' said Cabell.

The line of foliage across the road proved to be the tops of a line of trees, tamarisk and one or two laburnum, showing above a dip in the ground. At the bottom of the dip, which itself had once been a river-course, was a shallow stream, sluggish and yellow from its clay bottom.

Cabell took over the wheel of the car from Olga, halted the Rolls-Royce at the top of the dip where the road ran down to a ford. 'Okay, we camp here.'

'For how long?' Eden said.

'I don't know.' His voice was flat. He couldn't pump any false optimism into it, but he managed to keep the despair out of it. 'I don't want to think about it this evening. Tomorrow . . .'

The sun was still above the horizon when they ate, the day still warm. On top of the far bank some marmot appeared, blunt shovel-heads raised questioningly at the intruders on this side of the creek. They abruptly disappeared as a steppe eagle came plummeting down; the big bird appeared not to have noticed the humans sitting under the thin cover of the tamarisks. It landed with a flapping of wings on the opposite bank, saw the movement under the tamarisks and took off again at once, disappearing downstream. A large monitor lizard came out from a clump of wormwood to see what all the commotion was about, looked around and then seemed to dematerialize into the sandy clay that surrounded it.

After supper Eden said, 'Will you men please go for a walk? Olga and I want to take a bath.'

When the two men and Frederick had gone up on to the road and were out of sight Eden told Olga to strip off, then did the same herself. Even a week ago she would not have exposed herself so fully to the young girl, but now it seemed natural and, indeed, prudish if she had not done so. She had always rebelled against Victorianism, at least in her thoughts; but somehow there had never been any real opportunity to be relaxed and natural about her body. In the semi-detached house in Croydon her mother had chanted *modesty, modesty* as if it were some sort of invocation against the fires of hell; in the Gorshkov household in St Petersburg there had always been too many servants running around loose for her to expose anything more seductive than an arm or a lower leg. When they had moved to the estate outside Verkburg she had noticed that Frederick had begun to watch her with an eye too old for the rest of his face, a satyr crossed with a cherub, and she had felt it was not in her governess' duty to give illustrated lessons in anatomy.

'Will I be like you when I grow up?' Olga, slim, already perfectly proportioned if not yet womanly, looked at Eden with admiration.

'If you grow up to be like your mother, I don't think you'll have quite as much as me up here.' Eden pointed to her bosom. She poured water over herself from a cooking pot, began to soap herself. 'Sometimes you can have too much. You become top-heavy when you're middle-aged.'

'I think I'll just be slim and beautiful,' said Olga, quite certain she had no other choice. 'It's the hair down there I shan't like. I think I shall shave every day, like Father.'

Eden pealed with laughter, sat down in the water and splashed it at Olga. The two of them rolled around in the creek, the clay bottom giving under them like soft flesh. Eden all at once felt sensual, wished she were alone here with Matthew Martin Cabell. She hastily stood up, stepped on to the bank and began to dry herself.

'What's up, Miss Eden?'

'Nothing.' Why was she shivering? The evening was still warm. 'Get out and dry yourself. The men will want to bathe.'

Later she took Olga for a walk up along the road while Cabell, Nikolai and Frederick had their bath in the creek. When they came back Cabell was waiting by the car for them.

'You and the children had better sleep in the car,' he said. 'In country like this there'll be scorpions and tarantulas.'

Olga shuddered and Eden said, 'But what about you and Nikolai?'

'We're used to them. They don't bite tough meat.'

Olga went down to the creek to speak to her brother and Eden said, 'Do you think Nikolai is tough meat?'

He paused for a moment before he said, 'He's proving to be tougher than I expected.'

'You don't mind his being – what he is?'

'Why should I?' Then he nodded: 'I know. Decent chaps don't act very decently towards them, is that what you mean? He's all right. I just don't think I could discuss his – his *condition* with him, that's all. Have you?'

'Me? Good heavens, no.'

'You see? You're a decent girl . . . Poor bastard.' He looked down towards where Nikolai was laying out his own rug and Cabell's sleeping-bag. 'He's got no future.'

'Perhaps you could say that about all of us. Where do we go from here?'

She gestured around her at the vast steppe turning purple in the evening air. Some jerboa were venturing out early, moving in their peculiar hopping motion, their big ears looking like wings ready to spread and lift them into flight. All the birds were home for the night and there was no sound at all, just an immense soft silence, comforting rather than threatening, surrounding the girl and the man. The only threatening note was the feeling that they were utterly isolated, that there was no house or village within a hundred miles of them.

'I'll think about it in the morning.'

'No, Matt. It's not going to be any better in the morning. I looked at our food supply when I was cooking supper. We have about enough for two more days at the most. I suppose we can drink that water if we boil it first?' She nodded towards the creek.

'It should be okay. I'll walk upstream in the morning and see if it's any clearer up there.' He looked along the road, a narrow pale strip disappearing into the darkening steppe. He had claimed a fascination with horizons, but now he looked all round him and none of them beckoned him. 'We've got three choices. We go back to that little village we passed through this morning —'

'But that must be a hundred and fifty, nearly two hundred miles!'

He nodded. 'Or we head south and hope that there's a town or village not too far down the pike. Or —'

'Or what?'

'Or we stay here and hope for the best. This *is* a road – someone must use it some time or other.'

She pondered a while, then said, 'What I'm afraid of is that the dwarf or Captain Pugachov will be the first ones to come along.'

'I think I'd welcome Pugachov. We'd stand a fifty-fifty chance with him. But at the pace of his camels, I reckon he won't be down this far for at least five or six days, maybe more.'

'And the dwarf?'

'I don't know. Four days, five maybe. Depends how hard he drives his horses.' Or maybe the machine-gunners from the train had killed him. But that was a hope he didn't voice.

'Well, what are you going to do?'

'You wouldn't like to be the leader and make the decision? Be a suffragette and have a say in things?'

'No, I wouldn't.' But her tone was gentle. She knew he wasn't serious with his question, not entirely so, and she had faith in him.

He sighed, took her hand, but didn't look at her. Instead, he looked up and down the road, fading now, like his hopes, into the dusk. 'We'll stay here tomorrow and hope that someone comes along. If nobody does, then we'll start moving the morning after.'

'Which way?'

He nodded. 'South. I'm guessing, but I figure we can't be more than two hundred miles at the most from the Caspian. There's a phrase I once read in an old explorer's diary, one of the books my father gave me to read. The point of no return. I guess Columbus felt he reached it going across the Atlantic. Marco Polo probably felt the same way – his route wouldn't have been very far south of us. I think we've got to go on and trust to luck.'

'Then wouldn't it be better to start tomorrow morning? While we still have enough food.'

'Just like a woman. Won't make a decision, but does everything to make a man change his.'

'Where did you learn so much about women?'

He grinned and dodged that one. 'We're not going to have enough food anyway. We'll have to live off the land. Shoot some hares, maybe an antelope. Catch some fish — though I don't think we're going to be that lucky. My maps have no details, but south of here they do show it's almost desert country. Clay pans, maybe even sand dunes. But we'll make it,' he said with forced optimism. He put his arm round her shoulders and kissed her hair. 'I promise—'

Then he looked over her shoulder and saw Olga and Frederick standing on the other side of the car watching them. 'It's all right,' said Olga. 'Don't mind us.'

'I'm glad you approve,' said Cabell; but took his arm from round Eden. 'But something tells me you don't, Freddie.'

'Miss Eden used to tell us there is a time and place for everything.'

Cabell laughed and looked at Eden. 'What do you say to that?'

'I think it's time we all went to bed. Good night, Mr Cabell.'

'Good night, Miss Penfold.' He was still chuckling when he walked down to where his sleeping-bag was laid out waiting for him. But his amusement was only a defence, something to keep him from thinking about what lay ahead of them if no one came up or down the road tomorrow.

In the morning, before the day got too hot, he walked upstream with Frederick to check if there were any clear pools in the creek. He took the Winchester, in case a hare or antelope presented itself as an addition to their small larder.

He found no clear pools at first; the water was as sluggish and yellow as that down by the line of tamarisks. But in a soak where the creek bank flattened out he saw a familiar discoloration, the dark rainbow colours that always made an oilman stop in his tracks.

'What's the matter, Mr Cabell?' Frederick, several paces ahead, stopped and looked back.

'See that? That's oil. That's what we make gasoline from.'

'Could you do that now?' Frederick came back to peer at the swirl of colour bordering the soak.

Cabell laughed harshly, with none of the light amusement he had had last night. He was no stranger to irony; no explorer, whether for oil, gold or new lands, ever is. It waits, part of the price set by God or the gods, at every bend in the seeker's path. It explains, perhaps, the fatalism of the true explorer.

'No, Freddie. Oil has to be what they call *cracked* to get gasoline. And we'd need a lot of it before we'd get enough gasoline to take us down to the Caspian.'

'Do you think there might be a lot of oil here?' Frederick waved an arm up and down the creek.

'Could be. They've known about oil in this part of the world for centuries, even before Christ. The Babylonians used to use it to mix the mortar for their houses. But up till about sixty years ago no one knew how to produce it in large quantities. They used to just dig pits. Or even do that –' He scooped up a handful of the oil from the surface of the water.

'When we reach Tiflis, will you come back and dig to see if there is a lot of oil here?'

'I don't think so.' He wiped the oil from his hand with some sand, then washed his hand in the creek, using more sand. He wondered if the act was unconsciously symbolic, if he would ever return to Russia at all. He stood up, said with a yearning that surprised him, 'I think I'll go home to America.'

'Will you take Miss Eden with you?'

'I might do that,' he said with a smile. 'Would you miss her?'

'Very much,' said Frederick.

Cabell looked at him fondly. 'You're all right, Freddie. Even for a prince.'

Unexpectedly the boy smiled. 'So are you, Mr Cabell.'

They walked on, leaving the oil smear behind them. Cabell climbed up on to the top of the bank, stood for a moment as if trying to *feel* the oil beneath his feet, as if his legs were some sort of divining rod. How much oil was there here? Enough to make Pugachov's fortune seem like petty cash? He was too experienced to be carried away by an isolated seep; but he was beginning to feel that perverse optimism that goes hand-in-hand with frustration. As if he wanted, in the future, to read that there had been a big oil strike right here and he could then feel some sort of sweet pain from his chagrin.

Half a mile up the stream he and Frederick found a clear pool and they filled the water-skin they had brought with them. In the next hour Cabell bagged two hares and they brought them back to camp where Nikolai skinned them and that evening they had them for supper. They watched all day, alert to every shimmer on the horizon, but no one came up or down the road.

Cabell waited till they were about to turn in for the night, knowing that everyone had been waiting on his decision. 'Okay, in the morning we start walking.'

'Which way?' said Frederick.

'South.' The prospect frightened him, but he told himself they had no alternative.

No one slept well that night. Cabell took a long time to doze off and he woke early, just as the first light crept up in the eastern sky. He lay for a moment listening to some birds further up the creek, then he heard the other sound. He got up, motioning to Nikolai, who had also wakened, to stay where he was. He went quietly up to the car and in the gradually brightening light saw Eden and the two children sitting up in the car and staring up the road.

The caravan was at least half a mile long, coming out of the fading night like a caravan of ghosts. There were men, women and children; camels, mules and horses; and ox-drawn carts. The people were singing, a low sad song that was no more than a murmur in the vast silence of the dawn. They came slowly down the road, seeming to move without moving in the grey, illusionary light, just growing larger and larger. They were a hundred yards from the Rolls-Royce when their leaders suddenly halted; the procession con-certinaed in behind them, the murmuring singing dying away to a whisper and then to nothing. The long line stood there on the grey-white road in the grey light in a silence so still that even at that distance Cabell could hear the faint clink of harness metal.

'Who are they?' Frederick whispered.

Cabell had not brought the Winchester up with him from beside his sleeping-bag. But it would not be much use against such a large number of people; they were still too distant for him to discern what weapons they carried, but he was sure that he and the others were covered. He heard Nikolai come up the bank and stand on the far side of the car, but he didn't look around to see if the Cossack had brought the rifle with him.

'Stay here,' he said.

He walked up the road, moving steadily, wondering if this, by some freak refraction of light, was the procession he had seen in the mirage two days ago. He had gone no more than thirty yards when he saw the man detach himself from the head of the caravan and walk slowly down the road towards him. Cabell reached what he reckoned was the halfway point, halted and waited. The man neither slowed nor quickened his pace, but came steadily on, a rifle held on his shoulder, and finally came to a stop three or four paces from Cabell.

He said something and Cabell said, 'Are you speaking Ukrainian? I do not understand it. Please speak Russian.'

'I said I hope you are not going to stop us from continuing our journey.' He spoke quietly, without threat, but there was a crackle to his voice that suggested he was a man not afraid of argument.

Cabell looked at him, recognizing him now for what he was: a rabbi. He was a tall man, slightly stooped, with a grey-streaked beard and dark aggressive eyes; he wore a black skullcap and a thin cloak was draped over his shoulders. The rifle, Cabell saw now, was no more than a black furled umbrella.

'Rabbi, I'm not blocking your way. I'm just damned glad to see you.' Cabell explained who he was and their predicament. 'I don't suppose you'd be carrying any gasoline with you?'

The rabbi spread a hand; the aggression went out of his eyes and he smiled, showing yellow teeth. 'Not even a drop, sir. We cannot help you.'

'How far are you going?'

'To Palestine.'

170

'That's quite a journey.' Nothing surprised Cabell any more. But Palestine as a destination did make Tiflis seem no more than a short hike down the pike.

'It is necessary, sir. I am Rabbi Moshe Aronsky and they –' he waved a hand over his shoulder but did not turn round '– they are the people of Sulobelsk, in the Ukraine.'

'I don't know it.'

'Why should you? It is a small village, five hundred people – five hundred and twelve, to be exact. All those you see back there.'

'But why come this way, if you're going to Palestine? It's the longest route by far.'

'But the safest – we hope. We could not go down through Georgia – General Denikin's men would have stopped us. They were the ones who decided us we should have to leave Russia. Sulobelsk once had over seven hundred people, seven hundred and fifty-six to be exact. That was only six months ago.'

'What happened?'

'Do you know what a pogrom is, sir?'

It was a word Cabell had never heard before. 'Is it a Russian word?'

'Yes. It means destruction. For us it has a special meaning – destruction of the Jews.'

Cabell looked up the road at the long line of people waiting patiently (fearfully? he wondered) with their livestock and carts; then he thought of Frederick down the road behind him. Was this part of the boy's father's war, the murdering of Jews? 'General Denikin's army didn't – drive you out because you are Bolsheviks?'

'There are some Bolsheviks amongst us, one or two. But they were not the reason for the pogrom. We Jews have been persecuted in Russia for centuries. It is nothing new for us.'

Cabell did not want to pursue the subject. He felt a certain guilt; he could remember himself and other kids taunting the only Jewish storekeeper on his block on Prairie Avenue. He wondered when jeering turned to killing.

'Which way have you come? We didn't pass you.'

'We joined this road only yesterday, coming in from the west.'

'You are on the road early.'

'We travel early to escape the day's heat. You have to do that when you have only your feet to travel on.' He looked past Cabell at the Rolls-Royce. 'We rest from ten in the morning till four in the afternoon, then move on again till an hour before dark.'

'That will take you forever to reach Palestine.'

'Time is our only wealth. If you wish to move at our pace, perhaps we can help you? We bought camels when we came through a market town north of here. We can spare two to pull your motor car.'

Cabell went back to the car and told Eden and the others of Rabbi Aronsky's offer. 'At the rate they're moving it may take us another week before we reach a town. But it's our best bet. Maybe our only one.'

Frederick was watching the caravan, on the move again, coming down the road. 'Are they all Jews? All of them?'

'They are Russians, Freddie, like you and Olga and Nikolai. So don't start thinking of them as any different, okay?'

The boy sensed the sharp note in Cabell's voice, but he lifted his head with something of his old arrogance. 'Don't tell me what to do, Mr Cabell. I know what my father thinks of Jews.'

Well, there goes my ounce of influence. Cabell had begun to think that Frederick looked on him, no matter how temporarily, as a surrogate father; but he saw now that the boy's real father was still the dominant influence in his life. He suddenly cursed Prince Gorshkov for a son-of-a-bitch.

'Your father isn't here. Now get your ass out of there and help me tie the camels to the car!'

Nikolai said, 'I'll help you do that, sir —'

'You get down and get the bed-rolls!' Cabell turned his anger on the hapless Nikolai. 'Get the trailer packed and in a hurry!'

Then he stalked across to where Aronsky stood waiting while the caravan, all heads turned, some smiling tentatively, others staring curiously, went slowly by. The camels were at the tail of the strung-out procession, where their stink would drift behind on the empty air.

'They are bad-tempered beasts,' said Aronsky. 'Perhaps

by the time we get to Palestine I can teach them a little Jewish tolerance.'

You might try teaching some to the kid in the back seat. But he didn't say that. He had just entered the classroom himself.

The two camels chosen by Cabell, for all their bad temper, in the end stood patiently while he and Frederick hitched them to the front of the Rolls-Royce with rope traces. Frederick had not come near Aronsky, and the rabbi had watched the boy with curiosity but without saying anything. Eden and Olga stood in the background and Nikolai finished tying down the tarpaulin on the trailer.

When they were ready to move Cabell said, 'Rabbi, I'd like you to meet my friends.'

Aronsky acknowledged the introductions, raising his eyebrows slightly when introduced to Prince Frederick and Princess Olga. Then, seemingly for the first time, he looked at the Rolls-Royce. 'A magnificent motor car. Is it yours, Mr Cabell?'

'It is my father's,' said Frederick, now standing with his hands clasped on the hilt of his sword, the point of it between his set-apart feet.

'Beautiful manners,' said Aronsky to Cabell. 'Speaks when he isn't spoken to. Did his father teach him that?'

That's not all he's taught him. 'He has his lapses, Rabbi. I'm afraid I'm to blame. I've been teaching him a little American democracy.'

'That's democracy – children having a say?' Aronsky shook his head at how the world was falling apart outside Russia.

'Perhaps you would care to ride with us?' said Eden, feeling Frederick getting as stiff as his sword beside her.

'Thank you, no. I must lead my people.' He said it as if he were Moses. Then he looked down the road at the distant head of the caravan and suddenly laughed. 'What a leader – at the tail-end of the line!'

He went hurrying down the road, bouncing along with a peculiar stiff-legged walk, laughing as he went, taking everyone into the joke as he passed them, so that the laugh grew out of five hundred throats and rippled down the long line to its head.

'He smells,' said Olga.

Cabell held in his temper. 'Princess, most of the world's people smell. They all aren't as lucky as you, their houses don't have baths. Not so long ago the Tsars used to smell, too.'

He got into the car and after a moment's stiff silence the others followed him. He flicked the reins and after a short wait, while the camels made up their minds whether to obey or not, the car slowly rolled forward. As it did, both camels dropped manure in its path. Cabell looked at Eden.

'Now we know what they think of us.' Then he looked over his shoulder at the sullenly silent Frederick. 'And don't *you* give the Rabbi even a hint of what you think of Jews. You understand me?'

Frederick stared at him. For a moment Cabell thought, with sickening trepidation because he did not know how he would handle the situation, that the boy was going to defy him. Then Frederick lowered his head. 'Yes, sir.'

CHAPTER FIVE

It was remarkable how quickly the Jews accepted Cabell and the others as part of their caravan; and just as remarkable how those in the Rolls-Royce took it for granted that they were accepted. No matter how exotic their vehicle, they were absorbed as naturally as if a place had been waiting for them in the long line of refugees. And yet, riding in the Rolls-Royce behind the plodding camels, no matter how much the ugly beasts reduced the dignity of the car, Cabell knew that he and the others still belonged to an alien world. So far none of them had been subjected to persecution.

It had not occurred to him up till then to think of themselves as refugees. But of course that was what they were: one with the millions moving like bewildered ants across the map of Europe at this very moment, the vast slow avalanche started by the Great War. Strictly speaking, he and Eden were not refugees: they at least had homes to go back to. But Frederick and Olga and Nikolai: it struck him that perhaps their eventual home might be even far more distant than the Jews' dream of Palestine.

'Why Palestine?' he asked Aronsky.

They had stopped to rest during the heat of the day. There was no shade and the caravan had just sunk down where it halted on the road. Cabell had got out of the car and walked up the long line to its head. As he passed the people of Sulobelsk, they looked up at him and gave him friendly nods, welcoming him to their midst. And to their plight, he thought. Then he looked at them again and was surprised that none of them looked as unhappy as he had expected, that their faces, despite their weariness, were alive with smiles that could only suggest hope.

'Why Palestine?' Aronsky had taken off his cloak and sat on a wooden stool under the black circle of his umbrella. He was eating black bread and an onion, slicing the onion with a large sharp knife. 'We decided it was the only place where we might all remain together.'

Cabell had borrowed Eden's pale blue parasol, which had been strapped to her suitcase; he sat under it on a stool that a small boy had brought him on an order from Aronsky. The two men were sitting apart from the caravan, on a slight rise just off the road; Aronsky, a true leader, made himself visible at all times, even when resting. The pale blue and the black umbrella topped the rise like two tiny, formally trimmed trees.

'I understand a lot of Jews are going to America.'

'We thought of America. But we are rural Jews, Mr Cabell. Not all of us are farmers, of course, but even the tradesmen amongst us could not work in a big city. And if we went into your Wild West – well, what's worse? Being scalped by Apaches or carved up by the sabres of Cossacks?'

'The Apaches have given up scalping. They leave that now to the Wall Street barons, another tribe altogether.'

Aronsky laughed heartily, the umbrella trembling above him like a bush in a storm, and Cabell said, 'I always thought rabbis were mournful men.'

'Perhaps they are, most of them. We have plenty to be mournful about. But I don't think misery ever made anyone a better man.' He sobered, the laugh dying away in his beard. 'It is a dreadful handicap, being a Russian Jew. It is bad enough being a Russian when it comes to happiness – haven't you noticed how they love to beat their breasts? They're worse than women at wanting to be martyrs. Anyone who is Russian and a Jew and a woman —' He nodded down towards where a group of women sat with their heads close together in a pool of gossip. 'That howling wind you hear on the steppes in winter, that's not Nature, that's Russia enjoying itself. The worst of us were the Nogai Tartars – they were all that was left of what used to be called the Jewish Empire, which used to stretch from the Volga down to the Caspian Sea. I don't even know if they actually *were* Jews any more, if they practised our religion. But they were the world champions of misery. Their women, would you believe it, used to meet and have *wailing* parties! Can you imagine such a chorus?'

'In America, I've heard that it's Jewish mothers who keep

the families together.'

'What better way to be a martyr? A captive audience. Am I a misogynist, Mr Cabell?'

'I know one or two women who wouldn't nominate you as their patron saint.'

Aronsky laughed again, unafraid of what women might do to him. 'I think I inherited my feelings from my mother. A most formidable woman, always thought other women were far too weepy.'

'What about your father?'

'He was a great cantor, in very much demand. He could make thousands weep. My mother didn't think much of him, either. Is your Miss Penfold weepy?'

'Anything but. I shouldn't be too misogynistic if ever you get down to our end of the caravan. She has a pretty tart tongue when she wants to.'

'It comes with the sex,' said Aronsky, secure in his maleness.

'What will you do when you get to Jerusalem and you go to the Wailing Wall?'

'I shan't laugh, Mr Cabell,' he said soberly; then put a hand on Cabell's arm. 'No, you haven't offended me. But for a Jew to go home to Jerusalem after all these centuries — ah! I shall probably weep, not wail, Mr Cabell. Weep for joy.'

Cabell went back down the line to the Rolls-Royce. Some of the people laughed and made jokes about his blue parasol, but they were good-natured and not offensive; he was one of them now. A camel eyed him superciliously, chewed its cud and spat at him, but he managed to avoid the greasy mess.

Frederick sat sullenly in the car, slumped down in the shade of the hood, idly tracing the pattern on the silver handle of his sword. But Eden, Olga and Nikolai, despite the heat and glare, had got out and were preparing lunch. Eden had made sandwiches of sausage and black bread and Nikolai had the samovar simmering on a small fire, continually pushing stiff dry grass in to keep the flames going.

'What's the matter with His Highness?' Cabell asked.

Eden was apart from Olga and Nikolai, but still she kept

her voice low. 'He feels you're finished with him. He thinks you'd rather spend your time with the Rabbi than with him.'

'Jesus wept! Here, give me a couple of sandwiches.' He went across to the car, opened the rear door and got in beside Frederick. 'Lunch, Freddie. Eat up.'

'I'm not hungry.' The boy looked out of the car, his eyes squinting against the glare.

Cabell could remember doing exactly that whenever he had been annoyed with his mother or father and hadn't wanted to talk to them. It had been happening probably from the time of Cain and Abel, kids staring into nothing, seeing nothing but the reflection of their own self-pity. *Come down here, Rabbi, come down and see how kids enjoy being martyrs.*

Cabell shoved a sandwich into the boy's limp hand. 'I hate to press you, Freddie, you're only twelve years old, but I think you better start growing up.'

Frederick continued to stare out of the car, but he did lift the sandwich to his mouth and munched slowly on it.

'You're a pain in the ass occasionally. But other times . . . Freddie, for crissake, stop acting like a spoilt girl. What's the matter with you?' Frederick mumbled something, still gazing out of the car. 'Swallow what you've got in your mouth and say that again.'

Frederick swallowed. 'I said you're a Jew-lover.'

Cabell stopped chewing on his own sandwich, swallowed and took his time before he answered. 'Freddie, I don't believe that's you talking. I think it's some grown-up you've been listening to. You wouldn't know anything about Jews.' He knew very little, if anything, about them himself; but he wasn't going to confess that. He had all the enthusiasm of the newly converted; some day some of his best friends might be Jews. 'I think you'd like the Rabbi Aronsky if you got to know him. He's like you in many ways. For instance, he can't stand women.'

Frederick half-turned. 'Does Miss Eden know that?'

'About you or about him?' Cabell grinned and, despite himself, a smile flickered at the corner of Frederick's mouth. 'Come on, Freddie. Why the hell should you and I fight? When we start moving again, I'll take you up front and we can walk along with the Rabbi. Miss Eden can steer the car.'

'I shan't know how to talk to him.'

'It's time you learned. You've led a sheltered life up till now. But that's over.'

Frederick showed some wisdom to which his years didn't entitle him. 'I wonder what my mother and father will think of you when you meet them?'

They'll probably cut me dead when they learn what I've been trying to teach you. 'Let's hope their sheltered life is over, too.'

Frederick turned his head and looked out of the car again. Cabell wondered if he realized he was staring north, back to the life that was gone forever.

The caravan started off in the late afternoon. The day was still hot but the sun was lower, throwing longer shadows that gave the illusion of coolness even if the shadows were only those of the people themselves and their livestock. Cabell turned the wheel of the Rolls-Royce and the camels' reins over to Eden, having taken her aside earlier and explained what he and Frederick were going to do and why he was doing it.

'You're taking the place of his father, do you realize that?'

'Don't rub it in. If ever I have any kids of my own, I hope I do a better job than I'm doing now.'

'You'll do all right,' she said and wondered what he would be like to live with as a husband and father.

Cabell called to Frederick, who was standing talking to Nikolai behind the car. As he did so he looked beyond the boy and the Cossack, back up the road disappearing into the yellow haze of the afternoon. Something moved there, a dark mote in the far distance. Was it another, tiny mirage? An antelope? Some other travellers? Or the dwarf Pemenov? He squinted, trying to pierce the distance and the haze; but whoever or whatever it was had stopped, was getting no nearer. Then the dark mote disappeared, as if the ground had opened up beneath it. He shook his head, wondering if his eyes or his imagination were playing tricks on him.

'Is there something wrong, Mr Cabell?'

'Nothing, Freddie. Let's go.'

In the next couple of hours Frederick's education went a step further. He found Rabbi Aronsky far less awesome than

179

the Orthodox bishops who used to come to the Gorshkov home in St Petersburg, who always seemed to smile down at him from a level just below that of God's.

'That's a fine sword you're carrying, my boy. Are you intending to run someone through with it?'

'If I have to, sir.' Frederick shifted the sword in its scabbard from one shoulder to the other.

'Like all princes,' Aronsky said to Cabell. 'Bloodthirsty.'

'Are you a Bolshevik, Rabbi Aronsky?' said Frederick.

Aronsky glanced at Cabell, his eyes smiling. 'Am I, Mr Cabell?'

'I think you'd like to be, but I'm afraid the Bolsheviks would have no place for a rabbi. Right?'

'You see, my young prince? You and I are alike. There's no place for us in the worlds we want. How would you like to come to Palestine with me?'

'Thank you for asking me, Rabbi, but no.' Frederick found himself liking this gaunt, laughing man. He would have to tell Father that some Jews could be quite charming and amusing, even if they did not wash very often. 'I have to go where my father goes.'

'And where will that be?'

But Frederick could only shake his head.

[2]

Pemenov rode just below the horizon, like a giant below the low stone wall of the world. Only once did he make a mistake, in the late afternoon when he had come up on the skyline and seen the long caravan sprawled in an untidy line on the road far ahead of him. He focused his binoculars and at once, almost like a hit in the eye, saw the motor car at the end of the procession and the American standing looking straight back at him. He abruptly turned his horses and rode down into the dip of the road behind him.

From then he rode almost always out of sight of the caravan, occasionally coming up cautiously to the lip of a rise to check on the distance that separated him from his quarry. He kept glancing westwards, watching the sun go down as he might watch the hands of a clock, waiting for nightfall. Then gradually darkness came up out of the east, like a benign storm; then it was night, the stars were out and he rode up over the rim of the steppe. Far ahead of him he could see the fires of the caravan, like a line of stars low in the sky, and he knew he now did not have long to wait.

He swung down from his horse, fed and watered it and the second horse, then fed himself on cheese and bread, washing it down with water. The heat went out of the ground, the air turned chill and he wrapped himself in a blanket. He watched the stars, seeing them get brighter and sharper as the night got cooler; then he reckoned it was time to start moving. He got to his feet, hearing his knees crack.

He checked the hobbles of the horses, then, still wrapped in his blanket against the chill, he set off down the road. He carried only General Bronevich's pistol and a small silver-handled dagger, a *kindjal*, which he had stolen from a Circassian on Admiral Kolchak's staff. Borrowed weapons, but they would be enough. It did not concern him that in killing the American he might also be killed himself.

The moon would soon be up; he would have preferred a darker night. But killers, like beggars, could not always be choosers. He walked as quickly as he could, not wanting to be out of breath when he reached the motor car and its occupants at the end of the caravan. He had no plans to kill anyone but the American, but he also had no qualms if it should be necessary to kill the others. He plodded on through the thick dust, cursing his short legs as he had done all his life. He had taken off the farmer's wide-brimmed straw hat and was wearing his embroidered skullcap; he wished for his black fur hat, so that he might look like a true Cossack when he made his kill. But he knew that it also made him look ridiculous, as if he were all head and hat. If he should die in the next half-hour he did not want people standing over his corpse laughing at him.

Half a dozen jerboa bounced across the road in front of him like tics in his eye. Already up ahead of him, the sounds carrying easily on the still night air, he could hear the slub-bering sound of grazing horses and the hoarse cough of camels. The moon came up over the rim of the steppe, like a

181

voyeur's eye, when he was less than two hundred yards from the Rolls-Royce.

He saw it standing slightly apart from the end of the caravan, as if its occupants did not want to sleep too close to the smell of the camels. He dropped into a crouch, discarding his blanket by the side of the road, and looked for sentries; but could see none. They were either at the far end of the caravan or these people knew nothing about the dangers of being on the road.

He took out his dagger, fingered its double edge; he would use his pistol only as a last resort. Now he was so close to the man he was about to kill, he began to think of doing it quietly and without being caught. Perhaps there was a place in the world where he might live without being laughed at. He began to crawl towards the car, careful of the occasional thorn-bushes that lay amongst the stiff dry grass. He could feel the grass cracking under his hands and knees; it seemed like rifle shots in his ears. Twice he stopped, lying flat, sure that his progress had been heard; then he moved on when he saw no movement up ahead under the rising moon. The car stood out now and beyond it he could see the double-humped mounds that were resting camels. But he could see no smaller, lower mounds that would have meant sleeping people.

He paused, feeling himself beginning to tremble. Was it excitement at being so close to the kill? Or was it the beginning of fear, something he had always despised in others? He had known it as a child, but he thought he had conquered it once he had become an adult. But something was wrong up there twenty yards ahead of him and all at once he lost all the confidence he had had during the long ride to this rendezvous.

The moon rose higher, taunting him with its brightness, throwing everything into sharp relief: the car, the camels and mules and horses, the long line of sleeping people and carts stretching down the road. But there was no sign of anyone sleeping within twenty yards of the car.

Suddenly angry, careless of what might happen to him, he stood up and ran soft-footed towards the car, the dagger held out in front of him. He reached the car, jumped up on

182

to the running-board and raised the knife to plunge it into whoever was sleeping in the car, no matter who it was. But the seats were empty and he heard himself whimper with rage and frustration.

Then he felt the gun in his back. 'Drop the knife, little man, or you're dead.'

[3]

'I think he should be executed,' said Frederick.

'Children should be seen and not heard,' said Rabbi Aronsky. 'And in a matter like this, the same goes for women.'

'In your eye, Rabbi,' said Eden, setting no example for her charges either in respect for her elders or the proper use of English. Lately she had begun to *think* vulgarly and she wondered if all the years of repression had begun at last to crack, if, as Matthew Martin Cabell had advised, she was taking off her corset. 'But I don't think Major Pemenov should be executed. I'm speaking as an Englishwoman, of course.'

'Don't the English execute people?' said Aronsky.

'Only their kings and queens and common criminals,' said Cabell. 'They're very solicitous about prisoners of war.'

'Oh really?' said Aronsky with a note of disbelief in his voice, though he had never met anyone from England before this outspoken Miss Penfold. 'And what about the Americans?'

'We haven't had much experience with prisoners of war, except our own kind in our Civil War. But we're great ones for executions. Lynchings, hangings, electric chair, rifle squad – you name it, we'll try it.'

His cynicism was just words and nothing more. He was saying whatever came into his mouth, his tongue working while his mind worked on a decision he had never really expected to confront him: what to do with the murderous dwarf.

Last night's capture of Pemenov had not been a deliberate trap. He had moved himself and the others further up the line of refugees when he learned that Aronsky posted only two sentries per shift.

'My men have to save their energy for walking, Mr Cabell,' Aronsky had said. 'Especially in this country and in this heat. In the morning we let the sentries ride in our carts to catch up on their sleep. In this sort of country, so wide and flat and under tonight's moon when it comes up, do you think we shan't see anyone who would want to attack us? We'd hear their horses if they were half a mile away.'

'They might leave their horses a mile away and creep up on you on foot.'

'Why are you so worried, Mr Cabell? I should not have thought you were the nervous sort.'

But Cabell couldn't tell him about the dwarf who was tracking them. Aronsky might decide that, rather than endanger his own people, he would leave Cabell and the others behind, stranded in the Rolls-Royce. 'We've had one or two narrow escapes since we left Verkburg. I guess I'm just getting cautious.'

'Don't worry, Mr Cabell. My sentries will keep you safe.'

But Cabell said, 'Well, I'd like to volunteer. I'll take the first shift.'

'A splendid gesture, Mr Cabell, even if it does rise from selfish motives.'

'Jesus,' said Cabell. 'Are you so blunt in your sermons?'

'Do you think Moses was mealy-mouthed?' Aronsky wore his arrogance as easily as his prayer-shawl.

Cabell threw up his hands. 'You win. But I don't think I'd like to be circumcised by you. You'd be a bit heavy-handed.'

Aronsky laughed heartily, made a carving motion in the air that would have removed more than just a foreskin, and went back up the line, wishing everyone good night as he went. Cabell picked up the Winchester and, having made sure that Eden and the others were comfortable under their rugs, went down to the rear of the caravan and sat down in the shadow of an ox-cart. He decided he was not going to be a roving picquet, but one who kept low and in the same spot, one who kept looking in the same direction, back up the road to the north.

He had seen the dwarf when the little man stood up and ran silently across the moonlit ground to the Rolls-Royce. He had risen and, for the first time blessing the thick dust of the road, crossed just as silently to the car, coming up behind the dwarf.

And now there was the problem of what to do with Major Pemenov. 'He's *our* prisoner, Rabbi. I think it should be left to us to decide what to do with him.'

'An eye for an eye . . . The Old Testament knew what it was about, Mr Cabell. It is very swift and effective and final. I usually don't agree with children, but I think His Highness has the right idea. You should execute him.'

'No,' said Olga.

'Don't these children ever shut up?' said Aronsky. 'Sometimes I think King Herod had the right idea, even if it is heresy to say so.'

Several of the elders of Sulobelsk were included in the circle of justice squatting beside the Rolls-Royce. The prisoner himself was in the back seat of the car, a most elegant dock; he sat there trussed up like a big-headed turkey, staring straight ahead and not deigning to look at those deciding his fate. He had been kept in the car all night and he was beginning to feel stiff and cramped; but he would not ask for his bonds to be loosened or that he be allowed to relieve his bladder. He hoped they would shoot him before he had to ask for any favours.

Nikolai had been sent up to the head of the caravan at first light, when the refugees were readying themselves for the road again. He had returned with Aronsky, who had collected half a dozen of the elders as he had come back down the line. The start of this morning's trek had been delayed while the fate of the prisoner was decided.

'We shall have to be moving soon,' said Aronsky, one eye on the sun coming up over the horizon. 'You had better make up your mind, Mr Cabell.'

'I don't take a man's life on the spur of the moment. I think we'll have to take a vote. Eden?'

Eden hesitated, faced with a decision she had never expected to encounter in her lifetime. Back home in England she had been brought up to believe in the death penalty; but

185

the principle looked a lot different when one was on the jury. 'I – well . . . No, I can't say we should shoot him.'

'No,' said Olga. 'It wouldn't be right.'

'Shoot him,' said Frederick, a true prince, one for Russian tradition.

'You see?' said Aronsky to the elders. 'Some day they'll be giving them money to spend.'

The elders shook their heads, mournful at the thought of the world at the mercy of twelve-year-olds.

'Nick?' said Cabell. 'Your vote?'

Nikolai was ill at ease with this new thing Mr Cabell had told him was democracy. 'I – I think His Highness is right. The man should be shot.' Though no prince, he too believed in tradition.

'Two to two,' sa   den. 'Yours is the casting vote.'

Cabell looked at the dwarf in the car, saw, in his mind's eye, the little man staring straight at him as he sighted down the barrel of the Winchester; Pemenov, he knew, would refuse a blindfold. Still in his mind's eye, he tried squeezing the trigger. Then he looked down and saw the stiff claw of his finger locked in cramp.

'I vote he lives. We'll turn him loose when we get to the Caspian.'

Aronsky sighed, stood up from the stool that had been brought for him. 'He is your responsibility then. If he escapes and kills any of my people while doing so, then they, too, will be your responsibility.'

Only then did Pemenov turn his head. 'You would do better to shoot me now, Mr Cabell.'

Oh brother, thought Cabell, you're not going to miss a trick. 'There's still time, Major.'

The caravan at last got under way, the people of Sulobelsk restless to be on the road even if they did move at a funereal pace. Cabell, Eden, Olga and Nikolai rode in the car behind the two camels, while Frederick, complete with sword, mounted Pemenov's second horse and rode beside the dwarf, who now had only his hands bound in front of him. Cabell had sent Nikolai and Frederick back to bring up Pemenov's horses, the Cossack glad to go with his young master but scared stiff that he would have to ride a fractious horse that he would not be able to control. In the event he had found that both horses, worn out by their long trek, were remarkably docile.

When they had brought the horses back they had discovered the two gold ingots in the saddle bags. Cabell had instantly said, 'You got these at that wrecked train. Did you kill any of those Uzbeks? Answer me, damn you!'

Pemenov had been stone-faced and silent while Frederick and Nikolai had been away getting his horses. Now he said, 'That gold was no more theirs than it is yours. I took it, but I didn't kill anyone. I'm only interested in killing you, Mr Cabell.'

'I don't believe that. You're a real son-of-a-bitch, Major.'

'I've never denied that about my mother.'

'What a horrible little man!' said Olga.

Pemenov smiled at her, a fellow-conspirator in the nursery. 'Don't you hate your mother, dear?'

'Watch it!' said Eden and hit him with her handbag.

The dwarf reeled back in the seat, shook his head dazedly at such a method of assault.

'Leave the gold where it is,' said Cabell and looked down the road. The tail-end of the caravan was disappearing over a rise. 'Let's get moving or we're going to be left behind.'

'I don't think Rabbi Aronsky would mind if we were,' said Eden. 'You really are a problem, Major.'

Pemenov twitched the side of his face, trying to get some feeling back into his ear. 'I'm glad I am, miss.'

Cabell had the top of the car up and he looked out at Frederick and Pemenov riding in the growing glare and heat of the morning. The dwarf wore the farmer's straw hat and Frederick wore the white panama, crushed and dirty now, that Eden had brought for him. 'You're sure you don't want to ride in here, Freddie?'

'No, sir. Someone has to guard this man.'

Pemenov glanced at Frederick, then back at Cabell and smiled. It struck the latter that the dwarf looked like the boy's slightly older brother. But it would be years before Frederick reached the level of Pemenov's cynicism. Or so Cabell hoped.

They rode on, the road twisting and turning now through

the clay pans and grey ridges that looked like wrinkled dead flesh. When Aronsky at last halted the caravan they were in the dry bed of a river, some thin tamarisks offering the only shade. Cabell took out his maps, but he could make only a rough guess at their position.

Aronsky, floating awkwardly under the black parachute of his umbrella, came back down the line to Cabell. 'We are running short of water, Mr Cabell. You are a geologist, are you not?'

'I look for oil, not water. You want a water diviner for that.' Cabell was looking up and down the river bed. 'That's all sandy clay. You might try digging for water. I've seen the Indians do it back home in dry country.'

'It will be good practice. I'm told that Palestine is a very dry land.'

'You'll meet a lot drier before you get there, Rabbi. The Ust Urt can't be too far south of here – that's the worst desert in all Central Asia. My employers warned me to stay out of it.'

'We, too, were warned against it. We shall head west to the Caspian before we reach it. In the meantime we need more water.'

Despite the heat of the day work parties set about digging for water. They did not have to dig deeply: they found water, brackish and dirty, only three feet below the surface. Cabell and Nikolai collected three pots of it and lit a fire to boil and strain it. Pemenov, hands still bound, back in the rear seat of the car again, sat and watched them.

'He should be made to work,' said Frederick.

Cabell was still undecided what to do with the dwarf and it angered him that Pemenov knew of his dilemma and was enjoying it. 'That would mean letting him walk around loose. I don't think we could trust him. That right, Major?'

Pemenov nodded. 'Correct. I still intend to kill you, Mr Cabell.'

Eden, preparing the midday meal, could not quite believe what she was hearing. She had been through more adventures in the past week than she had ever expected to endure in her lifetime, but casual talk of murder was beyond her acceptance. She looked at Olga listening wide-eyed to the conversation, then at Frederick staring belligerently at Pemenov. Where had innocence gone? she wondered. And tried to remember what conversations she had listened to when she was the children's age. Perhaps her father talking about cricket at Lord's or, at worst, the arrival of Labour Party members in the House of Commons, an invasion, in her father's eyes, on a par with that of the Picts and Scots centuries before. Perhaps her mother rhapsodizing about Ellen Terry as Peter Pan or, at her worst, complaining about the vulgar behaviour of the Suffragettes. Death was sometimes mentioned, that of aunts or uncles, but murder never.

'Stop talking like that in front of the children, Major.'

The dwarf smiled, then said in English, 'Get fucked, whore.'

Cabell leapt up, wrenched open the door of the car and grabbed Pemenov by the throat. Olga screamed and Frederick shouted, 'Kill him! I'll get my sword!' and Eden rushed at Cabell and tried to pull him away from the dwarf. Nikolai just stood, not having understood what was said and wondering what all the commotion was about.

Eden thumped Cabell's back with her fists, yelling at him; but he was blind and deaf with rage. She grabbed her handbag from the front seat of the car, stood off and hit him across the back of the head with all her strength. He grunted, let go of the dwarf and eased himself back out of the car. Pemenov lay on the back seat, his throat red and bruised, his eyes closed as if he had been prepared to meet his own death halfway. Cabell slammed the car door shut and sat on the running-board breathing heavily.

Eden sat down beside him. 'Don't you see? That was what he wanted you to do.'

Frederick appeared with his sword drawn from its scabbard. 'Have you killed him already?'

'Shut your mouth!' Eden's command was almost a scream. 'Put that thing away or I'll hit you with it!'

Cabell, breathing a little more easily, aware now of what he had almost done, patted her knee. 'Steady, Eden. It's all over. No one's going to be hurt.'

She got up and moved away. Cabell, motioning to the children to remain where they were, followed her. They walked up the river bed, watched from the top of the bank by a crowd of Jewish children attracted by Olga's scream a few moments ago.

'It isn't over,' she said softly but fiercely. 'You'd have killed him then!'

'I lost my temper at what he said to you. But I didn't intend – *killing* him.'

'No? He'd have been dead before you woke up to what you were doing. Oh Matt – let him go! Keep his guns and dagger, but give him his horses and turn him loose!'

'Come with me.'

He took her hand and pulled her up the hard clay of the bank behind him. When they stood on the top he waved a hand at the surrounding countryside. It stretched away, semi-desert, eroded ridges and clay pans dotted with the occasional clump of camel-thorn or wormwood, a landscape that invited you to turn your enemies loose in it.

'Is that what you want to do? Turn him loose into that without a gun? He'd be dead in two days.'

'We could give him enough food. Take his gold and buy it from Rabbi Aronsky.'

'Well, maybe —'

'You just don't want him to go, that's it, isn't it?' There was passion in her argument; she was still upset at what had happened back at the car. 'You're afraid he'll turn round and still follow us, aren't you? That's what I mean – *it isn't over!*'

'Goddam it, what the hell do you want me to do?' Abruptly he was just as fierce as she.

She knew she was going round in circles. 'I – I don't know. Perhaps I should have voted to shoot him, got it over and done with. But I'd never have been able to face the children again. Not Olga, anyway.'

'We're stuck with him, Eden. When we get down to some town on the Caspian I'll take his guns and his horses, give them to someone, maybe Rabbi Aronsky, and I'll kick Pemenov in the ass – sorry, the behind – and we'll get on a boat and wave him goodbye. But till then we're stuck with him. But if he speaks to you again like he just did, don't get in my way. I may not kill him, but I'll sure as hell beat the

190

sh— well, I'll beat him. Don't expect me to act like a gentleman Quaker.'

They walked back along the bank like lovers on a Sunday stroll, his arm round her waist. A monitor lizard lifted its head and watched them with a baleful eye; a viper waited beneath some low camel-thorn ready to attack if they came close. But Pemenov, sitting up in the car again, gently massaging his throat with his bound hands, watched Cabell and Eden with more venom, because it was intelligent hatred, than the reptiles ever could.

Next morning, when the caravan was camped a further eight miles down the road, the dwarf escaped.

[4]

The wind began to rise just before dawn, lifting the dust off the road and blanketing the sleeping caravan with it. People sat up, coughing as the dust blew into their unwary faces. They turned their backs to it, but the wind increased and they looked over their shoulders and saw the end of the world. The eastern sky was one great billowing pink and red fog. They squinted into the wind and dust, increasing by the moment, and saw the huge cauldron of cloud, turning red now, rushing at them. The immense boiling mass covered the whole sky; behind it the sun burned like the fires of hell. Children began to scream, dogs whimpered and crept beneath any cover they could find, horses reared and began to whinny in terror. Only the camels remained calm: they turned their backs, faced west and put their heads down. They had been enduring storms like this for more years than could be counted, the acceptance was bred in their blood.

Cabell struggled out of his sleeping-bag, hustled Eden and the children round to the lee of the car. He had made them sleep on the ground last night, keeping Pemenov in the car while he and Nikolai slept on the ground on either side. It had meant that their prisoner was the most comfortable of them all, but it had seemed to Cabell the safest way of keeping an eye on him without having to sit up all night. He left the dwarf in the car now and made sure that Eden and

Olga were as protected as could be against the storm. Nikolai had pulled Frederick down beside him and they huddled under their rugs. Cabell, handkerchief tied across his mouth and nose, eyes slitted almost shut, took a last look at the storm before the full force of it hit them. The whole sky and steppe had disappeared in the violently whirling tempest; the storm rushed at him like the darkest, the last night of all. It hit him like a black surf as he sat down suddenly and pulled a rug over him. He lay there on the ground, Olga crushed between him and Eden, his arm clutching both of them to him, and wondered how long it would be before they all smothered.

The moan and hiss of the wind was deafening; yet at the same time it seemed to make the world silent. Eden lay with her eyes closed, her straw hat over her face, trying not to breathe too deeply of the tiny air pocket she had created for herself. She could feel Olga trembling in her arms, but so far the child did not seem to be choking for breath. The dust seeped in, insidious as water, and she could feel it building up in tiny drifts behind her ears, under her chin, everywhere it could find a crevice. Then she began to feel it in her nose and she knew that soon she was going to suffocate. She shivered with fear and felt Olga move in her arms; then Cabell's hand pressed her shoulder and she felt the comfort of it and tried to contain her panic. The wind whipped under the car, tearing at the rugs that covered them, and she grabbed at her rug before it could blow away.

No one knew how long the storm lasted: it seemed an eternity. It suffocated half a dozen dogs and a six-month-old baby; an old man and an old woman died from heart attacks. When it at last passed on, leaving dust still falling like a dry drizzle, the steppe to the east was just a vast pink mist, beautiful but terrifying, like the glow from the embers of the world.

The caravan, till it began to stir, was a long grey line of rocks stretching down the road. Then people began to stand up, dust falling from them like loose skin; a dog shook itself and seemed to fall apart. With the wind gone there was now just an unearthly silence, as if the dust had killed all sound. Then the dead were discovered and there was a scream, dry and harsh, and then the moaning started.

Cabell stood up, took a careful breath so that he would not take in too much of the still-thick air, and saw the empty car. He went plunging around in the low dunes of dust, as if he expected to find Pemenov buried beneath his feet; then he stumbled up along the caravan, past the bereaved wailing at their loss, but there was no sign of the dwarf. He had disappeared as completely as if the wind had picked him up, a tiny burden, and taken him with it.

Cabell did not trouble Aronsky with his news; the Rabbi was busy consoling the grief-stricken. It was an hour before Aronsky came down to the tail of the caravan; in that hour graves had been dug, prayers said and the young and the old buried beneath cairns of stones. The Rabbi was in no mood to accept the news Cabell gave him.

'But how? How did you let him escape?'

'Goddam it, Rabbi, don't talk as if I *planned* it!' Cabell was more angry at himself than the Jew could ever be. 'I don't know how he got away. I thought I had him well tied up, but I'm no expert at that sort of thing. Maybe his hands were smaller than I thought and he wriggled them out of the rope.'

'But he took his horses, too!'

'Well, that was pretty slick of him, I'll admit —'

'It was pretty stupid of you, Mr Cabell. He was a Siberian – he would know all about these sort of storms. He would know how to keep a horse moving in it, with its head covered . . . He's out there somewhere —' He gestured at the steppe, still lost in the pink mist. 'He'll be waiting for us —'

'For me, Rabbi. Not for the rest of you.'

'If he starts shooting from a distance, any one of us may be shot. Did he take a gun?'

'No.' That was the one smart thing I did, thought Cabell, hiding Pemenov's rifle, pistol and dagger in the trailer. But the gold bars were still in the saddle bags of Pemenov's horses and if the dwarf managed to reach a town or came across another caravan he would have no trouble buying more weapons. Unless, of course, someone killed him for the gold first. Cabell prayed for robbers lying in wait for the dwarf out there in the mist of dust . . . 'Do you want to leave us here, Rabbi? I won't blame you —'

Aronsky looked around him, as if debating the merits of the suggestion. Then he said, 'Hitch up your camels, Mr Cabell. But keep well behind us, so that he can see you. Make yourself a very visible target.'

'If Moses was like you, I'm surprised he got anyone to follow him to the Promised Land.'

'He *drove* them most of the time, Mr Cabell. And I'm going to drive my people to the Promised Land. Jesus Christ is the only leader I know who never had to use a whip on his followers and sometimes I think even He wished for one.'

At last the caravan got under way. It moved on, leaving the stone cairns, already coated with dust, just three more mounds amongst the dust drifts. Olga wept as they passed the smallest grave and Eden said a prayer for the baby, wondering if it was the fortunate one, to have died before it could know heartache. But she knew that she would not have wanted to die so young: her life so far was worth all the wages she had had to pay for it. And, still a romantic, if now a good deal more practical-minded, she hoped the best was yet to come. The infant and the two old people were left behind, lost in the pink mist before those who grieved for them had gone a quarter of a mile down the road.

Slowly during the morning the mist of dust disappeared, turning from pink to gold and then at last giving away to the blue of the sky. Cabell sat in the front seat of the Rolls-Royce, eyes aching with staring as he scanned the gradually emerging horizon for a sign of Pemenov. But the day passed uneventfully and so did the night.

Miles ahead of the caravan Pemenov plodded west on his horses. The road had taken a sharp turn as it passed between two high ranges of hills and now, as it went gradually downhill, dropping from a plateau, he could see a little more vegetation and the occasional glint of water in a not-quite-dry creek bed. Only another few days, he guessed, and he would reach the end of the road as it ran into the Caspian. There would be a town or a village there and, he hoped, someone from whom he could buy or steal a gun. For right now he had nothing with which to kill the American, not even his *kindjal*.

But his immediate concern was to stay alive till he reached a town.

On the morning of the fifth day, worn out by his vigilance, Cabell was dozing behind the wheel of the Rolls-Royce, the camels' reins resting loosely in his hands, when Frederick shouted from the back seat, 'Mr Cabell – look!'

Cabell jerked upright, looking for the dwarf and the threatening rifle. What he saw made him wonder if he hadn't fallen asleep into a wishful dream. Coming down the road, spinning dust over the caravan as it passed, was another car. It went past the Rolls-Royce, enveloping Cabell and the others in a cloud of dust. Cabell let out a curse against selfish, inconsiderate drivers, an incantation of the ages, against chariots, stage-coaches and motor cars driven by people who never looked to see what they had left behind.

'Did you see it?' Frederick, choking on dust, was jumping up and down in his seat, going close to harming himself with his sword and cutting off the future of the Gorshkovs. 'It was another Rolls-Royce!'

'It can't be,' said Eden. 'It was a mirage.'

'Mirages don't kick up dust.' Cabell pulled the camels to a halt and looked back. 'Here it comes again.'

The car had pulled up fifty yards down the road, as if it had taken its driver that long to believe what he had just passed. Now he swung the Rolls-Royce round and came back along the road and pulled up beside Cabell and the others.

The car was white and the driver wore all white: driving helmet, dust-coat, gloves, even his driving-goggles were white-rimmed. The effect was only spoiled by the dust that covered the driver and his car.

'Marvellous! Another Rolls-Royce! Oh, I do think this is absolutely unbelievable!' The driver had spoken from a white crepe-de-chine veil he wore over the lower half of his face. Now he unwrapped it, revealing a bushy heliotrope beard.

Cabell got down, put out his hand and introduced himself and the others. 'I take it we can't be too far from a town?'

The driver pulled off a glove, raised his goggles and put his hand in Cabell's. It was as limp and soft and damp as a calf's tongue. 'Oh, an American!' he said in faultlessly accented English. 'And an Englishwoman! Mother will be absolutely *thrilled*!'

Oh Christ, another one! thought Cabell and shot a wary look at Nikolai. But Nikolai, like the others still in the car, was too surprised at this new encounter even to be listening for intonations in a stranger's voice.

'I am Casper Mamoulian. How splendid to meet you! Where are you heading, pray?'

Cabell tried to look above the heliotrope (*heliotrope!*) beard, just glad that Mamoulian had not yet taken off his driving helmet. 'Well, we were aiming for Tiflis eventually. But what's down the road?'

'Kenchenko – an oasis! You must be our guests – Mother will be delighted!' His tongue was spiked with exclamation points. He looked up the road after the caravan disappearing over the rise. 'But who are your friends?'

'Jews, on their way to Palestine.'

A lip curled within the heliotrope beard. 'One can't invite them, of course. I don't mean to offend, but Mother —' Then he smiled, the smile of a host who had been turning people away from his mother's door all his life. 'There are too many of them, don't you think?'

Cabell felt inclined to tell him to shove his invitation up his heliotrope beard. Then he saw Eden and the children sitting up expectantly, already awash in the luxury promised by a gentleman who owned another Rolls-Royce. Nikolai too, he noticed, was now taking a new interest in Casper Mamoulian. That's two clubs I don't belong to, he thought: the Rolls-Royce owners and the fairies.

'I'm sure Rabbi Aronsky and his friends won't mind if we leave them,' he said. 'How much farther to town?'

'Ten miles. I was just out for a spin, do it every day, clears the head. Why the camels, dear boy?'

'We're out of gasoline,' said Dear Boy, only just managing to stop his nose from wrinkling.

'That all?' Mamoulian reached behind him, hauled up a four-gallon can. 'That should get you to town. I'll go ahead and tell Mother to expect you. She hates it when people just drop in.'

Cabell looked around him. 'Do people drop in very often around here?'

Mamoulian laughed, a fluting in the heliotrope beard; Nikolai sat up like a pointer. 'Oh marvellous! Mother loves dry wit. Well, cheerio! See you soon!'

'One thing —' said Cabell. 'Where do you live?'

'Of course! How silly of me. You can't miss our house. It's on the point above the town, anyone will show you the way. The Villa Heliotrope. You can't miss it. Heliotrope growing all over it —' He smiled and touched his beard. 'One has to amuse oneself.'

He went off down the road in a cloud of dust and further exclamation points and Cabell looked at Eden. 'I'm not sure . . .'

'I don't care what colour his beard is,' said Eden, 'just so long as his villa has a bath in it.'

'He's a gentleman,' said Olga. 'One can see that.'

'He's vulgar,' said Frederick.

Cabell didn't dare ask Nikolai what he thought of the flamboyant Mr Mamoulian. He poured petrol into the tank, unhitched the camels and took them round to the back of the car. Then he opened the Rolls-Royce's bonnet and looked in at the dust that covered the engine. 'Okay, Nick. Start cleaning.'

It took him and Nick half an hour to clean the engine. Fortunately, the dust had not got into the lubrication system; but Cabell was careful to check everything. Then two turns of the starting handle and the engine kicked over as if it had only just been turned off. Cabell decided that, if ever he could afford it, he would join the Rolls-Royce club.

When they caught up with the caravan they left the camels, which had protested loudly at being forced to run at a trot behind the car, with the camel-driver at the rear of the procession. Then they drove on up to the head and pulled up beside Rabbi Aronsky. Cabell explained what had occurred with Mr Mamoulian.

'I hope you don't think we're deserting you, Rabbi.' Nevertheless he did feel a deserter.

'Mr Cabell, we were always going separate ways even when we were travelling the same road. That gentleman – is he all

197

there?' He tapped his temple, but didn't wait for Cabell's opinion on Mamoulian's sanity. 'He pulled up a while ago and told us we are only ten miles from a town called – Kenchenko? We shall pause there a few days and restore ourselves. Some of us need to do that.'

Cabell looked back along the line of people, most of whom had already sunk down beside the road as soon as Aronsky had halted. They looked exhausted, utterly dispirited: their road was proving longer and more desolate than they had expected. But Aronsky was still full of faith and hope and bounce. So long as there was a road he would keep walking towards Palestine.

'Not you, Rabbi. They won't have to start restoring you till you're dead and buried.'

Aronsky moved his umbrella up and down in acknowledgement. 'If I'm to be resurrected, I must see they do a good job. They don't make things any more the way they used to.'

'Happy resurrection, Rabbi.'

They drove on, leaving Aronsky laughing and bouncing as he went back down the caravan, exhorting everyone to their feet again, dust rising out of the black shadow of his umbrella, a small storm that would blow them all the way to the Promised Land.

CHAPTER SIX

'Of course this is the wrong side of the Caspian. I can remember back home in London there was always a right side and a wrong side of the Park for one to live. I never dreamed I'd live on the wrong side of a *sea*. Where did you live in London, my dear?'

'Croydon.'

'Never heard of it, I'm afraid. If anything was more than ten minutes by carriage from Belgrave Square, I never bothered. Unless, of course, one was going to the country.'

'Were you going to the country when you finished up here?' said Cabell.

'Droll, Mr Cabell,' said Lady Vanessa Mamoulian. 'One doesn't expect Americans to be witty. Of course Mr Twain was, but he was a professional, wasn't he? Even when he came to dinner at my father's house in London. A most disagreeable man. I hope you're not disagreeable, Mr Cabell?'

'He's not,' said Eden.

She, Cabell and Lady Vanessa sat in the shade of the grape arbour on the terrace of the Villa Heliotrope. Below them, in a garden where orange and peach trees grew amidst a profusion of heliotrope, where fountains played and peacocks strutted, Casper Mamoulian was taking the children on a conducted tour, a gay uncle who couldn't have been gayer. At the back of the house Nikolai was washing the blue Rolls-Royce, sharing the yard with a servant doing the same chore on the white sister car. The washing was almost done and the two cars gleamed as if ready for a Tsar's progress.

The villa was large, forty rooms, a French provincial château that would not have been out of place in the Loire or the Dordogne but certainly did not fit in Kenchenko. The town lay below the high bluff on which the villa stood, a loose jumble of white-washed stone or mud houses scattered along streets that looked from above like nothing more than dry ravines. Parched-looking vegetable gardens backed the town, patches of green below the bare hills out of which Cabell and the others had driven an hour ago. The town was fronted by a quay along which grew a line of cypresses like tall blackened posts; their shadows lay across the houses and shops behind them like other posts that had fallen before a fire. Half a dozen fishing boats, a small trading steamer with a tall thin smokestack and several smaller boats were moored along the quay; red, brown and grey sails looked like huge sunfish hung out for smoking and fishing nets threw a latticework of shadows. Beyond lay the Caspian, a pale green desert stretching to the horizon, sunlight glinting on it like streaks of mustard-bush.

'More tea?' Lady Vanessa rang a tiny silver bell and a young boy appeared, dressed in a black kaftan and wearing white gloves, and poured tea from the big brass samovar into glass cups with silver holders. 'It's Earl Grey, from Fortnum and Mason. I never could stand the sort of tea they serve here in Russia. The biscuits are from Fortnum's too. One is fortunate, I suppose, to be able to get one's hampers, considering the state of the world. How is England these days, my dear? I haven't been home for – dear me – forty years.'

Eden, bathed and in a fresh dress, watched Lady Vanessa carefully, as if sizing up a new mistress. Lady Vanessa was that sort of hostess: you were there for her pleasure, not your own. She had once been a startling beauty; traces of that beauty still showed behind the lacquered mask that she now showed to the world. Her thick grey hair was streaked with black, like a negative of her head of twenty years ago. Her full-bosomed figure was dressed in peach crepe-de-chine, high to her neck; if time had ravaged her there it didn't show. Her hands were slim, elegant in their movements and remarkably youthful, as if they would fight to her death to beat off the wrinkles and dark spots of age. She had a deep throaty voice, full of authority, that made even a question sound like a command.

'I came to Baku in – good heavens – 1879. I was a romantic young gel – who isn't romantic when young? Even the poor are, I suppose. Are you romantic, my dear? Of course, you must be. You didn't go to St Petersburg just for the job, did you?'

'No.' Eden had never met anyone like Lady Vanessa before, though she had read of aristocratic Englishwomen who went off into the wilds of the world seeking adventure. Lady Vanessa had not mentioned who her father was, but Casper had already boasted that his maternal grandfather was the Marquis of Carmel. He had not bothered to mention his grandfather on his father's side and Eden had guessed he might have been a Roumanian gypsy, a class that would never have been allowed near Belgrave Square. Or Croydon, for that matter.

'I was romantic and looking for romance. I came to Baku *en route* –' she pronounced it with a French accent '– *en route* to Samarkand, to Xanadu. *In Xanadu did Kublai Khan a stately pleasure dome decree* . . . No, truth to tell, I was looking for Kublai Khan himself. Or some facsimile thereof.'

Both Eden and Cabell looked up at the villa towering above them. Lady Vanessa saw their glances and leaned forward to press their hands, Cabell's a little more firmly and longer than Eden's. She was still looking for romance.

'No, no, my dears. This is not Xanadu, but my dear husband tried to make it so. He wasn't Kublai Khan, either. Just a Roumanian oil – mogul, is that the word they use today? Thrillingly handsome, wonderfully virile, marvellously rich. What every young girl dreams of. He kept me happy every hour of the day, in all forty rooms of this house.'

'What happened?' Cabell said.

'Alas, he was a Roumanian. When the Great War broke out he was on business on the other side of the Caspian and the Germans captured him. He escaped and went north to join the Russians, who put him in prison because they thought he was a German spy. The Revolution came and the Bolsheviks wanted to shoot him, but he escaped and went south, only to be captured by the Whites, who also wanted to shoot him. He got away from them and got back to Baku just as the English occupied it. They shot him, by accident they said. Poor man. Roumanians are always expendable.'

'Do you still own your oil holdings over at Baku?'

'Of course. As soon as the English found out whom my husband was married to, they couldn't get across here fast enough. They invited me back to Baku, even tried to persuade me to return to England. But I couldn't go. This house is Alexandru's memorial.'

'Don't you feel – isolated?'

'Sometimes. Alexandru was a marvellous husband, but he had weird ideas of one's exclusiveness. He thought if he built on this side of the Caspian we'd be away from *hoi polloi*. He was right, of course. There is no *hoi polloi* here, but there's no one else, either.'

Cabell wondered if she ever looked down at the town. Perhaps its citizens did not even qualify as *hoi polloi*. In his time in Baku several years ago he had seen the mansions, extravagant vulgarities, of the oil moguls of that region. They had been built in the last two decades of the 19th century, palaces of bad taste; there had been one built of gold plate, another modelled on a house of playing cards. The rich oilmen had had their own harems of beautiful women, their own private armies to guard them; they had thrown their fortunes to the winds, secure in the thought that every day the oil gushers would continue to spout, black mints of money. They had paid their workers in bread and water and mortgaged their futures without knowing or caring. Perhaps they were the ones Lady Vanessa meant as *hoi polloi*. It was a strange sort of snobbery, but he didn't dare ask her about it.

Then her son, resplendent in a pink silk shirt and pale blue pantaloons, making his peacocks look like scrub turkeys, came back up on to the terrace. His hair was dyed to match his beard, Cabell had seen with a shudder, and one's eyes could suffer from strain if he stood too long in front of one.

'Prince Frederick is most impressed with our little abode, Mother.' He stood with one arm round Frederick's shoulders and Cabell saw at once that the boy was uncomfortable. 'We should persuade them to stay longer.'

'We can't do that,' said Cabell hastily. 'We have to be on our way. We're due in Baku in –' he grabbed a day out of the air – 'the day after tomorrow. The children's mother, Princess Gorshkov, will be waiting there for them.'

'Baku? But that's impossible. No boats go across to Baku from here, not since the English occupied it. The captains are afraid the English will impound their boats.'

'Why would they do that?'

'Oh, the English will do *anything*.' Casper looked at his mother and they bared their teeth at each other; bored with their life, they found diversion in minor warfare. 'Is that not so, Mother?'

'Just like the Roumanians,' said his mother, forgetting her sympathy of a moment ago for all Roumanians.

'You see, Mr Cabell? I am the product of both – what worse handicap could a man have? You are so fortunate, Your Highness, to be pure Russian.' He squeezed Frederick's shoulder.

'I know,' said Frederick and disengaged himself from the encircling arm. 'When can we go, Mr Cabell?'

'Oh, I should like to stay,' said Olga. 'This is such a beautiful house! Everyone should have one like it,' she added in a burst of socialism that she didn't recognize.

'I'm afraid you'll have to do some bargaining with one of the ship's masters,' said Casper, looking hurt that his guests were so eager to depart. 'One of the larger boats may take you and your motor car across Karoutai.'

'Where's that?'

'In Daghestan. There are some rather rough roads from there down to Baku or Tiflis. Through some thrillingly dangerous mountains.' He shivered with delight; the heliotrope beard quivered like a peacock's tail in a breeze. 'I drove through there once with Mother. We were almost captured, weren't we, darling?'

'It is dangerous country, Mr Cabell,' said Lady Vanessa.

'What's the alternative? Can we drive down the coast on this side and round the sea to Baku?'

'Dear Mr Cabell —' Casper put a beinged hand on Cabell's arm. He smelled of perfume and Cabell, a decent chap, wanted to shy away. 'There can't be anywhere in the world more inhospitable than the country south of here. No roads, no water – you would just *perish*! You couldn't inflict such torture on these beautiful children. Oh, and on Miss Penfold, of course.'

Eden, feeling she had just managed to get inside the doorway with those worth saving, said, 'The Jews we were with are going that way.'

'They'll never make it,' said Casper, waving a hand that dismissed five hundred Jews. 'Even if one could get through the deserts and down past the Kara-Boga-Gol, one still has to pass through Persia. And you know what those Persians are!'

'Okay then, I'll go down in the morning and talk to some of the captains,' said Cabell. 'But we must be in Baku or Tiflis as soon as possible.'

'We're so selfish, but we must delay them, mustn't we, Mother? Let's put on a feast tonight that will entice them to stay, shall we? I'll arrange it now!' He floated gaily away and the terrace seemed a little duller with his going.

'You must forgive Casper his enthusiasms,' said Lady Vanessa. 'He has to work so hard to keep them fired up, poor boy. I sometimes think we should desert the memory of Alexandru and retire to the French Riviera.'

'Oh, I shall see you there!' cried Olga. 'I am retiring there, too.'

'Dear child,' said Lady Vanessa, and the lacquered mask cracked in a smile that would have got an answering grin from a leopard. 'I can hardly wait for our reunion.'

Later Cabell went for a stroll through the big house. Eden had insisted that the children have a nap before dinner and Lady Vanessa had retired to her room. Occasionally Cabell could hear Casper's fluting voice, coming and going like a bird's call on a rising and falling breeze, but for the most part the villa was silent.

He wandered through the corridors, opening a door here and there and looking in on rooms shrouded with dust-sheets, tombs of dead hopes, of dreams of visitors who had never arrived. But despite the depressing atmosphere of the shrouds the extravagant luxury of the whole place showed through; and Lady Vanessa had someone who was evidently a proud housekeeper. The marble floors shone like mottled ice; the silk-clad walls, though faded, were not frayed; the silk and velvet drapes were not dusty and neglected. Even the chandeliers in the corridors and larger rooms gleamed like fresh encrustations of stalactites. He found himself being seduced, dreamed again of being rich, wondered how a house such as this would go in Bloomington, Illinois.

He opened a door on a library. It was a room with a twenty-foot-high ceiling, shelves of books covering three of the walls. There was a deep shelf containing large leather folders; he pulled out one and opened it on copies of *The Times*. A page fell open and he saw the date on the yellowed sheet: January 23, 1901. Queen Victoria had died the previous day and *The Times* mourned her passing. It was the end of an era and Cabell wondered if Lady Vanessa, when she had left England in 1879, had been trying to escape from the morality of that age. The tragedy was, of course, that Lady Vanessa no longer belonged to any time at all: Kublai Khan and Xanadu were gone forever.

He shoved the folder back into its place on the shelf, turned and found Eden standing beside him. He looked her up and down, at the pale blue silk kaftan and the kid-soled silk slippers she wore.

'I wondered how you crept up on me like that.' He nodded down at her slippers. Then he looked directly into her face. 'You look beautiful.'

'Thank you.' She had taken trouble with her hair, piling it high on her head like a golden burnous. In her room she had found a silver box full of cosmetics; Lady Vanessa thought of everything for those guests who had never come. Eden had never used cosmetics before, but this evening, tempted by the lushness of her surroundings, she had painted her face, though with restraint. She had left off her corset and, going all the way, even her chemise. She was heady with her nakedness, even though the kaftan covered her from neck to ankle. 'Lady Vanessa sent me this outfit. She said she likes her guests to dress for dinner.'

'Holy Toledo — I wonder what Casper will send me?' They went out of the library into the corridor.

'I don't think he will want you dressed up — he won't want any competition. What are we going to do about him? He has his eye on Freddie.'

'I know. I don't think he'd get too far – Freddie would yell his head off. But even so . . . I'm afraid for Nikolai, too.'

'Somehow I've never minded Nikolai being like he is. But Casper – he could be *evil*. He doesn't appear to have anything to occupy him. There's, I don't know, something – *decadent* about this house. Even Lady Vanessa. I passed her room on the way here and a servant was going in with a hookah. One of those hubble-bubble pipes they use for smoking hashish. I read about them in the *Encyclopaedia Britannica*.'

'That's a den of iniquity, that *Britannica*.'

'Don't joke, Matt —'

He took her in his arms, felt all that nakedness under the kaftan and eased his hips away from her, glad of the baggy trousers he still wore. 'I know it's no joke. I'll get us away from here as soon as I can. In the meantime . . .'

'In the meantime —' She gently moved out of his arms, aware of what was happening in the baggy trousers. She was afraid, of herself more than of him. 'One could be tempted in a place like this. I mean to be decadent.'

'Let's stay. To hell with the kids.'

'Be serious, please. If there were just you and I . . . But there's not.'

He nodded, looked at her again, gave himself a mental cold shower. 'Just don't look too tempting. A feller's human, after all.'

'I understand that's what all the – the fellers say. Have been since Adam first saw Eve.'

He grinned, took her arm and walked down the corridor with her. 'It's not a bad approach. You get about seventy per cent success.'

'Till we've delivered the children to their mother, you can count on a hundred per cent failure. Watch it!' As his hand slid down and patted her behind.

'The Garden of Eden,' he said. 'I'll look forward to it.'

Dinner was to be at 8·30 – 'When it is a little cooler,' Lady Vanessa had said. Just after 8 o'clock Cabell, dressed in his best and only suit, wearing a tie, clean shirt and fresh Arrow collar, was sitting out on the terrace, shaded from the westering sun by a large medlar tree. He always found the shade of a tree very soothing and it was one of his ambitions that when and wherever he settled down there would be trees beneath which he might sit to contemplate the passing of a day. He sipped his scotch-and-soda, brought to him by a servant, and thought again of the pleasures of being rich. But he had already decided that the Mamoulians, though they had money, were not rich. Not as he would want to be.

A bell rang loudly and demandingly within the house and he half-rose, thinking it was the call to dinner. But then Lady Vanessa herself came out on to the terrace and a moment later a servant followed and said something to her.

'Mr Cabell, there appears to be someone at the door for you. A Rabbi Aronsky.'

'I'll go see him —'

'No.' She waved him back. 'Let's have him out here. I've never had a Jew in my house, y'know. I suppose you think that's extraordinary?'

'I guess so.' But come to think of it, he could not remember a Jew's ever having been in the Cabell home on Prairie Avenue.

'My grandfather used to entertain Disraeli, but only because he was Prime Minister. I must see that my prejudices do not show.'

'I'd appreciate that, Lady Vanessa,' said Cabell. 'Rabbi Aronsky is really a splendid chap, as I think you English would say.'

'Some English might,' said Lady Vanessa, but she managed to op en the lacquer in a smile as the servant came back with Aronsky. 'Welcome to the Villa Heliotrope, dear Rabbi. Oh my, you are dirty and dusty, aren't you? Never mind, do sit here. The cushions can always be washed.'

Aronsky, umbrella loosely furled, leaned on it and crossed

one foot over the other. He had taken off his straw hat and was fanning himself with it. Cabell had expected him to be misogynistically surly or so overcome with his surroundings that he would be fawningly meek. Instead of which he was jaunty, ready to do battle with this English aristocrat looking down her long beautiful nose at him even though he was a good six inches taller than she.

'Madame, please don't let me put you out. Or dirty your cushions. I am only here to see my good American friend, Mr Cabell. I have a warning for him.'

'A warning?' Lady Vanessa, arranging her dress of royal blue silk as she sat down, posturing herself as if she were about to be painted, paused and looked up. 'How quaint! A warning against what? Or whom?'

Aronsky looked at Cabell, who said resignedly, 'Go ahead, Rabbi. You've pulled the pin out of your bomb.'

'The dwarf, Major Pemenov, has been down in the town. We arrived here an hour ago and when I went to make some purchases at a stall in the bazaar, the owner asked me if the dwarf had been travelling with us. It seems that he got into town this morning, bought a gun and some supplies and disappeared again. He is probably out there in the hills somewhere.'

'A dwarf? A dwarf who is a major? The officer class isn't what it used to be. Is he, too, a friend of yours, Mr Cabell?'

'No.' *He wouldn't be a friend of yours, either, if he were here.* 'He tried to kill me.'

Then Casper came out on to the terrace, resplendent in white silk: blouse, pantaloons, a silk tasselled cord round his waist, white silk slippers. A gold cross on a gold chain hung down across his wide plump chest. He looked like a fallen bishop.

He recognized Aronsky and looked with raised eyebrows at his mother, who explained the reason for the Rabbi's visit. 'A dwarf assassin! How quaintly thrilling!'

Jesus, thought Cabell, I'll assassinate this nancy before I leave here. But Casper had caught his look of angry disapproval and was smiling mockingly and yet disarmingly at him. 'You don't approve of my phrases, do you, Mr Cabell? But isn't that how you expect chaps like me to talk?

Of course you do. You'd be disappointed if I didn't. Well, what are we going to do about our tiny would-be murderer? Do we go looking for him?'

'Not before dinner,' said Lady Vanessa. 'Rabbi, I hope you will stay to eat with us. Casper, take the Rabbi inside so that he can clean up. Lend him one of your blouses.'

'I should go back to my people,' said Aronsky, but temptation was working on him.

'Nonsense,' said Casper, who seemed to have overcome his distaste for Jews; and also, to Cabell's suddenly keen eye, seemed less limp-wristed. The son-of-a-bitch is looking for excitement, he thought. If Pemenov comes tumbling over the wall, he'll be invited to dinner, too. 'Shepherds come and go, but flocks go on forever. I should put that to music on my lute . . . .'

He took an only half-reluctant Aronsky into the house and Lady Vanessa gestured for Cabell to sit beside her on the marble bench.

'You don't have to worry while you are here at the villa, Mr Cabell. You may not have noticed them, but we have a dozen armed guards about the place, very fierce Turkomen. They are on duty twenty-four hours a day. There is one now.'

Cabell saw the man, dressed in what looked to be a uniform, rifle slung over his shoulder, stroll by the far end of the garden below. 'Have you needed them?'

'Not lately. When my husband and I first came here, the local people thought we were fair game. They were always trying to get into the villa to steal things. I believe the guards killed twelve of them in our first year. Then the message got through that we were peaceful people and meant the locals no harm. Since then we have had a sort of armed friendship with the townspeople. They don't exactly love us, but they accept us. The Russians are like every other nation of people – they love to have someone to look up to. People are natural serfs, if the truth be known. Not all, of course. Not you, Mr Cabell.'

'You flatter me.'

'An old woman's coquetry, than which there is nothing more foolish. Except an old man's lechery. Don't worry, Mr

Cabell —' She put a hand on his, a girl's hand, warm and affectionate. 'The juices still run in me, but I'd never think of trying to seduce you away from your dear Miss Penfold. You are a very fortunate young man. She looks – *moist*, I think is the word. Is she a good lover?'

Holy Toledo! 'We only met a week ago.'

'A whole seven days – and nights! My dear Mr Cabell, you Americans are so slow. I knew dear Alexandru only two days when he was in my arms and everywhere else he was welcome. Ah, here comes your dear young lady – my, how beautiful she looks! – and the dear, dear children. Children are a handicap to lovers, aren't they?' she added in a whisper. 'Shall we go in to dinner? We have a chef who once worked at La Tour d'Argent in Paris – Casper enticed him out here. He is a hashish addict, unfortunately, but if we can keep him away from his hubble-bubble . . .'

Eden had seen dining-rooms like this in St Petersburg, but Cabell, a more plebeian diner, had never been in such a room before. The late Mr Mamoulian must have been expecting to hold State banquets; the room would have held a hundred diners without any discomfort to any of them. But if there had once been a table large enough to hold so many people, it was no longer in evidence. A table with only seven places stood in the middle of the room, floating on the largest Bokhara rug Cabell and Eden had ever seen. The huge chandelier was unlit and the room was illuminated with tall candles in ornate silver candlesticks.

'So much more flattering for us women, my dear,' Lady Vanessa told Eden. 'I think we shall start and not wait for Casper and Rabbi Aronsky. Jean-Pierre gets very upset if his main dish is not served just at the right moment. Caviar? We have our own boat go out to catch the sturgeon.'

'It is very good caviar,' said Frederick politely after a few mouthfuls. He was dressed in his best suit and a spotless Eton collar which Eden had had one of the servants press.

'It is the only way to start a dinner,' said Olga, equally polite. She was in her best dress, also freshly pressed and looked like one of those unreal children in a Gainsborough painting. Except that she was real and even more beautiful.

'Juvenile gourmets,' said Lady Vanessa. 'What higher

praise could one get?'

Casper and Aronsky arrived at the table at the same time as the fish course. Aronsky had had a quick bath and washed his hair and beard; his hair was slicked down and he looked younger and almost handsome. He wore one of Casper's more exotic outfits, a pale yellow silk blouse and green silk trousers. He surprised Cabell by not looking uncomfortable.

'Thank the Lord my flock can't see me now. What's that?' He eyed the silver caviar dish as a servant removed it.

'Caviar, Rabbi,' said his hostess. 'I shall see you are given some to take with you. You can have caviar sandwiches tomorrow. In the meantime do please get on with your fish. Jean-Pierre hates to be kept waiting.'

'Your cook runs your house?' Aronsky showed his surprise at what went on in the higher echelons.

'We all have our masters,' said Casper, tucking into the *coulibiac de saumon.*

'Mother runs our house,' said Olga.

'Dear child,' said Casper's mother. 'Don't choke on a bone.'

Aronsky, a man with an ear for nuances, looked at Lady Vanessa with new interest. 'I see that you and I share certain attitudes, madame.'

'Only just, Rabbi. I don't think you would have any love for women.'

'Oh, do you prefer men, Rabbi?' Casper lifted his head, surprised at where one found soul-mates these days.

'Please, Casper, not in front of the children,' said his mother. 'You'll give sin a bad name.'

'You believe in sin?' said Aronsky.

'Of course. One has to believe in it to heighten one's pleasure in being immoral.'

The dinner went on and Eden sat in a half-daze. The conversation floated back and forth light as ping-pong balls; servants in black uniforms and white gloves drifted in from the far shores of the huge room with successive courses; the food was superb, far better than any she had ever tasted before. Yet Rabbi Aronsky had come here to the villa to warn them that somewhere in the dark outside Major Pemenov was still waiting to kill them. She tried to focus her attention, looked across the table at him enjoying himself as he took huge spoonfuls of the *soufflé aux fraises*.

She could not help the spite in her voice as she said, 'What are your flock dining on tonight, Rabbi?'

Aronsky paused, a laden spoon halfway to his mouth. 'I do have a conscience, Miss Penfold, if that is what is worrying you. At this very moment it is stuck right between my taste buds.'

'Your taste buds seem to be winning.'

She was aware that everyone at the table had stopped eating to watch the small conflict and she was sorry now that she had spoken. But she was worried, on edge, her own taste buds just dry freckles on her tongue: her only taste was sour and she wished it wasn't. She felt unsafe in this house and not just because of the threat from Pemenov.

Aronsky put down his spoon, pushed his plate away from him. All his adult life he had been torn in his tastes, at least in food: his orthodox tongue constantly prayed for forgiveness for its unorthodox appetite. 'You win, Miss Penfold. I have been trying to tell myself that this is the last supper every condemned man is entitled to. You should know, I *am* condemned. My flock is very likely to carve up its shepherd tomorrow when it learns this is the end of our road. Mr Mamoulian has told me what lies south of here. I can't lead my people on into country like that.'

'Why will they condemn you?' said Cabell.

'Because I was the one who persuaded them to leave Sulobelsk. I told them about the Promised Land. *Next year in Jerusalem* . . . It will have a very hollow ring to it when I tell them in the morning that this is as far as we can go.'

'Can't you buy some boats and go down to Baku?' said Frederick.

Aronsky gave him a look that should have curdled the soufflé in the boy's stomach and Cabell said, 'Freddie, I think it's time you and Olga went to bed. We must be up early.'

He looked at Eden and she caught the hint, glad of the escape from the atmosphere she had created. She stood up at once, thanked Lady Vanessa for the excellent dinner and took the children out of the room almost on the run.

Aronsky said, 'That boy will never understand what it is like to be without money.'

'You may be wrong there, Rabbi,' said Cabell. 'Some day he may be just as poor as you are. When the rich lose their money, they always *feel* poorer than anyone else.'

'How perceptive of you,' said Casper. 'We must be careful, Mother, that we never lose our money.'

'What happens if you cannot move on?' said Lady Vanessa.

Aronsky shrugged. 'We go back or we stay here. It will be a tragedy either way.' He belched, grimaced as if everything he had eaten had suddenly turned sour.

'Are your people tailors or money-lenders?' Lady Vanessa's knowledge of Jewish trades was limited.

Despite his depression Aronsky smiled. 'They are farmers, madame. In a small way – vegetable growers. We had to be to survive. We were driven out of the towns as long ago as the 1880's. Sulobelsk was our own village, we created it. But General Denikin's soldiers took it away from us. Perhaps things will be better when the Revolution succeeds, but I have no faith any more.'

'I shall talk to my son,' Lady Vanessa rose from the table. 'Come up again in the morning.'

Half an hour later Aronsky, changed back into his own clothes, no longer an exotic figure, went back to join his caravan on the edge of town. Cabell went to the villa's gates with him. 'Thanks for the warning about Pemenov, Rabbi.'

'You should be safe enough here.' A guard stood just inside the gates, moonlight gleaming on the oiled barrel of his rifle. 'But he'll be patient and wait till you leave. You should have shot him when you had him prisoner.'

'Maybe.'

'You can't kill in cold blood, is that it? Sometimes one has to, to survive. But you have your problems here, too, haven't you? That pederast has his eye on that dreadful young prince. Children should be whipped for their own good, but not seduced.'

'I won't let him get near Freddie. Good night, Rabbi. I hope your flock don't whip you.'

'They'll do it. In cold blood.'

Cabell closed the gates on Aronsky, said good night to the guard and went round the back of the villa to the servants' quarters. Lady Vanessa, by totally ignoring Nikolai, had made it perfectly obvious where his place was: with the servants. Cabell found him sleeping in the back of the Rolls-Royce and woke him.

He told him about the warning on Pemenov. 'Keep an eye out, Nick.'

'The guns are here in the car with me, sir. And His Highness's sword. But will you please come quickly if I call? I don't think I could use either the guns or the sword.'

Another one who can't kill, in either cold or hot blood. 'I'll come running, Nick. Just see he doesn't hurt you.'

He strolled back round the house, went out on to the terrace for a final look at the sea. It lay there smooth and inviting under the moon.

'Your escape route, Mr Cabell?'

He turned. Casper sat on a bench in the shadows, smoking a hookah. *Goddam, he's the hashish addict,* Cabell thought. *Not the chef or Lady Vanessa.*

'I sit here every night and look at it myself. With my other means of escape —' He patted the hookah. He was silent a moment, then he looked up at Cabell. 'I'm not homosexual, Mr Cabell – that isn't my other escape or diversion, whatever you like to call it. My whole life is just all theatrics, something to keep me amused. I envy you, Mr Cabell. At least you have a profession. Boredom is not a career.'

'Why don't you leave then?'

'Mother refuses to. She dreams of another Kublai Khan like my father. She thinks England and Europe will never recover from the late war. She has started looking again for what she came here for forty years ago. I want to go to Paris. But I could never leave her. We are worth millions, Mr Cabell, but you don't know how poor in spirit I am.'

Cabell grunted politely but found it hard to feel any sympathy. The rich had their woes, just like the poor; but they could suffer them in more comfort. Silk rustled as Casper stroked his own thigh in self-sympathy.

'Mother is always looking for something to divert her. But what is there here? I have my little interests. I star-gaze, for

214

instance up there.' He nodded upwards. At the front of the villa a single square tower, almost Norman in its design, rose up against the night sky. Had Alexandru Mamoulian built it as a watch-tower, so that he might be warned of the approach of *hoi polloi* from across the sea? 'I lose myself amongst millions of stars, Mr Cabell, like a miser amongst his diamonds and emeralds. I go blind with their beauty.'

He sucked on his pipe and Cabell wondered how much and how often he was blinded by the hashish. 'It sounds interesting.'

'It is, Mr Cabell. But it is not enough — the days, somehow, are longer than the nights. I am bored and so is Mother. That's the only reason she has dreamed up her latest little scheme. She wants to set the Jews up as farmers, be their patroness. Lady Bountiful of the Cabbage Patch.' He sucked once more on the pipe. 'All it will grow will be trouble. The people in the town don't want any outsiders, especially Jews.'

Cabell thought of the other future that faced Aronsky and the people of Sulobelsk. 'Do you want the Jews to go back, maybe to be massacred?'

'If they stay here they could be massacred. And us too, for helping them.'

Cabell hid his disgust. 'If you're so rich, you could buy them boats to take them down to Baku. Or somewhere on the Persian shore. Spend a few bucks and get rid of them that way. Isn't that what money is for?'

'I have no money, Mr Cabell. My mother controls it all.' He seemed oblivious of the contempt in Cabell's voice; or else he was ignoring it. He smoked his pipe, drifting into his own diversion. 'I shall be the supreme hedonist when she dies, just live to enjoy myself. I'll be everything the Bolsheviks hate, so I shall have to leave Russia.'

'You'd do better to ask your mother for some money now and leave as soon as you can.'

'Ah no, I couldn't do that. My one saving grace is that, despite myself, I love my mother. On her off days she is a dear, dear lady. It is only when she is well and strong, feeling *juicy* as she calls it, that she is so hard to bear.'

'Well, if she wants to help Rabbi Aronsky and his people,

let her. They deserve some help after what they've been through.'

Casper smiled, the smile of someone lost in a dream: the hashish was having its effect. 'Why don't you stay a little longer, Mr Cabell? Perhaps you and I could go hunting your dwarf. It is a long time since I have been on a shooting picnic, not since my dear father died.'

Cabell was tempted to say, *He's all yours, Mamoulian*. But even Pemenov didn't deserve to be shot in cold blood by a man like this.

[3]

Pemenov slept peacefully, like a child, in the hills outside Kenchenko. He had ridden up the coast a few miles, found a lonely spot and, for the first time in his life, had bathed in a sea. At first the immense expanse of water frightened him and he ventured in only up to his knees. Then he waded in a little further, became exhilarated by the buoyancy of the water. Small and naked, he began to bounce up and down, showering himself, gurgling and laughing with delight. He rolled around in the shallows, then, greatly daring, waded out a little further and ducked his head beneath the surface. He came up spluttering, shook his big head as a dog might, laughed aloud, then ducked his head again. At last he came out, his bare feet crunching on the thick salt that encrusted the rocky beach, and stood with hands on hips, an infant Canute, and laughed at his triumph over the sea.

He put his dirty clothes back on, because he had no change of clothing, and rode on down along a narrow path to Kenchenko. People looked at him curiously, stopped in the narrow streets to stare at him; some of the adults and most of the children laughed at him, but he ignored them. He had no gun to shoot them down.

He bought food for himself, enough for three or four days, and a bag of mouldy oats for his horses. He let the horses drink at a trough on the quay, then he went to a town pump to fill his water-skins. The women at the pump, fascinated by his size and his unexpectedly charming smile,

216

stood aside to let him get to the pump. His belly and those of his horses attended to, it was time to buy the essential supplies.

He found a stall in the town bazaar where one could buy everything needed for extermination. Rat-traps, bird-snares, even a giant-toothed bear-trap, though the stall owner could not explain to him who would be trapping bears in this desolate area. There was also a variety of weapons: daggers of every size and description, swords, lances, pistols and rifles. He bought a Lee-Enfield ·303 rifle and a Mauser pistol and ammunition for both; he had no preference for the country of manufacture, the English and the Germans could both help him kill the American. He also bought another *kindjal*, a silver-handled dagger that he bought as much for its beauty as for its killing potential. When he at last rode out of town he had spent all his remaining money; from now on his only wealth would be the two gold bars in his saddle-bags. But he did not think that far ahead.

He had learned that a motor car had arrived in the town this morning and that its occupants were staying with the Englishwoman and her son who lived in the big house over-looking the town. He had also learned that the English-woman had armed men who guarded her house and that anyone who tried to enter the house or even its garden would be shot. He was content to wait till the American came down from the house into the town, as he surely must within the next day or two.

Camped on a high bald hill behind the town, sheltered from the burning sun by overhangs of rocks carved by erosion in the limestone, he saw the arrival of the Jews' caravan. He sat in his shallow cave, his two horses tethered in another, larger cave, and watched the distant villa slowly turn to a black silhouette against the setting sun. He wondered what it would be like to live in such a house, be surrounded by beautiful women who would love him because he was rich and normal-sized except for his member, which would be the biggest in the world. He dreamed just like other, ordinary men.

In the early morning, before the day got too hot, Cabell went down into the town and on to the quay. Men sat at rough tables slurping tea from glasses, watched him with eyes the colour of tea; there was nothing to do in Kenchenko but drown in the beverage. Women, who had work to do, peered at him above their veils as he passed them; he smiled at them but all he got in reply was the backs of their heads as they turned away. The children and dogs, all making the same noise, ran after him. His foreignness irritated him like a rash and suddenly, once again, he wanted to be home in America.

He wasted no time in choosing a ship: there was only one large enough to take the Rolls-Royce. The filthy tramp steamer, with its one tall funnel that looked ready to collapse and a hull that was ravaged with great eczema rashes of rust, had some spare space on its after deck and a winch that appeared strong enough to lift the car off the quay. The superstructure was as chipped and rusty as the hull and the decks looked as if the only time they were washed was when a high sea would swamp them.

The captain of this floating slum looked as if he, too, left his bath to the same chance waves. He was a Persian from Barfurush, but Persian only because he had been born there. He was a mixture of all the nationalities that had passed through that part of the world, a dirty mess of blood that had left him with no concern for anyone but himself. He had a wall-eye and the other eye was blind to principle, honesty or morals. He stank of onions and cheap wine and he regarded a fair price as an economic joke.

'A thousand dollars, American money. It is a dangerous voyage.'

'I'm told you make the trip twice a month.'

'It is still dangerous. The ship could go to the bottom at any moment.'

'Then what about insurance?'

'Another thousand dollars.'

'But what if we all go to the bottom, you included?'

'Then you won't miss the money.' Captain Zabari had a smile like that of a jackal which had just come on a herd of dead antelope. Even the wall-eye seemed to gleam with gluttony. 'And the money will be here in the bank in Kenchenko, waiting for me in case I should be fortunate enough to be rescued.'

'I'll bet you fifty dollars I know who has the only lifebelt on board.'

'I couldn't take your money,' said Zabari, but it obviously hurt him to say it.

After an hour's haggling the price was set at five hundred dollars for transport of the car and its five passengers. 'You don't want insurance, Mr Cabell?'

'We'll take the risk,' said Cabell, gazing around him at the risk; it seemed to him that even in an hour the ship had sunk lower in the water, though nothing was being loaded on to it. 'I'll put the car on board this afternoon and we want to sail before sunset.'

'I name the sailing time.'

'No, I name it. You don't get paid till we're five miles out at sea. That way you better make sure your ship stays afloat, otherwise your money will never get to the bank.'

'I have read of your American outlaw Jesse James. Are you related?'

'Only by marriage.'

Back on the quay Cabell found a secluded spot, took off his money belt and counted his cash. He had only five hundred and thirty-two dollars; they would be on a thrift budget once they landed on the other side. He took another look at the near-wreck moored beside the quay and once more knocked on the Church's door: he said a prayer for a safe trip. Then he walked out of town and along the coast road, past the straggly vegetable gardens, thin orange groves and rows of gnarled olive trees, to where the Jews were camped on a salt-encrusted beach. Behind them limestone cliffs reared up in fantasy shapes: needle-pointed spires, ice-cream cathedrals that had melted and then suddenly were frozen again as rock, castles pock-marked as if they were made of Swiss cheese. The Jews had found shelter in the numerous caves and under the overhangs and down at the water's edge the children were paddling, some of them gazing with awe at the vast blue sea that ran away to the very edge of the world.

Lady Vanessa was already there, dressed in white this morning: white crepe-de-chine frock, white hat and veil, white parasol: she reflected the morning sunlight like a vision, albeit a tarnished one. The Rolls-Royce, only a thin dust taking the sheen from its bright whiteness, stood in the background, a driver behind the wheel and two armed guards standing beside it.

Aronsky, sheltered beneath his own black umbrella, smiled broadly at Cabell as the latter approached. 'The good Lady Vanessa is going to be our patroness. We are going to stay here in Kenchenko and turn it into a garden city.'

Cabell cocked an eye at the surrounding cliffs and hills, bald of any promise. 'I don't think even Moses had your faith in miracles.'

'We can but try,' said Lady Vanessa. 'It is only a matter of finding more water.'

'Of course,' said Cabell, but didn't look at Aronsky. 'Who knows, the Alph, the sacred river, might run right beneath our feet.'

'There is nothing else for us.' Aronsky knew nothing of Xanadu and sacred rivers; but he could sense Cabell's scepticism. 'Of course I do have to whip up some enthusiasm amongst my people. I'm afraid at the moment they're blaming me for everything. They are starting to talk of Sulobelsk as if it had been the Promised Land.'

'You may have some trouble in talking them into remaining here.'

'My dear papa used to say, never over-estimate the will of the people,' said Lady Vanessa. 'Parliament would never have given them the vote if there had been any danger of that.'

'Marvellous,' said Aronsky admiringly. 'Aristocrats have such a sublime view of the world.'

'Just like clerics,' said Lady Vanessa, never without her ammunition. 'Confer with your people today, then come to see me this evening and tell me what you will require. You may have to go over to Karoutai and then down to Baku to buy pumps and well-digging machines, but that can be done.'

'The delights of money,' said Aronsky and jiggled his umbrella above him. 'Madame, we must pray together that the Bolsheviks never bring their Revolution this far south.'

'If they do, Rabbi, I'm afraid your patroness will be leaving you. May I drive you back to the villa, Mr Cabell?'

Cabell told Aronsky he would be leaving that evening and the Rabbi said, 'I shall come to say goodbye, my friend. In the meantime we shall keep an eye out for your dwarf.'

Cabell looked around at the bright glare of hills and felt his flesh creep: Pemenov could be anywhere in those folds and crevices, a rifle aimed directly at his target. 'I think he'll wait for nightfall. And we'll be gone by then.'

He rode back in the Rolls-Royce with Lady Vanessa, the two of them in the rear seat and a guard riding on the running-board on either side.

'Do me a favour, Lady Vanessa. Don't lose your enthusiasm for being the Jews' patroness. See them through.'

'You speak as if you have no faith in me, Mr Cabell. Is that gentlemanly?'

'Probably not. But I don't think you appreciate what is happening to a lot of people in the world today.'

'I may have a sublime view of the world, as Rabbi Aronsky says, but I am not stupid, Mr Cabell. I realize the Jews have no other chance but this, and even this is a very slim one. I don't even know if we shall find enough water to support another five hundred people. If we don't then it will cause tremendous trouble with the townspeople already here. But Kenchenko is dying on its feet – like me.' She didn't look at him for contradiction; she was too intelligent for that sort of flattery. 'We both need reviving and I think Rabbi Aronsky may be the man to do it.'

Cabell looked at her, one eyebrow raised. 'I hadn't thought of that. You as the wife of a rabbi.'

'Oh, I could never marry him, Mr Cabell. But I think we could be very good company for each other. All he needs is a good bath, some new clothes and his beard trimmed.'

Cabell grinned, shook his head. 'I don't think you are the fate that the Rabbi ever saw for himself.'

'A Circassian poet once wrote that the Promised Land was a woman. I shall just have to see that the Rabbi changes his concept.'

[5]

In the afternoon Cabell drove the shining blue Rolls-Royce down to the quay and with it the trailer. The latter was packed with food, water and spare cans of petrol supplied by Lady Vanessa. He took the Winchester with him, but left Pemenov's guns and the double-barrelled shotgun with Nikolai, who accepted them as if they were threats to his personal safety rather than weapons with which to defend Eden, Frederick and Olga.

When Cabell had gone Eden said, 'There's nothing to be afraid of, Nikolai. You won't have to use the guns. Mr Cabell has left us up here at the villa because we'll be safer with the guards round us than if we were on the quay or the ship. He'll come back for us as soon as the ship is ready to sail.'

The villa was quiet. Lady Vanessa had retired to her room and Casper had not emerged from his all day. Four guards were on duty, but they were out of sight, hidden in the shade of trees in each of the four corners of the garden. Frederick, his sword beside him, and Olga were playing backgammon on the terrace and Eden had come round to the servants' yard to reassure Nikolai that he would not be called upon to fire any of the guns at anyone.

'I shall be glad to be gone from here, Miss Eden.'

'There is still a long way to go.' But once they were on the other side of the Caspian she hoped that they would make it down to Tiflis in a day, two days at the most. The continuing presence of Pemenov was chafing at her nerves and she had begun to wish, if only half-heartedly, that he would come out into the open so that he might be killed. Though she was not sure who amongst them would kill him. Only Frederick seemed bloodthirsty enough to do the deed and she knew that she would stop *him*. 'But we'll be safe once the ship sails.'

She went back to the front terrace and Lady Vanessa came

out smelling strongly of eau-de-cologne and sherry. Eden had noticed last night that the older woman had prepared herself for dinner with several large sherries.

'I couldn't nap. My mind is too alive with ideas for Rabbi Aronsky and his dear Jews. Where's Casper? Is he still sulking in his room? He doesn't have enough to occupy him, that's his trouble. Oh, we're playing backgammon, are we, children? Don't rattle the dice too loudly — I have a slight headache.'

She looked nervous and flushed and Eden wondered if she had had some altercation with her son. She kept moving restlessly amongst the cushions in her big cane chair. She had none of the arrogant composure she had shown yesterday and Eden wondered how often she went to the sherry decanter when she and Casper were alone.

'Casper doesn't understand,' she said, not looking at Eden, arranging the cushions again about herself. 'He is jealous, of course.'

Eden assumed that Aronsky and the Jews were a bone of contention between the Mamoulians, but she didn't dare comment. Frederick won the backgammon game, stood up and picked up his sword.

'I'm going to the bathroom.'

'Do you always go armed to the lavatory?' said Lady Vanessa.

Frederick looked at Eden, who gave him an almost imperceptible shake of her head. The boy had been ill-at-ease from the moment of their arrival yesterday, aware that Lady Vanessa considered him and Olga as nuisances to be kept in the background. Olga, self-contained, was unperturbed, but he had always been sensitive to his reception by grown-ups. Deprived of the company of boys of his own age since the family had fled St Petersburg, he so desperately wanted to be grown-up.

He went off into the house, his sword over his shoulder, and Eden said, 'He wants to be a soldier like his father.'

'Thank God Casper isn't warlike. He's like his dear father, who always believed in negotiation. He would have made a marvellous Foreign Minister for one of the weak-kneed nations. What are you looking at, child?'

'Your frock,' said Olga. 'You have the most beautiful clothes, just like Mother.'

Lady Vanessa had changed from this morning's outfit, was in pale green chiffon. She smiled, softened for a moment by Olga's flattery. 'You have a very discerning eye, child. If ever you go into exile, do keep up appearances. It is most important. Every year M. Worth's establishment in Paris sends me a complete wardrobe.'

'One must always look one's best,' said Olga, 'especially when one is beautiful.'

'You think I'm still beautiful, child?'

'Of course,' said Olga, displaying a diplomacy Eden hadn't seen in her before.

'You're beautiful, too, now that I look at you,' said Lady Vanessa.

'I know,' said Olga, never denying the obvious. 'But thank you for the compliment.'

Eden got up and moved away, leaving the two beauties to their mutual admiration of each other. She wondered if Lady Vanessa had been like Olga as a child; and then, with a pang, wondered if Olga would be a lonely old woman like Lady Vanessa. She went down into the garden and walked to a narrow iron-grille gate in the high wall; from there she could see down across the path below it to the town and the quay. The Rolls-Royce was in mid-air, being winched up on to the deck of the tramp steamer. She looked for Cabell but couldn't distinguish him amongst the distant figures on the quay or ship. She looked for him not just for reassurance that he was *there* but because she now found she missed him when he was not close by. She was in love, much more so (was she ashamed to admit it?) than she had been with Igor Dulenko.

She strolled on through the garden, past the peacocks, which looked sombre as they stood, tails folded, in the shade of a row of cypresses. A guard, lounging in the same shade, straightened up and smiled tentatively as she passed him. Up on the terrace she could hear the murmur of Olga's and Lady Vanessa's voices; once Olga laughed and Eden guessed that Lady Vanessa had overcome her aversion to at least one child. She passed the tall iron gates that were the main entrance, where the road ended that led up from the town; another guard lounged in the shade of the wall. She completed her tour of the garden, stopping once to smell some roses; they were dried out by the heat, the petals like dead flesh between her fingers. But they reminded her of home, of the roses her father had grown in the back garden in Croydon. Suddenly she was homesick, for safety if for nothing else.

She went back up on to the terrace. Lady Vanessa and Olga were sipping lemonade and eating Fortnum and Mason's biscuits. But Frederick had not come back from the bathroom. 'Where's Freddie?'

Olga waved an airy hand. 'Probably practising with his sword in front of a looking-glass. I caught him doing that this morning in his room.'

Eden sat down, took a glass of lemonade and a biscuit. But she kept looking towards the house, waiting for Frederick to reappear. She glanced up along the row of windows on the upper floor, hoping she might catch a glimpse of him at one of them. But the shutters of most of the windows were closed. She even looked up at the tower, wondering if he had gone up there for a last look around before they departed; whether consciously or unconsciously, he had been looking around him a lot these past few days, as if, deep in his heart, he had begun to feel he was leaving Russia. But the shutters on the tower were also closed.

At last she could no longer contain herself and she got up and went into the house. She went up to Frederick's room, but he wasn't there. She went through the corridors, calling his name, but there was no answer. Then she went down to the rear of the villa and found Nikolai.

'I haven't seen His Highness,' said Nikolai and instantly looked troubled and nervous, as if he, more than Eden, was responsible for Frederick. 'We must find him.'

'That's what I'm trying to do!' Worry made her sound irritable. 'Come with me.'

'Upstairs? But I mustn't – the English lady would never allow someone like me upstairs in her house!'

'I don't care a damn about Lady Vanessa – we must find Frederick!'

She led the way back into the house, hurried through all the corridors on the ground floor, opening doors on rooms draped with the ghostly outlines of the dust-shrouds; but there was no sign of Frederick. She went into the big kitchen, found the French chef sound asleep on a big table amidst the ingredients for tonight's dinner, his head pillowed on a bunch of spinach; but still there was no sign of Frederick. Then, panic hurrying her, she raced upstairs, followed by Nikolai, who kept glancing back over his shoulder as if expecting to be hailed by Lady Vanessa for his trespassing. They went down the long corridors, Eden not bothering to knock but throwing the doors open on the dozens of bedrooms and ante-rooms. Then she came to the two big rooms at the front of the villa, one on either side of the main corridor.

The room on the left, she knew, was Lady Vanessa's; that on the right was Casper's. She hesitated, then flung open the door to Lady Vanessa's room. She had no idea what she had expected to find: perhaps Frederick, out of spite, doing something malicious to get his own back for being ignored. It was a room from the *Arabian Nights*. A silk-canopied bed, crimson-and-cream-striped like a desert sheik's tent in a musical comedy; heavy silk drapes that hung like frozen falls of cream; a crimson carpet in which one's feet would sink to the ankle as in a pool of blood; and every wall a mirror that reflected the room *ad infinitum* and would reflect every movement in it. It was a room made for love and love-making and Eden blushed that she should be seeing it with Nikolai standing beside her in the doorway. She closed the door, abruptly feeling sorry for Lady Vanessa for whom all that love was over.

Eden turned to the door on the opposite side of the corridor, hesitated, then knocked. There was no answer and she knocked again. Where was Casper if he wasn't in his room? She drew a breath, ready for apologies, and opened the door. Casper's room was also exotic. Black-and-crimson silk drapes; mirrored walls; the carpet a thick black swamp in which one might sink out of sight; and a hookah, like some antique douche, standing on a low table beside the bed. There was no love in this room, only a crying need for it.

'Miss Eden —' Nikolai pointed.

In one corner of the room a spiral staircase led up to an open trapdoor in the mirrored ceiling. At the foot of the stairs lay Frederick's sword. Even as she hurried across to the stairs Eden heard the voices in the room above, though she could not distinguish what was being said. Then she heard Frederick cry out, a mixture of terror and pain.

Grabbing up the sword, not knowing what she was going to do with it, lifting her skirts, stumbling in her haste, she clambered up the curl of stairs, thrust her head through the trapdoor.

The tower room was about twenty feet square, a stark contrast to the lush décor of the bedroom below it. Its only furniture was a desk and a chair; the largest telescope Eden had ever seen, with a tilted chair slung beneath it; and two huge globes, one terrestrial, the other celestial. The windows were shuttered, but a shutter in the roof, immediately above the telescope, was drawn back to let in the sunlight. Frederick, arms bound, crouched in one corner of the room while Casper, clad in a crimson silk dressing gown, tried to pull him towards the telescope.

'Look at the stars, boy! Ignore the Sun – the stars are always there despite it!'

'Get away from him!' Eden clambered up into the room. 'You – you vile beast!'

Casper spun round. His eyes were clouded, his face slack; he seemed to squeeze his features together from the inside, as if trying to focus on Eden. Then suddenly he let out a shout, half-laugh, half-roar of rage, and rushed at her. She fell back, dropping the sword in her haste. She tripped on her skirt as she went halfway down, stumbled and just managed to slip aside as Casper lunged at her. She heard Frederick cry out and she raced round the desk to be near him. Casper came at her again. As he passed the desk he grabbed up a long silver knife; he was crazed now, out of his mind. Eden backed away, pushing Frederick; they stumbled into a globe and it went down with a crash; the world cracked into fragments. The heavens followed, toppling over with the same loud crash. Eden was gabbling, hardly knowing what she was saying, just pleading with the mad

Casper for her own and Frederick's life. But he was deaf to any plea, an assassin in a red silk dressing gown.

Eden did not see Nikolai come up from the spiral staircase; terrified, she had forgotten him. Then suddenly there he was, the sword picked up from the floor and held with both hands; he stood for a moment as if afraid of what he was about to do. He didn't look menacing, just pathetic, the most unwilling killer. Then he let out his own roar of anger, high-pitched, hysterical. He rushed at Casper and the latter turned round, the dressing gown swirling open once more, this time to expose the big fat belly to the sword as it went in. Casper let out a cry of animal pain and fell backwards, crashing to the floor amongst the fragments of his worlds. Nikolai stood, both hands still holding the sword, staring not at the dead Casper but at the bloodstained blade. Then his knees buckled and he collapsed, going down with a faint moan.

Eden held Frederick to her, both of them paralysed for the moment by horror. Then she frantically tore at the ropes that bound the boy, pulling them off him, spinning him round so that he could not stare at the dead Casper, who lay, fully exposed now, like a great white seal, blood running from his belly down between his outstretched legs into the crimson pool of the dressing gown. The climactic obscene note was the heliotrope beard and hair, a dash of comic horror that turned the corpse into a sick joke.

Frederick struggled to turn round, unable to take his eyes off the dead man. Eden slapped his face. He blinked, burst into tears and she held him in her arms.

'Freddie – please get hold of yourself. We have to get out of here. Help me bring Nikolai round.'

Nikolai stirred as Eden dropped on her knees beside him. She patted his cheeks, revived him, got him to his feet and held him while he sought strength in his legs. He looked down at Casper and almost fainted again; but she held him up, turned him away from the horrible sight. Forced to take charge, she forgot for the moment her own horror at what had occurred. She picked up the sword, wiped the blood from it with the edge of the dressing gown, somehow managing to keep her eyes averted from the ugly fat corpse.

Then she pushed the still groggy Nikolai and the still horrified Frederick down the staircase ahead of her. She picked up the scabbard, thrust the sword into it and held it out to Frederick.

'Both of you – keep quiet! You understand? We go downstairs and we say goodbye to Lady Vanessa, then we're all going down to meet Mr Cabell and we're going to board the ship. Try and forget – for a while, anyway – what happened up there in that room and be natural.'

Nikolai looked as if he would never be natural again for the rest of his life. But Frederick was recovering, trying to be a brave prince again. He put the sword gingerly on his shoulder, as if he expected blood to run out of the scabbard, and told Eden not to worry, he and Nikolai would be natural.

They went downstairs, stiff-legged with control, not looking at all natural. But Lady Vanessa did not notice. She and Olga met them at the door that led to the terrace.

'Olga and I are going upstairs to look at my wardrobe. I have five rooms full of clothes, everything I have ever worn since I came here forty years ago. My dear husband so admired the way I dressed, I had to keep everything. Sometimes he would remember the way I looked on a particular occasion ten, twenty years before and he would ask me to wear the same frock. Olga wants to see them all. Dear child, she's so like me. Wrapped up in trivia.'

Eden suddenly wanted to weep for the older woman who had to live so much in the past to continue living at all. And now, with her son dead, murdered, in the tower room, she would be even lonelier.

'Have you seen Casper? Have you been with him, young man?'

'No-o.' Frederick coughed, cleared his throat. 'No, ma'am. I – I've been with Nikolai.'

For the first time Lady Vanessa seemed to notice that a yard servant, someone else's menial help, had just come out of a private door of her house. 'Don't take your servants through my house again, young man. I thought you would know better than that.'

'No, ma'am.'

Nikolai cowered behind Eden and Frederick in the doorway. He was ashen-faced and dumb; but Lady Vanessa mistook the reason for his appearance. 'Even your servant seems to know you've done the wrong thing. Now would the three of you allow me to go through my own doorway?'

Eden stood her ground. From here she could see two of the guards strolling in the garden; two others would be on duty somewhere on the other side of the villa; eight others were off duty, sleeping or doing whatever they did when not guarding Lady Vanessa and her son. They would all come running, guns at the ready, as soon as Lady Vanessa or one of the house servants discovered the body in the tower room.

'Miss Penfold – *do you mind?*'

Then Eden saw the crown of the wide-brimmed cowboy's hat down in the garden and a moment later Cabell, Winchester slung over his shoulder, came up the steps on to the terrace. Almost rudely she pushed past Lady Vanessa and ran towards him. 'Get us out of here at once! Don't ask me why – *just get us out!*'

He pulled up sharply, puzzled by the fierceness in her whisper. But in the past week he had learned to recognize signs: something had gone wrong, she was desperately afraid. 'Sure, we'll go right now.'

They went back to Lady Vanessa and the others and Cabell said, 'I'm afraid we have to go immediately. The captain is impatient to get away.'

'Oh.' Disappointment seemed to age Lady Vanessa. She looked down at Olga and put her hand on the child's head. 'I am sorry, young woman. Come back another time and I'll show you all my trivia.'

'Do we really have to go now?' Olga looked at Cabell. 'Tell the captain he has to wait.'

'No,' said Frederick and took his sister's hand, gripping it so hard that she winced. 'We have to go if Mr Cabell says so.'

'I must get Casper then,' said Lady Vanessa and was inside the door and gone before Eden could stop her.

'Quick – we must go!' Eden grabbed Olga's other hand.

'For crissake, what's going on?'

'Mr Mamoulian is dead,' Frederick said over his shoulder as Eden dragged Olga between them along the terrace.

'Nikolai killed him!'

Cabell looked at Nikolai, who was ready to collapse again. 'What happened? No, never mind – tell me down on the boat. Come on, start running. *Nick – for crissake, get moving!*'

Eden and the children were already down the steps, crossing the garden and heading for the grille gate in the wall. A guard stepped out of the shade of a tree, barred their path; then he looked over Eden's shoulder and smiled as Cabell and Nikolai came running down into the garden. He said something in Turkic, stepped back and swung open the gate and waved them through. They went out in a rush and a moment later were running, sliding, almost falling down the steep path that led to the town immediately below.

'Is the ship ready to sail?' Eden gasped.

'Steam's up. I'll hold this at the captain's head if I have to.' Cabell jerked at the strap of his Winchester. 'Jesus – where are the other guns?'

Nikolai whimpered, pulled up as if he were going to turn round and go back for the guns he had been minding. But Cabell clutched his arm and pushed him on ahead and they continued down the path. Once Olga fell, but Eden lifted her up and pulled her on, unmindful of Olga's complaint that she had skinned her knee. At last they came down into an alley that ran on into the town. Cabell led the way, hurrying them along past the stone and mud houses, through the narrow streets where children stopped playing to stare at them and women peered at them above the visors of their veils. Then they heard the three shots up at the villa.

Eden looked back and up, saw the gate swing open in the villa's wall and the guards, six of them, come streaming out and plunging down the path.

'We'll never make it!'

But Cabell was cajoling, cursing, hurrying them along. They ran out of a narrow street, came on to the quay and raced for the ship. As they did so people began to come like a slow dark tide out of the streets and alleys opening on to the quay; they shouted and laughed and cheered the runners, like a crowd at the finish of a marathon. Rabbi Aronsky, the race judge, stood under his umbrella at the foot of the narrow gangplank that led up to the ship's deck.

'Everyone wanted to come to say goodbye. I told them you were the one who persuaded Lady Vanessa to be our benefactor. They no longer want to go back to Sulobelsk. They've settled for less than the Promised Land.'

Cabell had pushed Eden and the others up the gangplank. He looked back the way they had come: the guards would be coming into sight at any moment. Then he yelled up at Captain Zabari who stood leaning over the side of the bridge immediately above. 'We go now, Captain – *now!* No questions – get the ship moving!'

Captain Zabari, whether because he knew where his biggest fare in years was coming from or because he was ready to sail anyway, did not hesitate. He had had to leave other ports in a hurry; he was well practised in quick departures. He yelled orders and seamen appeared at each end of the ship, ready to cast off.

Then beyond the crowd of Jews, now filling the quay, Cabell saw the guards. 'Tell your people to close up – don't let those guards through!'

'But why —?' Then Aronsky saw the urgency in Cabell's face, abruptly turned and shouted to his people. They all stared at him for a moment, then they looked back over their shoulders. The guards were halfway through the crowd; but on the narrow quay they had to struggle to make progress. Suddenly, yet almost imperceptibly, the crowd congealed, closing in on the guards. No one grasped the armed men; they were just imprisoned by a press of bodies. They shouted, cursed, waved their rifles above their heads; but the crowd pressed in round them and in a moment they could not even lower their arms. A rifle went off, but the shot went high and wild. The crowd let out an angry shout and there were no more shots. The rifles suddenly disappeared into the dark pool of people.

'Casper's dead, Rabbi! Nikolai killed him – I don't know why – but he's dead! I'm sorry to leave you to all this. Good luck with Lady Vanessa. Play your cards right and maybe she'll still be your patroness. And thanks for all your help!'

Cabell ran up the gangplank. A seaman stood there and he began winching up the gangplank as soon as the American put foot on deck. Cabell stood at the rail and looked down at Aronsky standing on the edge of the quay, tall and dark under the black hemisphere of his umbrella.

'Don't worry, Mr Cabell – we'll survive! We always have!'

The ship eased slowly out from the quay. The crowd raised its arms and a shout of farewell welled from five hundred throats; somewhere under the waving arms and the goodbye cry were the guards, silent and helpless. Cabell stared out at the dark mass of Jews. Dear Christ, he prayed, help them.

'Goodbye, Rabbi.' But his voice was just a croak in his dry, thick throat.

Then he looked up towards the Villa Heliotrope. Its white walls were as bright as ice against the sun; it was impossible to see anything clearly against the glare of it. But he imagined he saw someone standing on the terrace, a pale green blur against the brightness behind it. He felt as sad for the woman up there as for Aronsky and the Jews down on the quay. He could not bring himself to believe that Xanadu and the Promised Land really existed.

The ship moved slowly out past the breakwater. Cabell took one last look at the quay, then went along past the tiny saloon to where Eden, Frederick, Olga and Nikolai stood staring back at the Rolls-Royce and the trailer tied securely in the middle of the aft deck.

'Let's hope it gets us to Tiflis without any more trouble,' said Eden.

'Let's go up forward,' said Cabell. 'It's better not to look back. You can tell me what happened.'

Without a word they followed him back along the narrow section of deck beside the saloon and the cabins. They came to some steps that led down into the well of the forward deck. They pulled up sharply.

'Holy Jesus!'

Up forward, sheltered behind the high prow of the ship, were two horses. Sitting on a hatch-cover, a rifle across his knees, was Major Pemenov.

CHAPTER SEVEN

The s.s. *Perfumed Garden* steamed into the setting sun across a golden sea, the only blot in the whole vast beautiful scene. The two enemies sat on opposite sides of the forward hatch, each with his rifle across his lap. Up on the narrow passenger deck Eden, the two children and Nikolai watched fearfully, not knowing what they would do if Cabell and Pemenov should open fire on each other. Eden was certain that Captain Zabari, a self-concerned neutral if ever she had seen one, would not interfere. The crew, a mongrel breed of villains, would probably applaud the battle and then loot the body of the loser.

'You've got a nerve,' said Cabell. 'When did you come aboard?'

'As soon as I saw you leave the ship to go up to the Englishwoman's house. The captain was happy to have me aboard – at a price. I gave him a gold bar and he practically carried my horses on board himself.'

'I could tell him about your other gold bar. He'd cut your throat for it.'

'If he comes within ten feet of me, I'll shoot him.'

'I'm surprised you haven't shot me.'

'I'll do that after we land in Karoutai, Mr Cabell. If we have a peaceful trip across, Captain Zabari and his crew won't trouble us.'

'Aren't you afraid I'll kill you?'

'Of course not, Mr Cabell. That's why I'm here, travelling with you. You're not a cold-blooded killer. If you were, you'd have shot me when you had me as your prisoner. I feel perfectly safe with you, Mr Cabell.'

'I might just get *hot*-blooded.'

Pemenov smiled. 'I'll do nothing to raise your temperature.'

'Why are you so intent on revenge? Because of General Bronevich's death? I told you that was an accident. He was trying to rape Miss Penfold and there was a fight. Wouldn't you do the same, I mean try to stop a man who was trying to rape a woman?'

'No,' said Pemenov reasonably.

'I shouldn't have asked. Do you see all women as your mother? Wholesale rape is your idea of revenge on her?'

'Go back to your mistress and your snotty little friends, Mr Cabell.' Pemenov's good humour abruptly ran out; any mention of his mother provoked him. 'Enjoy the trip, because you'll be dead very soon after you land in Karoutai.'

Cabell got up, careful not to put his back to the dwarf. 'This ship does ten knots maximum. That means a thirty-six hours' voyage, Major. You think you can stay awake all that time?'

'Try me, Mr Cabell.' It was a smiling challenge.

Cabell went back along the deck, glancing over his shoulder every few paces, and climbed up the steps to the narrow passenger deck below the bridge. He sat down beside Eden and the others in the paper-thin canvas chairs and stared down towards the dwarf still sitting on the forward hatch. Pemenov looked up, saw them all watching him and gave a friendly wave. Olga gave a princessly wave in return.

'Don't do that!' Eden said.

'I was only being polite,' said Olga. 'You are always telling us to be well-mannered.'

'Not to scum,' said Frederick, whose education in scum had quickened. 'I still think we should have executed him. It is the Russian way.'

'For crissake, Freddie —' Then Cabell threw up his hands, shrugged, sank lower in his chair. He suddenly felt weary. 'There's been enough killing. Think of Nick's feelings.'

Frederick looked considerately at Nikolai. 'I'm sorry. You were very brave, Nikolai. My father will reward you handsomely for what you did.'

Nikolai, still recovering from the shock of what he had done, waved a limp hand. He had killed for love, something he would have thought a contradiction in terms if it had ever occurred to him to think about it at all. He had recognized, as soon as he had met him, what sort of man Casper was and he had been both fascinated and repelled. He wanted to love

235

and be loved, but not by someone like Casper. He loved Frederick as he would never love anyone else, but he would never seduce him. Not till the boy was old enough to know what love was about.

'How did you get up there in the tower, Freddie?' said Cabell.

'Mr Mamoulian invited me up. He said he had a telescope strong enough for me to see the other side of the Caspian Sea. Of course, I was stupid. One can't see over the horizon.'

True, thought Cabell, who had spent his life trying to see beyond it. He blamed himself for what had happened: he should have taken Frederick with him down to the quay. Yet in the two hours the ship had been at sea, as if with Kenchenko and the Villa Heliotrope fading into the evening haze memory would also fade, it seemed that the boy had put the whole horrible experience behind him. He appeared fully recovered, able to talk of executions if not of unpremeditated killings. Christ, thought Cabell, what sort of kid am I going to hand over to his father when we meet up?

'I think we should take turns in keeping watch on Major Pemenov.'

'Freddie, I don't think the Major is going to cause us any trouble while we're at sea.' Despite his shock and unease at finding the dwarf on board, Cabell felt that what he said was true. But it rankled that Pemenov thought he was chicken-hearted. Even Nikolai, the chicken-hearted Cossack, had killed when it had had to be done. 'If we keep our cabins locked at night, we should be okay.'

'Have you seen the cabins?' said Eden. 'Two pokey little cupboards. We'll have to sleep standing up. And they're crawling with cockroaches.'

'Ugh,' said Olga. 'I wonder what's for dinner?'

They ate in the tiny saloon with Captain Zabari. The meal was like something out of the Dark Ages compared to dinner last night: stewed goat, watery cabbage, black bread and cheese that looked ready to walk off the table any moment.

'I like to eat well,' said Captain Zabari, washing down the muck with a gulp of palate-rasping wine from a cracked cup. 'Major Pemenov does not know what he's missing. He's out there on deck – he brought his own food with him. Fruit and yoghurt. What sort of meal is that? No wonder he's only half-grown.'

'I thought for five hundred dollars we'd eat better than this,' said Cabell.

Zabari was unoffended. 'Where do you think you are? On the *Titanic?*'

'The comparison has occurred to me,' said Cabell, thinking how close they might be at any moment to sinking.

The *Perfumed Garden* wheezed, grunted and creaked its way through the night and the next day. Fortunately the sea stayed calm; Cabell was certain that it could not have weathered even the mildest storm. Pemenov did not move from the forward deck except to get up and stretch his legs, occasionally going up to the prow of the ship and standing there, looking like a figurehead sitting down. Cabell and the others remained amidship, keeping together, believing in safety in numbers.

Cabell talked consolingly to Nikolai. The latter's depression increased in proportion to the distance he put between himself and what he had done. 'Nick, try and put it out of your mind. You did it for the best of reasons.'

'How can one kill for the best of reasons, Mr Cabell?' But Nikolai looked at him warily.

Cabell was just as careful. 'Nick, I know how you feel towards His Highness.'

Nikolai was silent for a while, then he said quietly, 'I didn't think a man like you would understand.'

'When I first met you, I wouldn't have,' Cabell admitted. 'But it's hopeless for you, you know that.'

'I shall always be his servant.'

I guess so, thought Cabell, but that wasn't what I meant. 'I hope that will be enough, Nick.'

'It will be, Mr Cabell,' said Nikolai, who couldn't believe that the American might think he would dream of more. But he felt better for Cabell's talking to him. 'Thank you, Mr Cabell. You're a kind man.'

On the second morning, just after sunrise, the ship steamed into the little harbour of Karoutai. On deck early, Cabell saw the Caucasian ranges take shape in the rising sun. He had not expected to be driving through them as they soon would be, but he felt a thrill at the prospect. He had never come this far north when he had been working down around Baku, but he had been fascinated by what he had heard of the Caucasus. The name meant *white mountains*; even now, in late summer, he could see tattered shawls of snow on the distant, highest peaks. A hundred armies were lost or buried there atop the mountains or down in the narrow, steep-sided valleys: invaders who had been conquered as much by the mountains as by the people who lived there. Medes and Persians, Greeks and Mongols, Arabs and Turkomen had passed through, leaving remnants of their armies behind; if one listened to the wind, it was said, a hundred tongues could be heard. He suddenly wished again that he were alone, that he might linger and listen to the wind and, just as intriguing, the silences of the Caucasus.

Karoutai looked as if it were about to be pushed into the sea by the weight of turbulent land behind it; the mountains seemed to tumble down on to it. An offshore breeze blew steadily and a dozen fishing boats tacked in ahead of the ship, their decks silvery with fish. Cabell, Winchester slung on his shoulder, went forward to talk to the enemy.

'If you are going to try to kill me, Major, just be sure of your aim. I don't want Miss Penfold or any of the others hurt, you understand?'

'I am almost coming to like you, Mr Cabell. Somehow I never expected an American to be fatalistic about his own death. General Bronevich told me that my mother, even when she committed suicide, died complaining.'

'I'm sorry to hear that,' said Cabell, trying to improve his image even more in Pemenov's eyes. Christ Almighty, he thought, what a coward I am! Why can't I kill him and get it over and done with?

Pemenov brushed aside the sympathy. 'I shall be waiting for you.'

'I'll be ashore before you, Major. I've arranged with Captain Zabari for first use of the winch to get our automobile off the ship.'

But when the *Perfumed Garden* berthed at the narrow quay in front of the town, Pemenov was the first ashore. Cabell had overlooked how sure-footed a steppe horse could be.

Somehow Pemenov got his horses up the steps on to the passenger deck and from there led them off the ship down the gangplank. He waved to Cabell and the others, smiling cheekily like a schoolboy skipping class, and rode off along the quay and into the streets of Karoutai. It was another twenty minutes before the Rolls-Royce was deposited on the cobbled quay.

'Good luck!' Captain Zabari, a bad smell on the fresh morning air, wanted to embrace them all; they fled down the gangplank before they were overcome. 'You are my friends! I delivered you safely, didn't I? Come back soon! Bring American dollars!'

Karoutai, a fishing and port town, was early astir. The word got around that some grand foreigners in a grand motor car had just arrived; people flowed on to the quay like a landslide from the hills behind the town. These were different from the broad-faced people Cabell had seen on the other side of the Caspian; they were still in Russia, but this was another country altogether. The women all pulled black veils across their faces as soon as they saw Cabell, but the men stared frankly at the newcomers, especially at Eden. They were taller and slimmer than the workmen she had known in St Petersburg and Verkburg: darkly handsome, proud, they looked at the grand foreigners as equals. These people, she felt, had never been serfs, not even in the most tyrannical days of the Tsars.

A tall man pushed his way through the throng. He wore a dark blue uniform and a black lamb's-wool cap. He said in lilting, accented Russian, 'I am Lieutenant Taoush, master of the port, chief of police and commander of the garrison. Whom do I have the pleasure of arresting?'

'Arresting? Why should we be arrested? We are just peaceful travellers on our way to Tiflis.' Cabell introduced himself and the others.

'A dwarf who said his name was Major Pemenov told us you were thieves.'

'Where is he now?'

'He has ridden out of town. He said you should be inspected.'

'He wants you to hold us till he's out of town and found

somewhere to ambush us. He is planning to kill me.'

The crowd swayed closer; crackling murmurs ran through it like a wind through bracken. Lieutenant Taoush ran a finger up and down his long nose and cocked a quizzical eyebrow. He was a young, good-looking man, too young for bureaucratic cynicism: he would be a failure in the new Russia as he had been in the old. He held his job now because no one knew how the Revolution was going to go. He couldn't bring himself to believe what the American was telling him. Yet these people *looked* honest, they certainly didn't look like thieves, not with such a grand motor car. Unless they had stolen *that*.

'Are you a Bolshevik, Mr Cabell?'

'No, we're neutral.'

'We are not,' said Frederick. 'I am for the Tsar!'

'Kid,' said Cabell wearily, 'why don't you carry a banner? Shut up! While I'm leader, we're all neutral. And that includes you.'

'We are not for the Tsar here in Daghestan,' said Lieutenant Taoush and behind him the crowd shook its head as if another wind had passed through it. 'Nor for the Bolsheviks.'

'Then we're on the same side,' said Cabell. 'In the middle.'

'If you are neutral, why should Major Pemenov want to kill you?'

'Pure spite,' said Eden.

'You would be safer, then, if I arrested you.'

Cabell had had enough of being held captive. 'No, we must go on. We'll take another road down to Tiflis.'

'There is only one road, through the mountains. You really should allow me to arrest you.' Lieutenant Taoush was far too polite; he would never make a good official.

'Thank you for the offer, Lieutenant, but we'll push on.' Cabell looked up beyond the town to the mountains now lost in dark rain clouds. 'We shall keep our eyes peeled for the dwarf.'

'There are others to be looked for,' said Taoush. 'The Murids are moving again.'

'The Murids? Who are they?'

'Moslems,' said Frederick, the little fount of information. 'They fought the Tsar years ago in the Murid Wars. We beat them.'

The crowd stirred again and Cabell decided it was time to leave, Pemenov or Murids along the road notwithstanding. He had the feeling that Frederick might provoke another Murid War at any moment. 'Everyone into the car. Goodbye, Lieutenant, and thanks for the offer of jail.'

As they got into the Rolls-Royce an elderly man moved close to Frederick, helped him up into the car. 'Where did you get your sword, boy?'

'It was a present,' said Frederick.

'It was bought in a market town on the other side,' said Cabell. 'Why?'

'It is a beautiful sword,' said the man. 'May it take care of you.'

As they drove off the quay, the crowd parting to let them through, Cabell looked back at Frederick. 'Did you take your sword out of its scabbard?'

'No, sir.'

'Strange . . . Why should he say it was a beautiful sword then? All he would have seen was the hilt.'

Frederick examined the silver hilt, an intricate design that looked like interwoven S's. He had been examining it ever since it had been given to him, admiring it, polishing it with his handkerchief. He drew it half-out of the scabbard.

'Perhaps he was a silversmith or a sword-maker. Father told me the best sword-makers in all Russia came from the Caucasus. He once met a khan who had a sword that had been used in the Crusader days. Look at this —'

Cabell did not dare stop the car for fear of making them an easier target for Pemenov: the dwarf was certain to be somewhere up this road and not too far. But Eden took the sword and examined it.

'See?' said Frederick. 'All those decorations on the blade – what do they mean? I shall have them cleaned off when I get to Tiflis. A sword's blade should shine.'

The sword had been in Frederick's constant possession. Eden, not interested in weapons, indeed half-afraid of them, had not looked at it, not even when she had cleaned it of

Casper Mamoulian's blood. Now she looked at it carefully.

'Whoever decorated it was no craftsman. The paint is quite rough, too thick.'

'Do the decorations mean anything?' Cabell said.

'I don't think so. Just flowers and birds – funny things to have on a sword to kill someone with.' Then she looked over her shoulder. 'Sorry, Nikolai. I shouldn't keep reminding you —'

'He's all right,' said Frederick, patting Nikolai's knee. 'What he did was a brave thing. He's a true Cossack.'

The true Cossack looked as if he wanted to deny the truth of that; but he just smiled wanly at Eden. 'Let us hope it is not used again.'

Frederick was about to say something, then changed his mind. Thank God, said Eden to herself, looking back at him, he's learning a little sensitivity. She put the sword back in its scabbard and handed it back to him.

'We'll have it cleaned and shined up for you when we get to Tiflis.'

The town was now behind them; it had dropped away suddenly, chopped off by a turn of the road round a steep bluff. Cabell was alert, eyes almost somersaulting in his head as he tried to look in a dozen different directions at once. The road wound through the mountains, every turn presenting an ideal place for an ambush. The only thing to do was to drive as fast as possible, always praying that the car would stay on the narrow, stony road. The Virgin Mary was invited back once again to the company. If he remained in constant danger, Cabell figured, he might yet become a good Catholic again.

Up ahead the sky was almost black, veils of rain obscured the mountain tops. Thunder rolled down the narrow gorges like the sound of the mountains themselves tumbling; twisted lances of lightning stabbed at unseen targets, ear-shattering cracks echoing and re-echoing till the car seemed to be driving through waves of trembling air. Then the rain hit the car at the moment the first bullet hit the running-board just below where Cabell sat.

The rain came down as if a sluice-gate had been opened just above the Rolls-Royce. The hood was up and the water poured down off it, obscuring the view on either side. Cabell slowed, unsure of the way ahead; but he knew he had to keep going. He poked his head out of the side of the car, offering himself as a better target for Pemenov's aim; but it was that or drive the car off the road into the rock and gullies on either side. The rain beat against his face like soft leather lashes; he slitted his eyes against it, tried to breathe without drowning his lungs. He kept the Rolls-Royce moving, driving slowly into a torrent through which he could see no more than ten or fifteen yards ahead. Bullets were smacking into the road behind him, but he was unaware of them. Up the hillside, behind a barricade of rocks, feet braced to prevent him being washed away by the water cascading down behind him, Pemenov was savagely firing his rifle, cursing loudly in anger and frustration. He could see nothing below him and he fired wildly into the grey swirl of rain while the thunder hammered at him and the lightning bolts danced like the Devil's balls off the peaks above him.

Then just as abruptly as it had started the rain stopped. The Rolls-Royce rolled out on to a clear stretch of road; the road glistened and shone like a path of broken glass, but it was visible. Cabell had to make an effort to relax his grip on the steering-wheel; his hands and wrists and forearms fought his own will. Gradually the tension went out of him and he relaxed, sat back and peered ahead through the rain-streaked windshield. It was not going to be easy driving on this slippery muddy, stony road; but at least they were safe again from Pemenov. The dwarf was lost behind them somewhere round the last turn in the road. Cabell hoped the son-of-a-bitch had drowned in the downpour.

The outer side of everyone was wet through where the rain had poured in on them; only Olga, sitting between Frederick and Nikolai in the back seat, had escaped. Eden looked back at her and Olga smiled.

'I didn't get wet. I think I must live a charmed life.'

Even the rain spares her. But then Eden looked at Cabell and said, 'Did a bullet hit the car just as the rain started?'

Cabell had to admire her. She was squeezing water from her blouse, looking as unconcerned as if she had asked if nothing more lethal than a pebble had bounced up against the running-board. 'Yes. Just the one.'

'Then it must have been Major Pemenov. That means we have left him behind.' She looked up at the mountains ahead, now appearing out of the lifting clouds. 'I think we should try and drive right through to Tiflis without stopping.'

'Whatever you say, ma'am.' Cabell smiled at her, thinking of Tiflis and what he had in mind once they were there and he had her to himself.

She read the look in his eye. 'Watch it!'

The road began to climb and several times the Rolls-Royce skidded on the treacherous surface. The sun came out, blazing down, drawing steam from the rocks; they drove through a thin vapour that made everyone in the car sweat profusely. The road was twisting, narrow and lonely; they passed two ox-carts, whose drivers looked up startled at the machine bearing down on them; but that was the only traffic they encountered. The peaks towered on all sides of the car; they drove through narrow gorge after gorge, driving into the very heart of the mountains; the sun was shut out and they drove through an early-morning dusk. Then abruptly the road came out into the open; it ran as a ledge along the side of a sheer cliff. A rock wall towered five hundred feet above the car; the outer edge of the road ended sharply above a drop just as deep to a river far below. The roar of the river, a tumbling cascade of white water, came up as low thunder out of the narrow gorge. On the opposite side of the gorge, built into the steep side of a towering peak, was a large village, its flat-roofed rock houses brilliantly lit by the sun.

'How remote it looks,' said Eden.

'I shouldn't like to live there,' said Olga. 'One would never have any visitors calling. It would be worse than Verkburg was.'

'Would it be a Murid village?' Nikolai said. 'My grandfather used to tell me how he fought against them for the Tsar Alexander. Savages, he called them.'

'I can't see the road going up there,' said Cabell, 'so we shan't call on them. We're not stopping even for a pee till we're out of these mountains.'

'You're vulgar,' said Olga. 'But he's nice, too, isn't he, Miss Eden?'

'He needs working on,' said Eden.

'Any time you say,' said Cabell, and the look was in his eye again.

He took the Rolls-Royce carefully down the road, keeping to the inner side. Twice he had to brake sharply, the car skidding dangerously across the narrow track, as rocks plummeted down in their path from the cliff above. He came to a hairpin bend where the road switched back below itself; he made everyone get out and guide him while he manoeuvred the big car round the narrow angle. Then Eden and the others got back into the car and it was a straight, if steep crawl to the bottom of the gorge.

The road flattened out beside the roaring cataract, turned sharply on to a narrow bridge. On the other side of the bridge were fifty or sixty horsemen, dark as the rocks that surrounded them, a single black banner whipping back and forth like a staked bird at the tip of their leader's lance.

[2]

For a moment the confrontation was motionless, silent in the roar of the torrent beneath the narrow wooden bridge. A wind came down the gorge and Eden felt a sudden chill. In the back seat Nikolai and the children huddled together, as if they were all at once cold. It was gloomy here at the bottom of the gorge and it struck Eden that the sunlight probably never reached this dank depth.

The leader of the horsemen rode forward across the bridge and pulled up immediately in front of the Rolls-Royce. He inspected the car with the contemptuous but apprehensive eye of a man who hated progress; he pulled his horse's head back, as if insisting that it should show some pride. Then he inspected the car's occupants with the same contemptuous, but not apprehensive look. Cabell decided to remain silent, not trusting his voice to any argument against the thunder coming from under the bridge and rolling up the steep cliffs of the gorge. He smiled, raised the cowboy hat, tried to look like a friendly American; but the man on horseback was unimpressed. He turned his horse and jerked a thumb for Cabell to follow in the car.

Cabell drove across the bridge, the horsemen on the opposite side opening up to let him through. Then half of them closed in behind him while the other half rode on ahead with their leader out in front. They were all dressed the same: long, full-skirted tunics drawn in tightly at the waist, baggy trousers tucked into soft black leather boots, lambskin caps. Across the chest of each were double rows of silver cartridge-cases; rifles were slung across their backs and sabres hung in scabbards from their waists. They looked war like and yet somehow anachronistic, like figures out of old paintings Cabell remembered seeing in Baku.

The horses cantered along unhurriedly and Cabell kept the Rolls-Royce in low gear, his foot close to the brake: the horsemen immediately in front of him had a tendency to keep slowing down to look back at him and the others. He did not want to create an incident by running down a couple of horses.

Once they were round a bend in the road the roar of the wild river was abruptly cut off. Eden said, 'Are we going to be taken prisoner again?'

'I don't think they're aiming to give us an escort down to Tiflis. That leader of theirs didn't look too friendly.'

'They are Murids,' said Frederick. 'I can tell by their banners. They hate Christians.'

Eden glanced at Cabell. 'Are you suddenly a lapsed Catholic again?'

He grinned, but he knew that her attempt at humour was as forced as his own smile. 'Watch it.'

'Did you see the whip their leader had? What were those things skewered on the thong?'

'They all have them.' He nodded at the horsemen immediately in front: whips hung from their wrists, the thongs threaded through what looked to be a bunch of dried apricots. 'How strong is your stomach?'

'It used to be weak. But I think I could take anything now. Well, almost . . .'

'They're human ears.' He waited, but she did no more than pale a little.

'It is an old Murid custom,' said Frederick from the back seat, stomach strong as only those of some young boys can be. Jesus, thought Cabell, what did I know at his age? Maybe the pitching record of Christy Mathewson, but nothing about the scalp record of Geronimo. 'It is how they keep count of the enemies they have killed. They cut off the right ear or the right hand.'

'Ugh!' said Olga, right hand over right ear. And Nikolai put his hands between his knees and looked as if he wished he could pull his ears back inside the vault of his skull.

The column up ahead had begun to wheel, turning up a side road that climbed back above the main road. Cabell had to manoeuvre the car round the sharp bend and the horsemen sat and watched, laughing, as he wrestled with the wheel and gears; twice he had to back up, just squeezing the Rolls-Royce inside a huge boulder to negotiate the almost 180-degree turn. Then it was following the horsemen up a steep track that, Cabell guessed, had never had a motor car or truck travel over it before; he prayed that the flinty rock surface would not puncture the tyres. Then the road, or track, came out on a flat ledge; beyond it the path looked fit only for goats. The leader was waiting as Cabell pulled up the car and switched off the engine.

'You will follow on foot,' said the leader in accented Russian.

'I'd like to know whom we're following,' said Cabell, sitting tight.

The leader stared at him, then seemed to recognize an adversary, even if a prisoner, who merited some courtesy. 'I am Kibit Mohammed, Khan of Daghestan.'

He was a young man, no more than in his mid-twenties, tall and slim and breathtakingly handsome (which was Eden's and Olga's reluctant opinion, not Cabell's). He was dressed the same as the other Murids, except that in place of the *papakh*, the lambskin cap, he wore a black turban and over his shoulders, held in place by a gold chain, was the *bourka*, the black goat's-hair cloak. His uniform was sombre, but Eden, who had a quicker eye for such things than Cabell, saw that the materials were of the finest quality, the tunic and turban of black silk. The belt he wore was elaborately decorated and the scabbard hanging from the belt held a silver-handled sabre. He was a leader who suggested elegant austerity.

'The Khan of Daghestan?' Cabell tried to keep the note of mockery out of his voice. To his knowledge there had been no khans, the princely descendants of Genghis Khan, in this part of Russia for almost a hundred years. But this man looked every inch a prince, he did not look mad and he was backed by a troop of armed horsemen: it was no time to be openly sceptical or republican. Cabell introduced himself and the others. 'Just on our way down to Tiflis.'

Kibit Mohammed leaned forward and gestured to Frederick. 'Give me the sword, boy.'

Frederick held on to his sword. 'I, too, am a prince. Pay me the proper respect and I shall give you my sword.'

Kibit Mohammed slipped his rifle off his shoulder, aimed it at Frederick. 'One less Russian prince won't be missed.'

Eden reached back, grabbed the sword and held it out. 'Take it. We are not here to fight you.'

Frederick was about to protest, but Cabell looked over his shoulder. 'Okay, Freddie – shut up!' Then he looked up and saw the Murid chief staring at him. He reached down, pulled out the Winchester from beneath his feet and handed it to Kibit Mohammed. 'That is the lot.'

'What about him?' Kibit nodded at Nikolai. 'Doesn't he carry a weapon?'

Nikolai shook his head, held up empty hands. 'I am just a servant.'

'Servants ride in a car such as this? Are you some sort of perverted Bolsheviks?'

But Kibit Mohammed wasn't interested in their answer; nor did he seem very interested in them. He looked curiously at the sword he had taken from Frederick and frowned. Then he turned his horse away and led the way up the steep track, leaving his men to get Cabell and the others out of the Rolls-Royce and hustle them along on foot.

It was a steep climb, the track exposed all the way. Across the narrow gorge the mountains towered against the sun;

the peaks rose one above the other like battlements. The horses climbed steadily, sure-footed as chamois; but the prisoners stumbled and laboured, clumsy as goats forced to walk on their back legs. They climbed for half an hour, the horsemen never allowing them to pause for a rest, and when they at last came out on to the narrow plateau that sliced into the side of the mountain Eden and Olga were on the point of collapse. The two men and the boy remained on their feet only because Cabell and Frederick each had his own pride and Nikolai was afraid that if he fell down the tribesmen would kill him.

Cabell halted, ignoring the shouts of the horsemen nearest him, and made Olga clamber up on to him piggy-back. 'Sorry I can't accommodate you,' he said to Eden. 'I'll save you for Tiflis.'

She had just enough strength to smile weakly.

They moved on across the plateau towards the large village that dominated it. Cabell recognized it now as the village they had seen from the top of the road on the other side of the gorge. It was more a fortress than a village, a series of terraces of flat-roofed rock houses seemingly carved out of the mountainside; the villagers of one house grew vegetables and vines on the roof of the house below them. A mosque stood on the highest point above the village, its white minaret a challenging statement of faith against the wrath of Padishah and other djinns who had lived in these mountains since the imagination of the first men to come here had created them. A rock wall, the rocks dry-stacked one upon another, surrounded the village with a watch tower at either end of the main stretch of wall. A heavy wooden gate hung between two stout posts and seemed to offer the only entrance to the village.

The plateau and the mountainside rising behind the village were absolutely barren, but for a single tree. It stood beside the path that led to the gateway, a stunted walnut tree, grey and dead, looking like a rock sculpture; but its branches were blooming with fluttering rags, tattered flowers of cloth that threatened to blow away at any moment in the wind. Cabell recognized the tree as a shrine, the rags visible evidence of prayers offered to some holy man for whom the tree had originally been planted decades, perhaps hundreds of years, before. He had seen them in other Moslem regions, had compared them to the peasants' memorials he had seen in Catholic countries. At first he had been cynical about them, but his attitude had changed. Some day, he guessed, there would be shrines in America, though not to holy men.

By the time they passed in through the gate Cabell's knees were buckling; Olga, though not heavy, was driving him into the ground. He had not realized till the last ten minutes how high they were in these mountains; the air was thin and he was gulping it in great mouthfuls. Though the sun was blazing down on him, he could feel the chill in the wind as it came down off the great snow-streaked peak rising up behind the village. All the horsemen but Kibit Mohammed and the two men escorting the prisoners had gone on up past the village and disappeared over the rim of what looked to be a second plateau.

People came out into the long narrow open space immediately inside the wall; it was, Cabell guessed, the village square except that it was a long rectangle. Women at once pulled their veils across their faces as soon as they saw Cabell and Nikolai. They hung back as the men and the children pressed forward. Kibit swung down from his horse, tossing the reins to a small boy, and held out Frederick's sword to one of the men.

'What do you think, Jamul?'

The older man took the sword and ran his fingers questioningly over the hilt. Cabell watched carefully; he was suddenly aware that the sword for some reason was important. He took no notice of the crowd, except to remark that they, too, were staring at the sword. Jamul slowly drew it out of his scabbard and almost imperceptibly shook his head when he saw the painted blade.

'Take no notice of the paint,' said Kibit. 'That can be cleaned off.'

'It could be a trick.' Both Kibit and Jamul spoke Russian and Cabell wondered why. 'One cannot trust the Russians.'

'Their leader is an American.' Kibit jerked his head at Cabell.

'What is an American? Is he to be trusted any more than the Russians?'

Cabell felt it was time national honour was defended. 'Look, if you tell me what's going on, maybe I —'

Kibit, without moving any limb but his right arm, slashed Cabell across the face with his whip; a dried ear hit him in the eye. Eden let out a cry and Cabell staggered back, holding his face. When he took his hand away it was covered in blood, but fortunately he could see. The lash had just missed blinding him, but he would have a black eye from the ear that had hit it. Blood was pouring from a slash across his upper cheek and the bridge of his nose.

Eden wiped the blood from his face with her handkerchief. 'It will need bathing. Where can I get some water?' She spoke to the nearest group of women, but they all just stared back at her above the black masks of their veils. Then she turned back to Kibit. 'Damn it, I want some water! You've almost blinded him.'

Kibit gazed at her as if he did not understand a word she had said, even though she had spoken in Russian. She stared back at him and when he half-raised his whip she said in English, 'Watch it!'

Kibit Mohammed shook his head in mild wonder. Then abruptly he nodded at one of the men, who snapped something in his own tongue to the women. It was a language Cabell had heard once or twice when he had been in Baku but had never understood; it was Ma'arul-matz and it was spoken only here in these mountains. The women reacted at once to the man's command. They surged forward, grabbed Eden and Olga and before Cabell, still concerned with his bleeding, painful face, could protest, the women had swept Eden and Olga out of the square and into one of the houses. Frederick cried out and Kibit cracked his whip within an inch of the boy's face.

'Be quiet, boy, or I'll cut your eyes out!' Then, as if he had been no more than swatting flies away, Kibit turned back to the man with the sword. 'If it is a trick, we throw the sword off a cliff and these infidels with it. If it isn't . . .'

'Look —' said Cabell. Kibit half-turned, the whip arm raised again. Cabell backed off, but he was determined he

251

was not going to remain silent. He wiped the blood from his face with his sleeve, held his dirty handkerchief against the cut. 'If you listen to me, I can explain where we got that sword. There is no trick.'

Kibit said nothing for a moment, then he said something in Ma'arul-matz to the man who had got rid of Eden and Olga. The man snapped another command and all the children and the remainder of the women turned and went back to stand in the doorways of the houses and on the stepped alleys that led up to the higher terraces.

Kibit nodded to Cabell. 'Come. The three of you.'

He strode along the square, the two guards pushing Cabell, Frederick and Nikolai after him. The other men followed, their excited interest coming out of them almost as something to be felt. Kibit halted outside what looked to be a workroom carved out of the rock. He gestured to Jamul, who went into the cave and emerged a few moments later with a stone bowl containing some liquid, a piece of cloth and a rough file. He looked at Kibit for instructions and the latter turned to Cabell.

'Tell us where you got the sword. It had better be the truth.' He put his hand on the hilt of his own sword.

Cabell told the truth. '. . . We thought nothing of it till a man down in Karoutai asked Prince Frederick about it.'

'He is my man. He telegraphed me.' Kibit pointed and for the first time Cabell saw the wire, supported on thin poles, that ran across the square and plunged out of sight down a cliff. 'The Russians don't know that we here in Avarou have tapped into their line to Tiflis. My man warned me to intercept you.'

'But just for a sword?' Cabell was forgetting the pain of his face in his curiosity at this mystery.

Kibit nodded at Jamul. 'Go ahead. Remove the paint.'

The older man dipped the rag in the bowl of spirits, began to apply it to the blade of the sword. While he did this the crowd of watching men began to grow as the younger men, their horses left somewhere out of sight up on the upper plateau, came leaping down over the roofs of the houses. It was a game, a race, and, shouting and laughing, they came plunging down over the village in graceful leaps. But as soon as they joined the crowd in front of Jamul's workshop they fell silent, stood and watched as slowly the paint began to peel off the long, slightly curved blade. Cabell, standing in their midst, became aware of the smell of them, acrid, leathery; somehow it suited them and Cabell was aware of how soft and dairy-fed he must smell to them. Several of them wrinkled their noses and stood away from him.

Jamul paused, wiped a fleck or two from the sword. 'Blood?'

Cabell nodded. 'It was necessary to kill a man with it.'

'Who used it? You?'

'No. The servant Nikolai.'

He had taken a risk, but somehow Nikolai managed not to faint. Jamul translated what had been said and the tribesmen looked at Nikolai with respect and the latter, once he had got over his shock, straightened up a little. Frederick pressed his arm and the young Cossack could have wept at such acceptance.

Jamul worked on and Cabell, watching the lined, bony face, could see the scepticism dying out of it. Slowly the paint peeled off and an even colour began to show. At last Jamul lifted the sword and the bright sun gleamed on the blade. All at once it was another weapon altogether, its blade damascened with gold, a shining terrible instrument of death.

'It is Shamyl's.' There was awe in Jamul's voice, a reverence that impressed even Cabell. The latter now understood why Kibit Mohammed and Jamul had been speaking in Russian: they had been racked with doubt, afraid to believe that this might be what they longed for, trying to conceal as much as possible if it had turned out that they had been tricked. 'It is the Golden Sabre!'

'Shamyl!'

The shout that rose from the crowd of men was blood-tingling. It was more than just an exclamation: it was a challenge, fiercely passionate, a cry bottled up in generations of throats and now let loose to silence the wind and soar away to die as an echo amongst the peaks. Arms shot up, waving rifles; faces blazed with sudden fanatical excitement. There was another shout: *'Ourouss! Ourouss!'* Cabell saw and heard all this, yet only for an instant did he take his eyes from Kibit Mohammed.

The young khan had taken the sword from Jamul, stood holding it on both palms, gazing at it with a fixed stare that made him seem drugged. The sun caught the blade, was reflected into his face: his dark eyes shone with golden flecks. His mouth was working, but Cabell could hear nothing: it could have been a silent prayer or a curse or nothing more than the babbling of a man shocked by a miracle. At last, taking the sword by its hilt and lifting it high in the air, he shouted, '*Ourouss! Ourouss!*'

For the moment Cabell, Frederick and Nikolai were forgotten. A drum began to beat, slowly at first, then quickening; the men posed stiffly for a moment, then began to dance. Women came down from the terraces again, formed their own ring on the outside of the crowd of men and matched the steps of their menfolk, though neither sex looked at the other. Then there came the thin, reedy notes of pipes playing, barely heard above the now throbbing drum; someone started to sing and the song was taken up by both men and women. It was a sombre song, hymn-like; but deep in the notes there was passion, a declaration of faith. Cabell understood none of the words but he knew with certainty that it was a war song.

'What does *Ourouss* mean?' he said.

'It is the old Tartar war cry,' said Nikolai, who had fled from all war cries.

'Who are they declaring war on?'

'Us Russians. I think we shall all be killed.'

[3]

Pemenov rode dejectedly through the gorges, the dark green light of their depths suiting his mood. Cliffs towered above him, a thousand feet of black rock shutting out the sun; an eagle planed down through the dark, turbulent air, looking like a bat in some huge ruined cathedral. A few black pines stood amongst the rocks like pyramids of ashes. A waterfall dropped from the edge of a cliff, a towering white column that looked static as an ivory reredos in its steady fall;

hailstones from the thunderstorm of an hour ago still lay, like remnants of winter, in the black shadows of the rocks. The road wound through the gorges, seemingly leading nowhere. He had known other mountain ranges, the Yablonois and the Altai, but these were darkly sinister. He would be glad to be out of them.

He knew he had lost the American, probably forever. He and those with him in the big motor car would now be halfway to Tiflis; and once in that city the American would be safe. He probably would not stay there more than a day, would at once be on his way back to America. Pemenov let out a whimper of rage, jerked his horses to a halt. But what was the point of turning back? There was nowhere to go but onwards.

It was almost noon when the gorges began to widen out and he was riding down a narrow valley where a frost shone greenly in the sun and the rocky road had turned from dull grey to glaring white. He took off the embroidered cap he had been wearing and replaced it with the straw hat. The sun dried out his wet clothes and he began to feel a little better. The remaining gold bar in his saddle bag nudged his knee, reminding him that all was not lost.

Made sleepy by the sun, dozing in the saddle, he was almost upon the long column of troops before he saw them. His saddle horse whinnied and pulled up; he straightened up and looked down the road. The column stretched back for its tail to be lost round the shoulder of a hill: a troop of cavalry at its head, long ranks of infantry, horse-drawn mountain artillery and, just coming into sight, the supply wagons. There must have been two thousand men in the column.

There was nothing to do but ride on and meet it. He took off the straw hat, put the embroidered cap on again, wished once more that he had his black Cossack's hat. He tried to look outwardly like the Cossack he was in his heart, rode on down the road with his head held high, daring anyone to laugh at him but still afraid that they would.

Colonel Peter Marlinsky patted his sweating brow with his perfumed handkerchief and nodded to the sergeant who rode just behind him and his aide. 'Ride up ahead and see who the child is, Sergeant. These damned Murids may be trying some trickery.'

He sat his horse, the long column halted behind him, the infantrymen leaning gratefully on their rifles, even the cavalrymen glad to pause for a while. Marlinsky was a dandy, his thin bony figure a perfect clothes horse for the uniforms he loved; he was weak-chinned and not as handsome as he imagined women thought he was, but he was as brave as he was vain. He was also an excellent soldier.

'Perhaps he is a messenger from Kibit Mohammed.' Marlinsky's aide, Lieutenant Golovin, was plump, fresh-faced and not eager at all for the fighting ahead; at nineteen he was already convinced that the best position from which to fight a war was a desk. He had no faith that the Bolsheviks, or even these Moslems up in the mountains, could be defeated and buried in his valise were books about America, Brazil, Canada and Australia, though he had no idea where the latter country was. 'They may be asking for a truce. Or Kibit may even want to surrender.'

Marlinsky shook his head, not deigning to look at his aide. He rued the wages of climbing into illicit beds: the pox, a bullet wound from the pistol of a cuckolded husband, the blackmail by an ex-mistress that had resulted in his having to give a job to this doltish son of hers. He had no real enthusiasm of his own for this task, but he was a soldier who obeyed orders. General Denikin, fighting his own easier, more successful campaign further north had ordered that these mountains of the Caucasus had to be cleaned out. The Bolsheviks had propaganda presses hidden in the mountain villages and it was rumoured that Lenin had sent emissaries from Moscow to woo the Murids to the Revolution's cause. Marlinsky knew the history of the Murid Wars of the 1850's and he did not wish for a repetition of any of the frustrating campaigns of the long, bitter war. Wars should be fought on flat country, not in mountains like these.

'Why would Kibit want to surrender? He holds one of the world's great fortresses in these mountains. You have a lot to learn, Golovin.'

'Yes, Colonel,' said Golovin, who had no desire to learn

anything about war.

The sergeant came trotting back down the road with Pemenov. They reined in before Colonel Marlinsky. The dwarf saluted smartly and gave his rank and regiment. Marlinsky had never heard of it, but he recognized Pemenov for a Siberian Cossack. They were certainly cutting their officers out of small cloth in Siberia this year.

'I am pursuing an American spy and his mistress, Colonel. They have kidnapped the son and daughter of one of the Tsar's officers. Perhaps they passed you. They were in a grand motor car, an English one.'

The story sounded too improbable to be believed. Perhaps this dwarf was an impostor, a clown from some circus. 'Really? Do you know this officer whose children have been kidnapped?'

'Not personally, Colonel. His name is Prince Gorshkov. I understand he is fighting with General Denikin in the Crimea.'

'No, he isn't.' Marlinsky looked at the dwarf with less suspicion. 'He is ten miles down the road with his regiment at a garrison town. When was the grand motor car supposed to have come down this road?'

'This morning. It passed me no more than three hours ago. I tried to halt it, but couldn't.'

'We should have seen it, Colonel,' said Golovin, who couldn't keep his mouth shut. His mother had had the same failing, talking non-stop, if a little faster, even during orgasm. 'We have passed no side roads so far. None that a motor car could have taken.'

'They are still up there,' said Marlinsky, nodding towards the mountains, ignoring Golovin and talking to the dwarf. 'You saw no soldiers, no tribesmen?'

'No one, Colonel. I did see hoofmarks, a lot of them, in the mud of the road, but they turned up a side track.' Weary, half-dozing, he had not looked for the marks left by the tyres and he was not to know that they had been almost obliterated anyway by the hooves of the horses following the Rolls-Royce.

Marlinsky put away his perfumed handkerchief, sat up in his saddle, his languid air put away with the handkerchief.

'Sergeant, send a messenger at full gallop back to that telegraph station down the road. My compliments to Prince Gorshkov and I should like him to join me as soon as possible. Tell him I believe his children are in danger. Lieutenant Golovin will write the message for you.'

'But I don't have pencil or pen —' said Golovin.

'Holy Mother of God,' said Marlinsky. 'Get one! I want that messenger on his way in two minutes. Then get the column moving again.'

He put his horse to a walk, nodding to Pemenov to fall in beside him. 'Are you Christian or Moslem, Major?'

'Christian, Colonel,' said Pemenov, who was neither. 'My mother was a sort of missionary.'

'Oh really?' Marlinsky couldn't stand missionaries, especially female ones; they had some uncomfortable morals. 'What was your function with General Bronevich?'

'I was his personal aide. Through half a dozen campaigns.'

'Are you expert at anything?'

The supervision of raping and looting . . . 'General Bronevich was kind enough to say I paid great attention to detail.'

'Just what one needs in an aide.' Marlinsky looked over his shoulder at Golovin, still trying to borrow a pen or pencil from one of his fellow officers. 'Stay close to me, Major.'

'Thank you, Colonel. Where are we heading, may I ask?'

'We are seeking out a Murid rebel named Kibit Mohammed. Once I have found him, my orders are to destroy him. It may well be that he has kidnapped the kidnappers. In the meantime we shall press on while Prince Gorshkov catches up with us. If you don't mind my mentioning it, Major, you have an unfortunate stature for a Cossack.'

'We all have our shortcomings, Colonel.'

'Indeed we do,' said Marlinsky with another look back at Golovin and a thought to his own shortcomings, an inability to stay out of the beds of other men's wives. He should not have come to Georgia, where the air was good for a man's lungs but hell on his balls. 'Let's hope we all fight like true men when we finally confront Kibit Mohammed.'

'Yes, Colonel,' said Pemenov, buoyant again, confident

now that the American had not escaped him after all. His only wish was that this Murid, Kibit Mohammed, had not already killed Cabell.

Kibit Mohammed was a more lenient captor than Cabell had expected. He insisted that Eden and Olga, being women and therefore not entirely to be trusted, should be confined to the house where they had been taken. But Cabell, Frederick and Nikolai, though constantly under guard, were allowed out in the open. In the late afternoon the three prisoners, accompanied by Jamul, the swordsmith, and three young Murids, strolled up to the rim of the plateau above the village. Cabell had manoeuvred the walk to lead in that direction, wanting to acquaint himself with possible escape routes if an opportunity should present itself, and Jamul, intent on conversation, wanting to practise his Russian for the coming victory against the Russian infidels, did not seem to mind where their strolling led them.

'We could defend ourselves here forever,' said Jamul proudly. He had the look of a man who had absorbed some of the elements of his trade; certainly there was iron in him, perhaps not damascened, but heavy and reliable. 'There is no village like Avarou in all the Caucasus, except perhaps Gounib.'

'That was where Shamyl made his last stand,' said Frederick.

'Yes.' Jamul was impressed that this Russian boy should know. But twelve-year-old boys, once they had been tested, were accepted as men amongst these tribesmen and he was not to know that it was different amongst the effete infidels. 'We have never forgotten that. My father and Kibit Mohammed's grandfather died defending him. He was our hero of heroes, the Great Imam. Had he won the battles, had he not been betrayed by traitors, the Caucasus would be ours today, not Russia's. Shamyl —' he said it reverently, as if it were a god's name. 'He died in Medina in Arabia in 1871. The Russians could not kill him in battle, but they killed him by

259

degrees by exiling him. We have never forgotten.'

'Have you been waiting all these years for the return of his sword?' Cabell had recovered from the ordeal of the morning. Once he became accustomed to it, the high mountain air invigorated him. The wound across his cheek and nose had started to scab; it looked like a fresh tribal marking. He was still worried as to what was going to happen to them, but while they were still alive there was still hope.

'Some of us, yes. We knew it had disappeared. He gave it to Prince Bariatinsky when he surrendered to him at the last great battle at Gounib. Prince Bariatinsky gave it to one of his officers and the last we heard of it was that that officer's grandson, fighting with the Chevaliers-Gardes, lost it to a Tartar with the Bolsheviks. That was last year and we hadn't heard of it since. Twice, during the war against the Germans, we sent men north to steal it back, but they were caught and executed.'

The three young Murids did not understand a word of the Russian he was speaking; but they had heard the story before in their own tongue and they kept nodding their heads, knowing Jamul was telling the truth. The fierce passion of the morning had died down, but there was still an air of excitement, of expectation, simmering amongst the men, young and old. Kibit himself had for the last two hours been sitting on a rock at the far end of this plateau above which Cabell and the others now stood, a lone figure staring into the distance, to the wild high peaks above him and down into the dark gorges that led out of these mountains to whatever was his destiny. Jamul had told Cabell that Kibit Mohammed had left word that he was not to be disturbed till he got guidance from Allah. Cabell looked down towards him: himself a man of distant horizons, he wondered what Kibit Mohammed looked for beyond the close skyline of the surrounding mountains.

The small plateau was really a shallow bowl; sheep, goats and horses grazed on the carpet of grass that covered the bowl's floor. At the far end some women were harvesting a small field of grain; the wind whipped up a fine yellow dust about them, turning them into ballet figures. A spring somewhere up the mountain fed a swift-running creek that opened out into a small dam; from the creek a series of thin irrigation channels led into a grove of fruit trees and rows of vines. Avarou was indeed a fortress and Cabell wondered why Kibit Mohammed, if Allah should give him the message, would want to take his men from here down into the lottery of the gorges.

'Why does Kibit Mohammed call himself the Khan of Daghestan? That is a big title. Is he a holy man?' What Cabell meant was did Jamul think of the leader as a fanatic, but he didn't dare ask such a question.

'No, he is no *mullah*. Allah called him as a boy, but only as the sword of the *mullahs*. These mountains, Daghestan, were once our own country. We are now part of Russia, but no one has ever really conquered us. Not the Romans or the Arabs, Attila and his Huns, Genghis Khan, Tamerlane – they all tried and failed. Now, while the Russians are fighting each other, the Bolsheviks against the Tsarists —' He spat twice, to show he had no political preference. 'Now is the time for us to claim our own again. We knew a sign was to come – Allah spoke to Kibit Mohammed only two nights ago. Shamyl's sword is the message. Now we wait only the word when to strike.'

'What will happen to us?'

'Ah, who knows? Are you ready for death?'

'No,' said Cabell. 'We Americans never are.'

'Strange people,' said Jamul. 'Then you must all die unhappy. Your heaven must be full of miserable Americans. Don't the other Christians complain?'

'Only the English,' said Cabell, glad that Eden couldn't hear him. 'But then they think God is English.'

'Is he?' said Frederick. 'That will please Father. He is very much an Anglophile.'

Down in the village Eden, one of God's daughters, and Olga were complaining to each other about their misfortune. Eden, brought up in the smug security of pre-1914 England, was still adjusting to acceptance of the fact that in a war-torn land misery and disaster were day-to-day happenings. She had learned something of the history of Russia, of its excesses of violence and hatred and revenge, but her

Englishness, that which had got her her job as a governess, still got in the way of her resignation to fates such as or worse than death. Still the romantic optimist, she felt put upon by things continuing to go wrong.

'Damn it!'

'I feel like swearing, too,' said Olga, who had lost her poise and was feeling frightened. It was no fun being a princess when peasants spat upon one, as several of the Murid women had. 'Perhaps we should have stayed in Verkburg, waited for Mama and Papa to come home.'

'No,' said Eden, knowing that Prince and Princess Gorshkov would never go home to Verkburg; at least she had come to accept *that*. 'We had to try to get to Tiflis.'

'Do you think this horrible man Kibit Mohammed will spare our lives and make us his houris?' Olga looked for a gleam of the bright side: *anything* was preferable to being put to death.

'Perish the thought!' Eden had read of women captured by Moslem savages; even such an extravagant romantic as Lady Vanessa would not have welcomed their attentions. 'You're too young. Don't encourage them, be lady-like at all times.'

'I always am,' said Olga, who always would be, even as a houri.

The room they were cooped up in was small. It was no more than ten feet square, with low shuttered windows, a rough rug on the stone floor, some woollen cushions and nothing else. There was no personal furniture and Eden wondered if the room was kept solely for unwelcome guests such as Olga and herself.

The door opened and two women brought in food; a porridge of millet and yoghurt, some cheese and two tin mugs of water.

'May we have some tea?' said Eden.

The two women looked at each other, shrugged and went out again, slamming the door shut. 'No tea,' said Eden.

'They're rather rude,' said Olga. 'Ugh, what a mess!'

'Eat it. Yoghurt is good for you. Did you know that God Himself is supposed to have taught the Patriarch Abraham how to make it?'

'I shouldn't like to grow as old as Abraham. I shan't have any, thank you.'

'Eat it!' said Eden, being the governess; but also being afraid, letting the tension come out of her. 'Damn it, eat it!'

Then suddenly a hullabaloo broke out outside. Olga rushed to the window and squinted out through the shutters. 'What's happening?'

The village square was thronged with people, all of them swollen with excitement. Cabell, Frederick and Nikolai, standing on the roof of the house where Eden and Olga were held, still guarded by Jamul and the three young men, felt the vehemence strike up at them as something almost tangible; terror gripped Nikolai as men, whirling swords above their heads, swooped down, their faces contorted with a mad exaltation that was as frightening as the swords slicing the air. Frederick, too, was terrified; but he stood his ground beside Cabell. The latter felt no more comfortable than the Cossack and the Russian prince on either side of him. If the fever of this crowd continued to mount, it was going to draw no national lines as to whom it would or would not kill. All infidels would be good targets.

In the past hour, listening to Jamul, he had come to realize the hatred these mountain tribesmen had for the Russians. Then, when Kibit Mohammed, rising suddenly from his seat on the rock at the end of the plateau, had come striding back towards them, Cabell had known at once that all the pent-up fury for revenge, boiling in Murid breasts for sixty years, was about to explode.

Kibit Mohammed had strode up over the rim of the grassy bowl and jumped down over rocks to the tiny space in front of the mosque. He had stood there above the stepped houses of the village and shouted, the golden sabre of Shamyl held aloft like a slim gleaming banner. Cabell had understood only the word *Allah*, but he recognized a call to arms, one that brought a shiver to the spine.

At that moment, as if Allah had sent another messenger, a horseman had come galloping into the village, tumbled from his horse and shouted up to Kibit. At once there was an answering roar from the people now pouring out of the houses.

'What did he say?' Cabell looked at Jamul.

'It is a miracle!' Jamul's face was alight; he raised a fist and the string of prayer beads broke in the tightness of his grip; beads popped like amber drops of blood. 'Allah gave Kibit Mohammed the word that we must ride tomorrow. Then Talgik rides in with his news – the Russians are down in the valley heading this way! Allah has sent them to us to be killed!'

Then Jamul and the other guards had pushed the three prisoners ahead of them down over the terraces, the young guards pricking them with their *kindjals*, making them jump from roof to roof down over the houses. Twice Frederick and Nikolai, making the ten-foot leaps, stumbled and fell, but fortunately they suffered no more than skinned hands and knees. Tribesmen and prisoners alike hurtled down the giant steps of the terraces; but only Cabell, Frederick and Nikolai were silent. Yells, even screams, tore out of the wide open mouths of the Murids as they plunged down towards the square. Within a minute of Kibit Mohammed's call to arms, the whole village was a dark boiling mass in the square, a volcano ready to erupt.

Kibit Mohammed stood in the centre of the vortex, Shamyl's sword held high. He was the only silent one in the roaring crowd, but Cabell, looking down on him from the roof, could see the exaltation in the handsome face, a wild blazing expression that had no thought behind it, only feeling. When Kibit Mohammed led his men out tomorrow, Cabell knew, there would be no fear of death in him: he would lead them to mass suicide if that was what the sword of Shamyl demanded.

Then the Murid leader looked across the heads of the shouting crowd straight up at Cabell. For a moment his eyes cleared; intelligence showed through the fanaticism. Then he pushed through the throng, the villagers falling back, and came to stand immediately below Cabell.

'You will ride ahead of us in your motor car,' he shouted; then he pointed the sword at Frederick and Nikolai. 'The Russians can kill their own!'

CHAPTER EIGHT

Prince Alexander Gorshkov was an almost perfect example of the saying, Like father, like son. Pemenov had met the son; now he saw the son in the father. The physical resemblance was startling, Frederick seen large; and there was the same arrogant air. Prince Gorshkov believed in the Divine right of kings and tsars; as a prince he saw himself amongst the archangels and had always regretted that Archangel had not been his birthplace; it would have put a natural imprimatur on his opinion of himself. He was not as vain as Colonel Marlinsky, but that was because he was not concerned with other people's opinions of himself; vanity is only part of the search for other people's approval. He thought of himself as a good Christian but thought Christ had had one major fault: He had preached humility.

Gorshkov sat on a rock beside the road, stiff and sore from the long hard ride, but not relaxing, every aching inch of him still a soldier. His foam-flecked horse, galloped all the way from Karabek, had been taken away by an orderly. He sat and listened to Marlinsky, occasionally flicking a glance at the peculiar little man standing beside the tall, languid colonel.

'Why were you travelling with my children and Miss Penfold?'

'General Bronevich detailed me to escort them, Your Highness, when he learned they wanted to come down to Tiflis.' Pemenov had been a liar all his life and always a careful one, as a good liar should be. But there was no need to be careful now, there was no one within hundreds of miles to contradict him. Captain Zabari, who knew part of the truth, had probably already left Karoutai, taking the *Perfumed Garden* on its way to another port of call; and Rabbi Aronsky and the Jews, who knew all the truth, were still on the far side of the Caspian. He was safe, so he lied with all his old confidence. 'The journey was uneventful till the

American intercepted us south of Drazlenka.'

Gorshkov nodded. 'I know it. My family own that part of the country. How did you get this far if the American took the Rolls-Royce?'

'I followed on horseback, Your Highness.'

'You must be a very tenacious little man.'

'Thank you, Your Highness.' But Pemenov could have done without the second adjective.

Gorshkov looked at Marlinsky. 'What is the situation, Colonel? I believe Major Pemenov. I'm sure my children and their governess must be held somewhere up in those mountains. I can only hope the Murids have killed the American.'

'Yes.' But Marlinsky feared that the children and the governess also might have gone the way of the American. 'I shall do everything I possibly can to rescue your children. But with respect, I have to remind you that I am taking my men into battle. We start shelling Kibit Mohammed's village at dawn tomorrow.'

Gorshkov said nothing for a while, staring up to where the head of the valley narrowed into a dark cleft between two towering cliffs. Through the top of the gap he could see the peaks, their western walls shining like bronze shields in the afternoon sun. Like all the soldiers of the White armies, he had never fought in these mountains; that terrible experience belonged to Tsarist armies of sixty years ago. But as a soldier with a sense and knowledge of history, he knew the terrors and difficulties of fighting in such a terrain. It had taken his countrymen over twenty years to win the last war fought here, that against Shamyl; and the soldiers of those days had been more disciplined than the rabble one had to command today. Men in those days had fought for the glory of the Tsar, or so he believed, but today, with all the revolutionary ideas spreading like a pox all over Russia, one could not trust a soldier even to obey a direct command.

'It would be useless to try to negotiate?'

'General Denikin doesn't believe in negotiation.'

'No.' Gorshkov nodded hopelessly. He knew General Denikin too well. The summer campaign had gone so well in the Crimea and Don that Denikin believed the war was already won. Denikin would consider it beneath his dignity to allow any concessions to some mangy mountain tribesmen. 'No, we must attack.'

'First thing in the morning.' Then Marlinsky threw away his languid air again, showed the sympathetic side of him that, amongst other things, endeared him to the ladies. 'We can but hope. But there is no other way . . .'

Gorshkov slept only fitfully that night, the faces of his children, the sound of their voices, troubling him like sweet terrors. Near him Marlinsky slept soundly, neither excited by nor afraid of tomorrow; war was war and if he had any doubts at all they were to wonder what he would do when all the wars were finished. In a crib of rocks nearby, Pemenov slept like a child, a smile of anticipation on his face.

In the grey light of dawn, before the sun's rays had come up over the mountains to the east, Marlinsky woke Prince Gorshkov. 'Our guns are in position. We moved them up during the night.'

'Good.' Gorshkov struggled out of the web of sleep, stood up, was at once a soldier. 'I should like to ride at the head of your men when they attack.'

'Of course. There is one thing —'

'Yes?'

'Our forward observation post has reported there is a motor car halfway up the track that leads to Kibit Mohammed's village. It must be your Rolls-Royce. There are no other motor cars in these mountains.'

Gorshkov drew in his breath, a gasping sigh. 'Go ahead as you planned, Colonel. I should just like a few minutes alone to pray.'

Marlinsky left him, went across to his horse and mounted it. He looked at Golovin and Pemenov, both dim figures in the pale grey light. The early morning air was still cold and the men were wrapped against it, Golovin in a greatcoat that was as elegant as Marlinsky's own but a size too small, Pemenov in his rough, smelly blanket. The dwarf looked ridiculous and smelled abominably, but Marlinsky knew a soldier when he saw one.

'Remember, Major — you are on trial.'

'I shall follow you, Colonel, to the mountain peak.'

'A trifle extravagant, Major, but thank you. How far will you follow me, Golovin?'

'As my dear mother says, Colonel —'

But Marlinsky rode away before he had to listen to what Golovin's dear mother said. She had always had something to say about everything.

[2]

The first shell took the top off the minaret, a marvellous piece of shooting if it was intentional. Kibit Mohammed, mounted on a black stallion, had just led his men, five hundred of them on horseback, up over the rim of the upper plateau when the swift scream of the shell was heard. He reined in, shocked, recognizing the sound but not believing it; the Russians should be still down in the gorges, the angle of fire from their guns still impossible. Then the top of the minaret crumbled like a candy stick and fell, the boom of the exploding shell reverberating off the mountains. The second shell landed on the second terrace, opening up two of the houses; the dust cleared and the dead family inside one of the houses was clearly visible. The third shell fell right in the middle of the square.

Cabell, Eden, the two children and Nikolai were waiting by the gate in the rock wall, all five of them mounted on shaggy mountain ponies; they looked like a family on excursion to a fairground taking penny rides; only the four mounted guards beside them took away the picnic air. It had still been dark when Cabell and the others had been brought out into the open after a night during which none of them had slept; Cabell had expected that they would have had to walk back down to the Rolls-Royce, but the ponies had been waiting for them. Now, with the explosion of the shells, something they had never heard before, the ponies began to shy in fear, Cabell's to buck dangerously. He jumped down, yelling to the others to do the same; they slid off the ponies, letting them race away as another shell screamed overhead. Cabell pushed them all into the shelter of the rock wall, crouched down and looked back up above the village.

The horsemen were still there on the rim, outlined against the growing light in the sky. Then suddenly they were gone, wheeling and dropping down out of sight into the bowl of the plateau. Women and children and the old men of the village were racing across the square to the shelter of the wall; a shell landed and opened up the ground in a brown bouquet of rock and dirt and a woman and three children ran into it. When the dust cleared the four bodies lay in the one heap, as if they had rushed together in death.

The three young guards had turned their horses about and raced up to join Kibit and the other horsemen. But Jamul jumped down from the saddle and pushed his horse in against the wall. His rifle was slung across his back, but he held his *kindjal* in his free hand and stabbed it towards Cabell and the others.

'Don't try to escape – I shall kill you!'

'Kibit Mohammed should have ridden out last night,' said Cabell. 'He should not have waited.'

'Allah gave him the message – to ride today! One does not query God's word!'

Perhaps that's been my trouble, thought Cabell: all his life he had been querying God's word. But it looked as if Kibit should have taken less notice of Allah's advice. All last night horsemen had been arriving at Avarou, coming from other, smaller villages further up the mountain. Messengers had ridden out, going down the long steep track to the gorges and climbing equally steep tracks to villages on other mountains. Now this morning tribesmen were coming from a dozen points; they were to meet at the bottom of the gorge on the Tiflis road, ride down to meet the Russians and, Allah be praised, wipe them out.

All this Jamul had told Cabell while they waited in the fading darkness by the gate in the rock wall. And now the Russians had come sneaking in during the night, set their guns up on the far side of the gorge and made a mockery of what Allah had advised.

But Cabell, who sometimes mocked his own religion but never another man's, did not criticize Kibit Mohammed's faith in his God. He raised his head and looked over the top of the wall. The wall was about five-and-a-half feet high, sharp flinty rocks laid on top of each other: protection enough against bullets but not against shells. Even as he stood up to look, Cabell heard the whine of another shell and saw part of the wall blown out a hundred yards from him. Looking back across the gorge, he saw the thin belches of flame and the drifting smoke as the Russian guns continued their barrage. They were sited on the road down which he had driven yesterday morning, a descending line of ten guns firing as fast as their gunners could slam shells into the breeches. The village of Avarou would be no more than terraces of rubble in the next twenty minutes.

Dust covered everything, the morning air made thick and murky; through it Cabell could see figures running in panic. He flinched and ducked as another shell hit the wall; shrapnel whirred away into the dust cloud and he heard someone scream. Eden and the children pressed close to him, trembling; Nikolai lay flat on the ground as if already dead or wounded. Cabell's nostrils were choked with dust and the smell of cordite and his ears were aching from the thumping explosions of the shells. Twenty yards from them the wall blew apart with a roar and a slice of rock, like a knife-edged plate, flew past his face. He turned his head away and saw the top of Jamul's head taken off as if by the blow of a mighty sabre.

Before they could see the horrible sight, Cabell grabbed Frederick and Olga and started running, yelling to Eden and Nikolai to follow him. He had no idea where he was taking them, but he had to get them away from the wall and the falling shells. It was obvious that the Russians were going to demolish Avarou rock by rock.

Cabell and the others ran through the swirling brown fog. The wind had freshened, twisting the dust into thick coils that hit them in the face and blinded them; Cabell ran right over a corpse and fell headlong, bringing the children down with him. They scrambled up and stumbled on, deafened by the explosion around them. Fragments of rock and shell flew by them, but miraculously none of them was hit.

Then through the boiling dust Cabell saw the gate. A shell had hit it, blowing it off its hinges; beyond it one of the watch towers was now just a ruin. People were scrambling through the wreckage and Cabell and the others joined the panic-stricken rush. But once through the gateway they didn't turn with the villagers streaming up towards the upper plateau. They kept running down the track, past the tree-shrine where the rags whipped madly in the wind like desperate shouts for help to the dead holy man.

'Keep going! We're going to make it!' Cabell yelled.

Then he looked back over his shoulder and saw the horsemen, Kibit Mohammed at their head, come over the rim of the basin, down past the village and along the track after them, sabres glinting in the sun that had now come up over the mountains. And on the other side of the gorge the Russian guns were suddenly silent.

[3]

The Russian gunners had never fought in the mountains before. Made bold by intelligence reports that the Murids had no cannon in Avarou they had set up their own guns on the road below the towering cliffs. In front of them the cliffs continued to fall to the river far below; across the gorge the village stood out as a perfect target. Safe from any return fire other than rifle fire, they had felt, backed as they were by the sheer wall of cliff, as safe as on the practice ranges in the Crimea. Then the rocks, huge boulders weighing half a ton or more, had come hurtling down on them from above.

The Murid tribesmen did not all live on the one mountain, as Colonel Marlinsky well knew. He had proposed to destroy their villages one by one, beginning with Avarou, the headquarters of the chief Murid, Kibit Mohammed. It was Marlinsky's misfortune that he should have chosen the morning when Allah had told Kibit Mohammed to call the tribesmen together for an all-out attack on the Russian infidels. Had Marlinsky been a praying man his Christian God might have given him some warning, but unfortunately he had had no conversations with God since his confirmation almost thirty years before. But when a regimental runner brought him the news of what was happening he did invoke the Lord's name.

'All the guns are out of action, Colonel, and there are casualties amongst the men. Major Lazareff requests permission to withdraw.'

Marlinsky, at the head of the column at the entrance to the gorge, put his binoculars on the road carved out of the cliff-face. The rocks were continuing to fall and he could see the tiny figures, scores of them, working furiously along the top of the cliffs.

'Tell Major Lazareff he has permission to withdraw. Bring down as many guns as he can.'

The messenger went galloping off on his horse and Marlinsky turned his glasses on the village of Avarou. It was still half-obscured by a drifting cloud of dust, but even as he looked at it the wind blew away the cloud and he saw the horsemen come racing out of it.

'I think, Colonel, that you will have to change your approach. With the guns out of action, your men are never going to reach that high ground.'

Prince Gorshkov also had his binoculars on Avarou. He had seen figures running down away from the village, but they were too far away to be distinguishable; then they seemed to be run down by the horde of horsemen racing across the plateau. He lowered his gaze and saw the Rolls-Royce still standing on the ledge halfway up the mountain; he felt a sick welling of nostalgia, not for the car itself but for what it reminded him of. Happy times with his wife and children . . . Then he had to remind himself that those times had already been disappearing in the year he had bought the car. It was all so long ago, so much so that his memory was playing tricks. Perhaps the last happy times had been when the children were very young, before the war with the Germans, before he had even thought of buying the Rolls-Royce.

'We shall meet them at the entrance to that gorge.' Marlinsky snapped orders to his company commanders, who were grouped round him on their horses. 'If we can get into position first, we can bottle them up. At once, gentlemen!'

Pemenov sat his horse, wondering if he should quietly lose himself and fade away as the column started moving up.

Last night he had seen a new future for himself with Colonel Marlinsky, but now he wondered if the Colonel himself had any future. The coming clash at the entrance to the gorge looked to him as if it would be catastrophic for both sides.

The narrow valley was all confusion, dust and noise as the column got under way. The regiment of cavalry went racing by, spinning up dust behind them. Marlinsky watched them go, thrilled by the sight of the thundering horses, the flying pennants, the challenge of the rifles held high: war had its beautiful moments, far more exciting than anything else he had experienced. He had a convenient blindness when it came to viewing disasters . . . The cavalry would reach the defile into the gorge in time, but the infantrymen would be hard pushed. They had started to run, their packs bouncing up and down on their backs like loose humps; it seemed to Prince Gorshkov that they ran reluctantly, like men who no longer had any interest in this or any other war. He was surprised to find that he found it hard to blame them . . . Drivers were whipping up their horses to take the wagons carrying the machine-guns up the road; but everyone was now getting in everyone else's way. The road was too narrow and the rocks on one side and the swift river on the other prevented any spreading out of the troops for quick movement. The Russians were getting their first lesson in the difficulties of fighting in mountain terrain.

Then Pemenov, isolated from all this, unexcited by the beauties of war, unconcerned for the foot-soldiers, heard Marlinsky shouting at him. He looked across the road and saw the Colonel waving his sword and pointing up towards the gorge.

'To the mountain peak, Major!'

Marlinsky was laughing, as if suddenly everything was a great joke. His face was alight with anticipation: he could have been about to plunge into a horse race or the bed of some aristocratic whore. Pemenov suddenly realized he had attached himself to that worst of military masters, a fanatic who delighted in war for war's sake alone.

'I think we should follow the Colonel,' said Prince Gorshkov and spurred his horse forward. He knew he was probably riding to his death but there was nothing else he could do. No loving father could turn away to save his own life when his children lay dead in the mountains up ahead.

The three men put their horses to the gallop, went racing up the road. Lieutenant Golovin hesitated. Then he turned his horse and rode back the other way, shouting orders, looking busy as a good aide should, riding for Tiflis, his mother and some distant safe place where wars never occurred.

[4]

'Here!' Eden thrust the *kindjal* at Cabell. 'I grabbed it when Jamul was killed.'

Cabell took the dagger, pushed it inside his shirt. Next moment he and the others were enveloped as Kibit Mohammed and his horsemen swept down on them. He had expected to be run down, had tightened himself, waiting to be bowled over and trampled to death by two thousand hooves. But Kibit Mohammed still had a use for his captives.

He shouted something in his own tongue and Cabell and the others were grabbed and swung up on to the rumps of horses. Cabell clutched the waist of the tribesman in front of him and saw the others do the same. Then, with the prisoners hanging on for dear life, the Murids sent their horses racing down the track again.

It was a nightmare ride and Eden would never know how she managed to stay on the galloping horse. But it was stay on or crash to the ground and be killed. When Kibit Mohammed finally reined in beside the Rolls-Royce, she slid off the horse and, without looking at the Murid leader for permission, pushed Frederick and Olga into the car. Dimly she was aware that the trailer and all their belongings were missing; some tribesmen must have come during the night and effected their own small revenge on the infidels. She clambered into the front seat and fell back in a state of near-collapse. She heard Nikolai stumble into the car, but she was too exhausted to look around to see if he was all right.

Cabell, crotch bruised and aching, looked up at Kibit Mohammed. The tribesmen were already riding on down the steep track, losing no time in getting to the bottom of the gorge. On the far side of the deep chasm other horsemen had appeared on the road there, were galloping down towards the fleeing Russian gunners, firing their rifles and waving their swords. A gun went over the cliff's edge, fell like a toy to the river far below; another gun followed, and another. One of the guns must have had a shell in the breech as it was pushed over; it went off in mid-air with a roar that shot up out of the gorge. The shell hit the cliff, there was another roar and a section of cliff fell away below the smoke of the explosion, falling into the white eruption of water where the gun itself had landed. The tribesmen kept racing down the road and then there were tiny figures in the air, arms waving as they fell almost lazily down the five-hundred-foot drop.

'Leave the women and children here,' said Cabell. 'I'll drive the car down to the road, take it wherever you wish. But spare their lives. They've done no harm.'

Kibit Mohammed shook his head. 'The Russian guns killed our women and children. They stay in the car with you. Drive it!' He half-raised the golden sabre, for the first time almost smiled. 'It's a form of Russian roulette, Mr Cabell. Murid swords or Russian bullets. Drive!'

Then he set his horse to the path, riding it fast, holding it on its feet even though it slipped and slid at almost every yard, riding as only a man born in these mountains could. He left four tribesmen to see that Cabell got the Rolls-Royce moving.

Cabell looked over his shoulder at Nikolai. 'Swing the handle, Nick. Let's hope it's not for the last time.'

Nikolai, grey under his tan, got out of the car, went round to the front and somehow found the strength to swing the handle. The engine started up, ran smoothly and silently: oh, Mr Royce, thought Cabell, why couldn't you have let me down just this once? Nikolai came back, paused beside Cabell.

'You will get us through, Mr Cabell. You have got us this far.'

'Yes,' said Frederick and Olga, grabbing hope out of despair.

275

Cabell looked at Eden. 'Jesus wept,' he said.

She nodded, but said nothing. She could not burden him with her own faint hopes.

The rider nearest Cabell, riding on the inside of the car away from the edge of the road, kept jabbing his sword at the American, urging him to drive faster. But Cabell knew just how fast he could take the car down this steep, treacherous track. For one wild thoughtless moment he felt that urge for suicide that lurks in the hearts of all men caught in the hopeless moment; he wanted to drive straight at the Murids, taking them, the car and everyone in it over the edge and down to the rocks below. But the urge to survive, which is stronger, returned and he kept the car on the road, keeping it away from the edge as the tyres slipped on the rocky surface. Once he looked down, saw nothing but hundreds of feet of empty air beneath him and got an attack of vertigo. The car slipped towards the edge; somehow he pulled it away. At last they were at the bottom and he drove down on to the main road and pulled up.

The road was filled with horsemen, their horses jostling each other, the riders weaving and ducking to avoid the rifles slung across the backs of the men next to them. Somewhere back along the road the last of the Russian gunners had been slaughtered; having tasted blood, the tribesmen were eager for more. The bottom of the gorge was a seething mass of passionate hatred; Cabell suddenly felt he and the others might die from Murid swords before the Russian bullets could be fired at them. He looked towards Kibit Mohammed, trusting the Murid leader to keep them alive a little longer.

Kibit Mohammed raised his sword and waved to Cabell to bring the Rolls-Royce through. When the car drew level with him he said, 'You will lead our charge, Cabell. Drive on.'

Cabell let in the gears, none too smoothly, and drove on down the winding road between the towering black cliffs. Jesus, he thought, what a way to die! Between the swords and the guns of the two armies that belonged to the past. But for the life of him and the others in the car, he could think of nothing else to do but keep driving. He drove at twenty miles an hour and the tribesmen, Kibit Mohammed riding at

276

their head, kept up with the car. The Murids were singing a battle song, their voices bouncing off the cliffs, drowning out the sound of the cascading river running beside the road.

Eden glanced back, saw the long ranks of horsemen stretching behind, heard the thundering chorus. For a moment she felt light-headed, as if she did not belong to this moment; she saw it and heard it as if she were removed from it all. It was a magnificent spectacle, something she would remember for as long as she lived. Which might be only another minute or two.

Half a mile down the road Colonel Marlinsky heard the singing coming out of the gorge as out of a great megaphone. He urged his horse on, was followed by Prince Gorshkov and a reluctant Pemenov. The cavalry had already arrived at the entrance to the gorge, had swung off the road and were deploying themselves along the rocky slope opposite the river. When the Murids came out of the gorge they would find themselves between the cavalry and the river; they would either have to retreat back into the gorge, falling over themselves to do so, or plunge ahead down the road towards the infantry who had now paused and were setting up their machine-guns. Marlinsky knew he already had the battle won.

Then the bullet hit him in the chest and he died in a shock of disbelief. He fell out of the saddle and almost under the hooves of Gorshkov's horse as it came galloping up behind him. Gorshkov swung his horse aside, pulled it to a halt and hit the ground running, pulling the big gelding after him as he plunged for the shelter of some rocks. Pemenov dragged his mount to a stop, swung down, stumbled as he lost his footing, lost his grip of the reins and saw his horse whirl round and go racing back down the road. The dwarf let out a curse and ran as fast as his tiny legs would carry him into the rocks and fell headlong beside Gorshkov.

'Up there, Major!' Gorshkov pointed.

High up on ledges at the entrance to the gorge, like eagles in their eyries, Pemenov saw the tribesmen. They were shooting down on the cavalrymen below them and down the valley at the infantry who were now scurrying frantically for cover.

'They must have come in over the top, Major. This is what happens when one fights in country one doesn't know. Do you know anything about fighting in mountains?'

'I am a man of the steppes, Your Highness.' Pemenov squinted up towards the gorge. He could hear the singing, louder now, and he knew that at any moment the Murids would come charging out of the narrow defile. He hoped Prince Gorshkov would be sensible and give the order to retreat. He rolled on his side and looked at the Prince. 'Do you have an aide, sir?'

'Are you looking for a job, Major?'

'If we survive, sir.'

'I'm sorry, Major.' Gorshkov looked sad. 'I don't think I shall be needing an aide after this morning.'

Less than half a mile from him, his children were still alive, if already resigned to dying in the next moment or two. They crouched in the back seat of the Rolls-Royce, Nikolai huddled with them. Olga's mind was blank of dreams of the French Riviera, of growing up to be beautiful and loved by handsome men; Frederick wanted to die bravely, as a prince should, but he was only twelve years old and now he knew no one should die so young. Nikolai, who had died a thousand deaths before this, just sat mute, his arms round the boy he loved, and waited for what he had always known would come sooner than later.

In the front seat Cabell and Eden stared ahead at the black cliffs, waiting for them to open up and let the road run down into the valley beyond. They could see nothing of what was going on beyond the entrance to the gorge. They drove through the dim light of the mighty chasm and behind them the horsemen, hundreds and hundreds of them, sang their battle-hymn as they galloped down to what Cabell knew must be the gate to Hell. He took a hand from the wheel, felt for Eden's, missed it and clutched her thigh.

'Watch it,' she said automatically, then lifted his hand and pressed it against her lips.

Then suddenly there was the slit of sky in the cliffs, the gorge opened up and there was the valley beyond and the Russian cavalry trying desperately to escape from the fire coming down on them from above.

'*Ourouss!*'

Down the road Prince Gorshkov saw the Rolls-Royce come into view, saw Miss Penfold sitting up in the front seat beside some strange man, caught a glimpse of three people in the back seat. And saw the Murid leader, golden sabre held aloft as he called the charge, riding beside the car as he urged his horse to its full pace.

Gorshkov had no rifle, only his pistol and sword: commanders were meant to kill only at close quarters. He looked around, saw Pemenov's Lee-Enfield, grabbed it.

'With your permission, Major!'

Pemenov, too, had seen the Rolls-Royce, had seen Cabell but had not acted quickly enough. Another moment and he would have been sighting down the rifle barrel, aiming at the American still miraculously alive and ready for killing.

Instead, Gorshkov was aiming the rifle. He had to steady himself against the weakness of relief that had swept through him; he wanted to weep with joy, but there was no time for that. He had to keep his arm steady and his eye clear. He sighted on the Murid with the golden sabre and squeezed the trigger.

The bullet was too low. It hit Kibit Mohammed's horse right between the eyes and the beast staggered, going down in mid-stride. Kibit Mohammed felt it going, rose up in his stirrups and hurled himself sideways on to the running-board of the car.

'Drive!'

He clung to the windshield support, raised the sabre and glared at Cabell. The latter kept the car going, braking and swerving as he tried to take it through the wild mêlée on the road. Riderless horses were careering down the road; those cavalrymen who had managed to remount spurred their horses after them. The Rolls-Royce gathered speed, went down the road on a wild torrent of horses. Kibit Mohammed stood on the running-board and whirled the sabre of Shamyl, slashing at cavalrymen as the car caught and passed them. Behind the car the Murid tribesmen were racing out of the gorge as if nothing on earth could stop them, their black banners streaming in the wind.

Cabell, concentrating on keeping the Rolls-Royce on the

road, still kept flicking glances at Kibit Mohammed right beside him. The golden sabre was red with blood; Cabell realized with horror that he was making the Murid's task easier; the car was overtaking the fleeing cavalrymen almost as if their horses were no more than cantering. He saw a cavalryman look back; the man's face seemed to open up with terror as he saw the bloodstained sabre coming at him. In that moment Cabell acted. He dragged the *kindjal* from under his shirt, held the wheel with one hand and reached out and drove the dagger into Kibit Mohammed's back.

The Murid leader bent backwards, kept his grip on the windshield and turned back into the car. He stared at Cabell out of eyes that were already blind; his arm brought the sabre up in a reflex movement. But he was dead. The sabre fell into the car across Cabell's lap and Kibit Mohammed fell back off the running-board right under the hooves of the horses thundering behind. For some yards he was kicked along like a sack of grain, then the first horse came down over him. Another followed, and another, and in a moment the Murid charge was a rabble of plunging horses shuddering to a halt behind the struggling hurdles of horses and men blocking the road.

The Rolls-Royce sped on, past the machine-guns opening up on the wild confusion that a moment ago had been a stampede that had threatened to engulf them. Cabell would have kept going right on to Tiflis, but now he had to slow as the fleeing cavalrymen, realizing they were no longer being chased, pulled up their horses, turned round and began to re-group for a counter-attack. He took the car slowly through them, drove out beyond them and saw the Russian officer standing in the middle of the road, arms held up in welcome.

'Father!'

Even before the car had come to a standstill Frederick and Olga were out of it, rushing into their father's arms; the three of them stood there in the middle of the road, their arms binding them together like ropes that could never be cut. Thank Christ, thought Cabell, and meant it as a prayer.

He sat back, hardly able to believe that the long journey was over. He looked at Eden, then back at Nikolai. The sabre still lay across his lap, its blade still red with blood of the cavalrymen it had killed. He bitterly rued the day he had bought it, given it to Nikolai to give to Frederick.

'I don't think we should let Freddie keep this.'

'No.' Eden, now they were safe, could feel herself trembling and she struggled to keep herself from breaking down. She wished she were alone with Cabell, so that he could put his arms round her and she could give way to tears and anything he wanted to do to her. 'You don't mind, do you, Nikolai?'

'I still owe you for it, Mr Cabell.'

'No. I told you, I'm in your debt. We all are.'

Nikolai, embarrassed, looked back up the road. The Murids, those who had survived the murderous fire from the machine-guns, were streaming back towards the gorge and the mountains. He wanted to weep for the miracle that he and Frederick and Olga were still alive, but he would not allow himself tears in front of Cabell. He had never wanted to prove himself to anyone, but it pleased him that the American thought him a man. If his father and brothers were here, he thought he might even thumb his nose at them.

'Maybe we can send the sword to General Denikin.' Cabell got out of the car, carrying the sabre, and walked round to help Eden alight. 'Now I think you better introduce me to Prince Gorshkov. He's been on my mind long enough.'

Then Eden looked up past him, to the clump of rocks on the far side of the road and saw the dwarf aiming the rifle at Cabell's back. She screamed and flung herself at Cabell, pushing him down on the running-board of the car. The bullet missed his head by inches, went straight into Nikolai's heart as he opened the door of the car to get out. Eden felt herself shoved roughly aside, heard Olga scream and Frederick cry out, heard Cabell's terrible roar of rage. Then she saw him rush away from her and up into the rocks.

Prince Gorshkov raised his pistol to fire at Cabell, but Frederick grabbed his arm. 'Don't, Father! He's our friend!'

Everything that happened in the next few moments seemed to Eden to be seen through a cracked prism. She was lying on the ground, her head twisted back as she looked

281

over her shoulder. She saw Pemenov stand up, fumbling with the bolt of the rifle, his tiny arms trying to pull the butt tight against his shoulder as he aimed the gun at Cabell. The latter went up at him over the rocks, leaping from rock to rock with the agility of a mountain tribesman, the bloody golden sabre held out in front of him. She didn't see it go into Pemenov; Cabell's own body blocked that terrible sight. But she saw the dwarf stagger back, sit down on a rock, look up at Cabell like a hurt child, then slowly fall backwards.

She scrambled to her feet, clutched at Nikolai still hanging on the half-opened door of the car, knew at once that he was dead. She started to weep, grief and tension and relief coming out of her in a flood. She was dimly aware of Olga and Frederick close to her, then she felt Prince Gorshkov put an arm round her shoulders. She raised her head and saw Cabell.

He came slowly down out of the rocks, the bloody sabre still in his hand. He walked slowly past the car, across the road to the rocks that banked the raging river coming out of the mountains. He stared for a moment at the sabre, then he drew back his arm and hurled the sword high into the air and out into the middle of the white torrent. For a moment the curved blade caught the morning sun, gold shining as a thin edge through the blood, then it fell into the tumbling water and was gone.

CHAPTER NINE

'Nikolai was a sweet boy,' said Princess Gorshkov. 'He had so much sympathy and understanding, enough to have been a woman.'

Prince Gorshkov raised his eyebrows, wondering what his wife knew about sympathy and understanding. He sometimes felt he was married to Catherine the Great, though his wife did not take in lovers.

'I shall miss him always,' said Frederick.

'I, too,' said Olga, red-eyed from weeping.

Nikolai's body had been brought down from the mountains to Tiflis in the Rolls-Royce. He had been buried this morning in a quiet ceremony in a far corner of the cemetery reserved for foreigners; and the Georgian cemetery-keeper made it obvious that he thought even the Gorshkovs were foreigners; it was another lesson for Cabell in the matter of how loosely woven was the fabric of Russia. There were other burials that morning, but the city was not in mourning. It was celebrating the victory over the Murids and the latest news of the continuing success of General Denikin's armies further north. It was only a matter of time before all those who wanted to go would be back in, not Petrograd but St Petersburg. A thin summer rain fell on Nikolai's coffin as it was lowered into the grave; bells chimed in church towers, but they sounded lively enough to be celebrating the living, not mourning the dead. Eden, Frederick and Olga wept as if Nikolai had been family, which indeed he had been, though Prince and Princess Gorshkov might never know. Cabell felt sad and yet somehow relieved for the young Cossack. There was no world for poor homosexuals, only for rich ones. All his life Nikolai would have been the fairy at the bottom of his father's garden, no matter where he went.

'What will you do now, Mr Cabell? Will you go back to America?'

The Princess was one of the most beautiful women Cabell had ever seen, but it seemed to him that she was as self-contained and self-centred as a cat, though he did not think she would be malicious. Her children loved her and so, apparently, did the Prince; but their affection seemed to bring no reaction. She was the centre of the family, but all she saw in the loving eyes surrounding her was the reflection of herself.

'I am going to Batumi tomorrow to book on a ship for Constantinople. From there I can get another ship to England and then one for the United States.' He was dressed in the ill-fitting suit he had gone out early this morning and bought to wear to the funeral. It was tight under the armpits and under the crotch and he thought of Delyanov who believed that longevity lay in baggy trousers. He looked across the room at Eden and decided he wanted to live a long, long time. 'But first, this evening, I am taking Miss Penfold to dinner.'

They had come back from the cemetery and were having tea in the drawing-room of the house the Gorshkovs had rented. It had been the home of a Georgian princess: Prince Gorshkov believed in like renting from like. There was a sumptuous Oriental luxury to the house and Cabell felt uncomfortable in it, as if he were in a mausoleum that its occupants had not yet recognized as such. He could not bring himself to believe that the good news from the north could go on forever.

'Then we must see that she has a new frock,' said Princess Gorshkov, and Olga clapped her hands, grief forgotten at the thought of making Eden happy: love and pretty dresses would always banish woe from her mind. 'We shall go this very minute. Come! Before the stores close for lunch.'

Eden, with a sidelong glance at Cabell, followed the Princess and Olga out of the room. The two men and Frederick were left alone.

Cabell sat awkwardly for a few moments, looking at the father and son looking at each other with love. He knew, or sensed, that he had misjudged the Prince. Gorshkov had taught Frederick what had been right according to his class and the times; but that class was finished now and so were the times: he was not the first nor would he be the last father who had failed to give his son a true picture of the future. And Cabell sensed that Gorshkov knew it.

At last he said, 'Are you going back to your regiment, Your Highness?'

'Of course he is,' said Frederick, proud of his father the soldier.

'I'm afraid so,' said Gorshkov less enthusiastically. 'We are going north to join Baron Wrangel's army up on the Volga.'

'Oh, jolly good!' Frederick had all his old bounce. 'I wish I could have given you my sword, Father.'

'I'm sorry about that,' said Cabell.

Gorshkov looked at the American. There was a certain exhaustion in his lean, handsome face, a resigned sadness: like that in the faces of some of the Jews, Cabell thought. 'Perhaps some day we shall see you in America, Mr Cabell. You understand?'

'Yes,' said Cabell and hoped that some day Frederick, too, would understand that he could never belong to a past that was gone forever.

That evening he took Eden to dinner in the hotel where he was staying. It was the best in Tiflis, one with its own aura of history; it had seen the best of times and soon would see the worst. But tonight was the best of times; or a good pretence was being made. The dining-room was crowded with officers and their women. Cabell doubted that he had seen so many beautiful women in the one room: blonde Russian women from St Petersburg and Moscow, dark-eyed women from Georgia and Armenia, broad-faced beauties who were the wives or mistresses of roving Cossacks. But all evening his eyes kept coming back to Eden, who was as beautiful as any of them.

'What are you thinking?' she said.

'That you're a lady, in a class of your own. One that will survive.' He looked around the room, at the couples dancing to the music of the string orchestra half-hidden by the potted palms. The dance was a fox-trot, the music *I'm Always Chasing Rainbows*: Tin Pan Alley stretched all the way to Tiflis. 'I think I'm looking at the night before Waterloo.

The losing side.'

'I feel it, too.'

She heard the too-gay laughter, saw the flirting: she wondered how intelligent people could be such fools. Then she thought sadly of Alexander Dmitri Delyanov and Captain Pugachov and Rabbi Aronsky and Lady Vanessa Mamoulian, all of them still there between the Caspian and the steppes of Siberia, all of them with one eye on tomorrow. Laughing, yes, but not fooled by blind optimism.

She pushed away her dish of sherbet. 'Let's go somewhere else.'

'My room is upstairs. But I'm afraid you'll hit me with your handbag if I suggest . . .'

She held up the small evening bag. 'Are you afraid of something as tiny as this?'

They went up to his room and once inside the door he said, 'Will you marry me?'

'I was about to ask you the same question.' She went into his arms and kissed him as she had kissed no man in five long years. 'What's the matter?'

'My goddam trousers are too tight.'

She reached down and helped ease his discomfort.

'Watch it,' he said.

[2]

Prince Gorshkov went north with his regiment to join Baron Wrangel's army on the Volga and was killed a year later at Nikopol on the Dnieper. He died bravely but with a certain fatalism that some of his fellow officers recognized and understood. Princess Gorshkov took the news bravely, but if she wept no one, not even her children, knew of it. She left Tiflis, taking the children with her, just before the Bolsheviks, as she still called them, occupied Georgia and Armenia. She managed to escape with all her jewellery and some gold, and they went via Constantinople, Alexandria and Marseilles to Nice on the French Riviera, guided there by the entreaties of her daughter who knew a good destination when she had heard of it. Princess Gorshkov died in

Nice in 1950, from a stroke brought on by being addressed as *Hey love* by an Australian tourist. Unlike her husband, she died without resignation. Ever since leaving Tiflis she had always had one ear turned to the east, waiting for the call back to St Petersburg.

Frederick never lost his arrogance and grew up to be the ideal commissionaire for the best hotel in Paris, which, in view of the fact that there are six or seven best hotels in Paris, had better be nameless. He died in 1968 while out for a walk, hit by a stray bullet from a gun in the student riots of that year. His last words, according to the policeman who held his head while he lay dying, were, 'If only I'd had my sword . . .'

Olga married three times, all of her husbands handsome men and all of them rogues. She had a dozen lovers and loved each one as passionately as she had loved his predecessor. Today, an old but still beautiful woman, she lives in a small apartment in Antibes, poor in circumstances but rich in memories. She survives, as Cabell and Eden knew she always would.

Cabell and Eden married and went to America, where they lived happily ever afterwards. They had four children, all of whom were brought up to respect the lessons of the past but to keep their eye on the future. Cabell eventually left the American-Siberian Oil Company, joining Socony and rising to be one of their top executives, the only one to own a royal blue Rolls-Royce, which he bought in 1950 to celebrate his and Eden's pearl anniversary. Eden continued to tell people to *Watch it!* and to wield her handbag with devastating effect when the occasion called for it; in 1959 she was charged by a would-be mugger with assault, but the charge was dismissed. She and Cabell kept in touch with Frederick and Olga, going to visit them each time they went to Europe. They died in 1961. They were in a plane that crashed on its way to Nice, where they were to attend Olga's third wedding. They died holding hands, happy in each other's company even in such circumstances.

Prince Gorshkov's Rolls-Royce continued its travels, though no one has ever been able to trace all its owners and how it finished up in Australia. It was discovered in a woolshed on a sheep station outside Come-by-Chance in western New South Wales: perhaps the name of the place describes its history. It was restored by a vintage car buff who now drives it round the streets of Sydney and says he is sometimes troubled by ghosts who feel the car belongs to them.

The golden sabre of Shamyl? No one has found that again.